The Soul of Stone - © 2023 Florian Frank Fleitmann

CW00859894

This one is for all who tell their own story.

Florian Frank Fleitmann

THE SOUL OF STONE

Book I of the Cant'un Trilogy

1

Trees kept appearing in front of him like white, slim pillars in the mist. Line after line, like a form of defence, and he did his best to avoid running into them. More than once, he would bang his shoulder, or low hanging twigs would lash his face.

He could only feel the raspy breath and its biting cold at the top of his throat. His Composure was starting to get low, and the ocean was too far back behind him now. Water was the only element he could use to regain it, but he would not make it very far if he had no magic left. There was a river beyond the edge of the trees, he just had to get to it.

A larger branch hit his face and for a few moments, he had to blink away the irritating sting in his eyes. He was not worried about his sight, he could see perfectly without it if he had to, using his Composure. He was worried that he would slow down, or worse, fall to the ground, and then his pursuer would catch up entirely.

He could feel his weighty heart pounding in his chest, and his breath was rough and heavy. Ultimately, he would not be able to keep this up and then, the chase would be over. A tiny part inside of him was hoping this would happen.

He had been running and fighting for almost half the night and his magic was nearly depleted. He did not stand a chance against his former teacher and friend. He had no idea what happened that his mentor of over a hundred years would suddenly turn on him!

Dragus felt betrayed, and for the first time, in a long time, alone again.

Life had always been confusing to him, growing up without parents, mortals hating him and him being chased away, until finally, one day, a kind old man had taken him in.

This man had become his mentor, taught him all he knew about elemental magic ... – and now this?

From one moment to the next, he turned on him and tried to kill him? This did not make any sense! Had he fallen for an elaborate lie? Almost the entire night, he had tried to understand what was going on, but his brain was too busy keeping him alive.

"DRAGUS! STOP RUNNING!".

The voice was like a massive echo inside his head, as if it came from somewhere else but resonated in the young mage's skull.

He did not stop running. He could not.

Every instinct told him that his life, and that of many others depended on him to keep on running. More white trees, more mist, more short breaths, he had no idea how long he would be able to –

"DRAGUS! YOU PATHETIC LITTLE EMBARRASSMENT! STOP TRYING TO ESCAPE, YOU KNOW IT'S POINTLESS!"

Suddenly, he saw something moving out of the corner of his eye. Something very dark. He felt the cold presence of creeping shadows next to him. He must have sent them after him!

With a surge of his Composure, he sourced a rush to strengthen his legs and tried to pick up the speed again. He should be able to reach the end of the White Forest soon enough and then, he would be able to channel the river's energies to buy more time, he thought.

Again, a shadow appeared, this time on the other side. Dragus's chest tightened for a moment, and he felt hope withering away inside him. He was cutting it close *if* he was even going to make it to the edge.

The trees in the mist in front of him became thicker, and he could tell that it would not be much longer until he was out of the woods. He could not tell if he would have enough time and endurance to get there.

He glanced upwards quickly to see how dense the leaves above him were.

Their layers were getting thicker too, but it was still dark behind them. The sun would keep them waiting for maybe another quarter of the night until dawn. He just had to get to the river!

A very wide tree appeared in front of him, and he lunged to the left to avoid it. Right behind it, a slimmer tree was leaning over to the left. It must have been pushed to the side by weather or brought down by man. Dragus ducked and slid underneath it, only to hit his boot against a large stone hidden underneath a pile of leaves. He lost his balance for a breath and had to grab onto the next tree in order not to fall.

In this one breath that had slowed him down, two shadows had moved in front of him, blocking the way with their menacing, smoke-like movements. The young sorcerer had never seen such apparitions before. The shadows had a chilling aura with a growingly draining, almost choking effect. He could feel their magnetic pull, feeding off his fear, slowly getting bigger and more powerful. Sensing the cold, crawling feeling of his despair on the inside of his skin was amplified and almost vented out of every pore of his body. They were drawing energy directly from his … soul?

It was too strong to resist! This was not the magic he was used to from his mentor!

With a quick, silent spell, he shot a piercing glow towards them, which they easily dodged. In a small loop, their bodiless clouds swung further in his direction.

Using this fraction of a moment, he fell back and grabbed the tree behind him, pulled himself up and over it and then jumped onto the tree stump on the other side to get behind them. They turned and continued to move towards him, but he was a bit faster changing direction. He used his glow spell once again to hit them. This time, with success it seemed, because they dissolved with a crisp, crinkling sound and a faint, golden shimmer.

Dragus was alone. Or so he thought.

"Dragus".

He turned around as he heard his mentor's voice behind him.

The distraction had seemingly given him sufficient time to catch up. Dragus was close to just dropping to the ground and letting him finish him off. He was exhausted.

But he could not just give up. He would not. Fragir stood where the two shadows had hesitated to attack him, calmly, almost as if he was ready to apologise. Of course, that was not the case, and Dragus was certainly not hoping for something like this. He just had to escape, reach that river, and then, stop Fragir.

He could tell that his old mentor was injured just like him: burnt holes in his coat revealed deep wounds, a bruise on his arm was showing through a ripped sleeve, and dried blood covered a gaping cut on the temple of his head.

Clearly, Fragir's heart did not struggle with a bad conscience, regret or was anywhere near to understanding the betrayal Dragus felt.

He was strangely ... filled with hatred. Filled to the rim, nothing but, with nothing else left. Very new, raw emotion the student had never picked up on before, from anyone.

"Why did you run away, Dragus? You knew this was not going to work."

Fragir's tone was so cold. Vicious. That sensation from the shadows returned and flooded Dragus's heart.

He felt a knot in his throat, and he noticed once more how much he was out of breath.

The long period of fighting and chasing started to take their toll. He was a powerful sorcerer, but vincible, and certainly no match for his former mentor. He had healed the worst of his wounds, but his magic had limits. He was sure he still had a broken rib and countless cuts and bruises.

The fact that his talent was to use the life and regenerative nature of plants was key in curing himself and others. With the water's energies almost empty, he would only be able to perform magicless alchemy. His Composure needed refilling. He had to use the remaining magic carefully.

"What is going on, Fragir? You seem like a different person?! Why are you trying to kill me!"

The older man frowned but then, could hardly suppress a smirk. "I'm not *trying* to kill you. I *am* killing you, my boy."

Dragus was surprised at the viciousness of Fragir's intent. This was a complete turnaround; he had never seen his mentor so evil and brutal. He had never even thought it possible with how kind this man had been to him, taking him in when he had no one and teaching him the ways of the elements. He had been misled for over a century.

Yet again, he knew other people were not to be trusted. How could he have been so reckless?

He slowly took two satchels off his belt, carefully, so that Fragir would not see, hoping that he was not using his Composure right now.

"After all these years of training and friendship, you are willing to destroy what we have built? You are willing to kill your one and only student?"

Fragir stared with unchanged emotion. "Yes. It is your final test. Getting killed by a powerful sorcerer is the rite of passage for an amateur trickster like you."

This was part of the test? Surely, Fragir had lost his mind.

"You told me that death is final, and that I was never to use magic against another sorcerer!"

"Haha! Do you not think I just said that so you would never attack me? And yet, you have defied me and used magic against me, your own teacher."

Dragus let out a desperate laugh.

"Because you asked me to, do you not remember? Trust, you have almost killed me but if you think you can hunt me down in the woods to finish the job, you are gravely mistaken!"

With these words, Dragus threw one of the satchels on the ground between them. A small explosion of burning herbs created a dense, grey cloud, so Dragus could roll to the side and escape Fragir's attention for a few short moments.

It was a powerful little spell that he created himself.

It shielded all physical and spiritual sight for a few moments, and on top of it, temporarily blocked the target's Composure.

Cowering down on the ground near a tree stump, he emptied the content of the second satchel and arranged the items in a circle around him.

The smoke cleared up, and Fragir had not moved away from his spot. He turned to Dragus and put an even darker frown on his face.

"Oh, a protection spell. What a cheap trick! You may have pushed my Composure away for a few moments, but that will not stop me from using my magic to kill you. Did you really think, I would not be able to fight any spell of yours?"

This time, Dragus had a broad smile on his face. "No, but I bet you are not going to expect this!"

With a sweeping motion, he rearranged the protective circle into three curved lines without even touching the items and activated the spell. The lines raised a glowing set of barriers. As planned, Fragir shot his powerful energy arrows to break through the three layers of blue shining barriers.

Easily, the whirring red bolts penetrated the protective walls, but Dragus let himself fall backwards. After the arrows had left the air above his head, he could already sense that Fragir was creating new ones. Dragus quickly felt that his spell would not be strong enough though. What he wanted to use them for was something else entirely anyway.

He swung up, unseen by his mentor through the barriers, jumped into the air towards his master; silently, he moved through the air and landed behind him. Immediately, he shot his own glowing arrows into Fragir's back, wave after wave, again, and again.

His old mentor screamed in pain, and tried to turn around, but Dragus used this moment to kick his knees and force him to the ground. Meanwhile, he commanded the three walls he had created to rush forward, knocking his mentor down to the ground entirely.

The walls dissolved hitting Fragir with pure energy and singed his coat, hair, and beard.

The apprentice moved around his opponent and kept firing. Of course, there were new arrows being shot in both directions in deadly, flashing energy.

Dragus was barely hit but one of Fragir's arrows grazed his cheek. He warded off another one aimed at his chest with a small shield to deflect. Simultaneously, Dragus grabbed a few stones from the ground with his telekinetic powers and flung them against the sorcerer's head.

He only had a few instants until Fragir would get his Composure back and channel his element earth again, so he reached behind his belt and pulled out a short iron dagger.

Without hesitation, he rammed the small blade into Fragir's chest, making him scream out loud. He turned the blade inside the heart to inflict more pain and more damage, leaned down close to his mentor's face and looked him in the eyes.

"I am so sorry, Master. This is not what I had intended to do. Ever."

Tears formed, and Dragus let his physical vision become blurry. He could not hold this pain back much longer. Fragir looked up into his eyes.

"Oh boy, you have learned nothing."

A massive force pulled on Dragus and threw him with his back first against a tree. The air pushed out of his torso could as well have been his last breath if he had not used the very last of his Composure to repair his backbone right away. He hit the ground hard and rolled four feet away from the tree. The next thing that happened was the most powerful telekinetic spell he had ever seen – and well, felt. Again, something that Dragus would not have expected from Fragir.

It was as if the soil spewed out the nearby trees, roots were ripped off and pulled out of the earth. Just for a better part of an instant, about 15 trees were hovering a few feet above ground.

Quickly, and with enormous thumping and splintering, they pierced the earth around him. Dragus knew that this was meant to scare him, because the tree trunks had closed in on his position, making the circle smaller. The ground shook and most of the trees disappeared into the earth halfway, pushed in by Fragir's massive force.

Less than a breath later, the same trees lifted again, pulled out of the soil with even greater might. This time, as they got closer shooting back into the ground, two of the trunks almost impaled him. It happened so fast that it would have killed him for sure if he had not evaded. He rolled over a few more feet and jumped back up to avoid being stomped. Some of the trees fell over, other remained stuck in the ground in the most violent and unnatural way he had ever seen.

Fragir was still lying where he had stabbed him, almost lifeless and pale, did not look real anymore somehow. His quivering arms raised above his head, and the face stern and painful in concentration, he mumbled something inaudible.

Again, an extreme force pulled Dragus off the ground, this time across the magically created clearing. His flight was stopped by a tree trunk that he hit his head on badly. His senses numbed for very short period, and he was not able to use his Composure anymore. When he could focus his sight again, his mentor was standing above him. Healed to some degree, just a large blood stain on his half-torn shirt, he looked down to his apprentice with disgust and pity.

"You tricked me." Dragus coughed.

"You disappoint me, boy, of course I tricked you. You are a poor excuse of a street illusionist; it is not even entertaining. Let me finish this, once and for all."

Fragir created a ball of orange, cloudy swirls in his right hand and raised it as if he wanted to punch Dragus.

The younger mage pulled out a small stick from his shirt pocket with his bloody hand and quickly flung it into Fragir's chest. His mentor's expression changed from one breath to the next and he looked down to his chest.

Red, yellow, and blue streams of light and powerful energy started to form between the end of the pointy wood and Dragus's hand. Growing fast in intensity, the colours worked like a beam that connected Dragus and Fragir and prevented them to move away from or closer to one another.

"Do you know what you are doing, Dragus? This is not the smartest idea." Fragir had to speak through his gritted teeth, grunting with pain.

Dragus knew exactly what he was doing.

If he was going to die then, he decided he would take Fragir with him.

"You know, I did pay attention in your lessons. Especially when you told me about Soul Sorcery. I am sure you will recognise this blood-draining spell? Whatever happens to me happens to you now, so we will both die." he said with thick tears in his eyes.

He had tried hard not to show his emotions, but he could feel the ruthless embrace of death already.

With that, the disappointment and pain of violated trust came back in a big wave. The head wound was too severe, his body damaged heavily, and there were too many broken bones and inner bleeding that he had not been able to heal.

Fragir Tyrus Crim dropped to his knees, and tried to pull out the stick, without success. His energy was fading away too, and Dragus knew that they did not have much time.

His eyelids became heavy, and the dark veil of death wrapped him tightly in its grasp, leaving no more space for moving or breathing.

The shadow chill came back, engulfed his every fibre, and filled voids in his emptying body.

All motoric functions, pains, and thoughts washed away quickly, and he drifted further into a black corner of his being. The final resting place.

Still, he heard the voice.

"THIS IS NOT THE END OF ME, MY YOUNG STUDENT. YOUR SOUL IS MINE."

The two lifeless bodies laid there for an extended amount of time.

Long after the sun had risen, the young mage woke up, like from a long, deep slumber and unharmed.

Almost as if he was surprised, he examined his hands and arms. He got on his feet and stretched his muscles.

Looking around, he took in the full scope of the devastation, ripped out and fallen trees, blood and burn marks everywhere. He sternly stared down at the older man's corpse for a few moments, and then, stepped over him.

Slowly, he walked away, back to where he had been running from the night before.

2

She opened her eyes slowly, and then quickly turned away from the blinding windows to protect herself from the brightness.

After a moment, she was able to take in her new chambers. Shrill at first, lavish sunshine bathed it all into a golden, warm light that she started to adjust to.

Samjya preferred the cool, soft light of the moon that turned everything into a solemn blue, but she would never even imagine complaining about the sun smiling down on her day like this.

The room was very luxurious, large, with heavy drapes by the enormous windows, soft cloths around the bed and on the floors, a dressing table and bedframe from the most expensive wood that she had ever seen.

There were paintings of flowers and Cant'un landscapes on the walls. She did not recognise most of these places, but she was sure they were part of this kingdom. After all, she had not travelled much.

Fine crockery had been carefully placed on the tables as decoration, and bottles with wines from all over the lands were available not only in her chambers but in all reception rooms. She was not used to being surrounded by fancy furniture or paraphernalia.

It was an odd sensation, feeling out of place, different from herself, as if she was not herself, out here, all this way away from her father's lands.

She was still just a "farmer's daughter" as some people called her behind her back.

Her father was not poor, he owned seven farms, but that did not mean that they could afford silk and gold either. In addition, they used nice crockery for serving food in style, not style on its own.

The staff in the castle treated her already like the Queen, at least as far as she could tell.

She just was not sure, if that was because she was a Royal guest under some kind of protocol and Vonter would tell them off if they would not.

Or if everyone was generally welcoming and excited for a new Queen, as he put it. Today was the big day, to make it all official. She would get married to her love. A rush of whirring happiness entered Samjya Gardono and gave her the eruptive nudge to rise from the large bed.

Wiping the blurry sleep from her eyes, the sunlight became even warmer, fuller. Her heart on the other hand got lighter in every moment that she was awake. Wild butterflies spread inside her and surges of energy made her limbs jolt as she stretched shedding the soft sheets off her legs.

Later today, she would be his Queen, and all the lands from the Northern Seas to the Desert Mountains would be hers. The kingdom of Cant'un, her home that had been ruled by an old, strict King when she was a child, was going to be hers.

The new King, her betrothed, had chosen her, lifted her up in status and spirit – her, of all the women in the land. It was pure madness to her. A whole world that had quickly turned so very unreal.

In a way, she was more conscious of each step she took in this kingdom, and sometimes, it felt like she could not sense the ground beneath her feet.

There was a painting on the wall next to the entrance door of a religious symbol on a shaded background. Two half circles swapped in position were inside a larger circle, leaving oval and triangle shapes with curved lines inside.

The structure was bright yellow on a purple flag on a gloomy hill surrounded by dark, stormy clouds. Samjya had seen it before, but she was not quite sure what it stood for.

Cant'un had quite the mythical past. Yet so many things had been forgotten. All humanity was left with, were legends. There were legends being told by everyone who was interested in telling a story. And that was all there was. Stories.

One was more adventurous than another. People were in wide disagreement about what had happened generations ago, and stories has a funny thing about them. They would change depending on who told them. It was ever so moving and changing, so there was no way of being sure.

Samjya had always found it odd how there were so many contradicting legends. The most common theme of them all, however, was some influence that had man left at higher beings' plans.

Built by the Bronze Giants, and shaped by the Silver Spirits, the makings of the Powers that had made the kingdom what it was today, had thrown many tough challenges on the generations before hers. Or so they said. Death had swept over the lands many times, wiping out grand cities and flowering populations. Big dragons and earthworms had formed crushing mountains and sizzling deserts. Witches and warlocks had hexed their way to the top of the world, and back down. Countless good and evil men, women and children had lost their lives to famine, hard winters, and the most gruesome diseases.

Only about half a century ago, magic had vanished, and devastating wars had been overcome, and the people were truly thriving under the sun. It was believed that there were now Golden Gods that made magic obsolete and looked after humanity for once. Harvests were rich, the weathers had been very mild, and Fate was smiling down on fruitful families. They had even built new churches, and monks were spreading their new word. Hopeful and naïve were the words used by some to describe this new belief. But times were truly good for everyone.

Of course, there were sceptics as well. People who had a more traditional view of the world would dedicate their lives to preach about how the Bronze Giants were still in charge. They believed in what everyone referred to as the "Old Gods". Personalities with their own will and their own powers, Fate, Pride, Rage. They would play their games, plot, and plan, carefully, and sometimes mercilessly and determine the path for every miserable mortal in this world.

But the Old Gods were more self-involved and cunning than really interested in what the humans were up to. Their feuds and petty conflicts were what drove and shaped the human soul.

That's how the simple mind explained and justified their crimes and other immoral behaviour.

A thief was not inherently responsible for their crimes, they were just manipulated into their actions by Gluttony for example. At the same time, there was a certain powerless feeling of not being in control.

It was like Fate had their fingers clenched around each person and moved them around like a piece on a chess board.

These people were usually quite cynic, sad, or petrified of what life would bring. And still, for many, the belief in the Old Gods was still present in many traditions, like burials or things people said.

Samjya had never thought much about religion, or Cant'un's past at all. Her father used to call all stories related to the past "fables". He did not care about any of this, only whether it would rain or not.

He cared about the very real world with its very real people, simply for the reason of securing stability for his crops and cattle. He and his men would not waste any time on stories, so Samjya had heard of them from her teachers at home, travelling merchants, or people in small towns.

Most people though would only ever talk to her about religion, their everyday lives, relationships or hopes and dreams.

Even the housewives and the workers did not care much for the stories of old men or how the land came to be.

They were too busy with the here and now at any rate. Samjya was sure to meet more of the individuals in the castle and around the capital as well to learn about their worldviews and beliefs. It would be exciting to see life through their eyes, especially if they had received different teachings.

Like her husband to be, the King. Vonter had learnt everything he knew from either the educated staff, military school, or the Elders Council. On almost everything, they could agree, but that had not been the case from the very beginning.

She had seen Vonter for the first time on her home farm while she was working in a field. He was hunting a deer, and she spotted him crawling under a fence. She first thought he was an intruder set out to steal from her father's farm despite his clothing.

Fearlessly, she ran over and almost rammed her pitchfork into his leg and demanded he should leave at once. Obviously, she did not actually impale him, and he cleared up the confusion quickly, still lying on the floor. Samjya just wanted to die on the spot when he explained how he was the King – not only to assure her he was not a thief.

Luckily, she did not die, but it took her quite some time to recover from the embarrassment. She then insisted on inviting him for a meal, even her father did not think this was a good idea, but she had always had her own mind.

With Vonter's bold and forward manner, she gave in to the flirtation. It was the first time she had seen a man as something else than a brotherly or fatherly figure. It was a different feeling, so strong that it confused her greatly at first.

They arranged for picnics in the fields, and he took her out on a day to the capital, which was one of the most exciting experiences in her life. Everyone had been staring at them, as the King was leisurely showing her the sights and shops.

He wanted to take her to his castle after just a few meetings, but she had thought he was a mad man with an interest in someone like her.

After weeks of wooing her and spending a lot of time getting to know her on her father's land, she had finally agreed.

It was hard to leave her father behind, because she had never imagined giving up being with him on his farms and the work, but she knew that she could go see him at any time. Her old home was just half a day's ride away, and her father had a standing invitation to come to visit the Royal Court at any time.

Of course, Vonter would look out for him too knowing that Samjya's helping hands would be sorely missed in the Gardono keephold.

He had even promised to delegate a few more workers from the city for the upcoming harvest season, which was not hard for him to arrange as the King.

A knock interrupted her thoughts, and she gave permission to enter. Her childhood friend and confidant Yandra walked into the room.

"Good morning, my favourite person in the world!" she uttered winking at Samjya.

Yandra was just a little older than she was and had been in her life for as long as she could think. She was the only friend she had brought with her from home. More family than anything else, she had insisted on joining the young Queen to be in the castle.

Instead of a handmaiden that Vonter had offered to appoint to Samjya's needs, they had agreed that Yandra would be based at the castle and take on those duties. The woman she trusted most in her life, like an older sister that she never had, and in a way, the only mother figure she had ever known.

They had pretty much grown up together, and yet, Yandra had taught her so much, watching over her every move and being there for her, always.

Samjya slid out of bed from underneath the sheets to give her friend a hug.

"Please do not expect me to treat you any differently, and please never change, no matter what the castle staff say!" she whistled cheerfully and jumped up and down around her.

The slight hint or nostalgia mixed with her excitement for today made her exclaim this affirmation. "I would like us to stay friends, just like we have always been."

"You keep saying this, I am not going to change my mind and manner over night!" Yandra raised her left eyebrow and smiled.

"I know, but today changes so many things! And I do not want us to change, I want us to remain the same. Even though it is hardly possible as life goes on and change is inevitable sometimes, but I cannot lose you. Not here. Not ever." Her voice suddenly sounded so much more emotional than she intended.

"Yes, Samjya, I want this as well." was the reply, and then, her friend straightened her back, lowered her head and corrected herself with a silly glint in her eyes: "Forgive me, my Queen."

She and Samjya chuckled, hugged again, and Yandra moved forward to make the bed.

"Are you even more excited for your big day today?" she heard her say.

"Of course, I am! I could take off and fly, so many emotions are running wild inside me."

They had talked until late the night before, and Yandra knew exactly what Samjya meant by this. She shook her head, smiling, and turned around. She skipped to her dressing table and sat down to inspect herself in the mirror. She was young and beautiful, no doubt, but especially for today, her appearance was very important.

As the Queen Bride, she would not let anything interfere with looking the best. She had asked Yandra to make certain that all the arrangements had been made according to her and Vonter's wishes, and she would ensure that her new husband would have a truly wonderful day as well.

With a few brushes, she tamed her long, blonde hair, pinned it up and out of her face.

She washed herself with the cleaned water in the golden bowl next to the mirror.

Yandra handed her a soft cloth to dry herself and held out her arms for Samjya to hand it back to her. She got dressed in beautifully woven, blue, and bronze robes and a stunning silver belt with matching shoes and a small headpiece in the same colours. In Buntin and other towns, she had always seen rich women that wore the finest gowns and most expensive jewellery, and she had never really cared for it. She had not really felt like that sort of woman before.

Vonter had many pieces custom made for her, including this headpiece that resembled a dragonfly, a straight pin in the form of the creature's body and wings to the left and right making up the rims.

There were many more unique pieces in her jewellery boxes.

She had not asked him for that, and it made her feel overwhelmed. Then again, she adored Vonter's thoughtfulness and attention to detail.

Especially the little dragonfly embellishments made all of them very special.

They were her favourite animals – so majestic and simple, she had always wondered how it would feel to being able to fly.

Dragonflies were very precise in their flight, impressively controlled, yet so light and elegant. She used to watch them for long times during her days as a child. One time, she had even caught one, and become entirely obsessed with the silvery colours of its wings and body. Other girls loved horses and dogs, cats even, but not Samjya.

There was something about dragonflies that fascinated her. She did not mind other bugs or insects too much, but dragonflies were majestic.

She admired the headpiece one more time and reached for another piece of jewellery waiting for her to be worn. Yandra assisted her in closing the hook, and she adjusted the blue necklace around her shoulders.

It was a slim chain with blue stones, very tasteful. Blue was her favourite colour; many of the elegant pieces were silver or gold, with fancy blue and shimmering details. "How do I look, Yandra?"

Her comrade looked up quickly. "Such beauty, your kingdom will speak of it for years to come, my Queen."

"Oh, with all your gallant compliments, how am I going to keep up impressing you? And my King?" Samjya replied in a funny voice, and they both laughed again.

Yandra smiled with a sigh and copied her voice. "I'm sure you will experience no difficulties in this, my Queen."

She made way for her friend to pass, and Samjya walked to the door, giving her a fake gasp.

"Thank you so much, Yandra. You are such a good friend. Please inspect my wedding gown one more time if I may ask you, so it is perfect for this afternoon's ceremony."

Yandra nodded and smiled in excited anticipation. "Of course. I will do it at once."

Samjya blew her a kiss in gratitude and turned around to leave the room when Yandra called her back. "And Samjya, rest assured, nothing is going to change. Just your world!" she winked at her years long friend.

Samjya snickered, swirled out the door and down the corridor.

The large halls ran for many, many feet, it was a very big castle, as far as Samjya could say.

The opulent windows allowed for much sunlight to come in, and soaked everything into gold, warm light on a wonderful morning like this. Her robes swept across the marble floor and her soft shoes almost made no sound, she loved how comfortable they felt on her feet.

When she reached the stairs that led down to the ground floor, she could hear busy voices. With a big smile on her face, she quickly descended and found herself in a bustling hall full of servants and workers that went about their business to prepare and decorate for the big occasion, the wedding. She was surprised at how many people there were – working just for the Royal Court.

One of the maids saw her just before she reached the foot of the stairs and burst out: "By the Gods, Her Grace... Her L-Lady Samjya!"

Confused and shocked by her own surprise, she added hastily: "Good morning, we were not

expecting Her this early, my apologies."

She curtsied, and the surrounding staff stopped their work and joined in.

The shortest moment after, the entire room had greeted the Queen Bride accordingly, just as Samjya's feet touched the floor on the ground level.

This had never happened to Samjya, even when she arrived at the Royal Court, people had not bowed. It was as if she had already become the Queen.

Light nausea grew in her stomach and hot flashes ran down her neck. Nervously, she tried to wave this away. "Please continue, everyone, you do not need to stop what you were doing."

She had probably broken protocol again. Uneasy, and confused, she curtsied herself and as she was getting ready to rise back up, she looked up.

She was not sure at all whether this was one of the oddest displays of a Royal figure – even though she was not a Royal. Most of the staff smiled and returned to their tasks.

Maybe they were not used to this either. This was something they had in common, at the very least.

She knew her cheeks had gone from excitedly pink to embarrassingly reddish. She knew that Vonter would be teaching her how to be a proper castle resident very soon.

"Where can I find the King?" she asked a group of stewards by the foot of the stairs, trying to keep her eager voice down.

Several members of staff hesitantly pointed towards the Reception Hall, and the maid that spoke first said: "Let me show Her to him, Her Lady."

"Thank you." Samjya felt like the butterflies in her stomach were taking over more and more.

Just a few steps away, another large hall led to big, wooden doors. Behind those, there would be the Reception Hall with very comfortable chairs for family members to arrive and relax, and then, behind even larger doors, the Royal Ceremony Halls.

Samjya had never seen the latter. She had arrived only a few days ago, had a peek into the Reception Hall and she thought that was the room where they would get married. Vonter had laughed and said that was only the room where both their families would be before and after the wedding. Naturally, the other invited would never set foot into this space. When her escort opened the door, Samjya gasped again in surprise.

Yesterday, the Reception Hall had been a regal and impressive place with formal purple throws over the elegant dinner chairs, long oak benches, and very beautiful armchairs.

Today, all seating furniture with purple cushions and covers had been exchanged with finest blue ones. On the walls, big flowery murals in purple had been replaced with blue decorations that featured dragonflies and silver patterns.

She could tell that this was entirely new, and custom made, fresh fittings and brand-new cloth. Simply astonishing!

While she admired the detail and richness of the impressive display, she could hardly remember what it had been before. She had only seen the room twice before and it was all so different in blue. Even more so, she was puzzled by the effort and time this must have taken the King had asked of his staff.

"Vonter!" her breath had truly been taken away. "This is so different, and so... beautiful! But why did you change all the colours?"

He turned around as he heard her voice. His expression changed from focused to positively surprised. "Samjya! You look amazing! You are as radiant as the sun, my love."

He rushed towards her and lifted her up in a playful, but firm embrace. He stopped for a short while to look into her eyes.

After smiling at each other for a moment, they got lost in a long, passionate kiss. Then, she broke free and gasped for air yet again, looking around the Reception Hall.

"It must have taken you all night to arrange this! You really did not have to do all this."

"It was a lot of work, I am sure. But apparently, it throws off the entire room and all the colours if you change only one part of the wall from purple to blue."

He snickered with a glimmer in his eyes and tilted his head in Sir Thommus' direction. The head steward stood patiently in the same spot that he and Vonter were talking before Samjya had arrived and nodded in her direction as her glance met his.

"Our very diligent staff have made this possible. But for you, my sweet dragonfly, I would make the whole kingdom work for days, just to see you smile."

Samjya blushed. "You know that that's not necessary. My smiles come free of coin or favours."

Vonter laughed.

"And you know I only need you; I do not mind all these fancy things. It is nice, the jewellery and all, but you do not have to overdo it. Not for me."

The King stepped away from her, one arm in the air to present the room.

"Do you think your father will appreciate this?" Vonter was truly proud.

Samjya laughed again. "Your wealth will impress him, yes. But Vonter, do not try too hard, you are getting carried away.

"You know us simple people do not need all this fuss. And forgive me for being so blunt, I cannot help but think people might not like me because you are spending all this money on our big day for someone of a different social standing?"

"Please do not think like that! But yes, … I know, I know." Her lover almost looked discouraged. "This is all a bit much, is not it? I guess I just thought you only marry once, and this is what it should look like."

"Who would have thought that a farmer's daughter would marry the King anyway?" Samjya winked at him.

"I have. The moment I saw you. And I do not care what the people of my kingdom say or think. I love you, and you will be our Queen."

She sighed. Tears formed in her eyes. "It is all happening so fast, I never imagined I would ever be so happy in my life!"

Vonter grabbed her in a tight embrace and stroked her head. With his warm, strong arms firmly wrapped around her and her face against his chest, she could smell the scent of fresh flowers on him. Samjya loved his dark brown hair and blue eyes, his defined face, and the perfectly clean face that he always had – he did not want to scratch her soft cheeks with his beard, as he said.

The fine linen shirt in the Royal Court's colour purple and the fine, wild leather jacket in dark green were so simple, yet very soft and elegant.

She sighed and swiped a blissful tear off her face.

"But you see, it is all so confusing, I feel like I'm in a different world. I knew it would be a big change, but it is a lot more intense than I expected.

"People treat me very differently here, and it is not always easy to respond correctly. Some look at me like I do not deserve to be here. Everyone is so serious all the time."

"Yes, I know what you mean. And I'm sorry you had to hear the insults the other night. I do not see you as a 'simple' farmer's daughter, and I know for certain you have not put a hex on me. I love you, and I will always be one hundred thousand times behind you.

"And I do not care if go a little mad with my gifts, and all that fuss. I am just so excited to have you here, becoming my family."

When Samjya had arrived a few nights before, some citizens of the capital had assembled near the castle gates alongside the road and made themselves heard that they disapproved of the King marrying someone of no Royal descent.

Some fruit had been thrown, and some negative sentiments had been shouted. She realised she was called names, a thief and witch even, determined to take the kingdom with dark magic. Vonter had tried to keep Samjya away from any of this, but she had found a note saying the farmer's daughter had put a curse on the King, how else would he say he loved her?

Naturally, she was quite upset by this, she always wanted everyone to like her. She had a very open, kind, and honest personality, but she also knew she could not possibly make absolutely everyone like her. At the same time, she guessed that there were quite a few people out there who disagreed with Vonter's politics and Samjya was the perfect person to blame for this. That, and she was sure that some women were most likely jealous as the King was quite the catch.

She suddenly realised that the man Vonter had been talking to was still there, waiting politely to finish his business. In his hands, he presented two different bouquets of flowers, one light blue and one dark blue in colour, both very elegant and professionally arranged.

Samjya tapped Vonter's shoulder and gestured in the florist's direction when their eyes met. Her fiancé laughed and turned around.

"Right. Which of these do you prefer, Samjya?"

She had a closer look at the choices. There were light-blue cornflowers and gerberas in darker shades of blue. "Should we take the cornflowers?"

Vonter smiled, turned to the man, and said: "We'll take the cornflowers. Please make sure you place them in a clever way. I trust you."

"Of course. Thank you, His Grace."

The florist smiled, bowed to the Queen Bride, and rushed away.

Vonter turned to Samjya once again and said: "Would you like to see the Royal Ceremony Chambers?"

She felt the tingling sensation of utter happiness and excitement in her belly running up her spine and warming her neck and cheeks. "A world of yes!"

"Let's hope your Yes this afternoon will be just as enthusiastic." she heard him say with a broad smile, turning away from her, with his hand firmly grabbing hers to guide her into the next hall.

3

When Dragus arrived at the site where the fight between him and the sorcerer had begun, he looked closely at the ground. Mibb was sure, he was clearly looking for something. Dragus seemed very different since he had woken up after the fight, but it was hard to tell how or why. He moved differently. Calm and more serious, if that was even possible for a young man who always had a more sensible attitude.

He had been following the young sorcerer through the White Forest, and here, just outside the reach of the white trees, the chilling sea winds made him shudder. He had to wrap his bushy tail around to keep warm.

After a few breaths of checking the floor, Dragus appeared to have found what he was looking for. He bent down to touch it, carefully. He dipped his hand into something. And then, he continued his examination of the ground. Very thoroughly, he looked at the rubble and leaves. He kicked every stone and twig out of sight. Then again, he got on one knee and dipped his other hand in something. Making sure, his hands were not touching anything else, he moved back East. Back deep into the White Forest. Mibb was very careful to stay out of his sight while following.

After a walk of a multitude of breaths, he reached the old castle ruins. No one ever came here, not even the animals. This was a haunted place, they said. It was a very isolated spot, cold and … rotten. The trees had even backed away from the ruins, creating a small clearing around them.

The white grass had turned ash-like, grey, and darkly pale. It was almost like this monument and its surroundings had burned down and permanently spoilt the flora and the stones with decomposing poison. None of the ruins had grown over with weeds or moss like they usually do. The stones themselves were cursed.

The castle had not been very large back in the day, and most of the ruins had sunk deep into the ground, so they were well hidden in the forest. Whoever had ruled here all those centuries ago, was long gone, and forgotten. Mibb remembered the King and his family during his time vaguely, but none of the people outside the forest knew about them. No one would even think that something like this existed in the centre of the pale woods.

Dragus clearly had a plan. He moved further into the ruins and stood in one of the towers in the former square courtyard for a short while. Then, he walked around looking at all four walls and their gaps. Finally, he nodded as if he was happy with his selection. He touched a spot on one of the broken walls with both hands in every one of the four directions leaving a moist patch. Once all four sides had been touched by each of his hands, Dragus positioned himself in the middle of the square again and closed his eyes.

Nothing happened for a little bit.

Then, he spread out his arms next to his hips, slowly. A small vibration was spreading out across the ground, and into the walls. The stones began to move!

Every single piece of the castle started to vibrate, more and more. Dragus slowly raised his arms, and the stones moved towards the walls. All was soon moving and ... *rebuilding itself?*

The mage was building the castle back up again! This had to be a serious drain on his powers, but he did not show any signs of exhaustion at all. His arms were almost above his head when he was finished. The castle was pretty much rebuilt in its original architecture, with lifeless, black stones. He had not raised it out of the grounds entirely, so the walls were not in the right angle, still rough on all edges and not perfect, but rebuilt.

Very strange and suspicious, Mibb thought to himself. The two sorcerers had not been in the White Forest for long, and now that Dragus had killed Fragir. He was alone, yet he wanted to set up a base in a castle? Why?

The sorcerer went down on his knees and dug his hands into the grey soil in front of him. Like in a meditative trance, he was starting to chant and gently rock back and forth. This was his way of recharging his powers! Mibb had seen this from an earth sorcerer but he always had thought Dragus's element was water?

The small squirrel had watched everything, and he decided that this was probably a very bad development. He had to warn the others! And fast.

***

Samjya was such a whirlwind, so different from other women. She was truly a force of nature, defiant and strong, very much unlike the noble women he had met in his life. And if he was honest, she was the first woman to impress him that way in his life of 32 winters.

King Vonter III of Blood Taryien was proud to be with Samjya Gardono, finally and formally, and he could tell that she was proud to be with him. She did not care about the castle, the kingdom's affairs. Samjya just was not that kind of person. Not at all.

She had not even been impressed by his presents and wealth in the beginning. He had had to work hard to get her admiration. Even if some of his people made her out to be conniving and being just after his coin and status. He could not understand how people would think like that.

Vonter knew that not many in the castle agreed with his new Queen either. In the end, he even had to discuss the matter in front of the members of the Elders Council, and he had told all his advisors that there was no other way.

He respected the Elders as the people called them, he had trusted most of them all his life, but some really had put stones in their way.

In the end, he was able to persuade him.

After all, he was still the King, and his ruling would not be influenced by any woman he would choose.

His first duty was the kingdom and its safety alone.

Sometimes, he wondered what his parents would have said about how he had chosen to marry a woman of inconsequential social standard. But after the death of his parents, he already had made quite a few decisions that did not stand well with the Elders Council and the old ways at the time.

Vonter did not think much of outdated rules that preserved power for the powerful and brought in more money for the wealthy. If a man had worked hard for his status and standing, he deserved the payment and honour. Furthermore, every man and woman should have the same rights and chances. This was a hard one to get into people's minds.

But he had managed to make taxes fairer by reducing them for the ones who did not earn as much. He had put measures in place to make trade easier for merchants who did not own any land or shops, and instead had to rely on getting their caravans to the right place at the right time. And he had lifted the ban on honey, something that his father had established after a bee had stung him.

It had taken Vonter the better part of a decade to put most of these matters into effect, not only because of the work it had taken with the Council.

He also had struggled with making some decisions. It was tricky to keep in mind what effect a change would have on every single person in his kingdom. He was always second guessing every decision.

Never sure how people would react, it was hard to make the right one. Getting there had not been easy.

But he learned and was still learning that he did not have to be liked by everyone. Carefully, he had thought about any possible outcome, taken his time to work the Elders and other political figures in and outside of the castle, his advisors, and military leaders.

Even a few members of the Elders Council had to go as Vonter found out how corrupt they had been. But after he felt he had cleared out the vermin, it was time and opportunity for new rules, new laws.

It was always a strategy game, and a brutal fight against the status quo his father had left behind. In his ten years of reign, he had tried to get rid of most of his father's strange rulings and laws.

Yes, the late King Vinn had been very erratic and unreasonable at times. Vonter remembered that it had been difficult not to make him angry.

His mother and himself, they had always feared the King's reaction to something unexpected. With him, what was wrong in one moment, was the right thing in the next. It was tough on all of them, the Elders, the staff of the Royal Court, the people in the capital. All this anger coupled with the compulsive need to control everything, and everyone had created quite a few situations that Vonter had never agreed with.

His people loved his ruling. Yes, he broke with traditions, but he knew which ones he could break with small to no risk. Many letters and gifts had been sent to the castle from all corners of the land, praising the refreshing and just sentiment. Vonter had read stories of how citizens' lives had been transformed. People felt safe, and there had hardly been any resistance from soldiers and watchers. It seemed everyone embraced the changes. A few people were pleased with his bride, specifically.

Some, however, were just not too convinced of Samjya as the Queen. It was like they did not trust her, some even made fun of her behind her back, calling her names. She was referred to as the "simple farmer's girl" or the "Peasant Princess".

Even as a young Prince, Vonter had heard the murmurings and comments that came from within the Elders Council. His mother had been a bit of a rebel and had raised eyebrows on a few occasions.

Queen Yahl of Blood Prunh had made an appearance in trousers at one of the King's banquets, just to make a point. It was her statement against women having to conform to wear dresses and the world of men dictating what should be available just to them.

Vonter had still been very young. His father had been very angry with her for days, but deep down they had had a very strong, mutual respect, and Vonter was sure that a less rebellious woman would not have been the right one for the previous King and his bad temper.

He had to smile. It suddenly became very apparent to him why he liked Samjya so much. Since his mother's passing, he had never met a woman quite like that. His lover was a free spirit herself and would only agree with tradition and status if they made sense to her. She would challenge his authority within reason and present good argument with it. Vonter was more than convinced that she would make an excellent Queen. She would help him rule justly and honestly, despite the Elders' reservations.

And above all, she was not in this for the fame or glory of being a monarch. She was here for him. And all that she really wanted from him was love. Still, he would hand her the whole world if he could.

Suddenly, he remembered. How could he forget about her wedding gift? He stopped himself from just turning on his heel and running away. But he noticed how he had not been listening at all.

"His Grace, is everything okay?" Thommus, on top of the ladder, hanging up lights, was trying to be polite, but Vonter could hear the impatient undertone in his voice.

Only family and the very closest of friends to the Royals were allowed to use the addressing 'Your Grace' and 'My King or Queen' as it was a very familiar way to speak to members the Royal Family.

Everyone else inside and outside the castle was saying 'His Grace' and 'Her Grace' in their presence as a sign of respect and tradition.

It was the same for 'Lords' and 'Ladies', any citizen one would deem a higher standard, even if one wasn't sure.

"Is something the matter?" he asked again.

Vonter was back from his thoughts.

"Oh no, Thommus, excuse me, I just remembered something that I wanted to take care of, but it can wait until you are finished up there."

Thommus was halfway down the ladder when Vonter finished his sentence. "His Grace, you asked me to go through the ceremony with you again, even though you should really get ready yourself!"

Three more stewards nervously hovered around the ladder as the King had insisted to help, when really this was not his job at all. It would be catastrophic if something were to be happening to Vonter, but he thought that was just nonsense.

"I know!" his hand made a deflecting wave. "But yes, right now, I should tend to something else, and I should get ready soon anyway."

Just when Thommus' foot touched the ground, Vonter turned around without waiting for the answer. Rushing towards the entrance of the Reception Hall, he saw that Samjya was picking out more flowers. She was not paying attention to him, so she would not notice him dashing out.

Skipping past a few servers from the kitchen, and almost running into the musicians and their delicate instruments, he quickly arrived at the bottom of the stairs and leaped up to his chambers.

He entered his own private halls and closed the door behind him carefully. The large bedroom had separate corners for his clothes, for his personal weapons and a small collection of the finest wines and whiskies that his father had cherished so dearly.

Vonter was not a big drinker, but these bottles held the most tremendous liquors that no ordinary man would even have heard of. He was not even sure why he kept them around. Maybe his father would come back from the dead to haunt him if he were to sell them or give them away.

The soft carpets and heavy curtains were all purple, his parents' Royal colour. Vonter had never changed that anywhere in his home, up until this day. The Reception Hall and the Royal Ceremony Hall downstairs would be decorated in a different colour for the very first time in over 150 years. Blue, in fact, Samjya's favourite colour.

His large, inviting bed was covered in finest silk sheets and pillows. Underneath, he had stowed a few wooden chests, some of which were guarded with locks. One of these contained Samjya's wedding gift.

He had to have waited ten days to give it to her, so the old lady had said.

Not sure why, but she was very adamant about this rule. So, he had waited ten days, just to make sure, but he was also happy to follow her instructions. Even if this silly instruction was based on an old woman's superstition, but the day had come just in time. And this way, the wedding gift would not only make a nice welcoming his bride to the castle, but it would also make an excellent centrepiece and decoration. It really was one of a kind. He knew Samjya was not impressed by fancy gowns or real gold and silver, so this would be just the right thing to make a perfect gift.

After opening the lock on the chest, he lifted the lid and gently lifted the present wrapped in blue cloth that he used to protect it.

Carefully, he placed it into his left hand, and with the right one, he closed the chest and locked it again. Then, he moved back and left his chambers.

Running back to the stairs, and down to the halls, but this time, he was a lot more cautious and considerate of not only his staff, but also of his cargo, it took him forever and a day to get back to Samjya. At least that's how he perceived it.

Stopping on the freshly cleaned and waxed floor of the Reception Hall was not too easy. He slid the last few feet, catching the attention of everyone around him. The ladies working on the bouquets looked up in surprise, some smiled shyly at the King's unusual demeanour.

Out of breath, Vonter stood up and straightened his back in front of Samjya. She turned her head towards him, her hair flowing in the motion like a silk flag in a breeze, so elegant and regal. And her smile, oh, her smile.

"My King, what is this?" Her tone was cheerful but with a hint of sarcasm. Samjya was trying to get used to addressing the people in the castle in the proper way, but he could tell it was not natural to her at all.

She could very much tell that this was a surprise he had planned for her.

"My dearest partner and lover, please accept this as a symbol of my eternal love and gratitude.

"Thank you for joining me here at the castle, by my side as my equal, my Queen to be. For what you are giving me each day with your smile alone, and at night in my dreams."

Some of the ladies around them blushed as their attention was brought to what Vonter had to say to his beloved.

"You are my muse, my soul and everything that I breathe, eat, and drink. Your heart warms mine forever more."

Samjya blushed, too. "Vonter, you are too sweet. But I thought we were going to say our vows later, in the ceremony?"

"Yes, we will, my love, but this cannot wait until the ceremony. I acquired something truly fantastic for you. A fine rarity!"

Samjya's gaze focused on the blue cloth in his hand. "What is it?"

Vonter suddenly became quite nervous. Like a small boy who had handmade his very first gift for his love interest, he felt insecure and exposed. He shifted his weight from one leg to the other and back. When he spoke, he could feel his voice shake.

"A few weeks ago, I was out hunting. I got separated from my group, and I met this merchant on the street by the White Forest.

"She was a very kind, old lady, who asked me if I was lost. I stopped and said that I knew exactly where I was. Usually, I would just ride past and thank her for her offer to help, but this time, I got to talking with her a bit."

He knew Samjya loved stories and she listened, excited, and interested.

"About what?" she asked, eyes wide open.

"Oh, this and that. How I am marrying the most perfect woman on this earth on a magical late summer day, and she was genuinely happy for us." He caught himself in a lingering smile for a breath or two, then, drew the focus back to his story.

"I guess she must not have known that I am the King, so she tried to sell me something. She was talking about jewellery and the finest robes, but I brushed her off.

While she was presenting her trinkets and gifts, I saw this gem, and I knew that only this was worthy of being a gift for my love."

Vonter revealed the content of the light blue cloth by peeling back the corners of the cloth and looked at his Queen Bride's face that lit up in amazement and utter joy. He could tell that she instantly knew how special this was.

In the cloth, safely wrapped, was a delicate blossom, as big as his large hands, and glowing from the inside.

Many layers of thin, white petals made up this with light pulsating, warm flower, mostly white, with bright blue and silver shimmering edges.

The colours seemed to move around, and the light from inside the blossom shone through his fingers, it really was soft, but powerful.

Samjya whispered: "Vonter, what is that?"

He smiled. "The old lady said that it was not for sale, because it was not intended for humans. She called it an ambrosia. Only worthy of a God, she said. I convinced her to sell it to me anyway. It was not easy."

He was very proud to have found this. Her face was all he needed to see.

"How?" Samjya was still whispering, and he could tell that she was not able to take her eyes off the blossom, moving her face closer to it.

"I offered her ten times the amount of gold that she could have asked for all her cart. She refused, thinking I had lost my mind, but I was able to assure that I do, in fact, have that kind of coin. In the end, she sold it to me."

He smiled at her, she smiled at him.

"Take it." he whispered now as well.

Samjya slowly raised her hands, and gently touched his under the cloth. When he was sure her fingertips had their grip on the blossom, he moved his hands away.

He let her take the flower and noticed how the pulse of the glow appeared to grow stronger and lighter.

Samjya held her gift close to her face and leaned forward to smell the flower. When she looked up, Vonter noticed something.

Samjya's eyes flashed white and lit up. It was so intense that it startled him a little.

His face must have shown his shock, because Samjya instantly lost her smile too. And just as fast as the change in her eyes had occurred, it vanished again.

As if nothing ever happened, she asked, "What is it, my love?"

He must have imagined it. Or maybe the white glow of the magical item had caused a momentary reflection in this light?

"Nothing, I'm happy you like it!" he smiled, moving his thoughts aside.

"Enjoy it. We should use it in our ceremony and hang it under the flower arch or place it on the dinner table."

Samjya gave him a peck on the cheek.

"I will keep it safe until then!" she exclaimed and moved towards the stairs swiftly to transport the valuable gift to her chambers.

She would probably also spend some time now looking at it from all angles. It was a very captivating artefact.

Yes, it had probably been just the light, and the excitement about the wedding.

A small part of his suspicion remained.

4

What a glorious morning!

The sun was shining down on them, light, fluffy clouds floating gently across the blue sky, and Buntin lied peaceful in the gorgeous valley that had created the most beautiful and exciting city of them all. Even the capital could not possibly compare.

Syfur was always in awe when he was on his favourite hill. Sitting here for half a day, just watching the business around the Golden Cathedral or the magnificent marketplace, was one of his favourite pastimes. This was also when he created the most captivating songs.

Not this time though. Today, he was very moved. He would leave his hometown of choice for the first time longer than a few days.

It had always been his dream to travel around Cant'un, but he had never taken time to do it. Quite frankly, Buntin had always kept him in her thrall. She was his heart and soul.

He loved the farms on the Eastern rims, the riverside tavern, and the rich streets on the Northern hills.

Buntin had changed quite a bit, just like him. A very poor town that had grown over the last decade, had become wealthier and more successful with trade.

The position, surrounded by hills, with the forest on top, a shimmering stream running through the town square, and good connections to other towns in the area was ideal for safety and trading.

The houses built on the edge of the city, leading up the hills to the North had been particularly in demand as they offered the best view over the town.

Many rich noblemen from the capital had bought or built houses in that area and moved out here or rented their properties out to other citizens who could afford to live in them.

The low amount of disappointment and the rich architecture had made this a well-known and popular place to call one's home lately.

The fast-spreading belief in the idea of Golden Gods originated here too. A small group of priests had founded a new religion that a many people had embraced quickly.

Apparently, at the end of the 200-year long War in Darkness that almost wiped out all of man, a mysterious warrior armed with golden sunlight killed the last demons, dark conjurers, and evil witches, bringing a new era of peace and freedom.

No one could remember where this warrior had come from, not even the oldest men in Cant'un. People had always believed spirits saw to end conflicts and despair throughout the land.

They had not prevented the last war 20 years ago, but that had only lasted for three years.

Said to never have seen war known to man, Buntin was the cleanest, purest spot in the world.

Many different people from all over the land had come here to settle down, peacefully. It was the place to be to try your luck, change your life, become someone else.

Syfur was one of them.

Long, blonde hair, lean and tall, thin linen clothing, green and brown, he could almost pass for a hunter.

Sometimes, he pretended to be a man with lots of coin, just lying in the sun and not caring for making a living.

He was an orphan, who ended up in a dark alley, hungry, dirty, and ill. No home, too young to remember where he belonged and very shy, he surely would have died that cold winter night.

But luckily, that alley had been behind Yart's house. From the very first moment on, he kept calling him Uncle Yart.

A wealthy merchant and good at heart, he had taken the little boy in and raised him in a way that helped him to unlock his true gift.

His voice.

He was not particularly good with words, or with his lute even, but his voice had captivated many people.

They stopped, stared, closed their eyes, and smiled or laughed, all the emotions.

Well, some also hated him, and many times he had been attacked with foul tomatoes and eggs. Not a pleasant shower.

More often than not, they had asked him to sing somewhere else, but he was convinced of his talent.

If the people of Buntin would not appreciate his talent, his uncle at least did. Syfur knew that he believed in him, no matter what the other citizens were saying.

Uncle Yart had supported him throughout his entire youth and now that Syfur was a grown man, he had suggested to him that he should finally travel.

Gather experience. Collect memories. Forge friendships. Gain inspiration.

Share his stories and songs and create new ones. Syfur wanted all that.

It had not been easy saying goodbye to the only family he had known and standing up here on the hill that had been his refuge, thinking place and favourite spot of them all, did not make it any easier.

It was as Uncle Yart always said, you cannot look back without looking forward and looking back only held you back.

Syfur felt so deeply connected to Buntin, but he was an artist, and artists needed to be in movement. Standing still was not inspiration, and change would bring new impulses and truths, he was sure.

The view made him quite emotional. He had to sing his masterpiece one more time.

Well, not exactly his masterpiece, but it was his favourite ballad.

He was in love with this town, and he had created this song to show it.

Buntin, town of gold and art,
Let me do my humble part,
In 'his land, the gem yerar,
I'll tell 'hem of yer golden heart.

Yerar the beauty, radianth,
Wi'h the perfect ambienth,
In 'his land, the best yerar,
Ye make me joyful and contenth.

Ye truly are the only one,
Yerar the only, truly one,
In 'his land, the world yerar,
'Here truly is just but one.

The best about ye' overall,
All Bloods kin, tall and small,
In 'his land, a home yerar,
To the kindest of 'hem all.

Syfur let his lute sink down.

This felt like goodbye, and it was. Not for very long though. He was going to be back in a few months.

Once winter was done, he was sure Yart could use his help on the market again, and he could fill the days with more stories and songs than ever, earn good coin to support his uncle.

After all, Buntin needed her bard to take her glory out into the land, even if the people did not want to admit it.

With teary eyes, he turned around and started his walk down South.

***

This body felt amazing, and the eruption of power was overwhelming. This had been the best idea he had ever had! His old physical self was dead and uninhabitable, so the last resort had been to latch onto this one – and he enjoyed every breath of it.

Fragir had not been sure if it would have worked because he had been so close to dying, but not anymore. He was free once more, and in a younger body too!

How had he been able to spend all that time with the dreadful, stupid boy and teach him the ways of magic?

Not only had he been dead annoying and whiny, but he had also had the worst discipline and imagination. The seasoned sorcerer was furious about the time he had lost. Centuries, really. Over a hundred years he had wasted on that stupid boy.

Fragir felt a lot better now that Dragus was silenced. He had his apprentice's soul still inside of him to feed on, and the additional power gave his magic the extra boost. It was his turn now, and he wanted revenge, for all that was done to him.

Life itself disgusted him. There was nothing to live for, and no one else deserved to live!

The view was spectacular.

He took a deep breath and took it all in. Of course, he knew that the forest would not keep quiet about his arrival and the resurrection of the stone castle – even though the mortals did not know what was going on in this forest.

Words had the ability to travel, whether he wanted or not. He wanted them to know and be scared.

Now, he was just getting started. He needed more power to get where he needed to be.

To get another chance to crush humanity, his magic would not be enough, not just yet, he was sure of that. This time, he was determined to spread death and destruction beyond the

The day was still young, and it was not too far to the next town. Maybe half a day on a horse. If he left now, he would be back by midnight. Fragir looked down to his shoes. He would change those as soon as he would get to the city. Dragus had no taste at all.

Leaving for the front square through the large archway, he looked around and noticed a small pile of rocks in the corner. He concentrated on his Composure for a bit and raised his arm towards the blocks, which started moving.

In the same way he had built the castle with his willpower, he now commanded the rocks to do his bidding again. A black stone horse erected itself in front of him. Its posture and movements were very elegant and smooth despite it being solid rock.

Even though the stones were quite heavy, not shaped to the form of the horse, and the mount was anything but lean, it still looked very agile. A strong light with pulses of energy was emitting off its head, through two little openings, eyes that glowed like a powerful fire. He knew this was just a shell inside a shell, not a real soul, nevertheless, it was enough for its purpose. Yes, Dragus' soul energy was very resourceful.

The horse puffed steamy air out of its nostrils and moved its head towards Fragir. As if it had been his mount for many years, it let him mount, and he rode off into the woods made of slim white trees through the gateless, black stone entrance.

After almost half a day, he reached the edge of the White Forest, and gazed down to the valley and its town. It was more like a large village, but in the last few years, it had to have grown quite successfully, Fragir hardly recognised it.

His cunning smile grew darker when he thought about his first act of revenge.

With a nimble trot and a loud rumbling of grinding stones, he led his horse down the hill, onto a path that brought him to the main gates of the town.

The guards only glanced at him at first, but Fragir could tell, that once he came closer, they looked up in surprise of the mount's appearance. A moving animal made of boulders, trotting along with the crushing sound of stones on top of stones had to make them wonder what this was. It behaved just like a horse too while Fragir was riding it into town. It was causing quite the confusion, but none of them would live to tell anyone about it anyway.

One member of Buntin's guards stepped into his way as he was almost at the gate.

He was wearing a leathery armour with brown and copper embellishments, held a long spear and brown wooden shield in his small hands. "State your business, stranger!"

Fragir sensed the man's nervousness as he was trying to exuberate confidence. He looked up and counted about 12 soldiers in the close vicinity of the town's entrance and on the walls.

With an effortless hand gesture, he entered the men's soul and removed any suspicion. Soul manipulation was not easy and quite the drain on his Composure, but he needed to get into the town centre without issues, and this was the easiest way to ensure this happened.

As he continued his way to the town square, the large market, the poor peasants, farmers, and women and children stopped and stared at him riding by. A family squeaked and rushed away.

Some children started crying. They clearly had never seen a moving boulder horse, and especially not such a striking one.

He arrived at the market and jumped off his stone companion.

He stopped at a stall with a good selection of linen clothing, where he took a simple, black pair of trousers, a red shirt, and a black coat. His purchase was quick and almost without words, he did not even pay attention to anyone.

Turning to the next stall, a middle-aged fruit merchant caught his attention. His build was rather strong, and he could tell that the man had been strong. He started a conversation with the friendly man.

He had picked up a thought of his earlier. Reading his mind, gave him a piece of information that was of interest indeed.

"How much for all your cherries, merchant?" he asked him.

"All of them? Are you certain, my lord?"

The trader looked puzzled. Fragir assured him firmly that he meant earnest. Still not convinced, the man hesitated.

"I suppose I would earn 200 gold pieces with all of them." he exclaimed.

Fragir laughed quietly. "You seem to be a smart salesman."

"Thank you, my lord. I try my best."

The man glanced over to his stone companion: "What a peculiar horse you have, my lord. What is that?"

The warlock ignored his question: "My name is Fragir Tyrus Crim, and I come from a far land, we do not see cherries every day."

"It is a pleasure to meet you, my lord. My name is Yart, and I am more than happy to sell you all my cherries. Have you tried them from this region? They're very sweet!"

He continued to tell Fragir how he had been a merchant for over twenty years now. Glad about the big sale, he was more than eager to open and share his life story.

He bragged about his business and his brief career as a young soldier. He talked about his son who became a talentless bard and left, and a mother who passed away a few years back.

Fragir hardly listened while he started to channel his energies into the spell he was about to unleash. It was nothing that he did not already know after tapping into the man's soul anyway.

"To be honest, buying and selling makes me very happy. Before I learned the art of trading in my father's store, I had the mad idea to become a soldier, and I enlisted in the Royal Army." he explained.

Fragir gave the inkling of a smile. He did not really have to entertain the man, but he was still finalising the curse. "Really? How interesting. Were you any good?"

"One of the best in strategy. They wanted me to go for a General position, but it did not feel right. I realized that fighting was not in my nature. With all respect to the great warriors, I do not see an honour in killing or being killed."

"That's a shame, Yart."

The merchant was confused once again. His eyes went from Fragir to the black horse again.

"I was hoping you would miss those army days."

He could tell that Yart felt uneasy suddenly. Fragir's excitement grew as Yart got more nervous.

"Why is that my lord?" the mortal in front of him stammered.

There was no need for a response. The spell was ready.

Fragir summoned a black glow underneath his hand, touched the trader's arm, just briefly, and turned around. Even though they were in the middle of the market, surrounded by all these people, it went unnoticed by anyone. They all were captivated by the magical horse, except Yart, who stared down on his arm in disbelief and shock.

With no intention in finishing the cherries deal, Fragir grabbed some leather shoes from the neighbouring stall, walked back to his horse, climbed up, and looked back to the fruit stall.

Yart had grabbed his arm, clenched fist, and flexed muscles, looking up.

A woman next to him saw this and put a hand on his shoulder to check on him.

The fruit merchant, falling to his knees in pain, pressed his fists against his forehead.

Dark smoke started to whirl around him, the woman stepped back, and the sensation poked the interest of more and more peasants. No one dared to get near Yart. Close-by customers and citizens stood back, first in awe, then in fear of what was going on. A few women and children ran away, screaming.

Then, a bone-shattering growl burst out of Yart's mouth, and he lowered his fists. The growl was not human at all, it was a lot deeper and darker. With a loud crack that must have carried across the whole valley, his flesh turned into stone. At first, his hands, bursting open, emitting smoke instead of blood, and moulding into hard matter like cooling glass. Then, the arms and the torso transformed the same way, and just before his legs changed, he fell over with his front to the ground.

With another loud crack the head burst open and gave way to a much larger, black stone, with the skin melting into the stone, disappearing into blackness.

For a few instants, the lifeless rock just lied there, in the marketplace, in front of all those people.

A lot of the citizens had stopped to watch the tragedy shamelessly, astonished, and curious in equal parts, some were horrified, but unable to move their eyes away, let alone their feet.

Without a warning, the merchant jumped back up again, causing the crowd to step back further. Startled, and afraid, most people still stayed closer than they should have.

Yart had changed entirely into stone, but he was now almost three men in size, and his steps were as heavy as ten horses. The face was hardly a face anymore. There was a tear-shaped boulder left with a rounded tip at the very top, resting on broad rocks that were shoulders just a few blinks ago.

The mouth had turned into a large, gaping hole that did not close. The nose had disappeared, and the eyes were tiny, piercingly glowing dots in the darkest red that ever existed.

The soul was the best fire Fragir knew.

Yart's naked, cold pain, entirely trapped within the stone shell, was giving him an ecstasy like nothing else before. It had been so long he had trapped a soul, let alone in a stone body that would grow into so much more.

It was almost like the former soldier did not know who or where he was anymore, and all that had previously been now washed away. The new appearance was so obscure that there was nothing left for him than the void of pain, violence and well, death. Yart stomped the ground with his right stone foot and swung forward with a thrust. The plastered ground beneath his feet cracked and crumbled, some baskets fell over, women screamed out and children started to cry everywhere. Hot air left his wide mouth, and the darkest, deepest growl blew over the heads of the crowd.

Now, a full-fletched panic broke out and everyone tried to flee. The larger groups did not manage to get away quickly, because the alleys in the corners of the market were rather narrow, and the wider streets were already blocked with people running away.

The stone merchant began to swing his arms around, destroying his stall first, crushed fruit debris going in all directions. Then, he hit the first man.

Teeth landed in front of Fragir's horse's legs, and the poor man flew across the marketplace into a group of people. Soon after that, Yart had two women by their throats and flung them into the bread stall. One lady's neck was broken at once, and the other one rolled to the floor, unconscious.

By that time, the turned salesman had jumped to one of the corners where a group of people tried to escape through a narrow gate. Like a wild bear ripping through a deer, he grabbed into the crowd and threw men, women, and children aimlessly into the air. His stone hands smashed skulls, his heavy steps crushed hands and feet, and his grunts and growls filled everyone with petrifying fear.

Fragir was watching, glad that he had chosen so well.

His horse was as calm as a mountain and waiting patiently. While Yart continued to trash and kill everything around him, cold pride filled Fragir's heart. This was truly a great day.

With an ecstatic mood in his heart, he glanced over to the Golden Cathedral. It was a shame the magnificent building had to go. As beautiful and impressive as it was, it was nothing but a symbol of a silly religion that needed to be crushed. He was the new God. He was what they should build cathedrals for now. Except that there would be no one left to build them.

He pushed his heels against the rock body of his mount, so it would bring him back to the main gate. As he was leaving, guards rushed from the walls to the town square to help; he could see the fear in their eyes too. They would not survive, and why warn them, when they would miss out on all the fun?

One last time, he turned around. Yart was ripping bodies apart, spilling blood over the pale ground, crushed wood, tools, supplies, the living, and the dead.

He had a man and his daughter in his large stone hand, slamming their fragile bodies against his impenetrable stone head, until they were mush, limbs jerking, dripping with blood.

In a full frenzy, he pushed his shoulder into the chemist's shop and made the brick walls crumble like a stack of dice on a game table. Only in this case, the house would not win, and no one living in it either.

Just a few feet next to the spot where the Yart had been transformed, he noticed movement under the bread stall. Another stone arm emerged from the rubble. It was the first man that Yart had touched.

The second stone man was smaller in size, but other than that, no different from Yart. His soul too was now in a concrete cage and fed Fragir with its sizzling energy. He too would spread the contamination in a fired rage, and many of the citizens after him. Every soul was going to follow the same fate.

Fragir chuckled quietly as he made his way back to the gate.

His curse was an impact on the masses, a change that would affect every living thing.

As he popped a cherry into his mouth, he delightfully noticed that they were indeed the best ones he'd had in centuries. Yart did not disappoint. The warlock led the horse out of town back up the hill towards the White Forest. He would probably stop up there to enjoy the view. The new world order had begun. The first step had been taken.

Buntin's souls were about to birth him an army.

This town was going to be gone not long before the day was over.

5

The clouds parted and gave way to the sunlight that filled Samjya's chambers with warm, soft light yet again. Yandra finished up with her hair and smiled:

"You look stunning."

The Queen Bride laughed.

"Only because of your impressive talents. Without you, I would still wear my home apron and my hair would smell of hay."

"I must disagree, your hair hardly ever smelled of hay. And I am almost certain that any *proficient* handmaiden from the castle would have performed a much better service."

"Almost certain?" Samjya exclaimed with a sarcastic tone. Yandra looked at her directly, and she could see the playful glimmer in her eyes. She could not suppress a smile.

"I am so lucky to have you here with me, Yandra. You're like my sister, and I would not bear to live in this castle without you. You know, all these new faces, the large rooms, even the newfound excitement Vonter is showing with all this fancy jewellery and the decorations, it is…"

"Intimidating?" her friend offered.

Her chest felt a little lighter with relief. "Yes! It is quite intimidating. I want to embrace the change and just be myself, but how can I do that when everything is so…"

"Royal?" her friend was able to put the same pathos into the word that Samjya was looking for.

"Yes! And … can I share a secret with you?"

Yandra put down the brush. "Of course, Samjya!"

She got up, carefully, as she did not want to crease her wedding dress too much.

Hair, shoes, veil, everything was in place at this moment, and she intended to keep it that way.

She moved to the window and looked down to the wide fields below.

On this side, there were no houses, just fields; and in the far distance, she told herself, she could see her father's home.

That was not possible, of course, as it was too far away, but it gave her comfort to imagine her family's home was just at the end of these fields.

The capital's streets and buildings were just on the other side of the castle, and even though the Queen's chambers overlooked the Royal Gardens, Vonter knew that Samjya would enjoy the view of the empty fields more, so he had arranged for her to stay on this side of the building, and he was right.

"I am holding back. I know I should not, but ... you know, everyone is very serious. They are stiff and strict, and I want to say something, so much more, but I cannot. It's a heavy weight on my heart as I am constantly watching myself. I want to stay my own person, and be free like I was on the farm, and I do not know how.

"It has made me worry quite a bit, and I am scared that I am starting to feel very sad about it too. And the worst part is, I – I am not sure how to tell Vonter."

A flurry of uncontrolled emotions filled her.

She could not contain her joy about her present and future life. She was truly happy and overwhelmed. But as exciting as this all was, it was also scary. She was quite intimidated by her new surroundings – it was all so different from home.

Since the move to the castle, she felt insecure. Everyone else was so dignified, polite and, well, tense. Sometimes she caught herself thinking she might say something wrong or do the wrong thing.

And she did sometimes, especially in the beginning. Her direct way of saying and doing things seemed to surprise people. She realised that she was a very open and kind person, she was brought up this way, but it made the whole situation a bit complicated.

This was not her family or the farmers she had grown up with.

Not the strangers in the large capital, not the soldiers she passed on her roaming around the castle and gardens, and not the countless servants she ran into. Samjya was almost convinced there were many new faces among them every day.

At the farm, she knew everyone, and she mostly did not care what she would say or if she would offend anyone. But here, at the Royal Court, she had to respect the Elders Council and consider the etiquette among the noble people or whatever they were called.

And she was concerned whether she would get bored, living her life in a castle like this. Vonter had promised her a personal garden where she could work, plant flowers and vegetables, and create art surrounded by beauty, and of course, she would try to be with him in every breath's time possible. But this was a big place, far away from friends and family, with a busy husband, this could quickly get lonely. She was not sure what this would mean in a month, a year, gosh, 20 years. But she would certainly find out. Her life was changing.

"You have not told him about how you feel?" Yandra appeared next to her and gave her a comforting smile.

"I do not know how. I mean, he knows I feel overwhelmed and not sure how to always behave, but I haven't shared with him how restricted and hurtful it makes me feel. You understand me Yandra, I do not have to explain myself. With Vonter, I know he sees what he wants to see, nothing less, nothing more. In his mind, this is all just protocol and etiquette, and I will grow into it."

"He has fallen for you completely. I think that makes some men blind to the real ongoings of their tokens of affection. I don't mean to make excuses on his behalf, but maybe you need to speak truthful with him. And I am sure he will be able to tell this is coming from your heart. He loves you without restrict, so you shouldn't feel like you must."

Samjya could always count on her friend's wise insight.

"And then, we did not really have a moment to ourselves. It is a lot busier here at the castle, and he is always doing something. I am afraid to get lonely and turn into a scared little feather or a reclused snob." She suddenly realised that it sounded a little melodramatic.

"Do not worry Samjya, I will make sure to keep you on the ground." Yandra chuckled.

Her friend hugged her from behind for a moment, then turned around to get organised. "You will make friends here at the castle in no time, and I am sure your father will visit as often as he can. Speak to your King after the wedding, I am sure he will give you his time to really listen and help you get used to your new life together."

In thought, Samjya's hands played with her belt and the silver dragonfly just below her belly button. She was wondering whether her father had already arrived or if the carriage was just about to enter the city's gates. Vonter had ensured to send his best guards to get them safely to the capital. It was not long now until the ceremony, so they had better be on time, she thought.

A knock on the door brought her back to reality.

Yandra opened the door and exchanged a few quiet words with someone outside. When she closed the door again, she turned and smiled.

"Not very long until we should head down."

Samjya nodded and walked back to her dressing table. They spent the time applying lotions and perfumes, double checking her attire, final touches on her hair and face as well as preparing the second outfit for the evening. Samjya helped Yandra cleaning up and getting dressed as well despite her protesting. She insisted, they were family after all.

Finally, a last glance into the mirror gave her the assurance that today would work out just nicely. With a firm look into her eyes, she told herself that everything was going to be alright, and this was the beginning of a perfect life. With Vonter, her man.

She would warm up to the Royal Court to be a good Queen to everyone, and they to her.

In the background, Yandra was still folding robes and blankets, tidying up and rearranging the accessories on her jewellery table. The quiet of the room filled her, calming, and comforting her. And then, she noticed how she was smiling. She was ready to get married now.

She had never really thought she would marry one day, seeing men more as brotherly or fatherly figures in her life, colleagues at the most. But now that the moment was almost here, she could feel its sincerity and the emotional significance in its entirety. The ground beneath her feet, so tangible. Samjya stepped away from the mirror and signalled Yandra silently that she was willing to go downstairs. Her comrade smiled at her, turned to the dressing table, and lifted the small silver tiara above Samjya's head. She placed the light and elegant ceremonial piece onto Samjya's hair, and it was a perfect fit. This tiara would be swapped with the Queen's golden crown at the end of the holy wedding ceremony.

She had forgotten how many Royal women had worn the crown, but there had been many in the past centuries, she imagined.

For almost a thousand of years, they said. Never had there been a farmer's daughter though. Samjya, as humbled as she was to marry the King, could not think of a reason why that should stop her. It was fate.

Yandra cleared her throat. With tears in her eyes and yet, a cheeky smile she said, making a funny voice: "It is time, Her Grace."

Samjya placed one hand on the side of Yandra's shoulder. "What is the matter, my old friend?"

She shrugged and smiled at the same time. "Oh, it is just such a wonderful and special day full of... You were right, everything is about to change. It is quite overwhelming and moving, my sweet Samjya."

They embraced each other softly yet deeply.

"Everything is going to change, but we are not. I trust that you will remain the same Yandra I know, and I shall do the same! I promise."

While she was well aware she was saying this more to herself than her friend, she hoped whole-heartedly that it was true and that they would remain life-long companions.

Yandra wiped her eyes quickly and smiled, a little more reassured, collecting herself.

Another knock was the signal from Chamber Master Sire Thommus for her to go down.

He wanted to say something as soon as Yandra opened the door, but Samjya was too excited to wait. She walked right through, passed Sire Thommus, and ignored his urging.

"Her Lady, please, we need to speak!"

"I apologise. We can do that downstairs; I want to see my father!" she shouted happily.

Without looking back, the Queen Bride rushed briskly down the long hall to the large staircase. Making her way through the orange-golden lit corridor, she could feel the nervous excitement coming back in tides.

Wave after wave, the raving filled her gut and washed away the serenity that she had been able to experience just now.

Under her shoes, there was weightlessness lifting her up, a strange power elevating her mind and spirits.

By the time she arrived on top of the stairs, her hands were shaking, and her pounding heart was beating against the corset of her dress. Shallow breaths did not help either, she was truly nervous now.

This is the rest of your new life; she heard her father's voice in her head. She was sure he would be so emotional as well!

He was usually a very distant, silent man, a hard worker who rarely would voice approval or criticism as by the end of the day, the job had to get done and commentary was only going to hold people back.

With her mother dying when she was very young, he had built this wall around his heart that started to crumble with every major stepping-stone in Samjya's life. Especially since she was his only child, he had grown to be more sentimental in the last few years and she had thought they had been tears in his eyes when they said goodbye yesterday.

Her mood changed slowly as she was walking down the stairs.

Hectic voices, shouting and women that sobbed and cried welcomed her descent. What was this?

A stark and hard worry took over her heart, creeping into her limbs.

A group of people clenched against a pillar; some were sitting nervously in the corner. In shock and mourning, tears were on everyone's faces.

The two flower girls who loyally waited by the foot of the stairs looked up to Samjya, wet eyes and shaking with troubled emotions. They were not able to contain themselves, and Samjya's instinct was to embrace them both in comfort. As she did, the two girls started crying.

"What is going on?" she asked confused.

"Oh, ... It is unspeakable!" one of them burst out in horror.

This startled her, and her thoughts suddenly stumbled with a dark suspicion in the back of her head. Her glance searched the room for Vonter, but he was seen nowhere. She grew afraid that something might have happened to him.

The worry blew up into a full-grown fear. And a different nervousness crawled its way into her stomach, making her knees weak, and her hands tremble. She suddenly felt hotter, and sharper, the vibrations were starting to burn her up!

"Where is the King?" she demanded to know.

The girls lifted their hands and stepped away from their Queen to be. "We do not know, we have not seen him, Her Lady."

Now, Samjya was genuinely scared for her love. And her father!

She rushed towards the Reception Hall in the hopes of finding her father there, but the room was empty. Where was he? She asked the nearest people she could find, but no one knew about her father either!

They had not made it to the castle yet?

She could feel her heart pounding out of her throat.

She could hardly breathe.

What was she supposed to do now?

Why did no one know?

Where was Vonter?

Her eyes caught a man who rushed through the room carrying scrolls with the King's seal on them, pressed into purple wax, the Castle's colour. The capital's crest was the Proud Steed, a white stallion on his back legs, front legs up showing its strength and might.

Quicker than the wind, Samjya rushed to him. She almost fell into his arms, causing him to drop a few of his paper scrolls.

"I am so sorry; I am looking for King Vonter!"

Her voice did not sound like hers; it was a faint echo of someone she once knew. Her throat felt like it was clogged up, she wanted to cough but could not. There was something in her shoe. It was too tight. Her corset was tighter than it had been upstairs.

What was happening?

The man hastily reached down to pick up the scrolls, and then Samjya noticed how he was panting. "I am afraid, I do not know, Her Lady. He instructed me to comprise a warning to the other towns and villages because of an attack. I am sending ravens out and I should rush to do so. Her Lady."

Hot flashes ran down her back, and her heart's beat accelerated even more.

"An attack? What happened? I am desperate; I have not seen my father yet, is he okay? Vonter has vanished, and I have no clue what is going on. Please tell me –!"

The messenger nodded to one of the maidens, asked her to get some smelling salts and returned to collect his scrolls from the floor. Sire Thommus stayed by her side, holding her hand, probably making sure she would not faint. The girl came back faster than the Chamber Master had caught up with her from upstairs.

The Chamber Master released the messenger to his duties and helped Samjya to a chair.

The young Queen Bride took a few deep breaths and tried to get a clear mind. It was not an easy task.

Everything around her was moving, spinning in a groundless frenzy.

It was a new, wild feeling and made her very uneasy.

When she opened her eyes, Sire Thommus had left, and the girl who had brought her the smelling salts, stared at her in worry. A few other maidens and stewards stood in a little bit of a distance, just looking at her. Some had sadness and sympathy in their faces, with some it was pity. For her?

"Where is he? He wanted to tell me something?!" she started to panic again. All eyes were on her. It was too much.

She turned around and looked back to the entrance of the castle. Through the afternoon sun, she could see lots of men, servants and guards move hectically from one side to the other.

A tall figure was moving inside quickly. As the man moved away from the sunlight and into the building, Samjya could see his face. It was Vonter!

She immediately set out to rush to him, but the weakness and shock would not let her run in a straight line. He was clearly headed her way, but when he noticed her running, he moved faster as well. They met halfway through the Hall; her breath so heavy she could barely speak.

He caught her, slipping away at his feet. She realised how her knees were still very weak and the corset was too tight, tighter even. And there it was again, this pressing against her left foot inside the shoe. Very uncomfortable.

"Vonter?" she pressed out with pent up air in her throat. It was now that she noticed he was wearing his metal uniform in the Royal Guard colours, the Proud Steed on his chest, heavily armoured legs and riding boots.

"I am here, my love. I am terribly sorry; I am afraid the wedding must wait."

Her heart sank to the ground and melted like scalding gold. The burning and shuddering flashes took turns rushing under her skin up and down her back inside and out. She had never thought this possible.

"Are we in danger, my love?"

She had a hard time fighting her tears, and screaming, punching someone.

"Something horrible has happened in the Midlands, and I need to leave the capital at once." Samjya looked down.

"Buntin has fallen, we do not know how many dead."

Vonter paused, she could hear in the silence between his words how hard it was to speak them.

"There is something else, it is about your father."

She was too afraid to look at him, too afraid to look at anyone. Her arms trembled with anticipating agony. She could not believe what was happening.

Against her will, her hand reached for her fiancé's shoulder. She had no energy for tears, no strength for standing, but still, she felt her face welling up, she felt her body tense up. Her left foot started pulsing. She was so afraid, afraid of what would come next, afraid that she would not be able to do anything, that her King was unable to do anything and that it was suddenly all about the fear, pain, and loss.

She slowly moved her eyes up to read Vonter's face. Her heart was pounding, but all she could hear now was her raspy, heavy breath that was getting faster by the breath. She blinked the tears away so the blurry face in front of her would become clear. It did not work.

She closed her eyes, took a deep lungful, and then, she felt Vonter's hand on her shoulder. It had been there longer, but she only noticed now.

"I am sorry my love, but your father's carriage has not arrived. I must be honest with you. They are almost half a day late now, and with what's going on in the Midlands, … I have sent out my best soldiers to look for him. We will make sure he is safe."

Samjya's throat closed, she was unable to speak or breathe.

"Please forgive me, I must go, I must lead my men to Buntin. I must. I am sorry."

His hands rested on her cheeks for an instant, and he gently kissed her cold lips.

Within what she felt were mere moments, his face disappeared from her sight.

Tears blurred her vision entirely now.

All her joy was gone, only tremendous worry and pain were left.

Everything else she felt, heard, and saw, became suddenly very hazy.

Someone helped her to sit on a chair.

How did this chair end up in the middle of the room?

As she removed her shoes from her feet, whatever was bothering her toes, it was not there.

There was nothing. She silently cursed her shoes. It would have been quite the relief to take them off, but her toe still hurt.

She did not really feel it anymore.

She did not feel the ground anymore, or anything at all.

All she could do was cry.

6

The sun was still shining down on them, bright and warm, almost mockingly so. This would have been the most beautiful day for his wedding, Vonter thought. But the tragedy of Buntin had turned everything into desperation.

His father would have known exactly what to do. This was the first time a catastrophe like this happened in over 30 years. Was it a vicious attack on his kingdom? The slaughter of innocent lives for fun and games, or a very terrible and sad accident?

He had no experience in this kind of thing, and the word that had reached the castle, was not very specific in detail. He needed more information. Vonter had no idea what was waiting for them. That was the worst part. Not knowing was very bad for planning and strategy, so he needed to try and to find out more, and as soon as possible. If he had to go to war, then so it should be.

Even though Vonter knew that postponing the wedding most likely hurt Samjya tremendously, it was the right decision. What kind of a King would he be if he stuck to a celebration while his people died? He had to ride out to see for himself what had happened to the peaceful little town they called Buntin, and who was behind it. It had to be a very brutal and vicious attack; he had this feeling in his gut.

As usual, the two Generals of the First and Second Division of the Royal Army, rode next to him. The Seven Divisions, created to protect the kingdom, was the name of his army – though in the last few years, there had never been any conflict. There were three Divisions, usually based at the capital, with the First to be the Elite, the Royal Guard of 50 highly skilled sentries, 50 spies and martial arts experts, 600 formidable sword and dagger fighters, and 200 of the best archers. The other two were made of 300 sword fighters, 300 spear soldiers, 200 archers and 50 ballistae with four men each.

Other Divisions throughout the land had varying numbers of melee and ranged battle soldiers but all of them had horses for travel and combat. Ballistae were mainly stationery and did not travel well. Vonter's father had made sure that all major cities were protected with either half or a full Division.

The young King had not really had a reason to change this, and he was glad now that he never had.

His own priority were the people. He would not allow the killing of innocent souls as long as he was breathing. Again, his thoughts returned to Samjya.

Vonter knew that he would choose her over anyone else, and that was probably not right in his position. He also hoped that this was never going to be a decision he would have to make. Despite of the things he had heard other people say about her, he would do anything for them, he had sworn to protect his people.

The only one who had never voiced concern over or spoken out against marrying Samjya was his best friend and the General of the Royal Army's First Division, Sahdor Tonin. He had been a soldier for about five years longer than the young King before. As a very fast and early learner, he had received many years of strategic advising from the Senior Generals.

The ones that had the honour of teaching their subordinates were given the title "Sire", which was a well-respected achievement and status in the capital. They had the responsibility and privilege to sire the next generation of military men of all levels, refined fighters, craftsmen in any production work and artists in all areas.

Sahd was an excellent soldier of great honour and skill, in a multitude of weapons. He was just a few years older too, and they were like brothers. So, Vonter kept this man close to his side, he trusted him with his life. He knew Sahd had always felt the same about the young King.

Sahd had been there for him like no other when his parents had died ten years ago.

Vonter had been in the care of Sire Graynor since then, the Senior General, a close friend of his father's. It had really been Sahd, who had made his first few years of being the King of Cant'un bearable. Whenever grief and the feeling of being overwhelmed had taken over, his friend would get him to a place of calm and focus, so he could take on the responsibilities he needed, and in turn serve his country the way his parents would have expected.

He was the best among the senior recruits, and he had practised fighting with him after study time. They taught each other tricks and technique, in fighting and in negotiations, and they could talk about anything.

Without him, convincing the King to go hunting that day, he would have never met Samjya either. His father would have most likely not allowed this wedding. Unless Sahd had talked him into it. He had that special gift of finding the right words in any situation.

Sire Artius Graynor, the man his father had chosen to educate and guide Vonter after his death, had needed that type of convincing.

As a close friend of the late King, Sire Graynor was tied to the traditions and outdated rules. Luckily, Vonter and Sahd were able to change his worldview a little, and with his help, the view of the Elders too.

That was exactly why Sahdor had become his First General and valued confidant.

Another close friend, Draidr, Second General of the Royal Army, was very different from Sahd. He did not talk much, and when he did, he was always a bit of a cynic, often a bitter man even. Vonter appreciated his sceptical and questioning approach, and his honesty.

Where Sahd was his unequivocal supporter, Draidr was cunning, pensive, a quiet judge and yet swift challenger. Vonter was convinced that his intelligence was unmatched, and that he would one day join the Elders Council with all his wisdom and astuteness. The honour would suit him well.

Draidr had warned Vonter about how the public would react to Samjya before the announcement was made.

As much as Vonter had not liked what Draidr had to say then, he understood not long after the announcement how right he was. Then, and always. Draidr was brought up without a steady family, so he had a very good understanding of how rough and violent others could be, and more so, how tough, and smart can help you survive. He supported Vonter in his way.

That was not the case for all soldiers from the capital's Divisions. As a Prince, he never served alongside the other soldiers, and thus was considered to feel like he was above everyone else. But it was the proper way for a member of the Royal family to receive at least basic soldier's education. Because Vonter hated the court advisors and trainers in his young years, Vonter's father, and after his death, Sire Graynor had always made sure the Senior Generals would teach him in all disciplines.

His mother was the one then who had encouraged him to spend more time with the Generals as well. She had sensed the brotherly bond between her son and Sahd and Draidr. It was the main reason for Vonter to cherish their friendship the way he did.

Sahd, to his left, had not said a word since they had left the castle. He had a sister in Buntin, and Vonter could see that it was more than worry that made him rush his horse.

Draidr on his right, raised his voice: "My King, we will be there very shortly, it is just behind that hill."

Vonter could feel his throat close. In a few moments, they would know how many enemies they had to battle, and if he had brought enough soldiers to fight and healers to help the wounded. His eyes locked onto the top of the hill; it was just about a hundred feet away now.

For a long time now, they had been able to see the smoke darkening parts of the sky, and that had Vonter worry a lot. The villages in the area had to be alarmed, but none of his scouts or guards had returned yet. So, this could be the first, maybe even an isolated attack?

He made his horse go faster, and simultaneously, Sahd and Draidr did the same.

They created a bit of a distance between them and the about 2000 men that Vonter had brought. Signalling the army to halt, the three men continued to climb the hill fast. Shortly after, he reached the top and he was able to see the valley.

His heart stopped.

The town was gone.

Every house, every tower, each piece of the walls, the Golden Cathedral, the largest warehouse in the land, it was all just a pile of rubble! The whole valley looked like it had been stomped on by giant, repeatedly. There was not a single fence, stall or door standing. Smoke emerged from the scene, but it was a mystery to the men, what could still be burning with that intensity. Very small fires, but no person, nothing that was still living, could be seen. The silence was deafening. It was as if the dead town was just lying there, flat in the valley, still breathing but nothing but quiet smoke.

Then, he heard how Sahd cleared his throat. When he looked over, he could see the soldier's tears.

"This does not mean they did not get away." Vonter tried to comfort him.

"How could anyone have gotten away? Look at the town! It is crushed!" Draidr said, tactless as ever. Vonter gave him a stern look. He refused to believe there were no survivors.

He could feel his own tears creeping up behind his nose. Rage made its way into his stomach. He physically felt sick, but he would not let it fester. He needed to keep a clear head. His duty was to ensure peace and bring justice to the criminals, and this was not just a vicious attack. This was wiping out an entire town in the cruellest way possible, in his kingdom, which he swore to protect.

This was a declaration of war.

Sahd rammed his feet into the horse's sides and rushed down to the flat ruins. Vonter and his friend followed him. "Sahd! Stop! ... Sahd!"

His shouting was ignored, so he decided to try and catch up with his best friend.

By the time he did, Sahd had already stopped right in front of the place where the Northern gates had been. As if he was too afraid to lead his horse into the town, he did not dare to take another step. There was not a single thing or person moving in the open field. Just wood, broken furniture, crushed doors, and carts, and then, in between, they could see corpses of Buntin's people.

His people.

There were not many of them, but the ones they could see from here, were smashed into the ground, ripped apart, or wrapped around fallen trees or beams. Arms and legs stuck out of small piles of what used to be lovely homes and stores. This was a massacre.

Vonter could only guess how many bodies they would find underneath the rubble. He did not feel like a guess now. He felt like smashing the skulls of the ones responsible.

With tears running down his face, Sahd turned to Vonter. "My King, the monsters, who did this, need to be hunted down and punished!" he hissed between his clenched teeth.

"They will be. We will make them pay."

Vonter had no idea how to proceed.

Draidr was again very empathetic: "The whole town is dead, My King. No one survived. How are we going to find out who did this?"

"I do not know, Draidr. But we will. Get the other men to go into formation, and I will let them know my orders."

The soldier nodded and took off, back up the hill.

Vonter turned to Sahd, who had faced the crushed town once again. The two men stood in silence. There was no sound, no birds, no wind in the trees, even their horses kept the quietest they had ever been.

Then, suddenly, Sahd slid off his mount and started walking. "Sahd!" Vonter got off his horse too and went after him. He reached him just before his boot touched the splintered wood of the town gates and grabbed his shoulder.

"Sahd! Where do you think you're going? What do you expect to find out there?"

Under tears, boiling with anger, Sahd pushed the King's hand away: "You know who! I need to know."

"Sahd, I beg you not to go, this is pointless. You will spend weeks going through all of this by yourself. Our only chance is to search the entire valley for survivors using the numbers of the army. Trust me, we will find your sister and her children."

Sahd kicked his boot into a piece of wood several times, his fists clenched so hard that the knuckles went white and looked like they were ready to burst at any moment. His face quickly turned red, the boot hitting the immoveable board over and over until it started to break.

The King let him. He needed this. The demolition of the already damaged panel seemed to help him take back control. Maybe by controlling this pointless little act and inflicting more damage, he thought, Sahd slowly came to his senses again.

The hurt soldier turned around after a few kicks. "They were all alone, I left them all alone!"

Vonter put both his hands firmly on Sahd's shoulders, leaned forward and looked him in the eyes. "You are here now. We will look everywhere. And that is already helping her. You must believe that."

Sahd sobbed and snorted. His arms and shoulders sank down, and he looked to the ground. With quiet grunts and sighs, he sunk down and landed on his buttocks. Vonter decided to let him sit for a while and looked back up to the hill. His men had started their descent from the hills towards him and Sahd, and he had to make a plan.

A moment of quiet.

"Huh." His eyebrows at an angle, he had just noticed something peculiar.

When he spoke, he was not even aware or intending to speak to Sahd or anyone else. The thoughts just fell out of his mouth.

"Buntin had a lot of buildings, right? Made from bricks and boulders? There is not one single stone left."

***

Mibb tried again: "Yes, the stones were moving, because Dragus moved them with his mind!"

"So, he used magic to rebuild the castle?" the beaver asked.

The squirrel let his arms drop to the ground. "Yes! Now, do you understand? He used magic to build it back up again. The whole castle."

His friend still seemed to have a hard time understanding. "But how? His magic would not be strong enough to lift the cursed stones."

Mibb turned around and leaned against a tree trunk, his bushy tail between him and the tree.

He let himself sink down bit by bit, until he was sitting on the ground.

"Look, he seemed changed, somehow. I do not know what happened." He squinted his eyes and thought for a while. "I am not quite sure if it even was Dragus anymore."

The beaver was alarmed. "Mibb, are you thinking this Dragus is cursed?"

"Possibly. I was so sure that they both died during their fight. But when Dragus got up, there was this ... other energy about him. Like a different person, somehow." Mibb answered, uncertain of the matter.

The old friends pondered over what they had discussed for a few moments.

After the pause, the beaver inhaled and set out to ask another question. A deep, rumbling noise interrupted the two friends. It grew louder quickly, and it was approaching fast. Instinctively, the squirrel and the beaver jumped behind the trunk, thinking they would be safer there.

In the far distance, in the woods, a dusty, black force formed and rolled into their direction.

When the cloud got closer, Mibb was able to see what it was. He looked at the beaver in disbelief. His friend shrugged.

Out of the cloud emerged a huge, dark, man-shaped stone stomping its giant legs, one in front of the other.

The eyes were just two red dots, and the mouth a big, gaping hole. Fast, heavy steps were echoed by very similar creatures behind him. First a few, but their numbers appear to be ten, then twenty, and then a lot more than a hundred after a while. Smaller, but just as robust, these men made from black stone, marched like soldiers to the West, just about ten feet away from the spot where Mibb and his friend were hiding. The ground beneath their feet was vibrating. They could feel every single step.

There were so many of them! Hundreds of creatures made of stone stomped their way through the White Forest. They all varied in height, shape or form, but the stone and their glowing red eyes were always the same. The squirrel realised they were headed to the castle, to where he had seen Dragus last.

Mibb felt a shudder running down his back. Their hot, sharp aura made him feel very uneasy. The two animals were not noticed by any of them, but they stayed hidden and quiet for quite some time after the procession had passed and was not heard anymore, just to be safe.

Only after the silence had lasted a few long moments, Mibb dared to open his mouth.

"This is very, very bad."

***

Death. It is all that Samjya could think about. *Buntin has fallen*, what did that even mean?

How many had died in the city? Was it destroyed?

Would Vonter have to fight? Would he be attacked and killed?

And why was her father still missing?

The stewards had received no word from the Royal carriage that was supposed to bring him from the farm to the castle. Neither have had the messengers any news on the whereabouts of her father.

It was presumed that they had not arrived yet as they would still be on their way.

But that did not make any sense, they were supposed to be here a while ago!

The wedding had been meant to have finished by now!

Oh, the wedding.

It all seemed so pointless now.

She did not even care about the festivities anymore. She just wanted her father and her Vonter back in one piece.

In her darkest thoughts, she imagined her father being attacked and killed too.

He was living far away from Buntin, but another attack on the road would explain why no one had heard from his carriage. It was horrible to think that way, but Samjya could not help it.

This unbearable storm had invaded her heart, and she was not able to control it, or any of her feelings for that matter.

Pacing through her chambers for the better part of a day now, her thoughts and worries swirled around inside her like a tornado of unmeasurable proportions.

This room was too small for her alone. She felt cornered and trapped.

She could hardly breathe. But even more so, she would not dare to step outside her door. Everyone in the castle was very concerned, some terrified and hysterical.

Even looking at their worried faces made her sick to her stomach.

Like everyone, Yandra had tried to calm her down, but nothing had worked. At some point, Samjya had lost her temper and demanded to be alone.

She had never pushed her friend away like this. But then again, she had never felt like this.

And there she was, all alone in her bedroom, trying to not think about all the unthinkable things that could have happened to her dear ones, but thinking them anyway. Samjya could feel her body getting weaker. She had not eaten since this morning, and the tension was taking its toll. Slowly, she backed away to her bed, slumped down and stared into nothingness for a long time.

Looking around the room, restless, she noticed her wedding dress on the wall, which she had almost ripped off herself a while ago.

The thought of waiting around in it, waiting on a wedding that would not happen, waiting on a groom that would not come, was just too painful.

And her father, her dear, dear father!

After quite a while, she had no idea how much time had passed, the sun had gotten weaker, and it was about to be the mild summer evening that they had planned to spend in the gardens having cake. Her chambers had become darker. From the corner of her eye, she noticed a soft glow on her dressing table.

It was the flower that Vonter had given to her this morning as a present. The white petals emitted this light blue, pulsing shimmer, and an odd, comforting warmth. It was almost like the flower was calling out to her. And now that she felt it again, she remembered that it had been there all afternoon.

From the first moment that she had touched it, it was like it finally found what it was looking for, the reason to exist, like a long-lost baby that had found its mother. Its purpose was for her to feel the comfort and warmth, she was sure of it. How, she could not tell.

Samjya, now wrapped in exhaustion, got up, and moved to the dressing table. Tears formed in her eyes, not for the first time today.

She felt the longing pain to hug Vonter, to tell him how much she loved him and how much she appreciated his most wonderful present.

For some reason, deep down, she felt as if she would never get the chance to talk to him again. And this certainty grew with every breath, her heart sinking down into this dark corner of her mind.

With trembling fingers, she reached out to pick up the magical flower. She almost did not feel how her arms lifted and her hands turned to grab it.

As soon as she touched it, she felt it all. The pulsing energy of the blossom pushed itself into her fingertips, not to push back, it was more of a soft, welcoming embrace. Instantly, her pain, the worry, and the sadness were gone. The sensation was impressive.

Warmth and a sizzling power entered Samjya, and a big sigh of relief left her mouth.

As she raised the flower up to her face to have another smell, the rhythmic glows grew stronger and faster. Her heartbeat accelerated, but she barely noticed.

All that was left in her was the thought how everything would turn out okay. She was certain that in the end, all would be good.

7

The last group just returned as Vonter left his tent. His breath produced slim clouds in the cold night air. He could feel the sharpness of the wind cutting through his thin clothing. Was winter already coming?

The darkness around the camp was like a black blanket, shielding them from the outside world, at the time, threatening them with its endless void to swallow all life. From this darkness, his soldiers that he sent out to check for survivors, came back.

The flaming torch that Draidr carried had been burning for quite some time.

They had been gone all afternoon and evening, skimming through the rubble, the surroundings, and the fields in front of the White Forest.

Vonter fastened the sheath on his belt and grasped the handle of the sword he had inherited from his father. He was not alarmed, but his hand was resting comfortably on the sword at most times when he was outside his tent.

He nodded towards one of the stable boys to come and help Draidr get rid of his horse.

"Draidr!" he greeted him.

"My King." he hesitated.

Vonter's heart sank down inside his chest. He knew what he was about to hear next, so he said: "The others did not find anyone either?"

The stable boy took the mount's reins silently but stuck around to listen to their conversation. Vonter had heard earlier that he also had family ties to Buntin and was desperate for any news.

"No, I am afraid, there are no people around. If any were able to flee, they must have been flying. No signs of life whatsoever.

"There is something else though." Draidr looked nervously over his shoulder.

"There are large trails of many footsteps, like an army on many horses left the town on the road out the South gate across the river to the West.

"They have left dark markings on the road, leaving the path just uphill into the White Forest. It seems whoever walked away from this, went in there."

Draidr paused, then, continued: "Forgive me, my King, but the men are getting nervous about this place. Once the older ones started talking about magic, it had them all wound up."

The boy stuttered: "No one ever rode through the White Forest and lived to talk about it. It is impossible to -"

"Our enemy will be the first one then." Draidr interrupted the young worker.

"However, they did this, magic or not, we really should hunt them down and make them pay for this. And my King, if you ask me personally, I think we do not have time to listen to old men's fairy tales."

The stable boy looked to the ground and did not say anything. Vonter laid a hand on his shoulder, the boy looked up, and he nodded to dismiss him.

Draidr unmounted from his horse to leave it to the stable boy and turned to the King with a grim face. "How is Sahd doing?"

His concern was genuine. Vonter just shook his head. Sahd was concentrating on taking weapon and food inventory and making sure the troops were ready to ride on early tomorrow.

The King needed to make sure that his friend did not run off into the night and recklessly stumble into danger, so Vonter was trying to keep him busy. A purpose maybe, even? Plan the rations and making sure the weapons were all in good order.

That was not at all a task for a General, but Sahd was not in any condition to talk strategy.

They had to expand their search radius, go through the White Forest, and check on the other villages in the East.

"The good news is that no other village around seems to be affected. The messengers came back with good news so far, no further incidents."

Vonter sighed.

Now it was Draidr who put one hand on the King's shoulder.

"I have left a 20 to 30 men in each town as a precaution, and I will send more out tomorrow. That leaves the Second Division with mostly securing and continuous searching. The First Division should stay here and set up a base." the King said.

"That seems like a reasonable action. We would want to prevent something like this from happening again."

Vonter turned to his friend: "Can we?"

He could tell that Draidr knew exactly how powerless the King felt. "How can we stop a force that stomped an entire town into the ground? And fast, by the looks of it. We have found over 200 bodies already."

Draidr removed his hand and stepped away from the King, staring into the darkness past the camp. "I do not know, but we owe it to the rest of the kingdom to try. You cannot let this discourage you."

"I'm not. But it is overwhelming, we have no idea what we're up against."

He breathed in the crisp darkness and exhaled a warm mist slowly. "What if this is not the works of man's hand?"

Draidr turned around. "What do you mean, My King? Magic?"

"Have you seen the valley? The entire town is flat, and all cloth and wood, at least not what is burnt. There is not a single brick or cobblestone to be found.

"Where did the stones all go? Not any army that I have ever seen would be capable of this! This has got to be magic, surely?"

His friend could not contain a laughter: "I admit, it is very strange, but magic doesn't exist anymore! Don't you remember the stories of the War that brought back the Light, or whatever they call it?

"Old drunks and crazies are full of fables with creatures and witches. Especially after they had some mead at the tavern, and you get them talking about the olden days."

Vonter explained: "I know, these are nothing but stories. We have these old men that claim they have seen magic die, and others that say, magic is only a dormant force waiting to strike us down. What if it is the latter?"

Vonter began pacing.

"What makes these stories different from the new religion, the stories of the Golden Gods, and wonders from all corners of the land? Is this not magic? We have never faced something like this. Not in our generation. What if magic had never really left?"

A few moments of silence followed. And then, Draidr spoke again.

"Do you pray to the Golden Gods?"

"I did today. For the first time." It felt strange to say these words out loud.

"Do you think they listened?"

"Not sure. I do not even know if I want to believe they exist. If they did, none of this would have happened. Or they chose to ignore me. I do not know."

Draidr nodded. "I have the same thought, my friend. If they are really watching out for us as the monks say, they should have stepped in this time. This is an unspeakable tragedy. And this proves that they either do not pay attention, or they are again, just a fairy tale."

A soldier stepped behind Vonter and cleared his throat. "His Grace, forgive me, but you asked for a number. My men asked to stop for the night. The darkness is not making things any easier."

The King turned to face the man. "What's the number?"

"287, His Grace."

Vonter closed his eyes. Following a breath, he heard himself say: "Take rest until sunrise. I want the search to continue then."

The soldier bowed down. "Certainly, His Grace. Thank you."

Vonter turned around completely to face the man. "No. Thank you, and please thank your men from me too. Your task is not easy, and I will be eternally grateful for your brave service. Let's stay strong and supportive of each other in these dire times. Please make sure you pass this on to everyone."

"I will, His Grace. Thank you. Good night."

The soldier vanished again into the dark. In the far distance, they could hear shouting and groups of men moving in response to their new orders. Vonter remained in his position and spoke without addressing Draidr directly. "287 is not enough. There were over a thousand people in Buntin. I know the men have already checked a significant area."

Draidr followed his thought: "Yes, where are the other bodies? There must be survivors then. We will find them, My King."

"Yes, instead of you leading more men to other towns, I want you to take a few men into the White Forest to investigate. We will ask for volunteers first thing in the morning. I will do the same, we'll split up and find the source of this. Someone needs to check on Yopint, too. I think Sahd should speak to their mayor and arrange for their troops to be ready for a stronger defence and to move out for a potential battle. We need to stick together more than before."

He let out a short sigh, followed by a long sigh. "I cannot let this happen again." Draidr did not answer him. Vonter was not waiting for a reply either.

After a moment of silence, he walked back to his tent.

***

Samjya had stared at the ceiling for what felt like eternity. She had lost all sense of time and space. Numbed emotions were crawling around in the back of her head, somewhere far back in there.

Some background noise that was hard to make out and rather easy to ignore.

It felt as if a part of her had been haunted, by sadness and shock. But now, that she had allowed the wondrous comfort of the flower to take over, it was all so much better.

She did not have to worry; she did not have to be in pain anymore.

She did not have to do anything, really. Everything was going to be alright and work out just the way it was meant to.

However, she wondered why her dear friend had not come back. Yandra had been so adamant about Samjya not hiding away without food, because she was worried. Or so she said. Where was she now?

Samjya had been quite glad to be left alone at first, but now, she had the impression that Yandra did not really care as much as she claimed. There were no sounds, no knocks at her door, no one really asked her how she was doing. How could they go from being unbearably all over her to abandoning her like this?

And she had had the strangest dream last night. Something about how all she wanted to do was to look at the moon, but Vonter had taken it away from her! She liked the moon, but she had never been very passionate about it. What a strange thing to think!

And Vonter certainly did not have any reason to take the moon away from her. She could not think of one. Or a reason at all why he would want to take anything away from her. Unless of course, he was seeing her as some trophy – without the right to own anything else herself. Maybe that's why he had wanted her to join him at the castle in the first place?

Samjya had needed a lot of convincing as spent had spent her whole life on her father's farms and with her small family. And all this Royal business was an entirely different world to her. How could she really trust all that Vonter was telling her was true now that things had taken this turn? How could she trust in his love, his devotion?

Maybe she had been wrong to trust a man and follow him to this strange place. After all, he had left her behind on their wedding day!

Samjya lifted her head up and looked down at the flower. It was sitting on her belly, pulsing away in its peaceful rhythm, moving up and down in accordance with her breathing.

With a pensive sigh, she thought about the strange artefact. It was a complete mystery to her, why this simple thing had such impressive power. She was sure, it had to be of magical origin, and the woman who had sold this to Vonter, had to be a witch.

But she did not care. She was so glad that fate had brought them together. She was starting to believe that without this flower, she would not have been able to cope at all.

She took it back into both hands and sat up on the edge of her bed to take another close look. The individual petals shooting from the core were thick at the bottom, growing thinner and wider at the top.

They were larger than rose petals, and had a very soft texture, like satin. The scent was, oh, so magical. It was such a sweet and gentle perfume – like ripened fruit, but lighter, like a fresh morning in the fields, but fuller.

And the light was very soothing. Calling out to her, the silent sensation of experiencing this flower, created a subliminal but vibrant tone in her heart.

It was so intense and empowering that she wanted to crawl inside it. It had completely taken over and drowned out the storm that had filled her a while ago. A storm?

…

Pure serenity.

As she raised the flower towards her nose, she could feel the pulsing light warming her face. It smelled delicious. Water was collecting in her mouth. She wanted to get lost in this, it was so good.

Her lips touched the blossom, and the sizzling sensation left her even more ecstatic.

She could not help but think how amazing they might taste.

But could she eat it?

She would not think that it was meant to be eaten, but at the same time, it did not feel wrong.

On the contrary, the more she looked at it and took it in with all her senses, the more right it felt to take it a step further and put it inside her.

She was meant to.

It wanted her to.

Slowly, with eyes closed and lips just barely open, she moved the blossom closer to her face. She nervously licked her lips just an instant before they touched the petal below them. When it happened, all her senses exploded!

It was electrifying. The purity and sweetness were nothing like she had ever tasted before.

From her lips, the pulsing warmth extended into the back of her head, down her spine, into her arms and fingertips, her pelvis, the knees, and every single toe.

The only appropriate word that came to mind was whole happiness.

Her heart was beating faster.

Her tongue was licking the bottom of the petal, pulling it in.

Her hands lifted the artefact up even more, guiding the blossom into her face.

Her eyes still closed, she saw colourful shooting stars.

Her whole body was relaxed, totally still.

When she opened her eyes, the petal was gone. She had hardly noticed how it had disconnected from the artefact, whether she had chewed it, and how it had made its way down her throat.

But it filled her with such a comfort that she did not have to think about anything else.

This was not unusual.

It was the one, perfect, right thing to do.

She sank back, eyes closed, the flower still loosely in her hand.

She did not even realize how her torso leaned back, and how her back, and then her head gently set down on the bed until her body relaxed entirely.

She suddenly felt the softness of having arrived and the peace of the quiet cotton fabrics.

It was a sensation of utter peace, calm and true carelessness.

…

Samjya was very content with all.

…

No one could take anything away from her now.

It was all going to be good.

…

Better than that, even.

8

The next day started very early for everyone. With just a small piece of dried game for breakfast, the King stepped outside and ordered his squire to help him put on his armour. The large piece of iron breastplate was rather thin and light, so he was going to be able to fight should it come to that. His father had the purple seals added on each plate and cover. They had used a specially curated paint on the metal.

The Proud Steed of Cant'un, they called it. Its rearing hooves always pointed towards the wearer's heart in order to protect them.

The arm and leg pieces were slightly thicker and heavier, but like any other soldier, Vonter had trained to fight with and without armour. His helmet was of iron too, with subtle, purple markings on the back. The idea was that his Royal Guard was always going to spot him from the back to protect, but for the enemy, the King could easily disappear in a sea of helmets.

When Vonter stepped out, he could see that half of the tents had been taken down and the group that was assigned to collecting the bodies was already at work again. It was one of the toughest things his mean had had to deal with. Many of the 287 dead were in the worst state. The number of souls were crushing enough, but the mystery of the remaining citizens of Buntin had to be cleared up.

Vonter could not see the beautiful morning unfold as they were surrounded by death and cold steel. From the left, Sahd approached him: "My King, I would like to lead the search party into the White Forest. I need to make sure that my sister is safe!"

"Out of the question. I need my best strategist on a horse to Yopint.

"You need to plan with Sire Wern. It is imperative, that their army can join ours at any given point.

"They need to be warned properly and increase their defences too." Vonter said sternly.

Sahd stepped into his way as he was about to turn to the horses.

"Please, Vonter, let me do this. I am your best friend; I would not normally ask this of you. My sister has always been there for me, through thick and thin, and she is everything to me.

"Please." his voice was shaking. His eyes told him he would not let Vonter off.

The King stared at his friend for a few moments. "Sahd, you are too close to this. You will not be able to keep it together, I know you."

The General tried one last time: "I will not do anything that will put our forces here at risk. This is a pure investigative mission. I will find out what I can and come back as soon as possible! Please let me take charge on the search through the White Forest."

Suddenly, Vonter realised that Draidr had been waiting a few feet behind one of the tents. They had talked about it, it seemed, and Vonter could read on the other soldier's face that he did not agree with Sahd's plea.

But he did not have the heart to take this away from Sahd. He had already demoted him yesterday afternoon when he ordered him to do a squire's job. He was his most capable soldier, and he sensed every one of his men had their emotions riding high.

"Who is going to Yopint then?" he asked Sahd.

"With respect, My King, I think you should do this. You know Sire Wern, and you can make the best case to protect the kingdom. They will listen to the King more than a General. It will stress the severity of the situation."

Vonter thought about this change in plan. He had a bad feeling about this, but he knew Sahd needed this. And his friend was not wrong.

It would make the most impact if he went himself to warn Wern and request as many men as possible.

He raised his voice. "Right. You will lead a small division each and send back a messenger whenever you find anything, and I mean, anything, be it small or seemingly insignificant.

"I want all information to be collected right here. Please remember, this is a scouting mission only, no attacks and no risks. Track, follow, observe, and come back quietly. Nothing else."

He nodded, sent a long, determined look across to Sahd, and then, walked the men to their horses. Short embraces were exchanged, and Vonter told one of the soldiers on Sahd's group to watch out for their General. It was no secret that he desperately wanted to find his sister.

Only a half of the First Division had been left after he had planned the other six search parties: Two groups to skim through the woods led by Sahd and Draidr, one to go further North to secure Tramvil and Glaynth, the villages just North, and one to go East into the Planes of Llamar. Another group was to go South to Purdh and Ratsin, and the last to follow the river Southwest to cover any settlements closer to the mountains.

They all had the same orders: to warn and protect the kingdom everywhere.

In the meantime, he had left Sire Graynor in charge of the other Divisions, guarding the capital's citizens and its castle.

That way, Vonter was hoping to contain the panic and build a defence. Since they still had no idea where the danger came from, that really was the best he could do.

And if it really was in or behind the White Forest, then he would make sure that they'd take the fight to the enemy, whoever they were. Away from his kingdom, his people. He was determined to not let anyone else die, with or without the help of the Golden Gods.

When Vonter's squire was done, he had his horse brought up as well and rode to the men he had selected to accompany him to Yopint. He had one hundred men from the First Division with him to ride far East with their King.

The men did not comment on how they had been expecting Sahd instead of him, but he could tell, some of the younger soldiers straightened their backs and probably stayed more serious and focused than usual.

When he arrived at the group he had selected, their General nodded at the King, and he gave the order to move out.

They quickly left the campsite next to the destroyed Buntin and climbed back up the hills. Optimistically, they would reach Yopint in a bit more than a half day's ride if the horses were fast enough.

The fortress with the crest of the Trusted Eagle was not only a very resourceful and important place in the East, but it also housed the second largest army in the land. Their General and Mayor Sire Laint Wern, had the best strategic mind after Sire Graynor and Sahd. His father had put all his trust into the young Wern when they worked together in the capital. And just before his death he had him promoted to General of Yopint's Division and placed him in the trading city to lead the East and South defences.

Yopint was not a city the kingdom could afford to lose. Not that Vonter thought they could *afford any* city to be lost. Now, that was a silly thought.

He did not want any more people to die. But he knew this was not going to be avoidable. If this was a war, countless more people would give their lives.

After a tough and long ride of an uneventful better part of a day, they could see the towers of Yopint in the valley ahead. They had just left the trees on top of the hill behind them, and a small rubble path led them downwards. The roads in the East were narrow and uneven due to the hills and mountains.

The trees were a lot taller than in the White Forest, and their crowns did not give a lot of shadow. The valley was also not as secluded as the one where Buntin was. Had been.

It was even more beautiful, a few more trees, but no woods close by, and no river.

The fortress was on the hill on the edge of the valley giving it the tactical advantage to have a good view across the fields, the nearby coast, and the edge of the Desert Mountains.

The road going through the valley was an important connection between the Western traders and the Eastern havens.

All the major roads between the cities were quite busy. Lots of merchants bought their stock in Yopint from far away and exotic markets. They transported the wares to the other settlements and made sure that the citizens would have access to food and other items that they could not source in their area. It was vital to the villages close to the mountains as their crops were not fruitful at all. They would not be able to survive on herbs and wine alone, of course.

The small fortress looked rather peaceful despite being a fortress. If Vonter did not know about the looming danger, he would not think that there was anything wrong in these lands.

His men rode in a long line, now slower, that the safe fortress was in sight. Vonter could see movement up in the towers. So, the guards were alert at least, and not careless, he thought, slightly calmer himself now.

As they got closer, the gates were opened, and a few soldiers came out to take on a greeting formation.

On long poles, the green flags of the South waved in the wind, carrying the Trusted Eagle in black with its wings spread, just as welcoming as Yopint's citizens. A considerable number of citizens, mostly families and children, lined up to the left and right to greet their King.

Vonter smiled when they reached the walls, the children were waving at him, a few women looked up shyly, and the soldiers saluted their monarch. If only they knew, he thought.

Just behind the gates, Sire Laint Wern was awaiting them on his horse. He was a man around 55 years, grey hair, and rather tall and strong.

His uniform was of thick leather, finely laid around his body, but rather tight, and it made him sweat a little. That, or he had been in a hurry to get ready.

"His Grace, welcome to Yopint. We were not expecting your presence, and rather surprised to see the King's banner appear on the other side of the valley. But please allow me to say that I am delighted to call His King and his soldiers my guests."

He had a fatherly demeanour of being quite attentive and caring, but just the same, his eyes were caught easily by possible distractions. He was good at picking up on things that happened outside of a conversation without losing focus of what was in front of him.

"I am very grateful for your hospitality, Sire Wern, but I am afraid the reason for my visit is not a pleasant one."

The General's smile vanished. "Oh?

"Let's sit down first, my men need a drink, and I need to speak to you in private. Please have your men always secure all sides of the fortress with twice as much manpower."

With a worried gesture, Wern gave the order. They left their mounts in front of an impressively large tavern, and the King told his men to have a rest. Wern insisted on a free meal and mead for everyone. They had the King's soldiers sit down in the tavern, and the General led Vonter upstairs to a small room with a table and four comfortable chairs.

"This is your office, Sire Wern?" he asked surprised.

The General smiled. "Oh no, His Grace, I just thought this private room in our tavern would be a bit more accommodating after your long journey. You must have been on your horse for half a day, at least."

"We have come from Buntin, it was a very long journey."

Wern's eyes widened. The door opened again, and a waitress came in, put down some mead and water, but also a platter with the finest sausages, cheese, and hot potatoes.

"Please sit, His Grace. I insist."

He could definitely tell that Vonter was very tense.

The woman left the room, and the King sat down.

He took one of the cups of water and drank it all in one. Then, he reached for one of the sausages, but there were none. Maybe he had been mistaken? Instead, he helped himself to some cheese and started chewing.

"What brings Your Majesty into our beautiful town? It must be a pretty serious case if you are coming personally, bringing your personal guard?"

"This is not only my personal guard. I had to send out almost every single man of the Royal Army yesterday. I am afraid we are at war."

Wern sucked in the air quickly. "At war? With whom, His Grace?"

"We do not know. Buntin has fallen. Completely vanished from the land, actually. We counted almost three hundred dead until last night in the rubble, and everyone else is presumed missing. It is inexplicable, really."

The General's face turned white. He was about to grab some water too, but after hearing what the King was saying, he drank from the mead.

"How did Buntin fall – ... vanish?"

Vonter shrugged his shoulders. "We have no idea. The entire town looks like it was stomped into the ground. So many innocent people lost their lives. And there is not one trace of the enemy. I have never seen anything like it."

He tasted some of the sausages, only to realize that there had been no sausage just a few breaths ago. Nervously eating more than he would have normally, he noticed that he was quite hungry all of a sudden.

"I have men helping to enforce security in every town in the North and Southwest. My soldiers are also going through the White Forest as we speak, it seems that tracks lead right into the woods."

Wern's voice started to tremble. "His Grace, that is quite dangerous. Man has not been deep into the White Forest in centuries."

"I know. That's why it is so crucial that we investigate it. No one knows what is lurking in these woods.

"That's also why we waited until sunrise, and I have sent my best soldiers to search. We need to find the responsible force and deal with it."

"The responsible force?" Wern asked sceptically.

Vonter frowned.

"Forgive me, Sire Wern, but you have not seen the damage. There was not one house, one stable, not one bench left standing in Buntin. Any stone was gone, even the streets.

"It was unnatural. I have never seen anything like it."

The General pushed his chair back a bit. He was visibly uncomfortable, probably getting scared. "And you have come to ask for more men? We have just sent a large new division down to Ubbin, but I have at least 5000 men here that can fight."

"I mainly came to warn you. Your fortress is strategically important for access to the East coast and protection of the South.

"I wanted to personally make sure that you are safe, and that we take any precautions for war.

"But yes, if you can have men ready to join the Royal Army when things get more serious, that would be good. However, I would like to return to Buntin, or what is left of it, where we have set up our camp.

"I will have to ask you to check on the other towns and villages nearby to secure the area.

"We will stop in Lint on our way, maybe spend the night there."

Wern nodded, concerned. "As worrying as the situation sounds, I am glad His King is watching out for us."

"Any advice you can offer, old friend?" Vonter tried to smile at the General.

The older man smiled back as comforting as he could: "It seems you have a pretty good handle on things, your father and I taught you very well. It is important to gather lots of information first and to ensure armies are placed at smart points on the map in order to react quickly. I take it the capital is sufficiently protected?"

"Yes, I have left the majority of my troops, and only took the First and Second Division with me. A few of which are stationed in villages around Buntin, others have been assigned to search and secure."

Vonter decided to have one last bite of the cheese from the now empty plate. He had been starving, but he was equally determined to move on as quickly as possible.

In thought, the King straightened his back in the cushioned chair. He felt fairly tired, but the plan was to reach Lint before midnight.

"Can you pass a message on to the coast and Northlight as well? There is an easy road up there I remember?" he added. Sire Wern nodded. "Certainly."

"I can assure you we will find the source of this." Vonter rose from his seat.

Quickly, the General got up from his chair too. "Of course, His Grace. I will ask the girls to pack you some food for your journey."

"That is very kind, thank you."

On his way out, Vonter turned around and saw a few sausages left on the plate. These were certainly not there earlier.

The two men walked back downstairs, and as planned before, Vonter signalled his men to join him back on the horses.

It only took a few moments for everyone to finish their drinks and meals, and after a short while, all of them were ready to leave.

They only had a small while of sunlight left. Luckily, the next town was rather close, and their mayor was very easy to talk to as well.

It really was a beautiful day, and Vonter just realised how much he was not thinking of his wedding. By now, he should have been married to the love of his life for almost an entire day.

But it did not feel right anymore. He wanted to give Samjya all the happiness in the world, but not at the expense of his kingdom and the lives of his people.

And he was sure that she would understand.

Her love was unconditional, kind and forgiving, never unreasonable. She had to know that his duties would require him to be away in tough times.

A smile appeared on his lips as his horse started its way to the gates. He had let his guard down. He was exposed, which was frightening and beautiful in equal parts. But it was worth it, a million times over.

She was so gorgeous. And really, the most amazing human being in the world.

He did not care about being defenceless when it came to her.

As they rode to leave the trading city Yopint, he saw that the numbers on the towers and by the walls had already tripled.

9

The distant rumbling grew louder and was approaching the castle fast. He felt them. Every single one of those pathetic souls.

Fragir's thoughts circled around the black stone yard that laid in front of him, the last sunlight escaping behind the white treetops. This was a pretty good plan; he could not help but feel very proud of himself.

He had been quite lucky to have found the black ruins. Channelling the earth's energies was second nature to him, so building it back up as his new base was ingenious, and so easy.

Fragir had changed into the clothes that he had acquired in Buntin. Much better. His short, grey hair and the stubble had grown out a bit, but he did not mind. At least he had gotten rid of Dragus's old rags.

He could sense the young man's soul fighting him. There was no point, Fragir had him locked away tightly. Again, he was amazed at how easy it had been to take control over this body. Dragus clearly had underestimated his power as an earth sorcerer.

His trusted horse had been disassembled, and he was all alone in the old ruins that he had rebuilt. But that would change very soon. He was even a bit nervous in anticipation, delightfully nervous.

His first attack had been more than successful. And that was just the beginning. One town after the other, he would crush them and make them his. The capital was next.

And he wanted more. He wanted all the souls in all the towns.

Soon, he would let the world know who was behind all of this. And then, he would destroy the rest of humanity. He hated every single mortal in these lands, they had to pay, the King most of all, and he would make sure all their souls would be trapped in stone forever!

A shattering, continuous rumbling arrived at the open gates, and Fragir stepped out onto the front balcony. The first soldier to enter his castle, at the front of the black mass of gruesome stone men, was Yart. The poor merchant from Buntin he had transformed first, had become an infectious leader of his new stone army. A General to bring death and destruction to the other towns.

Yart's expressionless red eyes did not show any emotion whatsoever, but Fragir imagined pride in his eyes. He knew this was not the emotion of the soul inside at all.

With the silent mouth hole wide open, the black General was looking up to Fragir as if he was waiting for praise or orders.

Using a smooth wave, the sorcerer raised his left hand and nodded slightly. Yart had no problem understanding precisely what Fragir meant. The soul in its black vessel was under his control. He let out an earth-shattering roar and turned around.

Slowly, and with the rhythm of a heartbeat, the other stone soldiers came marching into the castle walls. The court between the main building and the gates filled up with live rocks that moved and behaved like real soldiers. They lined up in many rows surrounding their General in a half circle.

After a while, the area in front of Yart was filled with the stone army, a couple of hundred more outside of the gates. Silently, they stood as one dark ocean of solid matter that was patiently waiting for the storm to activate their crushing waves. The former merchant turned around to the sorcerer and looked up again.

"Souls!" Fragir spoke up. "Such delicate, lonely things. They blindly reach out to the world and get scarred with pesky emotions and useless desires.

"Most of you are in pain, confused and very much afraid. All sorts of despair, really. Isn't it dreadful?" he paused as if the dramatic effect would impress his audience.

"I have come to free you from this curse. Trust me when I say, all of your worries will be forgotten.

"You will not have to run anymore. No more fighting, no more longing for things you will never achieve. No more hurt, no more betrayal, no more loss. No more!

"I just need you to do one thing for me. One thing. It will be a new way of life. Well, not life as you'd define it, but it is some kind of life I suppose. You'll see."

He raised his hand again, and the stone soldiers started to move. They turned towards the walls in all directions and pressed themselves *into* the walls.

Faint screams and sighs emerged each time a soldier got assimilated into the bricks.

The souls were pulled into the stones, and it was a painful procedure.

Leaving nothing but black crumbles and their torturous echoes behind, the energy flowed from their hard vessels into the castle structure. As if the hard rocks were soft like butter, with an intense crumbling sound, they disappeared into the walls making them more voluminous.

The building took them in, entirely, one by one, and in the process, it grew thicker, stronger, more grotesk.

Fragir could feel the power of it all, the merging of the stones and the sweet release of the life of every single soul he had captured. Most of all, he felt the return of his own curse energy he had put on them.

It came flowing back into the fibres of his making, the combined power of their souls, the purest magic in this world.

The castle walls grew thicker and higher. Black stone grew out of black stone as the matter expanded, and the soldiers disappeared.

Long spikes and towers emerged from the black mass and weird, devilish, round, and bent shapes decorated the top and sides of the outer walls. The number of souls inside was overwhelming.

After the complete army had been swallowed by the walls around them, Fragir turned to Yart, who was still in the same spot as before, like a well-trained dog, waiting.

There were no thoughts, no sentiments, just a cold, empty shell behind those red dots. He did not want to release him just yet. His new soldier would be very useful in his current form.

Without a noise, the empty eyes just stared at Fragir. There was no doubt that the merchant was still alive in there, and suffering.

At the same time, unable to do anything. His soul was under the sorcerer's spell, ready to do his bidding, no matter what.

Fragir bent over to pick up a small stone, tossed it into Yart's mouth, and snickered. The soldier did not react at all. Still, as if nothing happened, he was just standing there, waiting.

With slow, relaxed steps, Fragir turned his back on the yard, and closed his brown eyes. He concentrated on the sounds of the White Forest. There was no birdsong, and he was not able to hear any other animals.

This area was avoided by any living soul, and with good reason.

Not too far away, he could hear ... thoughts. And the heavy breaths of just a few desperate men. He focused on their minds and closed in on their position.

They were quite close to the castle, Yart had made sure of that. The trail he had left behind was very clear, and nothing would have stopped them.

They were most likely not to attack directly; he could sense it in their thoughts. But it would not hurt to let his soldier stay guard – they would certainly get more than what they bargained for.

Whether they would wait until daylight or not, well, getting rid of them, was Yart's next assignment.

The sorcerer turned around and went to have an early rest.

***

The entire forest was unnatural. Everything was white, hence the name. White trees, from trunk to leaves in the highest crowns. They had found different tracks leading into the woods, and then, grouping together into a wider pathway destroying everything in the process. There were no pathways at all in these woods, and all the trees stood narrowly together, but luckily, the black trail was forming a road for them to follow, a very obvious trail.

It was as if someone had taken paint and coloured the grass and leaves behind them, the whole fauna was as dark as the night itself. It must have been a giant stampede that had destroyed Buntin, had made its way into the forest, and formed a passage through the woods, flattened all the trees in its way.

It had become clear that this was more than merely an army.

Draidr felt weary, the last night had been too short and cold. He did not sleep well in tents. But it mainly meant that he was not well rested and in a foul mood the next day. Even more so than usual.

His horse was getting exhausted as they had been following the trail for almost an entire day now, so he let himself fall back to his group, and shouted: "Halt!"

A spot on the side of the trail was as good for a rest as any; a couple of fallen trees on their right would make suitable benches to sit on, and a few feet off, he could see a stream behind a line of trees. He signalled his men to unmount, take a rest and get some food and water into their tired bodies.

Before getting off his horse, he tried to listen into the distance, but it was still too quiet.

He had heard the stories of the creepy White Forest without animals, birds or even insects, but this was definitely eerier than he expected.

A forest without life – that is why they called it the Dead Forest too.

It was literally silent, not even the wind was heard as the trees stood tighter together in this part of the woods.

Draidr jumped off his trusted horse, fixed the reins to a nearby trunk and walked over to the others to sit down. They passed dried meat and bread wrapped in cloth around. Two men walked over to the river to replenish the water rations.

He did not like this place at all.

Obviously, the black trail made everyone feel uneasy, but the fact that they were not able to spot even one enemy in this silent forest, made the whole situation even more threatening. Whatever danger was looming at the end of this pathway, could not be good.

Deep in thought, his mind wandered to the citizens of Buntin who had lost their lives. Or who may have escaped but had most likely lost their families. There was a lot of pain, he could see it in his friends' eyes, but he was not able to grasp it fully. Sahdor, for instance, his best friend had not been able to talk to him since they had arrived at Buntin. Not really.

He was not sure how he felt. Not knowing the fate of his sister and nephews, or any notion about the feelings people would have for their families, Draidr just could not fathom it.

He was an orphan; he did not even remember where he was from or if he ever had a family. And the nuns that had raised him, had been so religious that it had made him bitter.

He did not have anyone in this forsaken, broken world. And this horrific tragedy showed him once again that humanity was doomed.

Hundreds and thousands of years long wars that brought glory to the successful military men and Kings, but misery and death to the average population, that was the reality. Not whole-hearted Gods or Spirits that looked out for them. Not the Ungods or hags manipulating the hearts of mortals.

The way he was brought up, Gods ruled over this land, ensuring that man had all that was needed.

But he came to believe there was no higher power, no magical being that would guide their lives into whatever fate they deemed right for them.

He refused to believe any of it. Man was just sat in their own excrement, producing more excrement, hardly ever able to dig themselves out.

And now, there was a mysterious force that flattened towns and woods like a giant rolling pin. Maybe the King was right, maybe the magic was back. Back with a vengeance. To Draidr, it did not make any sense.

Screams of agony and terror ripped his mind away from his thoughts.

Flynn, one of their best, had jumped off the fallen tree grabbing his upper thigh, the eyes wide open in shock. His foot and shin had turned grey and rock solid!

With quite the pace, his transformation was going up his leg and moved across his fingers and hands. His screams filled the entire forest and had stirred up the other men around him.

Right after Flynn had started screaming, fellow soldiers started pulling him away from where this crazy change originated, but no chance. Flynn's leg was stuck, and only a few moments later, both of his legs and arms were covered, motionless, frozen.

No, they seemed to have *turned into* stone. One soldier started hacking the foot with his sword, another one grabbed Flynn's arm, but as soon as they tried to help the poor man, the infection jumped onto both of them as well. And very, very fast!

From the tip of the sword, the stone quickly grew up to the handle. The soldier dropped his weapon, but the stone handle still grazed his knee, and he was starting to turn into stone!

The other soldier that wanted to help Flynn, got stuck to his arm and turned into stone on the spot.

Before his arm vanished under the grey, he grabbed a fourth man in desperation, and as soon as his hand was infected, he could not let go.

The same effect started on the next man's chest.

Quickly, almost all his men were screaming in pain and turning solid, three of them already completely covered and silenced forever. Draidr didn't know what to do.

He realised that he had drawn his sword, but that would not do anyone good as he had seen just moments ago. Also, he was too scared to move as this was spreading way too quickly through touch. That's when he realized, no one had actually understood the situation!

"Stop touching them!" his voice was a growl that came through his closed-up throat, but it was not enough. Slim moments later, he stared at a statue.

17 men, completely made out of stone, like a motionless monument of terror. He let his sword sink down, powerless, and numb.

How was this possible?

From behind the statue, he registered movement. It took him a few breaths to come back to reality. Kvarn and Thrim came running from the place they were getting the water, weapons drawn and confused. They did not seem to notice right away.

"Where is everyone?" Kvarn said looking around.

Thrim was the first to even see the stone.

"Where did this come from?" he mumbled, and his friend was already reaching out to touch it.

"No!" Draidr awoke from his freeze, but it was too late. Kvarn's head turned towards his superior, the hand already touching his fellow soldier's shoulder. Thrim and Draidr both watched Kvarn's facial expression change from confusion to pain, and he let out the same scream that the others uttered before.

Thrim grabbed Kvarn's arm, but Draidr jumped forward and tackled Thrim away.

They both fell to the ground, Draidr rolling off him, making sure there was no direct contact between them. Thrim needed a short while to pull himself together, and then, leaned up to see. Draidr lifted an arm to indicate he should not move.

They both stared at Kvarn, who had now stopped screaming, because his mouth was stone. Just like the rest of his body. Just like the other soldiers, he was a lifeless, solid statue, with the horror of the transformation written in his face.

Draidr stared at Thrim for a long moment. Nothing happened. Good, he was safe.

Thrim looked at the Second General in disbelief.

Neither of them would speak for a long while.

10

With a silent sigh, Yandra let her head sink down in disappointment and doubt. Would she really had lost her life's long friend, or would she be able to reach out to her again and touch her in this difficult time? She had not seen Samjya in a day now.

After long and painful discussions with Sire Graynor, Yandra was not allowed to leave the capital, let alone the castle. She had given up trying.

She had planned to find Samjya's father, but they had told her that search parties were out there already.

She had wanted to hug and comfort her friend, but she was not even let into her room. She wanted to help out in the kitchen, to keep her mind and hands busy, just doing something, but they would not let her. Even the soldiers outside chased her away when she was having a look at the horse stables to see if someone would appreciate a pair of able hands.

She desperately wanted to do something, to help somehow, but she did not get a chance.

Yandra was walking down the corridor again, slowly, to pick up Samjya's tray with untouched food, her arms just hanging down aimlessly. She could understand how upsetting this situation must be for a young woman, especially not knowing where the rest of her family was.

But Yandra could not understand how Samjya could shut her out like this. She had locked herself in her room, and there was no movement, no sound, nothing.

In the 20 and something years that Yandra had known her and been there for her, as a friend, a sister in love and spirit, sometimes even substitute mother, she had never experienced this kind of behaviour.

Samjya was not like this, she never had been. Her kind, generous and always cheerful friend had locked herself away from the world and would not say a word.

Walking past the high windows that would let in the last few rays of sunlight, she caught a glimpse through one of them to Samjya's bedroom on the side of the tower. A strange, cold light emitted from the opening in the wall. It was rather faint, easy to miss, but peculiar in colour. Blue, silver, white? Yandra was not sure.

Shaking the thought, she continued her way down the hall, and after a few breaths, she reached the tray on the ground in front of the door. She stopped for a short moment and stared at the tea pot, the brown salad, the cold meat, and the flies that occupied the not so fresh fruit. What a waste, she could not help but think.

She knocked at the door.

Almost hesitant, but then, determined.

And a second time.

No response. Not a sound from the other side.

And of course, the door was locked, Yandra had tried many times, called out to Samjya, and even passed notes under the door.

But when she bent down to pick up the tray, she saw the light yet again from the corner of her eye. It was the same cold, blue shimmer that she had seen moments ago. This time, it was visible from underneath the door. What could that be?

Instead of getting the tray as intended, she knocked again, this time, without hesitation.

"Samjya? Please open the door!" still, nothing.

"Samjya, my love, please. What is going on? Talk to me."

Yandra was very worried.

She decided that she would not let Samjya hide away another day and try again in the morning. She might have to ask Sire Graynor to break down the door if there was no change. Her friend needed food and water.

Samjya's father would never forgive Yandra for not protecting his daughter.

Yandra walked down the corridor and the stairs, bringing the tray back to the kitchen.

All servants and kitchen staff had left, no one in the inner court to cook for, the wedding was off.

Her sad steps brought her to the shadowy Royal Dining Hall.

Everything appeared to be frozen. The food had been taken away, but the blue decorations, the flowers, the drapes, and the candles were still there.

Frozen in time. As if they were waiting for the wedding to commence like nothing ever happened. Only, it was the middle of the night, more than one day after the intended wedding day.

Nothing would happen.

Except for the war outside.

She was scared, and that was new. Life had been very safe, too easy for her to be prepared for horror and fright.

She found a chair and sat down in thoughts forgetting all about the tray.

Yandra had been so lucky, meeting the right people at the right time. She had not been given the best education, but what she had learned had given her purpose.

A good standing among other women in her situation, and she had made it from being a tossed-out soul from a shabby orphanage at the age of 14 to Samjya's father's farming estates.

She had never met her mother, never heard of her father, she knew nothing about her origin. Still, the farms had always been her home, and she felt that Samjya's family who had taken her in, was her real family. Samjya was her sister.

She loved her, and cared for her, even though she was often a mother figure, and had to be a stern educator to Samjya at times.

The days on the farms had always been filled with bliss. She was always so lively, daring and very strong-willed.

She also had to be, among all the men, with Yandra as her only female contact. Yes, the people at the farms had been very good to her.

There had been many days when Yandra did not believe that she deserved her good life and such good friends, her substitute family.

Maybe this war was how the Powers were finally taking it all away from her.

Incredible that they would. But also, so very painful.

If this was supposed to be the end of it all, she would want to curse the Old Gods, or the Golden Gods, or whoever was playing with their fate. Why give her a beautiful life, and then snatch it out of her hands like this?

The news about Buntin had everyone rattled and upset. There were no other reports of attacks, but that could be a bad thing too. The messengers might have never made it back, or they would have been attacked before they could send a messenger out. And hundreds of dead or missing people from Buntin was bad enough. They would not get any more information as they had been no other messengers. Again, a bad sign. Really bad.

Her mind was racing in circles, and it made her manic. She could feel her friend slip away into depression, the kingdom sinking into chaos, and ... then, it hit her!

Yandra was so full of doubt that she had lost faith in her King! Shocked by her own feelings, a short burst of air pressed out of her torso.

How could she doubt her own King? Of course, Vonter would overcome whatever threat this was and make sure there would be no more lives taken. He would fight for everyone, for the people and for Samjya, until his dying breath. It would be his single honour and duty to do so.

She sunk deeper into the chair trying to push her spiralling thoughts away.

Focusing on the clear and crisp moonlight gave her a little bit of silent comfort. Her cold arms felt momentarily warm, then, back to cold.

She wondered if the Chamber Master would decide to take it all down tomorrow. Or the day after tomorrow. Or if they would wait for word from the King. What kind of word that would be!

And Samjya, poor Samjya, her heart had to be broken, and her mind gone crazy with worry, she thought. Yandra could not imagine what she was going through, what she had to be thinking. And also, how she would react to the wedding set up that was still prepared down here, with no groom of hers in sight. What would she say, and what would she do? Yandra's thoughts were circled around her mistress, and how she could possibly be there for her.

Suddenly, she felt a lot colder. The winds had calmed down, but she sensed a cold breeze coming from the other side of the room, where the entrance was.

She pulled up her scarf, but it was no use. It dawned on her that the cold was not the night or the winds. It was probably her own worry and lack of sleep. The emotion was so powerful that her shoulders shivered.

She turned her head … and saw a shadow.

The figure was in the middle of the door to the hall, barely 10 feet away from her. It was a woman in a long dress, and her loose, stringy hair falling over her shoulders down to her hips.

She seemed to ... glow somehow. It was not overly noticeable, but there was a blue shimmer in her hair that could not come from any light source close by. And the room was quite dark.

Yandra wondered if that was Samjya. Her posture was different though, and there was an odd energy about her, almost sizzling. Was she a witch?

The woman started to slowly walk into the room, but the feet would not lift off the ground properly – almost as if she was sleepwalking. The darkness would not reveal any more details on her, and the glow was not strong at all to give enough light.

Yandra jumped up. She made out that this person was barefoot. "Excuse me, My Lady. Can I be of assistance?"

There was no answer. The head tilted abruptly to the left and then back, when Yandra started and stopped speaking, but her walking speed was not changed, and she did not change direction.

She noticed that the woman did not walk towards her, but to the window. The closer she got, the more moonlight fell on her, and Yandra was suddenly sure.

It was Samjya!

"My dear Samjya, please let me -" she was about to step closer, but something made her stop.

The eyes were so very sad, and there was a wet glimmer in them, very cold, and so deep. It was as if she had been crying for a century and more tears had been stuck just inside her eyes. Her face looked grey, and so did her hair, except for the blue shimmer in it. That had to be the moonlight!

The dress she wore was the underdress from yesterday, and it was all wrinkly, her arms hung motionless down each side of her hips.

She had to be beyond exhaustion, and she was pulling her feet across the floor more than she was walking.

There was a certain clumsy elegance to the whole scene. How she stepped into the pale white light, and the blue in her hair started to gleam even more, the blue dress became lighter and almost luminous.

But Yandra was frightened for her.

And … of her.

"Please, Samjya." she whispered. "What are you doing?"

Her friend tilted her head abruptly again. This time, towards Yandra which almost made her jump.

The expression on Samjya's face was ... sadness? Frozen happiness? Something in between?

"Yandra." her voice faint and crackling.

"I did not see you there. I needed to see the mess he left. I want to be sure. The sky and the moon."

She rocked her head back and forth in an irregular pattern.

It was as if she was not in control of it. Her arms were lumped down, her eyes had this wet shine and were not even blinking once. Yandra started to get more nervous: "Are you feeling alright, Samjya?"

"Did you know that I cannot see the moon from my window?" she asked without acknowledging that Yandra had spoken. She had almost interrupted her as if she had not heard it at all.

"No, my dear. I did not know that. Maybe we should sit down. -"

Samjya interrupted her again with the same monotone, weak voice: "I have never seen such a beautiful moon. She is very crisp and white tonight. I love it. I want to make sure."

Yandra stepped next to her and looked up. It was true. The moon was incredibly beautiful this night. Below the window, there were roofs, the castle square and a few trees that stood like dark green cotton balls under the moon. It was a dark image inked in black and blue. Very peaceful. Probably very unlike to where the King was. Wherever he was.

As if she had heard her thoughts, Samjya asked lethargically: "Do you think Vonter will come back? ... I think he may have forgotten about me."

Yandra wanted to scream. She wanted to grab her young friend by the shoulders and scream at her, that she should pull herself together, and that everything was going to be fine. That Vonter would return any breath now, unharmed, with all his soldiers, having returned peace to the land. But she could not.

Her fear for and of Samjya grew quickly. There was a large lump in her throat, and she could not even move. Let alone let a sound pass her lips. Unable to do anything, she just stood there, leaving the last words to the fatal echo of the hall.

For a very long time, no one spoke. They stared at the moon and breathed the silence. Yandra was struggling to fight her inhibition to speak, and her fear.

"I do not think Vonter is coming back. I had to be sure." the pale Samjya whispered finally in quiet lethargy. Her face remained in the same emotion, oddly happy, strangely sad.

Yandra was now also fighting the tears in her eyes, still unable to utter a single word.

Samjya's tone grew sharper, colder.

"Did you hear how sorry my Vonter is. He is so, so, sorry, he says ..." – *What?* – "... I think he will try and show me how sorry he is, it is all he says. I think, I am sure. Like how he is sorry for calling off the wedding and that my father went missing.

Oh, I am absolutely sure. But the King is sorry, did you hear?"

Her tone became quite vicious.

Yandra's speech returned suddenly and forcefully: "My Samjya! King Vonter is out there, trying to resolve the situation! He is doing everything he can to save lives.

"And they have soldiers out looking for your father, but there is no chance that Vonter would neglect you or your dear father. I will not give up on his determination, and neither should you. You must believe in him!"

"No."

The answer was defiantly determined. "I refuse to believe anything I cannot see. The King is just sorry, that's all he is. He is not helping, I sure know. The kingdom is lost, my father is lost, I am left all alone here with strangers, and the King is just sorry. I cannot see Vonter, so I know he is not with me. And if he is not with me, I am all alone."

Cold and hot shivers ran down Yandra's neck, shoulders and back. She wanted to scream, *what about me? I am right here, for you and only you!*

Her whole body started to tremble. This was not her Samjya. She was not making any sense. She was speaking in a fever or something! What in the Gods' names was happening? What was going on?

Samjya turned around, and walked back the way she had come in.

With the same tempo and dragging footsteps, her arms and hair just hanging down, her face in the same expression, she walked all the way back out the hall.

Her quiet voice echoed softly between them:

"I know. Do not take the moon, I like the moon. Do not take the moon. I sure know. My moon."

Why would I take –?

Yandra wanted to follow her, see that she was safe and sound in her chambers, tuck her into bed, and make sure that she would get a good night's sleep and a solid breakfast. Maybe this all was just the sleep deprivation and depression speaking?

But equally, she felt like running away from this cold, strange energy, this soundless threat that had taken hold of her friend – there was no other description for it.

She felt like screaming, crying, hitting the walls, knocking down the tables, running through the gates into the night, so the enemy could find and kill her, and it would all be over.

She could not move. Samjya had infected her with the cold state of being stuck.

She had frozen her. Yandra wanted to do so many things at this moment. Instead, she just watched her trusted friend leave the room, with an ice cold feeling in her gut.

An icicle, bleeding her out while she was unable to shout her name.

11

After a surprisingly good night, the King woke up to quite the peaceful morning since the day of his wedding that did not happen. From the balcony of the most generous room at the South Rocks Inn, he looked East.

Hoping to smell the salty sea winds again, he was out of luck. The Desert Mountains and their inland-reaching hills shielded the valleys here from the winds. In a way, this helped the farmers grow very aromatic and rich crops and fruits here. He knew that not everyone in the North would get the chance to enjoy them as the few supplied that made the journey, were mostly bought up by the castle directly.

This was his land, the beloved Cant'un, ruled by the Blood of Taryien for a long time.

Only after accepting the crown, he fully grasped the significance of the legacy of his family. Many Kings before him had helped shape the politics of the land, which was not always peaceful or reasonable.

Vonter had found his kingdom to be very interesting when it came to the characters and the regional peculiarities. He had travelled rarely with his father when he was young, and mostly the North.

But the more it had become his mission to serve his people after his parents' passing, the more he had undertaken journeys to show his face and support for the entire kingdom. If his people stood behind him, it was a more fruitful ruling, he firmly believed that.

For a long time, his ancestors had believed in the Bronze Giants that created this world, then the Silver Spirits that shaped it.

The newer belief in the Golden Gods that stepped in to fight evil and protect humans was something that he just could not warm up to.

He had never seen any magic or spirits.

His parents had taught him the ways of religion, but never spent too much time talking about magic as they had stopped believing in it themselves.

And Vonter was not comfortable with the thought that higher beings were in charge of his life. He made his own decisions and that was that. There should not be a mighty force, magical or not, that would be in control over life and death. Life was difficult enough as it was.

Yet, two nights ago, he had found himself praying.

If there was a small as it may be chance the spirits existed and listened in, he would gladly accept their assistance in preventing more bloodshed. He kept thinking, *as the King, I have the duty to use any help available, even a longshot one at that.* The only question was, why they had not saved the people of Buntin in the first place.

At the same time, he was not sure what to think of the world they lived in. Maybe it was created by Giants and Spirits who had left the people to their own devices and the Golden Gods were just invented by the monks as a way to maintain hope and comfort in dark times? Or maybe the world was just the world, and they were all making their own destiny, no help or guidance. He preferred the idea where he was in charge, and he believed he was.

Of course, he had heard a lot of fables too. Like when the last magic war was fought, Golden Gods helped banish the very last witch, destroying the remnants of darkness altogether.

And a few decades earlier, they had sealed away a full Circle of evil witches and sorcerers, and they created the White Forest as a symbolic warning against magic and its curses. Which is why no one would ever set foot into the pale woods, until Vonter had asked his two most trustworthy Generals to do so.

He was hoping they would not find anything. He was hoping that this was a simple, easily fought threat, and that he could just go home without having lost any more lives.

Vonter was glad that Lint was fine too.

If the other scouts would return with similar news, Buntin would have seemed to have been an isolated attack then, at least so far.

It was good for him and his men to get a proper night's rest at this inn, the owner had been very forthcoming with free drink and food too. The sun was almost up, so he decided to get dressed, go downstairs, and have his men prepare for their return.

He wanted to get back to the camp near Buntin as soon as possible.

Again, his thoughts came back to Samjya. She had to have been sick with worry. He was thinking, once back in Buntin, that he should send another message to her. His men might have gathered even more information on the threat to his land, which needed to be passed on to the capital anyway.

Vonter had to return, not only to find out what the scouting Divisions had discovered, so he could plan a counterattack and order reinforcements from the capital – the Senior General, Sire Graynor was awaiting orders to move more soldiers out, and he would be able to advise the King on further precautions or arrangements.

He also had to be back in Buntin quickly as he was eager to get word on Sahd's and Draidr's reconnaissance. He wondered how Sahd was holding up. Minher was close to his heart too, and it pained him to see his friend suffer.

On the ground floor, his men had already packed their things, and received some meals, courtesy of the inn's owner again. They were currently putting on their metal armour or getting the horses ready.

The inn owner, a small, overweight businessman with a sweaty forehead, came running out from behind the bar when he saw the King at the foot of the stairs.

"His Grace, we took the liberty of supplying you with packed lunches and waterskins, on the house, of course."

It was very important to this man to let him know he was not charging the King and his soldiers.

"Oh, you should not have, good man. We are very grateful for your hospitality and for letting us stay in your lovely inn.

"Please accept this as payment for food, your trusted services and a thank you for your selfless help." Vonter smiled.

He knew that the amount of gold in the little satchel he handed over was more than enough for the food and the room fares.

When the inn owner felt the weight of the satchel, his eyes widened. His delighted grin disappeared from Vonter's sight every time he bowed down to his King in exaggerated gratitude.

The King expressed his thanks one more time, turned around and stepped out into the cold morning. His horse was just a few steps away from the inn's exit thanks to his diligent squire. He swung himself up and gave the men the signal to do the same.

On their way out they passed a bard getting ready to sing. He announced a ballad about his hometown while stroking his blonde beard trying to look sophisticated.

Vonter wondered when he had last heard a bard sing in the streets. He could not remember. They did not have the time now to stick around.

The journey back would take them about a quarter of a day. They did not speak much during their journey back, but he could sense that the group was in higher spirits than they had been on the way to the city of the Trusted Eagle.

Morale was picking up, it seemed. The danger was not as widely spread as the King and his followers had feared, smaller settlements greeted them with joy and relief reporting no attacks whatsoever.

Yet, the shock from what happened to Buntin still was not properly digested, and that would potentially take weeks, months even, but the fact that this outing had progressed without any incident, lightened the mood.

Some soldiers seemed a little more relaxed, and Vonter himself was not as tense anymore as he was the day before.

The warm midday sun was very weak, but it helped to warm his shoulders a little.

He liked the colder months less and less, maybe it had something to do with getting older. It was true that the summer had been nice, but the fall was coming fast, with some cold, crisp mornings with winter like weather. They hardly ever had snow, even in the North it had become very scarce in the last winters.

He could not help but think if his and Samjya's children would ever even grow up knowing snow, or if they would have to take them to Northlight, past the lighthouse, on a ship to the Somber Islands. That would be quite the trip though, they would have to wait until the children were much older.

"Buntin will be just ahead, behind those hills, My King." the voice of his second in command pulled him out of his thoughts. He did not mind, of course, he had just been waiting for this moment.

When they reached the top of the hill, Buntin laid to their horses' feet.

Flat, like a crushed berry, the sad image had not improved from yesterday. About a thousand tents covered the East side of the site, and a few fires burned for heating rabbit meat, vegetables and for some, bread.

A short while later, they reached the stable boys' tents and got off their mounts. Immediately, a soldier approached the King, very agitated.

"His Grace, most of the scouts have returned with nothing to report, but I am afraid, there is no word from Lord Draidr or Lord Sahdor's men. So, it seems like it is the White Forest after all." he stammered.

"Thank you, good man. It does sound like it all points towards that damned forest." Vonter replied. "No information as to how far they have gotten?"

The man shook his head, and the King nodded to dismiss him.

They spent the night in the forest without a word?

He hoped that nothing had happened to them.

He was thinking whether letting Sahd go after the enemy had been a wise decision after all.

As he got to his tent, he saw that they had all the scouts come together for him to hear from each what they could report, but it was all the same: no town or village had seen or heard anything. In most cases, people were perfectly happy and unaware, but then got really afraid when they heard the news.

"Well, they should be scared! This danger, as evident in Buntin, should not be taken lightly. We should all prepare for the worst.

"Did you tell them to increase their defences and prepare their citizens for a potential evacuation to the capital?"

The scouts nodded in unison.

"Did you tell them that they can request soldiers from the capital if need be?"

"Of course, His Grace." some of the scouts murmured, others nodded again.

It was then that they noticed the scout from Tramvil was missing. Not a word from their soldiers either. This was concerning. They discussed how a small group of soldiers should carefully investigate. When the conversation was finished, Vonter instructed two of the messengers to travel back to get one more division out to Buntin, and they took off immediately to alert Sire Graynor on the same day, so the 1,500 additional soldiers would be here early tomorrow. He had also added a message to Samjya in a scroll. It was to be passed onto his strategist, so he would talk to her and share the comforting words with his love.

Just a few breaths after the last scout had left, another young scout stumbled into his tent.

"His Grace, I apologise." he was breathing heavily as if he had been running for miles. And he just might have. His name was Mil, and Vonter recognised him from another run he had done for them the day before.

"What is it?"

"I was hunting rabbits for the army and came across the large lake on the edge of the forest. Near Tramvil.

"And I saw something ... unbelievable."

Vonter had just barely sat down but straightened himself in his seat. "Go on."

"You ... erm, said that we should report anything, and I may tell you, even if it sounds very strange?" Mil stammered.

"Of course!" the King was getting nervous.

"His Grace. All the wild animals around the lake, deer, even birds, are just stone! Entirely frozen solid, just as if someone has turned them into statues. I believe, ... this is magic!"

12

Sahdor had sent the scout back just before sundown. It had been quiet ever since. No movement all night, and nothing the entire morning.

The castle in front of them was made of the blackest stones he had ever seen. It was so eerie that none of his men, including himself, were willing to step any closer. From their secure spot about 30 feet away from the entrance, there was no chance of telling what might be going on inside, it had been too dark to make out anything earlier.

And now, that the sunlight had improved their vision across the clearing, they could make out more details, but still, not a soul was seen. The suspicion for real magic had grown.

Sahd let out a short sigh. His patience was not the greatest at this point. Whoever was behind these stone walls, magic, or no magic, was responsible for the disappearance, possibly death of his sister Minher and her three boys. He felt the rage bubbling up again.

It had never been gone entirely, never fully quietened inside of him. But since he had seen Buntin's destruction, it had consumed him.

And he knew exactly where to put it. This horrible, horrible feeling of wanting to strangle the murderer to death would not just go away, he would have to strangle the murderer to death. Simple as that.

He remembered the times he used to drown his frustration and insecurities in mead at The Vagabond, the local tavern in his hometown. Not only had that jeopardised his apprenticeship at the carpenters, but it had almost destroyed his family too. Luckily, his sister had never given up on him.

Minher's kindness and confidence in him had been the best motivation.

To stop drinking, to enlist in the army when he needed a purpose, to stick with a career that would come as easy to him as getting up in the morning, to his own surprise. And most of all, to return the favour and be there for her.

When her second baby had been born dead, he moved in to keep her distracted and get back to loving life. When her husband started beating on her, he threw him out and made sure that he would not be able to see the children. And when her money was not enough to afford the house anymore, he bought it for her. He would have never left Minher out in the streets, let alone her children without a home.

He had promised their father to always support his sister in any way possible, and that was what he would do until his dying breath. And she had always done the same. Simple as that.

A rustling sound behind them interrupted his thoughts, and almost all the soldiers turned around quickly, to locate the source.

First, they could not see anything. Then, one of his men made a discreet clicking noise and pointed Southwest. Sahd squinted in an attempt to focus his sight, and after a few moments, he recognised the moving figure in the woods. His friend and fellow military man Draidr was walking in their direction, slowly. It was more like a cautious stumbling.

He seemed to be constantly looking down to the ground, making sure not to step off a path. Except, there was no path. He was walking almost in a zigzag.

The soldier looked very tired too as if he had been walking since they parted, without a break or sustenance, let alone a moment of sleep.

Sahd made the same clicking noise that they had heard before, only this time a bit louder, more noticeable. Draidr stopped abruptly, ducked down, and he drew his sword slowly.

It did not take him very long to notice the row of soldiers sitting in front of a natural dam on top of this small hill like chicken sitting on a beam in a coop.

He smiled, relieved that there was no immediate danger, and slowly, while still eyeing the ground meticulously, he moved further towards his friends.

Draidr pushed his shoulder against Sahd's in a silent greeting, looked around and whispered: "You would not believe what I have seen, friend! I'm so glad you are all still alive and moving."

Sahd raised an eyebrow, alarmed. The way he had said the last word was disconcerting. "Where are your soldiers, and your horse, Draidr? What happened?"

"We need to leave this place! It is not safe. They are everywhere!"

Ignoring Sahd's questions, he pressed the words out between his teeth, and looked around again like a hunted animal, his eyes jumping from one corner to the other in their eye sockets.

The First General grabbed him by the shoulders and tried to get him to focus, by giving him a quick shake. Draidr would not even look him in the eye.

"It is the stones. They are moving and then you are not."

"What nonsense is this?" Sahd was worried for his friend's state of mind.

"Are you saying that stones killed your men?", the soldier at the other end interjected, almost amused. Sahd gave that man a warning look, but turned back to his friend, only to see that he had tears in his eyes. A few breaths long, he let the last question ring in everyone's ears, until another man scoffed disparately: "Seriously? Moving stones?"

Faster than anyone could react, Draidr lunged forward and grabbed the man's chest plate, and almost shrieked: "All my men are gone! Forever! Even Thrim, he – ... All of them! There is nothing we can do except run; do you hear me?! Run!"

His face was red with anger and his eyes and mouth twitched with fear, his fists completely white from the tight grip, and his breathing was going fast, even faster than before.

He was clearly exhausted and too agitated.

Sahd grabbed his shoulder again with one arm, with the other one, he signalled the other men who wanted to get him off their fellow soldier to stand down.

"By the Gods, Draidr, you need to calm down, we are close to a castle that looks like the source of all of this. Please pull yourself together."

Sahd pointed to the gloomy black construct, but he had a hard time getting Draidr's attention.

"We need to leave! Now!"

Draidr screamed this time in naked panic, and Sahd could tell that his friend was beyond reasoning. He pulled him away from the group, only a couple of feet away. All his strength was needed to lift and pull him, but he obviously could not risk them getting caught.

It took Draidr barely a moment to realise what was happening. He struggled to get out of Sahd's grip. The two men fell back on their buttocks, and his friend immediately jumped back up and turned around, in fright, checking the ground around him. Sahd felt another wave of that rage coming up and washing all over him.

"What is wrong with you? Stay quiet!" he exclaimed with restraint volume but elevated pulse. As if that made him think, Draidr suddenly stopped and looked up. Slowly, his head turning back to the group of soldiers. His widened eyes fixated on something, and his mouth started moving, but no sound was heard. When he repeated the same articulation, he said: "Run."

Just as Sahd turned his head back to see what had caused that reaction, he heard him scream with all his strength: "RUN!"

Behind his group of soldiers, just up on the dam, a dark shadow had risen. No, it was not a shadow. It was a pile of black, smoky stone.

A part of the castle had become *alive*, in the shape of a man, but a lot more monster like, in a rough shape, ugly and surrounded by a dark cloud!

Where the face should have been, he could only see two red, glowing spots, deep inside the stone.

The mouth was just a huge, stiff, round shaped opening, and hollow – there was nothing on the other side. Sahdor's men gasped and were barely able to move away as the apparition had taken all the air out of their lungs.

The big stone man growled effortlessly out of the face hole, as loud as twenty trees falling in the very same moment.

"RUN!" Draidr's second scream made his voice go up as high as Sahd never had expected, which pulled his attention away from the black giant. He was on his feet quickly, reached for his sword and leaned in to start sprinting towards the others, but Draidr grabbed his arm. "No use, my friend, running is our only chance now."

The First General had only looked back at his friend for a short moment, but that was enough. He believed him. His head turned back to his men one more time, only to see one soldier being crushed entirely by the thing's arm. Another man's body turned to black stone because his leg had touched the creature's arm.

Sahd turned to Draidr and followed him dashing through the woods, East, and away from the pain filled screams. Away from the monstrosity that seemed to have a spell going on, turning men into black stone by mere touch?

He stepped sideways occasionally to avoid stumbling over a root and looked back again after a few moments.

The black giant had killed his group completely, blood and black stone everywhere around the corpses. The screams had stopped, but the growling was getting more and more aggressive.

He could see that the thing was getting ready to run too. After them.

"I think it is following us!" he snapped, turning his head back forward, noticing how Draidr was several feet in front of him. "What do we do? Can we fight it at all?"

"No freaking way! We need to keep running! Once the stones touch you, you die!", he heard from his friend, and so he tried to speed up his steps even more.

For a few moments, it appeared as if they could beat this by simply running, but soon enough he felt the vibrations behind him.

The ground shook, at first, only a little; and the stomping sound of big, heavy, stone feet reached his ears shortly after. He could feel its presence, the hot, dark, and violent smell, the heat emitting from the eyes, like a house that was burning with high fires. The shaking and rumbling of the stone became louder and louder. He doubted that they would actually make it!

Suddenly, a voice appeared in front of them, just above their heads. High pitched and hectic. "Follow me if you want to live!"

Something small and fast jumped to their right in the trees from branch to branch.

He could tell that Draidr did not even think about it, he immediately changed direction to follow the little brown ball of fur in the white treetops above him. Was that a squirrel?

His legs followed Draidr's trajectory and still, their enemy gained on them. They were led a bit South, and then around a formation of rocks next to a few fallen trees. Was there a group of foxes running parallel to them?

They ran further down a hill, and Sahd was very sure he started to feel the monster's breath on his neck! Just as if the ground decided to be on their side, a long, thin gap appeared in front of them.

"Jump in! Trust me!" the thin voice shrieked, and their little helper disappeared in the hole. His friend did the same, though he could tell that with his size, he was not as agile and fast.

Still, almost just as quick as the squirrel, Draidr was underground and crawled to the side, just down a narrow tunnel.

Sahd followed him as fast as he could, and not a breath too late.

Behind him, he could feel a ground shattering punch, or was a jump?

This caused the earth around him to loosen up, and for a moment, he thought the tunnel might collapse around him and he would be crushed by the giant through layers of forest soil.

But then, a small formation of moles appeared around them, and suddenly, the tunnel itself changed direction. Like living earth, the ground swallowed them deeper and deeper down, only that it was not the ground doing the work, but the moles, digging them in deeper. Sahd was so impressed by the speed and how they managed to grab the earth away from under his buttocks. The last bit of daylight suddenly vanished above him.

Sahd lost track of the direction in which they kept moving, and only after the sounds of their attacker died down, he noticed that he had held his breath since they were down here.

He forced his jaw to unclench and detected how dusty and dirty the air was around him. He was not able to suppress a cough. Deafening darkness surrounded them, but he could feel the tunnel widening and getting more spacious under the moles' digging claws.

Draidr coughed next to him, and the squirrel's bushy tail was in Sahd's face. They had stopped moving, but the ground beneath them was still in motion, due to the moles around them.

"Careful, there will be a drop!" the little rodent said, and just like that, the ground gave way to a small, dimly lit cave. About six feet deep, the two soldiers fell down into an opening. Sahd hit his shoulder quite badly, having not braced himself for the impact. Through the pain, he heard mumbling around him. When he opened his eyes, he saw the most incredible thing.

The cave was a few feet wide and long, just barely higher than 4 feet, so a small man could stand here, with three tunnels leading away.

Draidr and Sahd had been dropped right in the middle of it. Around them, a group of animals stood and stared at them.

He could see a few deer, a wolf, three foxes, a family of wild boar, and two owls.

The squirrel was surrounded by probably ten moles, who were panting and rubbing their stubby paws. Two rabbits hid shyly at the entrance of one of the tunnels that promised nothing but darkness.

"What is this place?" Sahd whispered.

The squirrel flinched and moved forward quickly like squirrels did.

"My name is Mibb, and you're welcome. We just saved your asses. And now, let me introduce you to the inhabitants of the White Forest."

13

Again, spending more time on the back of his horse than not, his buttocks were starting to feel sore. Vonter could see the lake in the distance. He could also see that Mil, the scout who had heard the soldier's report, was getting more and more anxious. This place had to frighten him a lot. After all, you do not see the living turned into stone every day. But why stone? And why animals? This was getting more and more confusing.

No one spoke, not even as they approached the lake. But they did not have to. What they saw, spoke for itself.

The lake laid in front of them, almost peaceful and quiet. The sun was reflecting in the water surface, illuminating the nearby treetops from below and bringing out the rich green of their leaves. The water was dark blue, serene, and almost inviting.

And then, Vonter saw the first stone animal. Just a few feet away, in the shade under a willow tree, a deer was drinking out of the lake. Feet just at the edge of the water, and the snout touching the surface, and that was the moment where the poor animal must have been turned into stone. As if someone had frozen this deer in concrete time.

He got off his horse and signalled his soldiers to do so as well. He had brought only ten men, and Mil.

"Please proceed with caution, we do not know what happened here!" he addressed everyone. He turned to the scout. "Did the soldier say he saw fish on the land as well?"

"Yes, His Grace, two of them, actually, ... I just found them." Mil was pretty far ahead already and pointed to the ground in front of his feet.

There was definitive fear in the young man's eyes. Vonter had turned to the willow tree, leaving his mount behind as well, and now moved back, slowly.

The soldiers, mostly with their swords drawn, stepped closer to the lake.

They advanced carefully, almost sneaking around as if any sound could alarm or attract the attacker. Fanning out, two soldiers and the King moved in the direction that Mil had shown them, three other men walked straight to the water, the other five turned left and looked out for an ambush from the White Forest.

Vonter noticed how silent the entire area was. No birds, no sounds from the fields, not even the wind produced any sound in the trees. The leaves were moving just slightly and without any noise whatsoever. The water was in the loop of its enduring movements within the borders of the lake.

When they got closer to the tree with its low hanging twigs, the deer looked even more unreal, just like any other statue. But it was hard to believe that someone would put a deer statue right here, far from any settlement of men and women to look at it. And then, there were the frogs. Scattered across the grass, some stone frogs were lying to Vonter's feet. He was about to nudge one of them with his sword, to see if they would move, but he was stopped when frantic, painful screaming arose from behind him.

One man of the group had walked further to the left and was bending down, holding his leg while the others pulled at him, trying to help. He must have caught his leg in a bear trap!

With the other two soldiers, Vonter turned around and ran towards them. Because there was already quite a distance between them, it took them a breath's moment to get close enough to find out that it was not a bear trap.

Quickly, some sort of grey matter was climbing up the man's body, and it had already started to cover the other three men where they had been touching their fellow soldier.

All of them screamed, and tried to rub it off, but once covered, the limbs would not move anymore! They were *turning into stone*.

One of the men lunged forward and grabbed a soldier who was with the King.

"Help me!" he pressed out of his thin lips, the lower half of his body was already numb and grey. The other man tried to fight him off, but while his arms were struggling with the other man's arms, the weight of his friend pushed him backwards and as he fell, his shin touched the knee of the first victim, and the stone spread by touch immediately. They both turned into stone!

The King was not sure what to do. Apparently, the touch was deadly, so he should stay away – but was there something that he could do? He was not able to decide whether to run or to try and cut off limbs, ...

There was an idea. In a flash, he was next to one of his men, who had just fallen to his knees. He had been touching another's shoulder and was screaming because his arm was disappearing under a grey, solid cover.

Without hesitation, Vonter swung his drawn sword up and with all his strength down onto the soldier's arm. Just before it touched him, Vonter's eyes jumped to the man's face, and he could see the terror in his eyes.

But that was not important now. The sword cracked the bone, was stopped halfway, and with a powerful thrust upwards, the King pulled his weapon back up.

Just a few inches before the moving stone, he hit the arm again, same spot as before, and this time, the bone was severed. He hacked his weapon down a third and final time to cut off any flesh connecting to the stone arm.

Now, the blood was not only bursting out of the wound, but it was also spraying almost everywhere. The chopped off half of the arm that was full stone now, motionless in the grass, heavy and dead. Vonter stepped back to gain some room in case his action did not help the man.

Under agonising screams, the man winched in pain on the ground, grabbing his stump with the other hand, the remaining one.

The King stared at him for a short while. No more stone transformation.

Vonter ripped a large piece of cloth off his cape and bent down to cover the bleeding edge and stop the flow of blood.

With a scarf that Mil handed him, he wrapped the wound tightly. He gazed over to the other soldiers as it got very quiet again.

There was no one else alive! All other soldiers had transformed and now laid or kneeled as heavy, lifeless statues in the grass. Only the scout was standing behind him, breathing frantically, short and panic filled breaths, cheeks wet with hot tears, hands dripping with the soldier's blood.

The man that Vonter had saved, looked up and uttered his gratitude even though he was under too much pain to use a lot of words for it.

The three men looked around. They truly were the only survivors.

"How do you feel?" the King asked his army man.

"A world of pain, … Apart from my missing arm, I should be okay. I think."

"Mil?" he looked over, and the boy's breathing had not settled yet. He grabbed his arm and pulled: "Hey! Mil! Look at me."

The scout moved his eyes to meet the King's and tears returned to them. "They went so fast!"

"Yes, they did. But we are still alive, we made it. You are okay!"

Vonter looked over to the stone bodies, then, back to the one-armed soldier.

"What's your name?"

"Ca'on, His Grace." he replied through his teeth.

"Ca'on, do you think you can get up and ride your horse?"

The soldier brought his knee up and put the foot down. "I need a moment, but yes, I … think so."

"Mil, we need to get our horses, and patch him up properly."

The boy hesitated, then ran back to where they had left the mounts. Vonter kept working on the improvised bandage, and after a few breaths, he was quite happy with the result.

The padding had slowed down the bleeding a little.

Unfortunately, they would have to get back to the camp or ride to Tramvil to properly take care of this wound. But if he could get Ca'on on a horse, they would be able to move.

Mil showed up behind him, the reins of three horses in his hands. His gaze was fixed on the stone soldiers on the ground.

Vonter stood next to him and looked at what had caught the scout's attention. In the grass, there was a little girl. Her face was turned up, screaming to the heavens, probably in pain. Her limbs were spread out in desperate anguish, and the left hand was clawed into the ground, surprisingly, fingers deep in the ground. The right hand was cupping a stone frog.

She had perhaps thought it was a toy, just like he had at first. And that was probably what had killed her. And the other soldiers. Like a disease, the stone had infected all of them. Probably because the girl had wanted to pet a frog.

"Mil, do you know the way to Tramvil from here?"

"Of course, His Grace, I do. We only need to follow the river that ends in this lake upstream, it will lead us to the road directly." He looked over to Ca'on. "It is also closer than the camp if you are thinking of getting him fast help, His Grace."

"That's exactly what I was thinking. Thank you, boy."

Ca'on produced a strained sigh as he lifted his arm to mount the horse. Instantly, Vonter was by his side and helped him up.

As soon as Mil and himself were on their mounts as well, they made their way to Tramvil. They made sure to move around the corpses and any animals or high grass in a safe distance and to watch out for any other small stones by the road.

After a large number of breaths on the roads, and many groans from Ca'on, who became paler and sweatier by the breath it seemed, they arrived at the wooden gate of Tramvil.

No guards, no people were visible from the outside.

Vonter and Mil exchanged worried looks.

Why was it so quiet?

The first people they saw after leaving the outer village fences behind, were a merchant and a younger boy. They were in front of one of the market stalls on the square around the well. The market was not particularly big, but it was famous in all the land for its clean water and the best fabrics in all imaginable colours.

The boy was drinking out of a cup holding it with both his hands, but he had an odd expression on his face, surprised, sad. The merchant had the same emotion on his face, but he was bending down, staring at the boy's hands, one hand on the young man's shoulder, with the other one reaching out to something behind him. They had turned to stone.

Vonter tried to find the detail that he was overlooking. They were not touching anything that was stone. The stall was at least one foot away from them and made of wood. The pathway was grained sand, not stone. And there were no animals around or anyone else touching them. As his eyes wandered about, he saw more.

There were maybe around 40 people, in one corner of the market, the Well Square as they called it. It looked like a monument of market frenzy, as if something had caught the moment of desperate people forever in stone when the very last item was on sale to a good price, and everyone fought each other with tooth and nail.

Looking closer, he saw a woman who had poured some water on herself. She was holding a jug with one hand. The painful look on her face was copied onto all the other faces, as they had rushed to help her, help the next person, and the next, infecting themselves in a horrible, uninterrupted chain of transformations.

"His Grace, this is absolute horror."

Mil's voice was quiet and surprisingly soft. Vonter was not able to talk. His eyes wandered across the Well Square and he discovered more and more statues.

He did not even notice at first, but surrounding the well, on the rim of the stone, and around the other animals and humans, there were two dogs, a cat, several sheep, a couple of birds on top of people's heads and the well.

At first, he thought these stones around the water belonged to the design of the well, but that was not the case. And that was the most peculiar thing, most of these statues were almost unnoticeable as their appearance blended into the town too well. As if they had always been part of the town. A dog owner had grabbed his dog in disbelief, which had been the last action in his life. The shepherd seemed to have done the same thing with one of his animals. A woman might have lost something in the well, her hands stuck in the water eternally.

"Is anyone still alive in this town?" Ca'on sighed.

"It is too quiet; I am afraid the chances are rather slim. Let's find out what happened here, but we should get you to a healer's house first." the King said.

"Follow me." Mil nudged his legs against the sides of his horse and moved forward across a small bridge. He knew the town and would be able to lead them directly to clean water and bandages.

Behind the cathedral, Vonter recognised the symbol above the door as the usual healer's sign and jumped off his horse. When he helped Ca'on, the soldier let out a scream as his arm grazed the saddle during the descent. And again, when he fell against the wall of the house, his knees giving in, and Vonter was not fast enough to catch him.

The King helped him up, and Mil tried opening the front door. It was locked.

Mil knocked three times without any kind of response before Vonter cried out: "Hello! Anyone here?"

He meant to get the attention of the healer inside, but he realised that his voice was projecting down the street, echoing in the archways of the cathedral.

After Ca'on made another sound that reminded them of the urgency of this matter, Vonter decided to kick the door in.

He nodded to Mil to support the warrior, and after he switched places with the scout, he rammed his foot against the door, targeting the area next to the lock, so the surrounding wood would burst. It took him three attempts, and the door flung open.

"Hello?" the King tried again just before his placed his boot over the doorstep.

They carried Ca'on inside, put him on a large table in the first room, and Vonter pointed towards the cupboards. Mil understood instantly and fetched bandages and clean cloths. When he turned around, he froze.

"What is it?" Vonter had just dropped the metal shielding from around his arms.

"I found the healer." Mil said very abruptly.

The King stepped closer and peaked around the corner. Just like the others, the healer was frozen in stone just as he was about to wash his hands. "This is turning into a very mysterious plague." he murmured. He raised his voice again: "We need fresh water and something for Ca'on to bite on."

A woman's voice sounded from behind them.

"Do not touch the water if you want to live!"

14

"My name is Mibb, and you're welcome. We just saved your asses. And now, let me introduce you to the inhabitants of the White Forest." said the squirrel.

Sahdor Tonin was still struggling with the fact that there was a talking squirrel in front of him. Now, there were all these other talking animals, living together underground, peacefully, hidden in the White Forest?

Draidr was faster than him, asking: "Are you saying you have been living here under the White Forest? Is that why there are no animals in the forest?"

The little furry creature frowned and folded his arms in front of his body.

"What reason do I have to lie? Besides, like I said, we just saved you. Do not be an ass, or I will start having regrets."

"Can you all talk?" Sahd asked. Some of the animals nodded, Mibb looked at him, impatient. The soldier sat up and wiped his forehead. The action reminded him painfully of his bruised shoulder, it had brought back the pain into his mind.

It was so warm underground, and the air was quite stuffy. Not the best surroundings to catch a breath. He took another look around the cave, and apart from the animals, that stared at them, it was rather empty. The occasional tree roots were sticking out of the walls, but it was very cosy and calm. They must have been dug in quite far that the stomping giant outside was not to be heard anymore. Also, the lights that made it possible for them to see, were fireflies! Tiny little bugs flying in several corners, lighting the entire cave.

Draidr coughed again, his short, black hair dropping dusty clouds. He sat up and looked around as well, probably just like Sahd for the second time, a bit more attentive to take it all in.

"Okay, so here is the deal. You will tell us all you know about that thing that tried to kill you just now, and I will tell you about us." Mibb proposed.

"We have never seen that thing before. We do not know anything about this." Sahd explained.

"So, you are telling me you were taking a walk through the White Forest on this fine day, and the stone monster found you by accident?"

"Stone monster – ...?" Sahd shook his head.

"The King's land is being attacked by something or someone, and we were trying to find out more about this threat. We did not know we would find that ... stone monster. Or rather that it would find us." Draidr explained. He still had not quite caught his breath.

"But I get the feeling that thing is the real reason why you are all underground like this?" Sahd added, pretty sure he was deducting correctly.

Mibb looked at the beaver next to him and exchanged a look with the foxes. They seemed to have discussed some sort of strategy beforehand. "Fine. I believe you. We'll share what we know. Maybe it will help you. But first, let me explain."

He sat down as he started: "A few hundred years ago, the White Forest did not exist. There was a forest, but it was not as big. I wasnot always a squirrel, you see. I was a lumberjack apprentice, working for the Court of the late King Arkus II."

Sahd interrupted the squirrel: "Wait, you were a human a few hundred years ago?"

Mibb frowned again. "Yes, please pay attention. So, there were large fields, beautiful hills and a magnificent city with happy men and women.

"A mysterious sickness came to light that only killed children, and the people grew desperate to find a cure. After a lot of failed attempts and many deaths, they sent messengers out to all corners of the land in order to find a solution anywhere.

"They asked a witch in the nearby forest for help, and she created an herbal potion that would heal the infected and prevent the others from getting sick. In return, the townsmen promised her a young man of her choosing, that she could marry. The witch helped the town willingly, and all the children got cured. The young man she had picked, refused to go to her, and the people decided not to honour the deal.

"Understandably angry, she not quite so understandably killed all adults in a frenzy and used their souls to create a forest made of white trees. She destroyed the town. The castle and the clearing with the poisoned stones that you saw in the woods are the actual ruins of the town's Royal residence. With the trees expanding into the world, she changed the landscape and killed many people in the process. That took up a great deal of her power.

"We assume, just before her magic ran out, she cursed every child in the forest to become an animal. She gave us eternal life at great cost. She said if we ever talked to another human, we would die instantly. If we left the White Forest, we would die instantly. And if we attempted to find her or oppose her in any way, we would die.

"Needless to say, her curse is not as strong as we thought, or she was lying to us, because here I am talking to you, and still alive. Figures."

Draidr wanted to say something, but Mibb would not have it. His little paw waved it away abruptly. "She disappeared, and so, we hid away. In between the ghostly remains of our parents, grandparents, and mentors, we stayed quiet and became forgotten by everyone because everyone was either dead or became too afraid to come into the forest. For many, many hundred years. New humans were born to the land, but the silenced forest was avoided by anyone and everything, so we remained forgotten."

The pause was filled with the faint humming of the fireflies.

A cursed forest full of animals that had not spoken to humans in centuries!

Draidr asked the first question: "So, you have been living in hiding the entire time? How long ago was his?"

Mibb shrugged. "We do not really know. 800 years, maybe more? We have lost count."

"And you were all children?"

"Yes, when we were cursed, we were. I was 17 when I got sick and was healed by the witch. Since our leader has left, I am now the oldest."

Draidr was sceptical: "You said you were cursed with eternal life – so you are immortal?"

"Well, we may be immortal, but we can still be killed. Chop a head off an animal, and it will surely be dead, trust me. We have run into humans that have hunted us, and others have been bait to mortal animals, you know, the non-verbal kind. Some got on the witch's bad side, and she struck them down." Mibb's voice cracked on the last part, and he swallowed with a mourning look on his face. Then, he started again.

"I am currently in charge. And before you ask, yes, it is a big risk to talk to you. It is not actually part of the curse that we die when we talk to you, but we still need to be very careful.

"We have not seen the witch in a very long time, but she has always seen almost anything that went on in this forest, so we should proceed with caution."

Sahdor exhaled as Mibb paused again.

An intense sadness had grown inside him. He could not begin to express what he was feeling. His own life seemed so insignificant all of a sudden. Not only losing most of the family and friends in your town, but also being cursed with sticking around for eternity, in the midst of trees that once had been your own people, isolated in a lifeless forest, that was beyond cruel.

He was amazed that these children had stayed so composed. "I am so sorry."

Some animals were apparently very surprised to hear that from him. The squirrel looked directly at Sahd, probably wondering why he said it.

"My heart goes out to all of you. This is a very sad story; I am sorry that you had to go through this. Losing your families like that and living with this pain for centuries."

Some of the others turned away or looked down.

Mibb only smiled in melancholy. "Thanks. But let's talk about the present now. I have reason to believe that we are in grave danger. This new force in the forest, ... the one that rebuilt the castle, and created these creatures, … it feels very similar to the witch's powers. The magic is so dark, destructive and a threat to us all. I think there is an evil warlock behind this. This stone monster is not the only one I am afraid; he brought an entire army into the forest.

"An evil warlock? How? Do you think he may have destroyed Buntin as well?" Sahd asked.

Mibb got slightly annoyed again. "Yes. I have no idea what a buntin is, pal, but it is probable. Whatever the stone army may have done, destruction sounds like it. The warlock probably recently got stronger because he killed another just before. I saw evidence of a fight and how one walked away, stronger."

Sahd cleared his throat and asked another question: "What is the warlock's name?"

"His name is Dragus. The older one was Fragir. Something happened between them, we do not know what." Mibb answered coldly.

"So Fragir died when they fought, and Dragus became stronger to raise this army of stone monsters?" Sahd wanted to know.

The furry fella nodded. Again, more questions arose in Sahd, and by the looks of it, in Draidr too.

"Where did they come from?" his friend asked cautiously.

Mibb shook his head with a sigh: "Well, we saw Dragus for the first time about 150 years ago, he was living and travelling by himself outside of the White Forest as far as we could tell.

"Then, he met this older sorcerer, Fragir, and became his young apprentice.

"Naturally, we had to stay quiet and keep our distance to avoid the witch's wrath, but there seemed to exist a peaceful relationship between them.

"Suddenly, it all changed. We do not know how it happened, and why, but they fought to the death. Dragus was later resurrected with some dark magic. At least, that's what we think. More and more stone soldiers appeared shortly after, and we figured that he had to have some sort of plan. Sounds like he came for your buntin and started attacking your King's land.

"If there is one thing we do know, it is magic. We do not have any ourselves, but we have been exposed to so much that we can sense its energies and determine what's good or evil."

"Why are you convinced it is not the witch's work?" Sahd was not even sure what he himself was talking about.

"It is a slightly different vigour, a lot darker. We know the witch's energy well enough. It is hard to explain." the squirrel's tail twitched twice.

Sahd looked around again. All the animals had been listening very patiently. This Mibb character was indeed their leader, despite his size.

Draidr had been relatively pensive too, no big surprise there, but he was more reserved than usual. This was a lot to take in. Talking animals, a cursed forest, witches, and warlocks. If he had not heard it from a talking squirrel, he would not have believed it, which made it even more absurd.

Mibb got up and paced in front of them, slowly. Well, slowly for a squirrel. "The big question is, what do we do now? I personally believe, we should get you out of the White Forest. It will be a lot safer to get some distance between you two and our kind. But also, the further you humans run away from this as possible, the safer you are. You need to warn your people."

"Running away is not an option." Sahd heard himself say.

"Well, you just did, pal. And it saved your life." Mibb replied snappily.

"No, I meant, we need to fight this. Together. There must be a way. You can explain the magic things to our King in more detail. And we have a large army. We'll come back with reinforcements and crush those stone bastards!"

No one said a word for a while.

Mibb only raised an eyebrow. After moments of silence, he finally said: "I seriously doubt your army will be sufficient. Have you seen what just one of these soldiers did to your men in an instant?"

Sahd did not know how to respond to that. Mibb was right. They needed more than an army.

The little rodent raised his voice again, more determined: "We will think about it. We will not sacrifice ourselves for humans. But we will discuss once you're gone."

There was a slight hostility in the little furry helper's voice. The awkward pause that followed was paired with even more awkward looks among the animals.

"Do you remember the witch's name?" he wanted to know.

The animals exchanged looks. Some of them seemed to not be comfortable thinking about her. Mibb's face turned sinister.

"Her name is Tessel."

15

Yandra plucked up her courage and knocked on the door. Again. *What must Samjya be thinking right now*, she pondered.

Truthfully, she was not entirely sure what she had seen last night. If she remembered correctly. And if she believed her own memory. Maybe she had been tired, and was recalling a strikingly vivid dream? There was no doubt that something was seriously wrong here. She just could not put her finger on it. Nonetheless, whether the frightening situation was real or not, she was still very worried about her friend.

Samjya probably did not sleep at all, did not eat or drink nearly enough, and she most definitely was not behaving like herself. Maybe she had been sleepwalking and was struggling with fever dreams! She would probably not even remember the last night.

After a couple of instants, the door flung open, and she braced herself for a painful discussion of whys and hows. But Sire Artius Graynor smiled at her.

"Yandra, what a surprise for you to knock on my door." he nodded respectfully, and she did the same. "You are as beautiful as ever."

"Sire Graynor, please." she could feel that her cheeks flushed with rosy embarrassment, and she did not even try to move the hair out of the way that had just fallen into her face. He was probably just being courteous.

"I am terribly sorry to disturb you this early, but I have a favour to ask." she stammered timidly. The grey-haired man continued to smile.

"You are worried about Lady Samjya since we have not seen her in almost two days." he said.

Yandra nodded, her lips pressed together. She hesitated speaking, but the words still came out, almost without control: "Actually, I think I have seen her last night."

"You think?"

"Yes, well, I was very tired and quite frankly, still shaken up by yesterday's news. But she came downstairs into the Royal Dining Hall. Sire Graynor, she was truly not herself! I have never seen her like this. She is either very depressed or going mad! Possibly both."

"How do you mean?" his smile had now made room for genuine concern.

"I do not know, she was talking nonsense, and it scared me. It was almost like she did not recognise me. She was convinced Vonter was against her. She became very bitter all of a sudden how the King was just sorry for her but not doing anything to help. It was so unlike her!"

Sire Graynor turned and walked towards the window, Yandra followed him but stopped after three steps. Her heart was beating in her throat, thinking of last night was making her feel shaky and weak.

"Well, she certainly must deal with the troubling news as well. We should check on her. Thank you for including me, I'm sure Vonter will appreciate your reaching out. Has she eaten anything at all?"

"No, the trays we left in front of her locked door remain untouched. I do not think she will survive much longer like this."

Graynor raised his hands. "You would be amazed at what the human body is capable of. Believe me, I have seen extraordinary things in the military. It was my duty to train and guide the young recruits. My soldiers could live weeks without food."

"But you talk of trained soldiers, Sire Graynor. Samjya is a farmer's daughter. And you know, our winters have not been that harsh." Yandra lamented. She knew Samjya was tougher than other women, but was she absolutely sure of it?

"No woman is just someone's daughter. I may not be married, but I know women too have more strength than one thinks. Trust me."

The soldier winked and turned around, walking further into his room past the window. Yandra stayed where she was, close to the open door.

He grabbed his leather jacket and threw it over his linen shirt. Only now, she noticed that he had not been fully dressed, and she caught herself staring at his muscles before his arms disappeared in the jacket's sleeves.

He was a burly man, quite hairy from the looks of the front of his neckline, and mostly grey without covering his natural black hair entirely. She had also caught a glimpse at the scars on his arm, though they looked to have healed nicely. A strong man beyond his sixties, he still looked very strong, limber and he was a handsome fellow.

The light blue eyes promised wisdom and kindness, but she had noticed a few times, that there was also great sadness.

He mentioned that he was never married, so maybe he had lost a young love? Maybe even his family? He must have been quite young during the last war. Also, losing a lot of his soldiers and the fast promotion in the army had probably changed him to become more serious early on.

She did not like thinking about war too much, not now. So, she stopped her thoughts and noticed how she was staring at his chest again.

Graynor smiled. "See anything you like, Yandra?" he said playfully.

She suddenly looked to the ground and started to ramble nervously: "I was not really, I mean, just thinking, ... I did not! Honestly, ... -"

He quickly stood in front of her, ready to leave his chambers. "It is all right, Yandra, we're both no spring chickens anymore!" he chuckled. "But I am much too old for this kind of thing. I apologize for making you uncomfortable."

His strong hand touched her arm for a breath, and she impulsively sucked in the air in between the both of them. So much in fact that she got a little dizzy.

Her shoulders quivered for a moment, and she backed away.

Realizing how that must have seemed, she looked up and smiled at him, reassuringly, trying to appear confident.

Graynor smiled back, closed the door behind him and turned to lead the way. She was expecting an awkward, silent walk down the hall and up to the Queen's chambers, but he would not have it.

"So, how long have you been in Lady Samjya's service?"

"Well, I am more of a family member, really. Samjya's family took me in when I was about 12 summers old. I'm an orphan, you see, and I needed a home and work. They quickly grew to like me so much, they almost treated me like their daughter.

"Shortly after, Samjya's parents were expecting a child and I was so excited. When Samjya was born, her mother died, so I became the most important person in her life, after her father of course.

"When Samjya met the King and he had finally convinced her to move to the Royal Court with him, she only agreed on the condition that I came with her. Of course, Vonter wanted to do anything to make the transition to the castle easier for her."

He pursed his lips.

"Very well. Sounds like you and Samjya have quite the family bond then. I would have never thought you were older than her?"

Yandra was grateful for the conversation to overcome her embarrassment.

"Well, I am not young anymore, to be honest. I had to become very responsible after Samjya's mother passed. But yes, the King trusts me just as he trusts Samjya, and I certainly would not want to disappoint him.

"Just like her, I am new to this whole Royal business. I do not know how to talk to the staff most of the time. And some do not seem to be overly impressed with her or me either.

"But I'm putting my head down, and I'm always respectful. At the same time, I would not forgive myself if Samjya got hurt in any way."

"Naturally. But you know, there are so many things in this world that you cannot control. We cannot be responsible for everything, not even for most of the things around us. In fact, very little can actually be controlled by us. Most of the time we only have the choice to react and counteract."

She thought about that for a little while.

It did make sense in a way. She could not control Samjya's emotions, or any of the events outside of this castle.

Still, her duty was her friend's wellbeing. And she was determined to try everything in her power to keep her promise.

"Do you believe in Fate?" she asked the Senior General.

"I do. We can make our own decisions, but Fate has this path for us, and if we deviate too much from it, there might be consequences. She is a kind, and powerful ally if you play by the rules and follow your heart, your soul, your destiny. Force Fate's hand, and she might strike you down where you stand." he made it sound like he was reciting a poem.

"Oh, so you know of Her?" Yandra asked.

"Yes, she is the Goddess of prophecy and all that should be. Some call her Destiny, the Oracle, or sometimes even the Keeper of What Will. At least that's what I have heard. I know the priests are talking about Golden Gods these days, but I believe in all the old Gods still. They make more sense, there is more order to things."

"You have thought about this a lot?" she wanted to know.

"Yes, I have always questioned my own decisions, beliefs, and even myself. Not because I was doubting who I was, but I was critical towards things I have done, things I have felt. I think it is important to think about what you are doing, and what it does to you.

"I can say now with certainty that my faith has made me stronger. Relinquishing the concerns and trusting in the order of what is meant to be, has helped me find an element of acceptance."

She glanced over and caught a glimpse of this sadness again.

When he noticed her look, he blinked it all away and asked: "So do you believe?"

She had to think about that.

"Yes, I think so. I was also brought up with the knowledge of the Gods and Ungods like you. I must admit, once I heard about the Golden Gods, I wanted to believe in them.

"They promise more hope. But lately, I am not sure if this true. There are so many unanswered questions about the Golden Gods.

"Why are they not getting rid of all the pain and suffering? You know, they claim they are here to protect and serve us, but it's all so cynical. I wonder if they are playing with us like toys.

"Why are there people in this world so rich they get bored, and so poor they cannot eat? Why do they not take better care of us? I have been very lucky in my life and blessed with so much kindness, but I have also seen the sick and the unfortunate suffer and die.

"And now, this new danger that no one knows where it is coming from, and why it is attacking the kingdom? I just do not understand how they can let this all happen! I thought they were supposed to be different from the old Gods!" she noticed how she had talked herself into a kind of rant.

Her heart was pounding, and the frustration of the last few days had finally burst out.

Sire Graynor had stopped two steps behind her, and she turned around to him.

His serious face was honest and open.

"The Spirits may well have a plan, Yandra.

"And be it these new age Spirits or the old Gods, any Power to be, even if we do not understand their reasoning behind small, feeble actions, or their inexplicable absence, there is a bigger picture and the power that lies in each one of us.

"You and me, Lady Samjya, Vonter and his kingdom may be in danger, but life is a challenge, a trial, and we must prove ourselves. Not necessarily to them, but to ourselves. We need to grow and make good in this world. Because only that way, we can build a better future and make sense of this life. That is why they do not give us everything we desire or make it so that everyone is happy and healthy all the time. They need to leave things in our hands, for the most part. So, we have the motivation to create, destroy, touch, live and die."

"You should have become a poet, Sire Graynor." her tone was much dryer than she intended, but she could not take it back, so she turned and started walking again. Maybe she was a cynic after all.

She could feel his grin behind her.

"What makes you think I am not a poet?"

Yandra shrugged and picked up the pace.

When she reached the foot of the stairs, her companion had caught up with her.

"You're a soldier."

"I cannot be both?" he exclaimed. "I try not to overthink it. And I concentrate on the good I can do to make this world a better place." he said, still grinning.

"That sounds too good to be true, and a bit rich coming from a General, who fought in a war." she instantly regretted saying that. *What was going on with her manners?*

But Graynor did not seem insulted in the slightest. "Like I said, we cannot control everything."

She hesitated for a moment, and then decided to just ask. "What was the war about? No one ever speaks of it. And the past is always such a big secret, things get forgotten. People only ever say that it was the last war against magic and that we had overcome it forever."

"Well, it was about the last witch, who had done horrible things. She attacked the towns in the South of the land with curses and plagues, killing hundreds of men, women, and children with her army.

"Her crimes were so great, and the price paid so high, but we were not able to kill her. In the end, she was banished beyond the Desert Mountains."

"The fruitless planes no one ever goes to."

"Yes, apparently, the passage was blocked, so no one could cross the mountains ever again."

Yandra did not quite understand.

"How was she banished without the use of magic?"

"Oh, we did have magic on our side. There was a powerful tree, and its fruits made quite the effective weapon. We used it to injure her army and diminish her powers.

"I could feel it, it was powerful stuff. It was just not enough to kill her. So, it was decided to find another permanent solution. I fought in the war, but even I did not see her or how she was banished with my own eyes. They say, the Golden Gods stepped in. It was the last time they were ever seen.

"And that was also the last day this kingdom saw any magic. Believe me when I say, magic is really gone. I have not seen anything like that since the war. And I do hope we are not on the brink of a new one.

"A magical tree and its fruit. This sounded like a fairy tale. Her thoughts circled around that witch. Could she be the source of what was happening now? Could she have escaped her exile and attacked Buntin? A grudge could be a horrible thing to hold on to, and revenge was so easy to give in to.

"Why is the witch not mentioned in any stories?" she wondered out loud.

"She is. But mostly in scary bedtime stories the parents tell their kids in the South. Magic had already been a rarity, and people stopped believing.

"They did not trust magic, they never had, because people fear what they do not understand. We have a hard time remembering what was, and magic was something so old that people were not comfortable with it.

"And even more so now, I believe the whole matter of the war and its evil witch was too painful to keep in people's memories. Most of us wanted to forget. I have told the violent tales of the war to a few of our soldiers, but it was too much even for them. And it is better to look ahead than back. Forget the pain and get on with a good life."

There it was again. He most definitely lost someone dear to him along the way. Had he been alone all this time? Did he feel regret because he had gotten his revenge? He seemed to be a little too calm to still be holding a grudge?

"We will beat this, Yandra. Please do not worry too much." his voice changed back to the more comforting, fatherly tone.

They took the next few steps in silence. It was a comfortable one, but maybe that was just because her nerves had calmed a little. Sire Graynor surely had a lot of patience. She was not sure how she was feeling about this entire situation.

And she was far enough away from home to feel even more unsure. Apart from Samjya, there was only Sire Graynor to talk to. The capital was a strange place to her, and to Samjya. And these strange and worrying times were not helping.

"Sire Graynor, I cannot keep myself from wondering", she started.

His voice was more like a soothing sound: "Yes?"

"Why does the city of the Proud Steed not have a name?" she wanted to know.

After a short pause, the soldier replied: "The capital? Lady Yandra, I have to admit, I do not know." He chuckled. "That's odd, is not it?"

"Yes." It was indeed odd, she thought. "And the castle? No one ever named the castle? Other places have names and titles."

"Well, we do not have any for this place. I never asked myself why."

Somehow, it was bothering her. She could not shake the question. "But someone made the decision to not give the capital a name. When it was founded, I am sure people must have given it a name, no?"

The General was indulging that assumption. "It was most likely forgotten. Cant'un is full of legends and stories, some are bound to get lost or left behind."

"But to forget the past of the capital, is that something that sounds likely?" she prodded. It sounded unlikely.

"I am not sure what to say, Yandra. It never occurred to me that the capital is just what it is now. My guess is that the Elders know a lot more."

Maybe that was the case, she thought.

They had crossed the other hallway almost entirely. The day's sun was still young, so full of potential and promise. Yandra hoped despite her dark thoughts that it was the same for her friend.

"Would it be too much to ask of you to break down Samjya's door if she doesn't open?"

The old man pulled one corner of his mouth up. "No, I believe we should do what it takes to ensure the Lady Samjya is up and well."

She was glad he agreed with her plan. Only if it came to it, of course.

When they arrived at the door, Yandra exchanged a quick look with Graynor and knocked three times.

16

He was absolutely certain. He felt it.

These were just two humans, they would bring word to their King, who would grow desperate for action, and might become reckless and send more soldiers. More souls to collect. Word would travel further and put the fear into other corners of this land.

Then, Fragir realized something else. The last soldiers, that Yart had killed, their souls had not come to him. The spell had started to wear off.

Maybe Yart had reached the limit of his potential, the curse of the black stones might have been depleted. Which was also an acceptable explanation as to why the other two had been able to escape. Why Yart took longer to come back to his castle. Longer than he expected.

He was coming, slowly, but surely. Maybe the soul was being tormented too gravely, maybe his power was weakened altogether. But Fragir would deal with that once he was back. He wanted to send the King a more personal message, and turn the capital, and the Royal residence into a warzone. That should shake things up, he thought to himself.

The black castle was still a very cold place in the middle of the White Forest. Colder than the forest itself, even with the searing power of the consumed souls he had collected.

He could feel them breathing, beating against their cages, ghastly screaming into the dense hollowness of the stones. They were heating up out of rage, pain, and pent-up despair, but the stones would not dissipate any temperateness at all.

His warm hand touched the cold stone of the wall near him. The room was a grand hall, or at least had been before they had left it to ruins.

The King who had ruled here, had been a lying tyrant, but people had still adored him.

Now, these walls were filled with nothing but wind and cold air. Well, and souls, but no one knew that, except for Fragir.

He walked across the hall and onto the balcony where he had addressed his victims once before. Parts of the balustrade and the walls were crumbling off, the boulders were old, the curse worn and ancient. He could still sense its power. He was not sure what had happened here. It was a magical energy that still lingered on, light as the wind, yet heavy with pain.

The yard was empty, just a few random stones and leaves lying around. He was trying to imagine a market, horse stables and fighting pits, maybe some horribly annoying children hunting pigs or chickens, or a few salesmen praising the quality of their fresh goods, some stone soldiers stomping it all into the ground crushing skulls and limbs.

A gust of wind moved the grey dust and dried, white foliage in front of his feet.

Fragir had the deepest respect for his power, and the element that he had control over. Earth was so powerful. The best thing was, that he could access its mighty source from anywhere, as anything was grounded somehow and connected to either soil, sand, or stone, and he had the energies of his element easily available.

He remembered how he had struggled to master his abilities, and he kept digging himself in. Or make people suffocate by filling their lungs with dirt.

Because of his special talent of soul sorcery, he was also able to capture their deepest inner selves, emotions, and thoughts. It didn't quite work like telepathy, it was more of a stream of information, a kind of energy he picked up. That gave him more information than he liked and provoked many fights and deaths that he was responsible for.

It had definitely not been easy.

But luckily, his parents had recognised the first signs of magic early and put him in the care of the White Circle of Ancients's education and their ethic system.

Not that he had cared much for their morals, he was just too much of a free man to restrict himself under rules that another had created.

He had always believed in healthy anarchy, not brainless submission. To think he had to run every spell past some self-proclaimed committee in the hopes they would grant permission! He was not a blind sheep!

When the humans, their King and his men, had decided to strike them all down through the biggest deceit of their past, they had solved that problem for Fragir. But unfortunately, they had also killed his parents in the same blow. Never ever would he forget or forgive. They had to pay!

After the others had died, she had been the only one left. And the initial spells they used to rain wrath onto humanity had been much fun. It had been more than liberating to retaliate and scheme with her. Tessel.

They had had a few good centuries, fighting, loving, torturing each other. She had been his everything. Even more so, he had been hers. Until ..., well, his love had never been enough for her. Because he would never make her as happy as she had expected, she kept asking for more and more. He had pushed her away, and she had cursed him with this ... benevolence.

Somehow, she had been able to hex him, manipulate him into being someone else, *something* else than he was. For the better part of two centuries or so, he had been turned into a naive, solemn wizard living by the coast. He had felt compelled to do good, to take in a miserable apprentice and create a somewhat meaningful life.

Whatever that was. While under the spell for that long, he had had no recollection of his previous life. Now, the memories came back.

And he was furious.

Turned out, in the end, she was just a crazy hag, who could not deal with Fragir being an independent man with his own life.

Fragir wondered where she was now. Tessel had to still be alive, it was hard to believe that she put this powerful curse on him, and then disappeared to never return.

She would have wanted to see him as her little puppet, a good little wizard making house and peace with nature and all that. It would not be like her to just turn around and walk away. He would not be surprised if she was watching right at this time and merely waited for a moment to reveal herself. It was just a matter of time.

He had to be prepared for that! Getting this army together was something that could prove useful. In the process, he would be collecting as many souls as possible by killing as many mortals as possible.

Thinking about his long life, there were some regrets. Letting others get close to him. To know what connection would be and than abusing this or corrupting him with unnatural thoughts. Tessel, the woman, that had taken his best centuries away from him, good solid seven of them! She would have to pay for what she had done to him. Not just the curse, but the lying, manipulating and betrayal. If she would show her face again, he would definitely get even. That bitch better stayed away. He would *destroy* her.

And Dragus. He did not regret taking over his apprentice's physical form, but he felt remorse about the good he had done while his student was around. No, remorse was not the right word, it was more fury than anything else. He was angry at himself, the curse, all the good in the world that he had helped prevail.

Whatever had broken the spell, was a complete mystery to him. He was just glad that it was over. Fragir, the earth sorcerer and soul master. He was finally back.

The rest now was so easy. It was like he had never done anything else. That was exactly what he was going to show the world.

How easy it would be for him to take it all away. Stomping it all into the ground, taking away their souls and destroying all life as they knew it.

It was a good feeling to mine souls again.

It was even more delicious to put them into stone, he thought to himself. Into the most lifeless matter he knew, to contain, concrete and crush their will, and their lives. Once again, he felt this rush of might and fulfilment.

Fragir closed his eyes. Apart from the souls, the castle ruins were very quiet. And so was the surrounding forest. He could not even sense the animals anymore. They must have left the woods. There was not a living soul in the White Forest. No other than himself.

Dragus. He was still there. Deep inside. He was not even fighting anymore, dormant, muffled, paralysed. Fragir had to keep him alive to maintain this body though. Otherwise, he would start to decompose, and he could not afford to look like an undead sorcerer. That was not very attractive at all. And besides, the silent soul of Dragus gave him more power. Souls of the immortal were a manficient source to fire his magic. This one would slowly go insane in the cage and with that, exert even more energy. That he controlled his former apprentice's body, and sanity was an extra kick. The best revenge he could take on him.

He could feel how close Yart now was. His willing soldier had made good progress in the last part of the day. In a very short while, he would be able to make him stronger again and send him on the next attack. He decided to go downstairs and greet Yart. Slowly, he descended from the upper floor down the dusty, spider-web decorated staircase. He did not mind that the castle was still rough and appeared mostly unused and decayed. It was meant to be his base, but not forever. Fragir was sure that the ruins of the capital would make a much better place to build his throne.

Yart's stomping feet created a faint echo in the yard. As the sorcerer stepped out, he noticed how the sun was already starting to set behind the treetops.

He thought he should start right away if he wanted the warrior to get to the capital tonight.

Like a menacing shadow, Yart appeared in the asymmetrical archway, which had been the former castle's gate.

His hands hanging low, and the red eyes merely faint lights anymore. The spell had been used up almost entirely.

"Hello, my favourite soldier. How did it go? ... Well, I hear." he did not expect an answer of course.

"You let two humans get away, but that's okay, they are important for our plan to stoke their King's interest. He'll come. And do not worry, I will load you up with more power, and get you to a whole new playground. How does that sound?"

Yart's expressionless face was turned towards him. Motionless, voiceless, the small lights just glowed back at him. Fragir was really just entertaining himself.

The former merchant would hardly be able to hear him by now. The shell had become weak, and the soul almost dried up. He could revive the spell for a bit, extend the life of the soul, and that meant it would not be long until Yart ceased to exist. That was exactly what he was planning to do.

With one hand, he reached into the earth and pushed his arm deep into the ground. He was holding on to strings of the soil's energies underneath the surface, and then put his feet into a balancing position. The other hand was raised in front of his head with the palm towards Yart.

Eyes closed, Fragir channelled the earth's essence and pulled it out the ground into his arm. It was then moved into the other arm, and at its end, right in front of his hand, formed into a grainy, heavy cloud of dark orange light. This apparition of energy would not stay there. With swift movements, it entered Yart's black hard shell and filled the stone with a bit of magic.

Fragir repeated the action a large number of times, with more orange clouds leaving his hand and entering Yart.

The eyes started to glow fierier again, his mouth let out an obscure growl, and at the same time, a somewhat relieved sigh, and the arms moved up as more and more energy flowed into him.

Then, the stone grew.

Not much at first, but there was a significant difference of at least three feet after just a few moments. Yart was getting bigger, stronger, and more powerful every passing instant. Fragir wanted him to be as intimidating as he possibly could be. When Yart was almost twice as large, the sorcerer stopped.

That spell was so intense that we had to catch his breath. He pulled the hand from the ground and let the other one sink down. The small burning sensation in both of his hands was wearing off slowly.

His trusted stone soldier stared at him, with newfound light in his red dots, the feet almost shuffling nervously in anticipation. But something was missing, Fragir thought.

He would have liked for the infection spell to work again, but that was not possible, the spell had been too powerful, and it would take too long to refill his magic for this. And his army was already very impressive. He could increase the range of his punches though!

The sorcerer held out both arms towards the yard's walls, and with all his soul wrenching power, he pulled two extra souls out of the castle.

Two long and painful howls emitted from the white ghostly shapes that formed and moved from the walls into the black giant, slowly. The souls were screaming in agony yet again when they entered the stone of Yart's chest. Their voices were still so loud and strong, Fragir thought, the pain had to be unbearable. This filled his heart with great satisfaction.

When he opened his eyes again, Yart had this darkly smoking glow about his shape that he had had in the beginning. The vaporing stone was almost shining in the last day light. And even though he knew that the soldier would not last forever, it would be enough to serve his purpose.

"Yart, my friend, we have come so far. I will send you on your last mission. Maybe you will survive, then, I will come for you, and you'll build me a throne.

"But I'm not going to lie, they might fight back, and if they're lucky, they could put an end to our good times. I know and trust your might, so I am convinced, you will prevail."

He stepped back and raised his arms abruptly. "Go and attack the capital! Tear their defences, towers, and houses down. Hunt all men, women, and children, and kill every one of them, until there is nothing left.

I would like you to turn the King's home into the same flat graveyard than Buntin." he lowered his voice as Yart turned around slowly. "Do not come back until you have accomplished this. Do not disappoint me."

Yart stomped off into the White Forest that got darker by the breath. He was able to run now, and it would not take him all night to reach the castle. He should be there just after nightfall.

The King was in for a surprise!

Fragir wiped his hands on the trousers and thought of the next phase of his plan. And he needed a lot more souls for that.

17

Vonter and Mil stared at the young woman holding the blade of her sword to Ca'on's throat.

Her expression was not exactly hostile, but sternly interrogative – after all, there was this weapon that underlined her confidence and seriousness.

Her black, straight hair fell to both her shoulders, covering the top of her thin, tight linen shirt. Her soft, dark brown trousers were a little tight but still appeared to give her the ability to move around quickly. Vonter would have thought her to be quite the warrior, and not to be underestimated.

"Who are you? And why did you break in?" she demanded to know.

Vonter raised his hands and turned towards her, slowly showing his arms and upper body to prove that he did not mean to attack her.

"Our friend is hurt. We were about to put proper bandages on his arm, so he doesn't bleed out." Without moving a muscle, she looked at Ca'on's arm. The fabric was soaked in blood, and some of it had already dropped onto the table.

"We do not mean harm, and we were only going to take what we need. I am King Vonter, -"

She immediately interrupted him.

"King Vonter?! My sincere apologies, His Grace." her head bowed down quickly. "My name is Grunia Pardhua, Daughter of Lartm."

"That's okay, Grunia. It is good to be vigilant these days." he said, relieved. He pointed to the scout.

"This is Mil. And our friend on the table is Ca'on. We really should stop the bleeding!"

She nodded in Mil's direction and turned her head to the soldier next to her.

He was quite pale by now, but he was still able to joke: "Do you mind removing the sword from my throat, or did you intend to make me bleed out faster?"

She put her sword away swiftly and stepped back closer to the kicked in door, almost embarrassed. Then, she rolled the sleeves of her blue shirt up and wiped her hands on the leather trousers.

Vonter gave Mil the signal to get the bandages and some alcohol, and they rushed to patch Ca'on up.

They moved him to a smaller table in the middle of the room. Mil held him down, and Vonter was cleaning the open wound. With pain filled screams and a lot of tears, the man twisted and turned under Mil's hands, so Grunia had to assist them by holding Ca'on's feet. Vonter made him bite down on a washcloth, but it hardly helped. Finally, the soldier passed out from the pain. Mil was getting nervous, but Vonter would not let him panic.

"He is going to be fine! Keep pushing this into the wound, while I get the bandages folded." he said and gave Mil the bloody rags that he had dunked into the alcohol.

"There is so much blood." the young man murmured.

"Ignore it! We need to close the wound." the King explained.

He used needle and thread to close the largest part of the wound, with shaking hands. Sweat was running down his forehead, and he was not entirely sure what he was doing. Halfway through, the young warrior took over, and Vonter instantly recognised, she was so much better at this than him.

They used the bandages to create a thickly layered patch to press against the blood flow and then, wrapped it as tightly as possible around the wound with Mil's help. He could feel the blood pumping underneath the bandages, but at least it looked firmly wrapped and clean now.

Vonter let himself fall onto a chair. When he looked at Mil, he started to worry about the boy once again.

He was just standing there by the window, staring down on his palms open, covered in blood.

Mil's eyes were filled with horror and disgust. This had to be new to him.

"Go wash your hands." he suggested.

"No!" came the immediate reaction, but not from Mil. "No one can touch the water. It will turn you into stone!" the woman said.

The King looked up. "Yes, you said something about water earlier. How?"

"I do not know. It just does. I cannot explain it."

Mil hid his shaking hands behind his back and blinked tears away.

"Who are you again?" he asked with a crackle in his voice.

Vonter was glad that the young scout was still able to focus, so it seemed.

"My name is Grunia." she answered with a half-smile. "Grunia Fanda Pardhua. I am a seamstress at the town's tailors. Or at least that's what I was until yesterday."

This time, her voice broke a little.

"Were you born here in Tramvil?" Vonter asked gently.

"Yes, lived here all my life. And I love this town, and everyone in it. … Loved."

He could tell that she was fighting tears too.

"Is anyone else alive? Your family?" he uttered, with the worry of making her cry.

But she did not cry. She slowly shook her head. "No, everyone I know is dead. They either drank from the water, washed themselves with it, or they touched someone who did. You see, t is not only the water, but also any stone that was cursed by the water."

Her voice failed her on the last word. She had to battle a lump in her throat, and Vonter and Mil gave her the time. During the pause, he checked on Ca'on's pulse. Weak, but steady.

When she started to speak again, she hesitated and paused a lot: "The first, I think, … were the goats, and their shepherd. They must have been drinking from the well. …

"It spread quickly, they said. I heard so many screams. Not long after, … I saw the first townspeople change in front of my eyes. They, they were drinking the water."

Grunia paused again, clearly struggling to hold it all in.

"Children jumping into the river and, … never coming back up again. And they started to turn after touching each other. All these screams… It looked so painful.

"I did not understand it at first. When I did, I tried to warn them. No one would listen to me. I had even convinced a young mother and her family to stay away from the water, but then, her youngest son touched a water bucket at the well."

She swallowed hard. "He turned so fast, she cried out and embraced him willingly, knowing that it would kill her, and that … got all her children."

Vonter felt a shudder running down his back. He could tell that it was all happening again in front of Grunia's eyes.

"I saw my parents change just this morning; they were so thirsty. They had decided shortly after the Well Square reactions to drink mead that was produced a while back, so it was safe. My father got so drunk; he fell into the river. My mother … jumped in after him."

"I am so sorry, Grunia."

"Thank you, His Grace." she cleared her throat and wiped her wet eyes. "I just wish I could undo this. I wish my parents were still alive."

The King had to swallow as well, and said: "Are you thirsty? We have water from the South, it is safe to drink."

Grunia nodded and Vonter passed the waterskin to her. She took a big gulp, stopped herself, and looked at the container. "We might have to save some for later."

For a long time, no one spoke.

The King checked on Ca'on regularly, Mil stared out of the window and Grunia sat quietly, until she got up and looked around for food, carefully.

She came back with an apple and two dried sausages. They divided evenly and ate in silence.

When it was almost dark, Mil sighed and looked at his hands again. "How are we going to get rid of all this blood? I do not want my hands to be red for the rest of my life."

Grunia again half smiled. "I have some white wine at the house, it is two years old, so it is safe. Your hands will be just as sticky, but at least cleaner. We should go tomorrow morning first thing; it is probably safer in the light of day."

"Yes, thanks." Mil looked at his hands, still very pensive.

Vonter's thoughts circled around this place. They should not stay here, but with an unconscious Ca'on, the journey would be quite impossible. Even he would not be able to carry him on his horse. But the longer they stayed here, the more dangerous it became for them to be affected by the same fate than the townspeople of Tramvil.

Grunia did not look so good either. She had drunk half the waterskin, and she still looked very thirsty. He could tell that she was pacing herself, so there would be a bit of water for everyone else. She had to have strong willpower and immense control over her actions.

As soon as Ca'on would be awake, they should make their way back to Buntin and warn everyone.

When Vonter woke up, his eyes opened abruptly, and his whole body shook suddenly. It appeared he had fallen asleep. The last night had been rather short, and he was more exhausted than he let on.

Grunia was startled by his rapid activity, her eyes dark and with a hunted expression. She had taken Mil's place by the window. The daylight was almost gone, and it was just as quiet as before.

Until he realized that Ca'on was snoring quietly. He could not suppress a smile.

"That's a good sign." he commented.

"Yes, he came to for a few breaths, mumbled something about gold, and then he fell fast asleep." Grunia explained. She made it sound like this had been the only development in their situation. Maybe it was.

"Where's Mil?" he wondered.

"He wanted to look around for food and prepare for our way back."

"By himself?"

"Yes, why not? This house is safe, as long as he doesn't touch the healer."

Vonter jumped up. He had a very bad feeling about this. He rushed into the other rooms and called out for the boy. Nothing. There was a back door which was unlocked, and it dawned on him that Mil had gone out.

When he walked back into the front room, Grunia had gotten up, worried now too.

"He left! This is too dangerous. What if this is not just the water? What if there is also someone attacking people in this town? Mil is definitely not doing well enough to be alone!".

His heart started to beat out of his chest, Mil had already been through so much! "How could you have let him go alone? He is just a boy."

"I did not know he would actually leave the house; we had talked about this before; he knew the risks!"

Grunia turned away from the window and placed her hands on her hips, arms in an angle that made her look more intimidating than the King was expecting.

"I could have hardly known that he would run off like this without saying a word. And even so, that boy can take care of himself. He looks weak, and young, but he is not, and he really wanted to do this."

Vonter was just worried, but she was right. They would need food and supplies for their way back, but especially if they would have to make camp here for the night to get Ca'on ready for transportation in the morning.

Mil was just looking out for the group, but they should have had an agreement to only go out together, and potentially barricaded the house.

Feeling Ca'on's pulse and checking the bandages, he tried to calm down. When he glanced over to the young woman, he could see that she was trying to do the same.

There was still this fighting glimmer in her eye. And she had not moved one inch.

"Look, we should prepare ourselves for anything. I think more supplies will definitely come in handy." she said with a contrite tone. "And I apologize for speaking against you, His Grace."

He sighed silently. "That is understandable. This situation is very unusual for all of us. I just feel I need to protect Mil. Anyone, really."

She did not say anything. Instead, she loosened her stance, and turned her head towards the window.

Vonter looked to Ca'on's feet. Someone had already put together whatever this healer's house had to offer. A bag with cloths and clean rags, and another bag with herbs and small phials with alcohol. Just what they needed to renew the soldier's bandages and have some emergency supplies in reserve.

"Good job on collecting these." he said.

"You should tell Mil that, Your Majesty. He wanted to be useful and start on getting you back on the road."

"Us." he corrected her.

"Excuse me?" she seemed puzzled by that.

"Getting us back on the road. You should come with us."

"I don't know." she moved her head again to watch the outside, followed by a long sigh. "My life is here; this is my home."

"Forgive me for saying, but what life? Your life is filled with stones here. Your home is empty. And it is too dangerous to stay here. You need to drink clean water and wash yourself."

As soon as he said it, he regretted it. His tone had been a lot sharper than he intended.

She had her face turned away from him, so he could not sense what she might be feeling or thinking. The silence, that followed, was heavy. Just when he finally decided to get ready and go find Mil, Grunia raised her head and pushed against the side of the window. "Mil?"

She shook her head. The King was still determined.

"I should go out and get Mil." he said. "Who knows what kind of trouble he is in?"

She did not protest, just looked at him. She had been crying, silently, while she was facing away from him just now. Had he hurt her with his brutal honesty? Was she feeling bad because the boy had gotten away?

Vonter walked over to the door, opened it, and saw Mil! The boy had just approached the front door in the intent of walking in. His eyes were filled with tears. In his hands, he had two large bags, filled with food.

"Mil!" it burst out of the King's mouth.

The scout entered the house and dropped the bags onto the floor. He kept on walking, to the end of the room, and back, his eyes jumping from one side to the other.

"This town." he stammered. Over and over. "This town. This town."

Grunia, now very alert, closed the door, and grabbed Mil by his shoulders. "What did you see?"

Mil focused on the seamstress and raised his voice: "So many stones. They are all gone. I mean, they're everywhere, so still."

Thick tears rolled down his face.

"Children and women, everyone. … We need to leave this place. … It is a town of human gravestones."

18

"Come in!"

Samjya's voice sounded absent, far away, quite not herself. But at least, this time, there was a reaction to the knocking, Yandra thought relieved. Her hand moved down to turn the door handle, and her eyes met with Sire Graynor's again. He nodded encouragingly.

To her surprise, the door was not locked anymore.

Yandra opened the door and found the room in quite a state, simply put. The bed fabrics were pulled off and shoved into a pile on the floor behind the door, and the pillows were on the other side of the chambers. Some clothes covered the ground between her and her friend, and a brush had been pushed into one of the potted plants, in between the leaves.

Samjya also had torn down one of the curtains, and the water jug had been tipped over, soaking one of her morning gowns in front of the window.

The new Royal was sitting at her dressing table, the face hidden between her hands and the hair standing in all directions. Even her dress was ripped in three places, and it was dirty, even though there was no easy way to see how this could have happened.

Yandra spoke softly: "Samjya, are you okay?"

Samjya turned around, she had an expression on her face, the same mix of happiness and sadness that Yandra had seen last night. Again, the eyes were very smoky, wet as if she was about to cry, or would have been crying all night. The hair was just a mess, knots, and broken hair around her face. She was very sure she could see that blue-silver glow again, just lightly.

So, it had not been the light? The young bride put one arm on the back of her chair and bent her back, like an old woman. Her eyes squinted a bit when she talked, and the movements of her limbs were very limited, abrupt.

"For the most part," her tone was hostile, almost accusatory. "Thanks for checking on me."

Her posture was so tense, and the eyes were shooting cold energy their way, it was very apparent what she was feeling. Sire Graynor shrugged his shoulders when Yandra turned to him. "I have been checking on you for two days now, you have not touched any of your food, and we are worried, my love. Worried about you."

Samjya cocked her head back and cackled: "Worried? You were happy to not see me! Because I am just a burden, another mouth to feed, Vonter's blind love slave! Where is he? I bet you are keeping him from me!"

"That's not true, Samjya. Trust me, I am on your side." Yandra tried her softest voice, but inside, a violent storm of confusion and frustration attacked her patience. She was so glad the General was with her, and that she was not going mad. Samjya was not the same person anymore, but she had to remind her! "These are your chambers; you are safe here. And Vonter will be back before you know it."

Without a warning, her mistress jumped up and screamed: "You should stay away! You took the moon, and my family away from me, I curse your blood! … Bugs!"

"Samjya …" Yandra tried, but Samjya would not let her. She was so confused! Did she say *bugs*?

"I want to see him again. You're just locking me up like a wild animal. Does he want me as a trophy – or are you keeping me from him? Is this you or him? Tell me!!"

While she frantically screamed at them, she picked up her things from the dressing table, jewellery, brushes, hairclips, and threw them towards Graynor and Yandra.

What was going on here? What had happened to Samjya? Yandra was so confused, she did not even raise her hands to protect her face. She woke up from her freeze when the first brush hit her forehead. But Sire Graynor was faster than herself. He stepped in front of her and raised his arms to protect her.

"Tell me! Which is it? Tell me!!" Samjya kept going on in her frenzy.

"My Lady, please calm down! You are not making any sense! We are here to help."

And then, suddenly, she stopped throwing and screaming. Yandra risked a peek. Samjya looked as if she had just remembered who Sire Graynor was. She could see how her brain was working on grasping the situation.

"Keep talking." Yandra whispered. "She appears to respond to you."

Graynor stepped forward and bent down a little.

"Do you know who we are, Lady Samjya?" he said softly.

"Of course, I do. Sire Graynor, can you please get me out of here?". Her voice sounded so different suddenly, soft, almost sweet.

Samjya fell to her knees and started sobbing. It seemed so genuine. Was it?

"I feel so alone and betrayed. Every bug is looking at me, all the time."

"What do you mean, who is looking at you?"

"In the loud space, that is empty when it is quiet. Bugs. They are so full of anticipation and questions. I cannot hear their muttering anymore. I cannot. So many dirty bugs."

Yandra did not understand. There were no bugs. She grabbed Sire Graynor's shoulder from behind. He did not react.

"So many bugs, it is getting louder again. They are worrying and crying again, with all my blue and silver."

Graynor turned to Yandra. "She is talking about the wedding preparations and the people downstairs."

"Oh.". She still would not dare to speak up.

"Samjya. Please look at me.". He reached in between the wild hair and pulled her chin up gently. The Samjya's eyes were red from crying. And she had to be so exhausted. She shuddered when she saw Yandra again, but she remained calm.

"Do you remember your friend, Yandra?" he asked in the same tone.

Samjya nodded, disgusted and hostile.

"She locked me in here! She is keeping me from my King."

Yandra could not hold it in. "No, I'm not, I just want you to be safe and well! Can't you see that?" She touched Samjya's hand. It was ice cold. And it definitely was the wrong move.

The Queen to be pushed her away and ran into the far corner of the room. Was the silver glow in her hair getting stronger? She pressed her back against the wall and eyed her handmaiden with hatred. Cold hatred. No, it was very different from that, but Yandra did not have a more suitable word for it.

Something on the dressing table caught her attention. It was the white and blue glowing flower that Vonter had given her two days ago, still pulsating with the same light. That must have been the source of the odd light that she had seen last night from underneath the door.

Was this somehow affecting Samjya? Was this flower the reason she was behaving like this?

Just as Yandra was about to take a step towards the table, Samjya pushed herself off the walls and ran towards her.

"DO NOT TOUCH THAT!" she screamed on the top of her lungs. In a flash, she was at the dressing table, grabbed the large blossom and then, she broke off one of the inner petals and *shoved it into her mouth.*

Half turned away from them, she gulped it down, like a starved bear would swallow a whole fish, barely chewing.

Yandra felt as if her eyes would fall out. She was unable to blink, or even breathe.

When her head turned towards Sire Graynor, her eyes had a hard time following. The General's face mirrored her disbelief and lack of comprehension of what was happening.

Just as slowly as she had looked away, she forced her attention back on Samjya.

Now, the silver in her hair grew more apparent, fuller, and stronger.

Her skin was getting even paler in rhythmic surges, and when she turned towards them with new fury, her eyes turned silver too!

"Get away from it! Leave! LEAVE IT ALONE!" *What*?

Samjya extended her arm towards them, and a crackling sound filled the air, as if someone would hit the air with a whip.

Yandra jumped back, she wanted to hide behind Sire Graynor again, but he was backing up too. He bent down to hold his shin and cursed quietly. With a firm hand, he pushed Yandra back and out of the room. Before the door closed, she could see Samjya standing there, frozen, looking down on her arm in shock. Or was it fear?

Sire Graynor slammed the door shut and turned the key that he had obtained from the other side. Then, he sank down, and sat on the floor, obviously in pain.

"It is so cold!" he pressed through his teeth.

She got down to get closer to his leg, and she saw a blue cut, surrounded by black, freeze burnt blood and skin.

***

"Come in!"

Samjya's own voice was so close to her own head that she almost jumped. She was not expecting her voice to be that close. The knocking on the door had also been very clear. Unlike the muttering of the other voices, she had in her head. Everything was buzzing.

She had a slight headache from the constant buzz. The warmth made it all sound so fuzzy, so far away.

It was very chaotic. Where did all this noise come from? Maybe they had a party downstairs? Despite the wedding being off now? However, she could not make out any words.

The knocking was very clear. That felt … more real than anything else.

She could hear them sneak in. Was it time? Was Vonter finally back?

"Samjya, are you okay?" Yandra's voice was also closer than the others were. Samjya decided to turn around. As soon as she stopped touching the flower, the warmth was gone. But she was trying not to give it away. Her secret.

She rested one arm on the back of the chair and looked at them. Her childhood friend had a cold, stern expression on her face.

Sire Graynor was standing next to her. Her first instinct was to run to him, but she was not sure. Could she still trust him? Probably not.

"For the most part. Thanks for checking on me." the young Queen was trying to be not too obvious; she should try to get more information first. If they were going to take her away somewhere, she wanted to at least know where to. If they were going to keep her here for longer, she wanted to at least know where and for how long.

"I have been checking on you for almost two days, you have not touched any of your food, and we are worried, my love. Worried about you."

She could not suppress laughter. This was rich! Yandra's voice could not sound more dishonest! First, they would lock her in here, and now they pretended to care?

"Worried? You were happy to not see me! Because I am just a burden, another mouth to feed, Vonter's blind love slave! Where is he? I bet you are keeping him from me!" she heard herself say. The two exchanged another look, as if they were silently communicating with each other.

She wished she could leave this room, run away to find him. Her Vonter.

"That's not true, Samjya. Trust me; I am on your side. These are your chambers; you are safe here.

And Vonter will be back before you know it."

Another rush of rage took a hold of Samjya. Yandra was not the same person anymore, she had changed!

There was a glow in her eyes, so aggressive and mean.

It was painful for her to realise that her friends were not her friends. They probably never had been! This entire undertaking had been a trap!

Like wardens, Yandra and Sire Graynor took position next to each other and blocked the way to the door. Samjya jumped up.

"You should stay away! You took the moon, and my family away from me, I curse your blood! … People!"

"Samjya -"

No, Yandra would not get to say anything! That stupid bitch!

"I want to see him again. You're just locking me up like a wild animal. Does he want me as a trophy – or are you keeping me from him? Is this you or him? Tell me!!"

She turned her head, grabbed a few items on her dressing table, and just flung them towards her captors. Her anger needed an outlet, Samjya had been cooped up in this room for too long.

"Tell me! Which is it? Tell me!!" she demanded.

"My Lady, please calm down! You are not making any sense! We are here to help." Sire Graynor's warm timbre made her stop. He had always been so understanding and kind. The way he said the word Queen was not as ironic as Yandra did it. She did not understand why he was supporting this. All she wanted was to get out of this room and find Vonter. Thick tears built up behind her eyes.

Yandra whispered something to Sire Graynor. Samjya tried to hear what had been said, but the blood was rushing too loudly in her ears. And there were still these other voices. Thoughts invading her mind. Why?

Her former friend had been hiding behind the soldier like a coward. The Queen knew that her handmaiden was eyeing her with hatred.

She did not even have to look. And she did not have the energy to throw brushes and towels at them anymore.

Instead, she just sunk down to the ground. Her body was so weak, her knees gave in, and her head hung low between her arms.

Silent tears ran down her face and then she had to gasp for air. Breathing had become a challenge at this point. She was too agitated to concentrate. And she was tired of holding it together!

"Do you know who we are, Lady Samjya?" Sire Graynor said, softly. She needed a little while to just breathe. *Calm down.* This was all so pointless without her King. And if she wanted to see him again, she probably had to be collected and appear more reasonable than this.

"Of course, I do. Sire Graynor, can you please get me out of here? I feel so alone and betrayed. Everyone is looking at me all the time."

"What do you mean? Who is looking at you?" he asked softly.

"In the loud space, that is empty when it is quiet. People. They are so full of anticipation and questions. I cannot hear their muttering anymore. I cannot. So many people." Samjya was relatively calm again.

Thinking of what was going on downstairs made her very anxious. All of the people that were probably pretending like nothing had happened. Celebrating the wedding that never was. Mourning the wedding that took place. Or did it?

It felt good to finally share this, let these thoughts escape and run free.

That much she knew.

"So many people, and it is getting louder again. They are worrying and crying again, and I am just afraid for my Vonter." she added, turning more desperate. "She is talking about the wedding preparations and the people downstairs." Sire Graynor said.

"Oh.". The stupid bitch was apparently out of words. Those voices, so far away again.

"Samjya. Please look at me."

She felt his warm hand on her chin. Softly, he pulled her face up. It felt like he was digging her out of the dirt that was dampening her hearing.

But just sometimes.

It was changing all the time, so exhausting.

"Do you remember your friend, Yandra?"

Her heart skipped a beat. Her former friend's evil smile jumped into her field of vision and stayed there. Brutal, cold, and full of the worst possible intent that she had ever seen.

And felt!

She could feel the negative energy attacking her.

And the worst part was, she could not lose it. It would just stay there!

"She locked me in here! She is keeping me from my King." it burst out of her.

"No, I'm not, I just want you to be safe and well! Can't you see that?" her so-called friend said with a vicious smile on her face. She had turned her face away from the General as if she did not want Sire Graynor to know her true intentions.

And then, Yandra grabbed her wrist, pain surged through Samjya's arm, and she tried to get away. The stupid cow had burning hands!

Shaking the hot grip, she fell back, and almost crawled backwards to get away from her. She did not stop until she felt the wall behind her. Staring at Yandra, her heart began to race.

Could she make a run for the door? Would her so-called friend attack her or grab her again? Would Sire Graynor help or stand back? Whose orders was he following? Had the bitch finally done harm to Vonter and was covering it all up?

Yandra leaned forward and wanted to pick up the flower.

"DO NOT TOUCH THAT!" she cried out and rushed to the table.

She grabbed the blossom, and suddenly, was hit by the warm feeling again, the sensation of being cared for, not hungry or sad anymore.

She knew that it was all not so bad.

Samjya wanted to get deep into this emotion and hide away in it.

Her hand was almost acting on its own when she grasped the petals in the middle of the flower, and she suddenly felt the sweet taste of love on her tongue again.

This was the third time she allowed herself a piece of the flower. It filled her with so much comfort and energy.

This was the purest feeling she had sensed. The softest softness, a tight embrace, a giant wave of all the happiness in the world, and all that in itself.

It was the golden moment that she had been craving from her friends and family, who had abandoned or captured her.

The ecstasy that she would never feel with Vonter again.

And then, it hit her.

Yandra wanted this as well.

For herself!

Samjya had failed in keeping the secret. Was this the reason why they had her locked up?

Was this why she had brought the General? Thinking that Samjya would trust him, and willingly hand it over? Or to take it away from her by force? She had to protect her precious gift!

And they were closing in on her to take it!

"Get away from it! Leave! LEAVE IT ALONE!"

She screamed as she turned around. A hot flash rushed from her shoulder into her hand that she had extended to defend and push back.

But this was not the only thing that happened. The heat produced a ... flash of lightning? Like an arrow of blue light, energy left her hand and hit Sire Graynor's leg!

Unable to say anything, she just froze. What was that?

She did not even realize how they left the room in a hurry.

She did not want to hurt him.

She did not even know what that was.

And how she did it.

All she was able to do was to stare at her hand.

All she thought was, how and why this was possible?

All she knew was that she had to protect herself and her flower at any cost.

They would never understand.
People.
Bugs.

19

Mibb sighed long and deeply. After hearing their story, he really could feel for them. Even after hundreds of years of watching humans from a distance, they had become such ... animals, but he could still relate to their desires and pains.

Maybe this was a part of his humanity that was still intact. Maybe it was some quick thinking, flexibility in that way, that came naturally to squirrels, as he knew the others would not think that way. At all.

Or would they? He did not know. He had never thought of squirrels as very intelligent, self-reflecting and empathetically grasping their environment back then. Until he had become one himself. And that was not the right thing, of course.

He was not even a real squirrel. He was not sure if he would be able to communicate with another rodent. Would they speak the same language? Have the same body language? He had never met any. Except the other immortals. But they were foxes, owls, and deer. And they spoke. Words.

So, he was neither squirrel nor human anymore. And it had never been clearer to him than in this moment. For some reason, he felt like he could trust Sahdor and Draidr. They needed his help to escape this forest. And Mibb thought that they all should help each other. The threat was very real. The only question was how they should work together to overcome this new danger. The two humans did not seem too concerned for the animals, however.

"Well, if you ask me, we have all the information now, we should get back to the King as soon as possible." one of the men said.

The other one nodded silently and turned away from Mibb. There was some indistinctive muttering, but the squirrel did not have to hear. He already knew.

They would try and convince the animals of the White Forest to help them in their war.

Mibb turned and walked to the foxes and the owls. "What do you think, my friends?"

Kalia, one of the owls jerked her wings and squinted. "I do not know. We really should get rid of them as soon as possible. Toss them out at the edge of the woods and forget we have ever talked to them. It is risky enough as it is."

"We cannot let them go, really. They know now that we exist, thanks to Mibb!" some creature in the back shouted, hiding.

"But we cannot really hold out underground forever. Sooner or later, this will concern us! We need to do something." Mibb tried.

"Do something?" Sihgr the fox, who was the second oldest after Mibb, expressed his scepticism. "Do what exactly? There is nothing we can do. Human matters should not concern us."

"We do not have hands large enough to hold any weapons, and we do not possess any magic. There is not much we can, let alone should offer." the vixen agreed. She was siding with the majority of the animals on this, Mibb could tell by their postures and the expression on their faces.

"But what else is there? Hiding away underground until what happens? We run out of food, go crazy, suffocate to death?"

Mibb was getting impatient. That was probably very squirrel-like.

"We can always try and leave?" Sihgr said.

"Leave the White Forest?" the other two foxes were shocked.

"No, no, no, no. We cannot do that, dear," said his female. "We absolutely cannot leave the woods; the witch would never let us! We would die instantly."

"She also said that we would die if we ever talked to a human. We have taken huge risks by saving those two idiots." the male fox nodded into the soldiers' direction.

"Hey! I heard that!" Draidr's eyes shot arrows.

Mibb smiled. Apparently, the humans had better hearing than they thought.

Draidr shook his head and turned back to his conversation with Sahdor.

The fox corrected himself: "Forgive me, I misspoke. Mibb has taken a huge risk by saving those two idiots."

Kalia sighed, and shared her thoughts: "Well, we did not die talking to the humans, maybe leaving the forest would be worth a try. Maybe the witch is not around anymore, or her magic is not as strong as it was?"

"Maybe she lied to us?" Mibb added thoughtfully.

The female fox raised her voice again, more into Sihgr's direction that the group, actually: "But we would subject ourselves to the cruelty of humans. We would give up our secret, even by letting those men leave the forest. We are letting the world know that we exist, and we'll be hunted down like ... well, animals. At least here, we are safe. We should stay." said the vixen. She was really worried. Of course, she wanted to protect her family. Her speech earned nods and wordless approvals.

But Mibb felt this was so much bigger than what they saw. It seemed to him, they had reached a point where they should not hide anymore.

"What if this is our time to prove how human we still are? What if it is our destiny to help the humans? The redemption we were supposed to inherit from our parents and elders' mistakes?"

Sihgr and some of the other animals snorted disapprovingly.

"Seriously, my friends. If our past has taught us anything, it is that we should help each other and honour and respect others in our community."

"*Our* community." Sihgr interrupted him. "They are not part of us, or our kind."

Mibb raised one hand. "Our kind? We were humans once. What we are now was meant as a penance. We should never forget that."

Some muttering emerged within the group.

The fox smirked. "Well, I see it as a blessing. We have been given a new chance, to be free from pride, greed, and envy. Can't you see that this has liberated us from human flaws?"

"I do not think so. If that's even partly true, we are doing something wrong. We are giving in to pride. We should not try to lose ourselves; we should do better than the ones before us."

The fox pushed his chest out forward and looked down on Mibb, more than he had before.

"Well, if you feel like that, maybe you should bring the humans back to the fields. Make sure they get back safely. But I think they should leave for good, and never speak of us. Never."

"Is that what you all want?" the rodent asked his friends.

Most of them nodded, a few looked away, but the general consensus was clear.

Mibb nodded and decided: "Agreed. I will lead them away from this place to the Eastern edges of the woods where they will return to their own."

He did not have to say that he was disappointed. The animals were able to see it in his eyes. It was not so much that they would not listen to their leader, their group did not work like that.

Still, it made the entire situation disappointing.

Many years ago, they had decided to never turn their back on anyone. And to see now, that his friends were breaking their own promise, just because this was about humans, and not animals, it made him sad.

And he apparently was not able to argue this case, or to even convince any of his group to rethink their standpoint.

"Hey, asses. We should go. The sooner, the better."

Draidr frowned, Sahdor smiled.

"Yes, we need to return to Buntin." Draidr said.

"Alright, let's not waste any more time." Mibb clapped his paws and turned to one of the tunnels.

"This should be wide enough. It leads to the surface not too far from the fields and the river."

He jumped to the opening of their pathway. The two men followed him, crawling. One of them was still moving funny – he had probably bumped his leg or something when they fell.

Mibb moved ahead nonetheless, making sure that he could always see or hear them behind him. It became quite dark after a while, as apparently, even the glow worms had decided to stay behind. There was no chance to get lost, so they should be okay, Mibb thought.

One of the soldiers was complaining that it was quite stuffy and hard to breathe. Humans!

No endurance, he thought. But it was indeed easier for a small, quick animal.

After what felt like half an eternity because they were so much slower than Mibb usually was, they finally arrived at the tunnel's end. At the hole in the ground, he did not want to wait a few more moments until the others emerged as well, so he quickly jumped up a tree to have a look around. No sign of any stone men. Good.

The men stretched their muscles and breathed in deeply, but Mibb pressed forward. It was a fairly easy walk. Draidr had warned them about touching or stepping on any stones, so they made their way carefully. The squirrel was up in the trees most of the time, easier to see over their surroundings and keep track of the humans.

A few long breaths went by, and the edge of the forest was already visible. Through the slim white pillars shone the luscious green of the open fields. Another tree with green leaves was standing just outside of the White Forest's grasp, casting its shadow on a deer. Mibb was wondering who it was.

There were no other animals around than the cursed children that he had been living with in the last centuries.

Sahdor was the first one to notice that his attention was fixed on one particular point in front of them. "What is it, Mibb?" came the voice from behind, slightly concerned.

The squirrel only shook his head and jumped ahead. On one of the branches, he stopped, because he recognised him.

The deer was solid stone. At first, he looked like he was asleep. Peacefully, he was sitting in the shadow, head turned around onto his legs and feet in a puddle. Mibb swallowed audibly and let himself sunk three branches lower.

When the men caught up and saw the same thing, Sahdor immediately froze. Draidr shouted up: "Someone you know?"

With tears in his eyes, Mibb nodded and mouthed a silent yes. His voice was gone for a breath, so he cleared his throat and said: "His name was Gartt. He was one of the older ones, a very good friend. He went missing two days ago. About the same time as this attack on your people happened as you said." the rodent answered.

He did not know what else to say. It was all so empty. The animals were not safe. He had to talk to them again.

"Do you want to come with us to Buntin?" Sahdor held his hand out.

"What?"

Why would he follow them to Buntin?

"Well, I just thought you had quite an argument with the others, and it is not very safe in the woods anymore." Sahdor seemed unsure about how Mibb would take what he just said.

But he was actually surprised by himself: "We did not have an argument; we discussed your fate. But thanks for your concern, I will be certainly not be joining you."

He did not think leaving the others behind like this was the right thing. Mibb was their leader after all.

They had every right to know what happened to Gartt. And they would join the humans together or find a different solution.

"Alright." Draidr rolled his eyes, and stepped to the right and towards the fields, always looking down, checking the ground in front of his feet.

Sahdor looked up to Mibb.

"Thanks for saving our lives. I will not forget this. And do not worry, we will not tell the others." He smiled.

Mibb wiped his eyes and smiled back. "Take care of yourself, good Sahdor".

The two men walked out of the White Forest into the sunshine, in a safe distance from poor Gartt.

As soon as the energy would return to his feet, he would make his way back to his group. They were not safe, not at all.

***

Oh Father, I celebrate ye
Such strong hands, so honest and tru'hful,
Just like yer heart, open and courageous.

Oh Father, I salute ye
Blood or not, we are kin and loyal,
Love, Trust and Soul are more precious.

Oh Father, I revere ye
Yer chose compassion and service,
Before dea'h and orders, wi'h a heart so full.

Oh Father, ... I mourn ye
Yerar always here, ... always here,
I shall never forget yer, by my soul.

Syfur let the lute sink down onto his lap and wiped tears off his cheeks. His nose was all closed up from writing, reciting, and practicing the verses.

They were in no means finished, and there was probably no stage at which he felt they were doing justice to his old man. "No survivors", the words rang in his head like a church bell.

He wished he had the strength to go and see Buntin, but when people had told him about the scale of destruction and death, he froze, and he was stuck ever since.

He was afraid of himself and his emotions. Buntin had always been his home, and he loved his father. Thinking about how he would have to face the extreme destruction and death in person made him sick to his stomach. In his soul, he admitted to himself that he was a coward.

He was not made for fighting, killing and death. Magic was completely new to him. His strength ws telling stories, and he would definitely use his emotions to tell his father's story. He would make sure that everyone would hear about this compassionate, supportive and kind man. How he had given up the duties as a soldier and dedicated his life to taking care of his adopted son, Syfur.

The bard suddenly realised how much Yart had given up for him. How much love there had been for someone who wasn't even his own flesh and blood, but he never noticed for a breath! He really thought that his father had no regrets or resentments to the chosen path.

That was probably the most moving and inspiring part of his life – while he had the deepest admiration for all the qualities, benefits and care he had been able to enjoy, it was very impressive of his father to fully embrace his life.

And that was what Syfur was going to do. Once he would arrive in Yopint, safe behind thick walls and military defenses, he would make it his life mission to honour his father and stick to singing tales and legends, just like his father's. Like he would have wanted for him. Like he would have. No regrets, no resentments.

As he put out his little fire and wrapped himself in his blanket, his thoughts circled around the verses he had composed.

He would continue his work on them on the road between Lint and Yopint, and if he arrived early enough, he might have a chance to play in one of their taverns to earn some coin for a room even.

The back streets were no place to sleep, but he didn't have the money today.

His eyes teared up again, and the soft glimmer of the moon became a glistening wave of light through his half-closed eyelids.

20

She still did not understand what exactly and how it happened. Was she starting to see things? But surely, what she felt and heard was real?

Samjya stared at her hands, again. Naturally, she did not mean to hurt anyone, let alone Sire Graynor, who had ever been so kind to her since she had come to the castle. But how long has that been? A few days, a week, a few weeks? She could not remember!

Vonter.

Her thoughts returned to her fiancé. Her magical, amazing, beautiful, and warm Vonter. She missed his kiss, his touch, his embrace, and his smile. She grew more and more frightened that she would forget what his smile looked like. Or his eyes. The eyes that she had always gotten lost in. Her heart became so heavy, it stung like a thousand needles.

She only now realised that she was crying. Again. Yandra's change confused her most. How could a friend she had grown up with and been so close with so quickly, rapidly change this much? Had Samjya done something wrong? Maybe Yandra was not feeling well? But why would Sire Graynor let it all happen? And the nagging rage came back. Bugs.

Not understanding, feeling powerless and the fear of losing everything that she had and would ever have, made her so angry. Mostly angry at herself. At least that's how it felt.

She was angry at herself because she could not understand. It was all so empty and hostile suddenly. In her new home that had been a dream come true so beautifully up until a few days ago, she now perceived herself a prisoner.

It did not feel right at all anymore, something was off. She was not angry at herself; she was truly angry at Vonter and Yandra. But why? Or was she angry at her father?

The only thing that made sense to her was the flower. It was so delicious. She had already eaten seven petals. And she could not stop, but she also did not want to stop. Her body craved its silvery rich release of comfort. Her heart was screaming for it, pounding up her throat like a baby bird waiting for mother's worm.

It gave her a tremendous amount of warmth, and a strange sense of happiness, bliss, joy, and wholeness. She could not explain it.

The truest and purest emotions filled her, from head to toe, and other thoughts would disappear. She could trust the delicate and absolute taste of the blossom, and herself, when she was letting the silver and blue light pass her lips and let it dissolve on her tongue.

She did not have to chew, the petals were just melting in her mouth, running smoothly down her throat, and warming her stomach from the inside, soft and tender. It felt more than right. It was meant to be. Samjya had never felt something like this before. Through the tears, she had to smile. Her ecstasy grew stronger and stronger, convincingly, and gently conquering her heavy heart.

But it would only last a few moments now. And then, the longing and confusion would come back. Her head would not stop circling the same matters.

Her captivity, the bugs, how she hurt Sire Graynor, and her beloved King Vonter.

Vonter, always Vonter. Why was he gone for so long?

She could not fight the feeling that he had maybe gotten away from her on purpose. That he and Yandra were executing this cruel plan together. Bugs.

Why did she have that dream that he would take the moon away from her? Wasn't that a silly idea!

Yandra had said that the moon would not to be taken away by any man.

And surely, her King would not have the power. Or would he? How well did she know this man? Did he like the moon as much as she did, or did he know for sure that she liked the moon more than him?

She looked down at her hands again.

The flower's blue light was so intense that they looked blue. Lines of the same colour were running up and down her sleeveless arms, it was strangely pretty.

She could taste another petal of silver magic unfolding in her mouth. Her eyes fixed on the white and blue light of the artefact; her vision became blurry once again. Thick tears rolled down her face. Why were these feelings so confusing? Why did she have to feel so much? All these whys.

Samjya hated all bugs. She could not remember a time when she had liked them. And it felt like they were everywhere outside. She had felt safe in her chambers, but no more. Following her, talking to her, inside her head, and in front of her face. It became harder to focus on thoughts, as they kept dripping into hers. So many confusing thoughts and feelings. And they were loud. So loud, that the fuzzy warmth that had invaded her head, was replaced with their insect like buzz of annoying vibrations.

She wanted them to stop.

Vonter. He would know. He always knew.

He had never left out a chance to show her that he knew more than her, because he had had military schooling and a sophisticated family. Unlike her.

No, he did not! What was going on? Why was she thinking these horrible things? Was she going insane? Or had her love left her blind, and she was just waking up to a most deceiving dream of a love for a man that had never been?

Vonter. Bugs. Eating. Peace. Bliss. Vonter.

The buzzing came and went. She had had a headache all day now, from all this thinking and especially from them, their thinking.

They worried and complained, a lot. Short lives, infidelity, sickness, their stupid bug babies, bug food, bug money, bug love.

They were pathetic. She was pathetic.

Yandra. Hating. Eating.

Bugs. Touch. Happiness. Vonter.

Her mind was all jumbled up. She noticed it, and then, fell back into the chaos. Bugs. Was this going to be like this for the rest of her life now? Was she going to be kept here until she got old and wrinkly?

And suddenly, her hands were empty.

The flower was gone.

It was inside her. All its light, the softness, the warmth, all its magic.

Oh, and it was a strange sensation, utterly pleasant and calm, which confused her even more. She should be sad that it was gone, because in a few moments, the craving would set in.

But it did not.

It was changing. She could *feel* that it was changing. The craving was not there, and it was … changing her.

Her thoughts were still whirling around, but there was a calmness on top of it. She was sure of ... something. It was like the comfort that everything would be okay. But this was stronger, deeper. Kind of a peace.

Inside of it all, there was a happiness that slowly pushed it all away. She could feel how her thoughts became quieter. A broad smile occupied her face. With her eyes closed, she listened to her own heartbeat. It had slowed down. Just like her thoughts, it just was not disturbing her anymore. Peace.

She could finally sleep. Finally turn her mind off and stop. Forever.

A loud thumping woke her up. Darkness had fallen into the room, and it was all cold and damp, but Samjya barely noticed. Alarmed by the loud noise, she was on her feet at once.

But her head would not be as quick. Dizziness overcame her, and she had to lean against the wall for a moment.

The loud noise was heard again. And it felt very close. The ground was vibrating, and in the distance, she could hear some roaring, fighting maybe?

She was not sure of anything at this moment, but she had to try and leave this room and find out what was going on!

Her feet brought her to the chamber's door quickly. As she tried the door handle, she was not expecting it to be unlocked. The entire door came undone! Wood splintered in all directions and metal folded like cloth, commanded like nothing, by a brute force. Her hand.

Her hand? She looked down at her hand and dropped what she was holding. The large wooden door fell to the ground with a loud clonking sound, and she moved back two steps.

Unbelievable. She had just broken herself out of her room by ripping off the locked door. She must have gotten stronger. A lot stronger.

A smile appeared on her lips, and without any more hesitation, she ran outside. Down the hall, down the hall, quickly.

The thumping grew louder, and Samjya realised that it was a continuous sound, almost rhythmic. Walls and the stones underneath her naked feet rumbled with the constant shattering sound.

As she ran down the stairs, she could see the people. The bugs. Crawling all over the floor, crying and screaming. They fled in a panic.

She could feel it. It was such an overwhelming sensation, a wave of pain and fear, crushing down on her. However, the newly found strength she had, helped her keep the gushing emotions at bay.

Barely anyone paid attention to her. Very few stopped and stared at her. They had to be surprised how she had escaped her cruel prison.

But no one said anything to her.

She could tell that the looks were not only those of surprise. There was something else. Fear? She hardly paid attention; it was not important.

Lots of them were running into the castle and hid behind pillars or tried to get into one of the more secluded rooms. She turned back and saw that a few bugs also ran upstairs where she had come from.

With minimal effort, she pushed herself against the masses and went outside, to see. The roars became more distinctive to her now. It was a roaring like a wild animal, a bear, or a tiger, but very big.

She could also finally see where the thumping noise came from. A couple of feet from the iron gates, the stones were shattered into the inside of the walls. Someone or something was trying to get through, with quite the success!

Bugs, everywhere. They were running in all directions except to safety. Why were they so disoriented? That had to be their naked fear. She could sense everyone's very own senselessness. What an odd emotion.

The final stone smashing thump was heard, big blocks dropped and rolled, gave way for a large opening in the castle walls, and everyone in the courtyard could see the attacker.

A large, black stone ... thing stepped through the newly created hole. Its man-like shape was almost steaming with a dark glow, and the black was so hot in colour and consuming any light, that it fascinated the Queen. It was entirely made of stone, but surprisingly agile. The stones were connected, and rubbed against one another, giving off little clouds of black dust whenever the giant moved. The face had no expression, just a large, empty mouth hole and two small fire pits as eyes. Piercing, but deep embedded inside the stone.

With handless arms and feetless legs, it stomped through the fleeing bugs, smashing, and hitting them, without aim or definitive goal. But very effective.

Skulls were smashed, limbs torn off by the simple power of punches, and blood was spilled, a lot of blood.

But the violence was not confined to the masses, the monster was also crushing market stalls and houses, slowly working its way in. It was destroying the capital!

Samjya might have been a prisoner in her own home, but this was still her kingdom! Whether they had performed her wedding or not, even without being married to Vonter, she would claim this land to be hers!

She did not even care about the bugs. But this castle was meant to be hers. And she would have no stone monster take it away from her!

The rage was back.

And oh, was it sweet. She finally knew what she had to do. What she was able to do – with this rage, with her frustration. She was not powerless!

Pushing back the bugs and stepping over them, she made her way towards the monstrosity. When she had almost reached it, she noticed how big this thing really was. It was at least twenty feet larger than her, and as wide as a house. But that did not stop her.

It had its back turned to her, so she jumped up on a small cart nearby, and flung herself towards it. With all her strength she pushed both her hands against its back. To her surprise, it fell flat on its face, immediately. With a loud crash, the stone flumped to the ground, crushing two more citizens.

Samjya looked at her hands. She was so powerful! Quickly, she jumped up on the stone creature's back and punched its body. Black pieces of stone flew around in all directions and her knuckles were not even sore!

After a two more punches, the monster pushed itself off the ground with the stumpy arms and threw her off like a buckling horse. The Queen landed on her back and the thing turned around to face her. This time, it raised one arm for a punch, but Samjya had another surprise, for everyone including herself.

She pulled up her hands, and like the movement that she made when striking Sire Graynor by accident, she fired a cold bolt of energy – on purpose this time.

The result was cataclysmic!

The icy arrow cut through the arm and grazed the stone body and pushed it back. The black arm fell to the ground, and a loud, forceful growl left the thing's mouth. It stumbled back a few steps and glared down at Samjya with flaring red eyes. But she did not waste any time.

Her hands produced more freezing energy that she shot towards the stone warrior. Now, it was prepared for the impact, and despite the velocity and force of her magic, this thing was able to raise itself off the ground and slowly move forward. With one arm, it leapt in her direction, and kicked her with its gigantic foot.

Samjya was not able to brace herself for this attack and soared several feet through the air until the wall stopped her body's flight. It was not graceful at all, and painful.

Her head was buzzing. Her shoulder hurt. For a moment, she had to fight passing out, and a new feeling joined the rage and the pain. How dared this monster to touch her? To fight back and hurt her?

This was a surprise. But it made her excited too. It was a welcome challenge, and she could give in to it all. Sweet rage, embracing and empowering her, no longer burning her up anymore!

Vonter might have turned his back on her, and his kingdom, but she was still here to defend it. With all her power.

She would end this. At once.

21

Poor Gartt. He had always been so wise and compassionate. His advice and wisdom had helped them through some tough times. They had lost more members of their community than they should have.

They were all immortal, dammit! Why was dying always so sad, and what was the point of being immortal?

Granted, turning to stone would kill anyone. But how would the others take this? It became even clearer to Mibb that neither inside nor outside of the forest was safe. Nowhere would be safe with this threat.

He jumped from one tree to the next, at first fighting, and then wiping off the tears. It all became a blur. The white branches and leaves were starting to blind him, make him dizzy. Despite the pain, exile, and punishment, this had been his home for centuries. It now had become even more evil and cold in just two days.

With the feeling of being powerless, it cost him more effort to grasp the next branch and pull himself up whenever his paws slipped.

After some time, he realised how he had not been paying attention as to how far he had gone. He had missed the closest entrance, and he was too far gone to turn back.

Climbing up on one of the larger trees, he had a quick look around and got his bearings. He then decided to go Southwest.

There was a relatively secluded tunnel that he should be able to reach without getting discovered. It was closer, and he did not want to lose any more sunlight as it was already very late.

Mibb moved back down and continued his way, changing the direction he had chosen, and tried to occupy his mind and not think of Gartt.

His mother. She had been the single most wonderful person in the world.

An Elders Council member and loving parent, she had achieved so much in her life. There was no pain in the memories he had of her because this was at least 800 and something years ago. And yes, there were days when he wished he could ask her for advice, like today.

Apart from his father walking away when Mibb was still very young and her having to work really hard to keep them afloat, she was still able to make a real childhood possible for him.

When he was fourteen years old, and he noticed how things got tough on her, he decided to grow up, do his part, and started training to become a lumberjack. He had always been drawn in by trees, the smell of wood and the freshness of the forest smell after rain.

And he loved the physical aspect of the job too. As a human, he had been very attractive, with strong arms and shoulders. All the girls had stolen glimpses at him, but he had always known being nothing more than a lumberjack, that physical labour was not the most desirable career a man could have, especially if women were looking for a husband with a bit more than just a reasonable income.

And back then, he never thought it possible to go into politics like his mother. But now, he had become the animals' leader, and it was very hard. It made him think his previous notion was correct, after all.

He just held the deepest respect for her and admired all that she had done for him. She had tried to save the town. She had voted to repay the witch for her aid as agreed, but the vote of the Elders Council had gone the other way. She had tried to save the children.

As new leader, Mibb was trying to be more like her. To lead by her example, benefit from her wisdom. Luckily, all decisions were carried by the group, so he could only try and push something through, if he seriously thought it would endanger everything they had here. This was it.

He should have asked the animals to keep Draidr and Sahdor around for a little bit longer, to plan and work together.

And that was what Mibb wanted to press for now. They needed to help each other, to preserve life, and fight the sorcerer together, with whatever means possible, while they still had the numbers and the magic had less of a chance of growing further.

His tears had dried for a quite a while when he reached the hideaway entrance. With a quick jump, he was underground and running down the tunnel. This was a particularly long one, very dark, but he knew it quite well. When he saw the lights, he could also hear the voices, arguing loudly and chaotic. What was going on?

Mibb ran into the room, only to find the youngest fox in the corner, crying.

"What is this?" the squirrel asked.

"I was saying how I thought you were right, but then everything went bad. I am sorry." he said under tears.

Their leader turned to the other animals and was very surprised to find them not arguing with each other over the humans. They were arguing against him! He could not believe what he was hearing.

"He is not fit to be our leader. He may be smartest, but still too young and naive. We should challenge his authority." said Sihgr, a few around him were nodding.

"He was just looking to help; I still trust him." someone said.

"We should take a vote against him!"

"We should have never voted for a younger one to be a leader!"

"But he is a really smart squirrel, maybe he will turn around?"

"Let's ban him from the woods! If he is so keen on being with the humans, he should be with them."

"Do you think he'll hate us?"

"So what? I do not care."

"I feel we're letting him down. But all that he has done was letting us down."

"No chance I am following him anywhere anymore."

And then, the group noticed that he was in the cave.

The heated discussion stopped instantly, and some interesting expressions appeared on their faces. Some looked embarrassed, caught, sad and ashamed even. But others were obvious in their anger, defensiveness, and aggressiveness. Could it really be that almost everyone except the little fox was against him?

He spoke first. "Gartt is dead."

Silence. The rabbit mother hid her face in her paws. He could see some quiet tears on other faces. "He was turned to stone. Just outside of the woods. Sitting by a tree in the fields. It must have happened very quickly."

"Oh no." someone whispered.

"Listen, friends, it is *not* safe outside this forest. Still, the threat is very apparent in our own home too, inside the forest, do you not see? We really should do everything in our power to get away from this thinking that isolates us from all help. We should meet the humans halfway and make peace. Let's forget our differences and work together. Maybe we will have a chance to fight this. We do not have to live together, but we will certainly die alone."

A pause ensued. But not for very long.

"Good speech. But we are not coming with you." said Sihgr. "We must not trust the humans. And we feel, spending too much time with them has clouded your judgement. We do not want you to be our leader anymore."

Mibb was not surprised, because he had heard it just a few breaths ago. But he was surprised by the way he phrased it. What the fox said to him directly had quite the effect on him.

"You are speaking for everyone now? Even though your conversation was still ongoing, and I heard very clear voices to speak against what you just said?"

No one said a word.

The fox kept his stern face, eyes fixed on Mibb without any indication to look away. The silence went on, while the squirrel turned around in the cave. The others were just staring back at him, or to the ground, or up to the ceiling. What a shame.

"So, a few breaths with humans, and I am leprous? Is that really how you all feel?" he asked, folding his arms in front of his chest.

The group stayed quiet, until someone uttered a clear and unhindered Yes. This was unbelievable. His heart sank low and great sadness extended inside him. He had to decide. Right here and now. Like his mother, he would have to take a vote that could go against everything he believed in, but he needed to save this community with any means necessary.

"I vote to veto your consensus and demand we leave this forest to join the humans in their fight. We do not even have to fight if you do not want to. Let's ask for refuge and safety. Or let's find a place in the mountains, away from the humans, I do not care. But I am asking all of you to come with me. For choosing life, not death. It is not safe."

Some murmuring arose, and large eyes popped up and stared. Sihgr looked down to the ground, with an odd expression on his face.

"It saddens me to see you're still not seeing clearly." he said. "We are not with you; we will not obey."

Mibb could not think anymore.

He noticed how tired he had become. Too tired to argue, too tired to give everyone a break, too tired to try to keep it all together. And this was not because being a leader was suddenly too much for him, no, this struggle had been going on for years.

There had always been doubters who disapproved of him as Gartt's right hand, and as their new leader in the last two days.

Yes, him, not his choices. And it was very clear now that this was because he had become weak. Human, apparently.

What a disappointment, a real shame. But there was also the pressure of the curse, it was getting too much. So, what, the witch would kill them if they left the forest?

She had not killed them yet for talking to the humans! And Mibb was tired of being an animal in captivity.

"Okay. If you stay here, you will die. If you run away, the stones will catch up to you, and you will die. If you fight the humans, you will die. Just wanted to make this very clear to you."

His eyes were fixed on the fox's. His look was returned with coldness.

"Thank you for these uplifting words. Please leave."

Mibb hesitated.

"Now." Sihgr ordered.

With a sigh, he turned around, meeting the youngest fox's shocked gaze. He could not leave just yet, he had to try one last time.

"Are you absolutely sure you do not want to come with me? Anyone?"

Again, his reasoning was met with silence.

"Think of your younger siblings!"

"Just leave, Mibb. Leave and do not come back." he had to hear one final time. He gave in. There was nothing else he could do. He was not welcome here anymore. They had chosen their fate.

The squirrel touched the little fox's arm and whispered: "I'm sorry. Good luck!" and with that he dashed off.

Running up the dark tunnel again that he had taken with Draidr and Sahdor, he did not feel too sad anymore. No, this was anger now.

If they wanted to die, so they should.

They did not want his help, so he should not waste any more time and energy. He could still catch up with the two soldiers in the fields, it should not be too hard to track them, he thought.

The sun had almost entirely set now, and the trees were a dark kind of shade of white. It would make it easier to get ahead and jump through the treetops quickly.

But then another very troubling thought came to mind.

What was he going to do once he reached the humans? Had Sahdor and Draidr believed him fully, were they willing to help? And what did he alone have to offer them?

He was not a fighter; he did not possess any magic.

He had not really thought this through! Doubt filled his mind and dampened his mood. But he had to try, it was his path now.

This was life, and he had chosen life.

***

Cherries, finest cherries. Again. Cherries, a supple skin bursting with flavour that delights children and parents alike. A fresh snack for young and old to enjoy on their own, or maybe a sweet surprise to woo a special someone. Their red flesh and the tangy juice that never is quite sour but not always purely sweet either. Cherries, ripened in the warm sun of Cant'un, hand picked on the orchards that make sure the trees are healthy and fruitful. And we select only the best ones for Buntin. Only the best ones.

Cherries, finest cherries. Bursting with flavour, ... Cherries.

Why was it so hot? There was a rage he couldn't shake, didn't dare to look at. A rage so deeply disturbing that he was afraid of seeing it, made him sweat. He didn't know which way was up, what this place was or what he was meant to do, what he could do. It was very, very hot.

There was no body, no space. He wanted to scream, always scream, every single breath. There was no air, no sound. There was only hot nothingness full of heat and ... nothing.

Cherries, finest cherries.

He was trying to remember what was before, and he struggled to keep any other thought. Slowly, the cherries made way to wood. A sturdy wooden plank, no, a wall. No, it was a door, a small door on high hinges, maybe. And wooden wheel. Cherries. Yes, a wheel and a small door, two actually. A cart with cherries.

Nothing came back with hot nothings to wipe it all away. The rage was washing over him like poisoned clouds of fire. He was desperate for a scream and to hit anything and anyone, but there were no hands. No fingers, no fist, no arms. Cherries.

Then, a boy. Blonde hair. Eating cherries, the finest cherries.

His boy, no, a boy, part of him though. He was his boy. He had a son! A son, who loved cherries and who loved to tell stories and sing. He had no talent, but that didn't stop him. He felt a surge of purest, warmest love for this boy. Every fibre of his being was pushed and pulled towards him, to protect and care for him. His reason and his reason. He was his, and everything that mattered. Cherries for the boy and no more death. The soldier life was not right, he wanted the boy to live, love and prosper with the best chances he could have. And cherries.

This boy was meant to be his legacy, the energy and soul of what was meant to be left behind. His reason, and – his reason? He was ready for Serenity to take him. But she was not here, this was different. And his boy was gone. Yart had been taken away from his boy, his gentle, sweet, innocent boy. It was not right. He wanted to scream. Pain. Poison. Fire.

It all went dark, then white, then dark again, a void so empty it was unnatural, ill, and unreal, nothing and yet everything that was wrong.
The rage returned with an all-burning power. No chance to feel anything else any longer, the void was only rage. The power was rage, and the rage was power. Hot nothing rage and hot nothing rage, and hot, nothing, rage.
Cherries, finest cherries. Again, and again.

22

It had become almost dark. The sun was not seen anymore, instead, the Royal Courtyard was illuminated with the menacing flickering of fires. A lot of fires.

Samjya shook her head and pulled herself up from the dirt. She could feel the magic of the flower pulsing inside her. It was so exhilarating! She would show this monster how she would defend her kingdom!

The dizzying pain was gone quickly, and entirely. She was ready now.

She pushed a woman out of her way, grabbed a whole fruit cart and threw it towards the stone warrior. It raised the single arm it had and blocked the attack off easily.

The cart's wood panels shattered on the stone like matches, but she had only intended this as a minor distraction anyway.

Effortlessly, she jumped onto one of the intact stalls, took a secure stance, and started firing powerful ice blasts down on her opponent.

One after the other, she was able to just generate them without interruption. They were not very powerful against its stone shell, but they packed a certain punch and hardly missed their mark. Samjya was fully caught in this flurry of power. It was a new, and liberating feeling, but very strange at the same time.

She had never felt so … in flow before.

Then, she noticed how the growling giant started to punch its way through her cold hail, barely being able to hold its footing, but repelling most of her blasts now.

Sometimes, Samjya would miss and hit the ground, or even one of the bugs. But she was determined and focused on the task at hand, defending her land.

She had decided she would win this fight. It was quite fun too!

When the stone monster was tumbling back for a moment, she concentrated her full attention and power on her fists, collecting as much energy as she could in a few breaths. And then, she pushed it away from her, released it directly at the aim. The black warrior was able to brace itself for the impact but underestimated the power of her magic. With a loud clang and a strong thrust backwards, the hit burst a giant hole into what was the chest and scattered black, smoky pieces of stone all over the ground. The monster was not able to comprehend, or look down at the damage even, but it was considerably weakened and hesitant.

"Still alive. No heart, then." With a triumphant yet intrigued smile, Samjya jumped off the stall, ripped off a pole on one of the smaller stands, and froze it in her hand with her willpower, hardening the pointy tip as much as she could. She threw the spear taking aim confidently, and quickly turned around to get another one ready. And another one.

Because she kept her distance to avoid the monster's punches and debris, there was really no offense that posed a danger to her at this point. The warrior was hit with the ice lances violently, and repeatedly. Some spears even got stuck, and some chipped the surface of the stone and separated parts of it.

After a dozen spears, it fell to its knees and growled a long, sad sound, and tried to push itself back up again with one arm. But Samjya would not let it.

She ran closer and made the last spear count! Determined to go in for the kill, she aimed right for the face, between those red, dotty eyes. It all seemed to pass in slow motion.

She could see her weapon cut through the air gracefully, with her running after it, to engage her enemy with final attacks.

The lance pierced the stone head and a large, blue, and silver explosion of sparking power emerged into all directions.

The sound echoed through the entire capital and was followed by one last final roar. A bone shattering and nerve-wrecking roar of a dying animal. The stone almost crumbled entirely and lumped to the ground like a sad little pile of burnt coal.

There was still some light in that thing's eyes, so Samjya went for them. With a broad, but powerful stream of more freezing blasts, she shot at the tiny little glows and drowned them in blue and white ice.

With the occasional silver ice shard inside of her whirls, she cut the larger stones of the back, the legs, and the remaining arm into small pieces.

And suddenly, it got very quiet. The stones were not moving anymore, and the bugs were not screaming and running anymore. There was still some distinct crying of small children, and the soothing crackling of fires spread out in the yard.

Samjya could not suppress a smile. She had won the fight. A fight that she had never deemed possible. And she still had more of that magical force inside her. Like an ocean, the rage had calmed down, but the mass was still there.

Her hands were burning slightly with the aftermath of all this energy that she had released. And it felt so good! She was hardly able to contain herself.

A little girl, close to her, came up and whispered with her insecure, thin voice: "Thank you."

The Queen looked down and frowned. What was she thanking her for? She had not done it for this little bug. She did not want any thanks. She had only fought for her kingdom not to be destroyed.

Behind the girl, a few other bugs appeared, they all looked scared and confused. Quickly, another bug jumped forward and pulled the little one away.

New thoughts and emotions started to seep into her mind. Some were scared, still, of her because they did not understand what just happened.

She could feel the joy of the happy ones, the flesh-eating pain of the injured, and the mourning traumas of the suddenly lonely ones. Oddly, quite a few felt grateful. And proud of what Samjya had done for them. Saving their lives.

But she did not want to be a hero, she could not care less about how they saw her. She did not want to bring them salvation, she could not care less what they might need from her. She did not want their pride or their love. It was only asking more from her, and she did not want anything to do with these bugs.

They were nothing but weak, insignificant insects. And she had to get away!

Samjya jumped over the pile of stones, and ran towards the hole in the castle walls, pushing through the groups and gatherings, sometimes stronger than she had to, causing some bugs to fall over. She slipped through the gap in the stone wall next to the gates and ran past the houses outside the first walls.

This stone warrior had wreaked quite the havoc on the capital. A lot of buildings had turned into nothing more than a pile of rubble and wooden splinters.

Some fires were burning up remaining huts, and a lot of bodies were left it its path. People mourning their loved ones, and others helping the wounded. Some survivors stopped when Samjya ran past them, with big eyes, pointing at her.

Finally, she looked down on herself and was surprised to see how much she had changed. Her hands and arms were light blue with dark blue veins running up and down.

Her dress was quite dirty and had a lot of rips and holes in them. She was barefoot and covered in mud and blood. And then, she noticed her hair. It was dark blue with silver streaks in them.

A horse carriage appeared in front of her. Quickly, she jumped over it, and mid-air, she looked down. Probably as surprised as the bugs around her, she easily jumped over the carriage.

Landing safely, she glanced around.

She could not believe how easy this all came to her. Still, she had to get away. And fast. More emotions were gushing in on her. Waves of feelings, thoughts and worries made her choke.

A few moments later, she was already at the second gate and ran through the other hole that the monster had produced next to it. The iron city gates had probably been too strong for its force.

As Samjya left the capital behind her, she also noticed how her breathing was steady the entire time. She was not getting tired. Good. She could run away without slowing down.

She was planning on finding her father. Since he had not made it to the castle, he had to be home still, so that was where she wanted to go. And if Vonter really had been keeping him from her, she would hunt him down.

Samjya remembered him when he had been younger and travelling a lot. There were times of the year where he was away for weeks, sometimes months, working on the other farms. She had always wanted to go with him, but he had most often asked her to stay home with... She didn't recall, but someone to care for her.

One of his farms was particularly far and she loved to visit there. It was a small house with the smallest beds that she had ever seen one time she came with him.

They hadn't been able to build something larger as the ground was difficult to work with, it was close to the swamps.

The moisture in the soils was needed for the vegetables and burning materials they farmed there. She remembered the smell and how she snuck out one evening and got herself into all sorts of trouble.

She had her dress and herself washed by ... she couldn't recall, but it was someone who was always around.

Why couldn't she remember?

Her father had always been so kind. Strict and shouty with his workers, but always gentle and kind with her.

He was a hard-working man with a strong sense of duty and a dislike for laziness. That's why she had turned out so strong, because of him.

It was very quiet on the roads. There were no sounds other than the wind,

The road split in front of her after a couple of miles. Which way was her father's farm? She did not remember. She roughly knew that it was East, so she picked the road that led that way. It had become entirely dark now. And apart from the smoking dark shadow of the capital and the far away Northlight flame, there was nothing to see beyond the hills.

The moon was there, however, whose light helped her to see the road and her immediate surroundings. She was still running, so the road had become this grey band of ground flowing beneath her feet. The shapes of the trees and bushes on the sides were easily replaceable shadows in front of a dark nothingness. She was not scared of running into a wolf or bear, she would be able to fight them off without effort. But she feared what she would find when she arrived at the farm.

It was odd how no one knew what happened to her father's carriage. Vonter had arranged for her family to be picked up and safely brought to the castle himself. Unless, of course, it had been part of his plan that this would not happen.

After what felt like half a night, a new shape appeared in front of her in the darkness. And some movement. Two white horses were standing in the middle of the street, nervously kicking the hooves. Behind them, one of the King's carriages. Empty. Where was everyone?

Then, Samjya had an idea. With one finger, she produced a light blue, ice cold flame that grew to the size of her head and lit up a small circle around her.

With the light floating above her face like a petroleum lamp, she walked around the wooden vehicle.

The doors were open wide, so whoever had been in there must have left in a hurry.

She could not see anything else, not on the side of the road, and not in or around the carriage that would give her an idea as to what had happened here, so she tried listening for any suspicious sounds. She closed her eyes, concentrating to ignore the magical humming inside her and her own heartbeat.

In the distance, she could hear some animal snoring, a wolf panting, the wind howling in between rocks, and water. A river. Should she check out the river? It did not sound to be very far away.

She turned left and walked over the grass. A wide field laid in front of her, and she moved farther inwards silently.

The river was quite big and would have been easily visible from the carriage during the day. So, maybe they had gone to get some water?

They had. She saw a stone statue lying in the grass, not far from the water.

It was one of Vonter's soldiers. His face showed signs of pain and despair, and he seemed to have tried to get away from something. Closer to the water, there was a second soldier, bending down, stone as well. His mouth was open in a silent cry, but Samjya's eyes quickly jumped to what he was touching.

Her guts cramped up and a new kind of rage grew inside of her.

He was an old man. On his knees, the man was crying out to the skies in agony. Entirely motionless, the last thing that he had felt was now frozen in time. Forever. All the pain that he had felt, cold stone for her to find in the middle of darkness.

It was … a man she knew, someone very familiar.

He had been washing his hands or something, and the soldier's hand had grabbed his ankle, but that had not helped anyone, apparently.

Her eyes produced thick tears that turned into ice drops without her noticing.

This man was important, someone she should remember.

Someone she wanted to remember, as clear as the love she felt, or perhaps the absence of that love.

And then, suddenly, the rage exploded in a high-pitched shriek and with it, the light above her head. Her body exerted a blast of silver and white energy and created a surge that pushed anything away in a wide radius.

Her pain, betrayal, hatred, loathing, and jealousy, but also all the happiness, warmth, laughter, affection and all the love that she had ever had for her own, it all came crushing down on her, and she could not bear it.

Her long cry filled the silent night around her, and as she stopped to catch her breath, she sank down to her knees and cried. She cried so hard that she had trouble breathing.

For a long time, she stayed next to this man she believed she loved with all her cold heart, just giving in to all her suffering.

When her heart was numb of empty emotions and the ground beneath her was covered in little, frozen drops, she suddenly felt the warm sun on her skin. She had not noticed how it had become day already, and how her face had dried from the tears.

Finally, she was able to let the rage in again. This was all Vonter's fault; and he was going to pay for this!

23

Fragir woke up and sensed right away that Yart was no more. It was to be expected, his soul had been fading anyway. Still, it made him angry that the humans had been able to destroy him.

There was only one way to find out what happened. If he channelled the forest's soil to access Yart's soul, he would be able to see what his soldier had been experiencing in his last moments. It would take some time, but it might be worth it in case they had any weaponry that Fragir should better be preparing for.

Yes, that's what he was going to do this morning. But he had to be quick.

He got up from his bed, walked downstairs and brewed some herbal tea over a small fire he set up. The herbs that he had collected were quite bitter, but he liked his brew like that, and it helped him focus.

Once he had emptied his cup, he made way into the old, empty garden. The soil was softer and milder, the energies would flow a lot better here. He sat down with crossed legs, bent over, so his arms were stretched, and the hands pushed into the dry, grey ground, not as deep as his arm went in yesterday.

With eyes closed, he started the spell to go in.

His plan was to go into the Myrcer, the Soul Midpoint, where all souls would go first after leaving this realm, after lives ended, even only after Fragir was done torturing them, to transform and shape them to his will in this realm. His stone curse for the army was holding them here, but any dead ones had moved on, and while they were confused and stuck in Myrcer, he could still reach and read them.

Easily, his mind shifted and detached itself from his body. Working through the barriers, he concentrated on Yart's energy.

It would be too easy to get lost and lose focus on the objective, Myrcer had that effect on most souls and visiting sorcerers.

Since he had not performed this spell in quite a few centuries, he had to be careful.

Thick layer after layer was penetrated, and dark wall after wall was crushed with his willpower. He could smell the sweet scent of fear and loneliness that any new soul was emitting after the transition.

Going into the Soul Midpoint always made him remember the story of the first mortal soul – at least the way that they had taught it to him when he was just beginning to understand that he was an immortal.

Long before Cant'un became what it was today, the land and ocean were very different. Volcanos burst heat from underneath onto the land, and strong storms brought mountains down and masses of water up the coasts, destroying and re-shaping the landscape.

Through Fire, Earth, Water and Wind, the Gods carried out wars and games, for thousands of years. There was no other living thing around, just their might and will. They loved to play and feud using the forces of nature.

But after millennia, the Gods became bored playing the same old games. And so, they sent for comets that crashed onto the ground.

The destructive power of their impacts, new patterns and exotic energies mixed with the powerful matters of this world, until a spark flashed up.

This spark was true, pure energy. It died quickly, but others would come. The Gods took great pleasure in trying to refabricate the sparks, again, and again, to throw them at each other, manipulate them and collect their essences. These sparks left black, soft mud behind whenever they perished.

Dark matter that quickly clogged up the land and made it dull. This mud swallowed each of the sparks a lot faster than it would disappear on its own, and faster than they were recreated.

The almighty beings decided to collect the black matter and comprise it to a secured realm, a sphere of its own, where it would have to exist by itself, isolated.

That way, they were able to keep it away from their creations.

And soon after, the sparks lasted longer, brought more energy exchange to the world, and they perfected their death. The Gods played with them for many thousand years, until one of the Gods found a way to give one spark a much longer lasting life and a mind of its own. It was meant to think, and act like them.

And it worked – the spark turned out to be very resourceful. The God created a shell from the land and stone around it, a body. It was not pretty at all, but it was able to now use the elements to create a life for itself.

Through this transition, something else was created. Thoughts and desires led to emotions and experiences that shaped the very essence of the being. The personality was born. And it was different from everything else. It wanted more and demanded more.

The God realised that they had produced much more than just a spark in touch with the space around it, they had created a free, living soul.

In proud admiration for this wondrous and entertaining thing, they made more of them. Soon, these sparks in their shells with their personalities populated the world, making the elements their tools, and creating a home for themselves. Then, emotions and experience took over, the personalities outgrew the sparks and managed to prolong the endurance of their bodies. They became Immortals.

This was most fascinating to the Gods. The power struggle between raw vitality and its product was so captivating that they sat back and watched.

The essence of the sparks was tamed, and these immortal beings mastered this across their surroundings. They became so potent that they were able to harness not only the elemental magic, but also use their spark's power, Composure.

Soon, some of them started to neglect their heritage.

They stopped relying on their magic and focussed on other things, materialism, greed, lower needs, and their bodily instincts.

Some would only watch what others did, and be as inactive as an old mountain, or pointlessly dance in the same spot as a dying fire.

Physical attraction became sexual, and they produced the first offspring. This freak of nature was the firstborn of this world, and it was almost empty.

A physical shell, blessed with a soul, but having lost the connection to the sparks, it was the first of its kind with a limited lifespan. A Mortal.

Cant'un was formed amidst the spread of the Mortals. To this day, Elders and scholars have argued over how they had been able to grow their numbers to what they were today. Especially as the powers of the Immortals were making everything possible.

They would become witches and sorcerers and they really should have ruled all of existence.

Frankly, it was not very attractive, nor practical to shorten life and listen to their own shells for desires and ambition. Even more of a reason for Immortals to keep their bloodlines pure and not reproduce in the same mindless manner.

Fragir was glad that his Composure was bound to the element Earth and his talents were telekinesis and soul magic. This put him in the unique position of being a master of controlling souls.

His concentration returned to the journey to Myrcer. Soon, the last border was demolished, and he found himself right in the middle of blackness, surrounded by pulsing walls with an organic texture to them, alive and trying to pull at him, to pull him in.

Even the floor had this effect, mildly.

That's how Eternity was absorbing the souls back. They actually ingested them, and their energy would then move on after that.

Most souls stayed in the limbo quite some time as they never understood their purpose. And letting go was never easy for any mortal, or the immortal.

That, and these walls were quite intimidating. Scared and confused, anyone and anything would stay away from them, until they gave in, went crazy or were too weak to withstand. And then, they would be pulled through any surface into nothingness as soon as they got too close.

He looked around and saw some lights ahead. Yes, there they were. Most souls would also be drawn to each other and try to cling to any connection they could find, as it was really the only thing that would remind them of their worldly lives.

As he walked towards them, he made sure to roll his steps off the entire length of his sole, so he would not get stuck.

He certainly did not want to get pulled into the void. Carefully, manoeuvring down the corridor without getting too close to the walls, he moved forward. Step by step, he went on, still focussing on Yart and his soul, who was not part of the group in front of him, but he could still feel his presence, close.

The souls he passed by, hovered away from him. They would not recognise his appearance, he was just a faint apparition to them, a ghost, if anything, something sinister rather then something they would welcome. If only they knew.

Two or three of the light orbs got too close to the wall and got sucked in. Quietly, and without any struggle. It was rather painless, sadly.

But any soul in here was already out of the sorcerer's real grasp. He would not be able to get anything from here except information.

He could sense Yart, closer now. The tunnel bent to the left, and then, there was a crossroads.

The walls drifted apart a bit and contracted, like the whole system was breathing. Brightness appeared in front of him, more souls lighting up sections of the passageway.

He took a left turn, continued his way down, passing light after light, changed direction three more times, until he finally found him.

Just silently floating in the middle of a wide corridor leading further down into this realm's depths, Yart was immobile, as if he was waiting for something to happen. Maybe he was waiting for his master?

As Fragir approached, the orange orb moved away, just a bit. Because the mage avoided any abrupt movements, he managed to get quite close.

He used his Composure to ward off the pulling effect of the organic surroundings, and simultaneously, he executed the Soul Entanglement to pull Yart closer.

Almost touching it with his expanded hands, he was able to feel what happened. A warm, vibrating sensation moved from Yart to his hands to his shoulders and up and down his spine.

When the sizzling energy reached his brain, passed impressions exploded inside his mind, and he saw it all through Yart's eyes.

The vision was not clear, and it was more emotion than actual image.

The castle walls bashed in, crushed skulls and soldiers flying. So much blood and destruction, it filled Fragir with delight. Yart started fires, stomped women and children into the ground and easily flattened entire houses. This was very similar to his and the others' rampage in Buntin.

He could feel the power of the souls fading, but his spell would have been active for quite some time, still.

And there were hardly any defences or weapons that inflicted enough damage to even penetrate the rock skin!

But then, he saw her.

A woman, so full of anger, pain and confusion, an immense power.

Her face was determined, she had light blue skin with large blue veins and her hair was blue and silver.

She wore a ripped wedding dress and no shoes. Her movements were so wild, frantic.

She had to be a witch with that kind of chaos power, Fragir thought. He watched her attacking Yart without any regards to her own or the other people's safety. And very effectively.

She was barely hit by his warrior at all, and her magic was unlike anything he had seen. At least not in a very long time. When he saw her up close, she rammed an icy spear into Yart's face, and the impressions stopped. He got what he had come for, moved away from the orb, and turned around. Naturally, he did not want to spend more time in the Soul Midpoint than he had to, so he walked back the same way he had come.

When he reached the portal back to his realm, he took one last look back.

Myrcer had some comfort to it, it was nice to be remineded of this. He had rarely visited. It was good practice though, to keep his summoning and transition energies flowing and to make sure that he was comfortable with souls in all their stages.

Slowly, he entered the portal that had brought him here, and similarly to breaking through the water surface after a dive, his consciousness broke through the layers and walls back to reality.

The way out was always easier as his spirit was not wanted in the limbo of souls, so this way took less energy and concentration.

When Fragir opened his eyes, his body was in the same position as before, torso pushed forward, arms stretched all the way, hands pushed into the ground. His back hurt from staying in this position for so long.

That was the main problem with going into Myrcer, time was going so much faster in this plane of existence. The day was almost over, he could see that the sun was already descending.

With his Composure, he tried to flex and relax his back muscles, rubbed his eyes, and prepared for the impact.

Going to a different plane always changed the ability to perceive and experience emotions of the souls he would interact with while under.

He had numbed himself to this in order not to lose focus and get exactly where he needed to go, and it would now crash over him like a flood, ruthless and uncensored.

There it was already!

He knew this was coming. The witch's hatred, and jealousy invaded his heart.

It was so powerful and so strong that he had to push it out. He fired a thick, black bolt out at the walls in front of him out of reflex.

Hot thunder echoed through the area, melting the rock a little where the pressure had hit the wall, and sending hot air with high velocity into all directions.

A relieving scream came across his lips, and he had to pull himself together. It was the purest feeling he had felt in a long time. He was quite surprised by the intensity of this rage. No mortal had ever possessed this kind of cold fury, this much hate.

This was some influential witch!

Not only was she responsible for killing off his trusted warrior, if she was against his power, she was likely with the kingdom!

He was glad now that he had checked Yart's soul for this information.

This witch meant serious resistance to his plan! He had to stop her; she was too much of a risk.

Captivated by her emotions, his own rage grew and took over. The mortals that killed his family came back into the forefront of his mind. Tessel, who betrayed him. The new witch that he had to destroy.

He had to follow his attack up right now and crush the King's capital!

Now, while her magic was most likely depleted, and before it was fully refilled.

***

It was so bright. Why was it so bright? ...

Was he back? Did it work? ...

Was Fragir still there? ...

When the disorientation was over, and he found his bearings, he was able to sense him. He could feel the trees and the ground. ...

He should probably try and find a place to hide! But there was nothing ...

He should probably stop thinking ...

24

Vonter knew that he had to tread very carefully now. They had only been on the road for a short while, and he could see water wherever he looked. There were a few puddles on the path, ponds that he could see in the distance, the river as a constant temptation to quench their thirst, and sometimes, more people that had turned into stone. He caught himself looking down to the ground pretty much all the time.

And for his peace of mind, he had finally been able to convince the young seamstress to go along with them. Grunia would be of great help to spot danger and avoid it, and she was skilled with a sword too.

She was the only survivor of Tramvil, after all, he thought it might not be a bad idea to be overly cautious. And he would not have left her behind either way. She had not been very trusting in the beginning, but Vonter had good arguments, and, in the end, she probably did not want to be alone for long.

And now, more than ever, they needed a plan.

First, they had to get back to his men and warn them about the water. If they had not already killed themselves drinking it.

Ca'on was not ready to ride a horse at all, but after he had regained consciousness during the night, he had insisted on getting back to the others as soon as possible.

So, they used a little wagon to lay him flat on the King's banner in the Royal colour and had him pulled across the roads.

They would not be able to go very fast, so it would take them a small part of the day until they reached Buntin.

Vonter's thoughts came back to Samjya, wondering what she was doing.

It now had been four entire days that he had not been at the castle.

At least his messages were not too worrying, so she would not lose hope.

But maybe they should retreat to the capital and plan for the citizens to be protected and more defences to be put up. He still did not know if they had heard back from Sahd and Draidr, or if they were even still alive.

He had already sent Mil to the castle to warn his home. Since they did not share the same river, there was a chance, the capital was not compromised, but he was not sure about rain. Or if there was a curse on all fresh water, this would mean the entire kingdom was in danger.

Wine and mead from the last harvests would only last for so long, and it would make his soldiers only drunk, hardly ready for battle.

The young scout should be at the capital in less than a quarter of a day to warn them, he thought. He also had the fastest horse, as a precaution.

Another reason why Vonter had decided to take Grunia with him: he would not have wanted to be alone with Ca'on in case something happened to himself or the soldier.

Their new friend had been awfully quiet since they had left the town. She did not seem like a woman of many words. But she probably missed her family and her home as she knew it. While he was watching her guide the horse down the road avoiding any bumps and humps as best as she could, he thought about his life when his father took him travelling around the North to get to know the nearby towns.

He remembered the first time going to Tramvil as a teenager, seeing all the great pottery and sculptures; it had always been the town of artists and poets. And as soon as he had seen the place, he was captured by the beauty and talent of the amazing people there.

His father had introduced him to a lot of authors and painters, and he was able to learn a lot about making and appreciating art.

But over the years, hunting and politics had not allowed him to be creative himself.

And since his parents were dead, being a King also played a huge role in him not having an unlimited amount of free time, so it had been years since he returned to Tramvil.

Little did he know that one day it would die, enclosed in stone without an engraved tombstone with goodbye songs or farewell poetry.

It made him sad to see that there was so much death in his land. Was one city after the other getting attacked and destroyed now?

The two attacks seemed so random, so very unconnected, but his gut was telling him something else.

Buntin and Tramvil were the closest towns to the White Forest, and there was no attacker or left-over magic to see, apart from the stone people.

There was no way these two incidents were coincidental. He was not ready to believe it.

But just the same, his efforts seemed rather pointless. The enemy was always two steps ahead, and he was arriving not only late, but merely finding empty remnants of the tragedy, bodies, and death.

Suddenly, he caught himself clenching the horse's reins in his fists and tapping his toes inside his boots. Following deep breaths, he stopped himself, tried to relax his neck and shoulders.

No luck, he just was too tense. This ride took too long with a hurt Ca'on and avoiding puddles.

Grunia seemed to have read his mind.

"His Grace, when do you think we will be there? Forgive me my impatience, but I have never

travelled outside of Tramvil."

"Never?" Vonter was surprised.

She had mentioned before that she had been in her hometown all her life, but he had not really paid attention to the fact.

"No, my parents did not have a lot of money, and whatever they had, they put into their store.

"Buying good fabric from the travelling merchants was not very lucrative, you see. So, my parents were not in the position to show me the world. We concentrated on the business rather than exploring the country."

Her face wore this grey mask every time she talked about her parents. Vonter had noticed that before.

"My mother had this fascination with silk. A very luxurious fabric – as you probably know, His Grace."

She mumbled the last part as if she was more reminding herself rather than talking to him.

"Silk is quite difficult to work with though. It is very thin and rips easily." The corners of her mouth were raised for an instant. "I think that is why my mother liked it so much. It was a challenge to her. She always tried to find an exciting new piece to produce involving silk.

"And my father ended up having to ask for a very high price for these items because my mother spent so much time on them."

"She sounds like quite the strong-willed woman." the King said.

"Yes, she was. It was always her who made the decisions between my parents. Whatever my father said, she was always able to persuade him otherwise. But mostly, he would let her decide anyway. Except -" she stopped for a moment.

Vonter looked up, alarmed, but there was nothing on the road.

Grunia swallowed some tears away.

"Except for the store. That was my father's second child. The son he never had, even. I was never able to compete with the fabrics, the clothes, the price tags; it all had more importance to him that any other thing in this world. He was working all the time."

A small period of silence followed. Grunia sighed and turned around to Ca'on. He could see that he had fallen asleep again, his bald head resting on woollen rags, the look on his moustached face was rather peaceful.

Vonter would not have been able to sleep on a cart like this, he thought. But soldiers were used to unusual comforts and trained hard for these things.

He suddenly became aware that he did not know a thing about the warrior. The man was a total stranger to him. That was so odd, that he did not even know the soldiers that were closest to him. Out of the entire army, he only really knew Sire Graynor, Sahd and Draidr well, like they were family. All the men that had died by the lake yesterday, he did not even know their names.

Again, Grunia was in his head. "Where does Ca'on come from?" she uttered.

"I do not know. Why do you ask?" he said.

"He has these tattoos on his neck. I have heard the stories."

The King's curiosity was peaked. He looked back and saw the unique markings on his olive skin. Underneath the left ear, there were parallel lines shaping into triangles on opposite ends, running towards the back of his neck. "What stories?"

"The legends of the Cant'un Pirates? You have never heard of them?" her voice was raised slightly, and immediately, she leaned back a little. "Excuse my manners, His Grace, but every child gets told these stories."

Vonter just shook his head, and Grunia gave him a very apologetic look.

"Well, many centuries ago, before men and women had even set foot in Cant'un, they were travelling the Northern Sea and tried their luck to settle on the icy islands. But the land was not fruitful and life in the cold realms came at a high cost.

"Because they had been on their ships since they could think, they knew how to survive without crops, some even never ate at all." she caught his doubting look. "I know! My mother was very convinced of this! Never mind.

"On one of these icy islands, they encountered natives that did not want to share their food or their land.

"A simple conflict started a whole chain of failed negotiations and violent battles, until the sailors had them all killed and taken all they had. By spilling all this blood onto their own hands, the men and women felt warmed and ecstatic in the cold weather. And all the looting made them only want more. So, to ensure the success of their next attack, they started training with their weapons, and prepared their ships for the next conquest.

"From then on, they travelled around the seas, attacking anything and anyone they could find, like pirates. Sometimes, they would take prisoners, and if these prisoners would prove useful, they would let them join their fleet.

"As they grew in numbers, they stole more ships, bullied defenceless villages into producing food for them. They also decided to dress in a certain way and mark their faces and necks with symbols. That way, in a large battle, they could recognise each other and not slaughter their own. The symbols were associated with successful kills, honour, and astounding achievements."

Grunia stopped talking while she slowed down, redirected the horse around a large puddle to her left, keeping one eye on their tattooed friend. Vonter let her catch up.

"When they finally reached the shores of what we know as Cant'un today, a lot of them were intoxicated by the wide, open fields, the lush nature, and green trees. The climate was so much milder, the land very nurturing, and there was not another living person in sight. Legend says, some of them were so moved by the silence and the peace, they cried, not knowing that this was what their souls had been craving all along.

"This led to another conflict. The majority wanted to explore the land, peacefully, no more bloodshed, no more pain, but they feared that the others would come back and rob them of food, goods, and all their newly found comforts.

"The other faction wanted to remain on the ships but did not want to leave forever as they would lose the connection to resources and manpower.

"A horrible last battle decimated the masses, and the larger group that wanted to settle in the land, won by killing the others.

"They vowed to never kill again after that, and to leave the seaside empty so they would not attract more raiders. They also demolished their own ships so that no one else would get ideas, sail away, and come back ashore again to pillage their new homes.

"And then, they decided to split up into smaller groups, but sworn to keep the peace, they forged trading relationships and established pathways through these fields. That's how the first towns were founded we have today, and the travelling merchants came to be."

She looked back to Ca'on again. "And that's why markings and symbols can still be found on some people's faces and necks. Some of the merchants. Mostly peaceful folk. They are either very aware of their roots with the pirates' true stories and traditions passed down throughout generations.

"Their stance is to honour the past, and make sure it doesn't repeat itself. Some simply stand for an independent, free life, no settling down, without real ties to Cant'un. Either way, they are very peaceful despite their intimidating looks. I'm surprised he joined your army. The legend says they abdicated from performing violence."

Vonter was amazed by this story. "Is this tale what every child grows up with?"

"Oh yes. ... – What did they tell you?" Grunia asked.

The King could not suppress a smile.

"That man arrived from beyond the Desert Mountains to escape the fruitless lands. The journey across was so hard, that the Bronze Giants were impressed by their perseverance, they molded the valleys and rivers, so the people could settle, plant crops, and raise cattle."

Grunia laughed. "Forgive me yet again, His Grace. The priests taught us about this old religion, back in Tramvil, but I suppose not a lot of people believed that."

"I know, after that, stories of the Silver Spirits came up, and now, a lot of people have left all this behind and believe in the Golden Gods. I'm not sure what to make of this. Was Tramvil very religious?" he added.

The young woman shrugged her shoulders. "Not really. I think the town had always very liberal sentiments, you know, with artistry and craftsmanship. There is a church, but not many believers. I heard some religious followers moved to Buntin after the Golden Cathedral was built."

"I never talked to anyone outside the castle about this. And my ancestors and all our staff have always been very traditional in their beliefs.

"Except for my parents, they had never discussed what they believed in. I was raised learning about religion, but not in a way that I was meant to follow the family's faith, their belief."

He felt the need to justify his education.

"*Their* beliefs? What do you believe in now if you do not mind me asking?" the seamstress smiled.

"I do not know." he muttered. "The Bronze Giants and Silver Spirits have always been a part of my world, but I stopped believing the priests and the new stories of Golden Gods long ago, especially after my parents died. ... With everything that's happening, I wonder if the Gods were going to step in and help at some point. I would have had to start blaming them for the bad. ... Or maybe, they just did not exist at all." he added after some hesitation.

"Your story is so compelling, there must be some truth to it!"

"Maybe both legends are true."

Grunia shrugged again and silently focused on the road.

Vonter turned his head to watch Ca'on.

Was he a pirate at heart? Was he travelling around, without a proper home, and being a soldier was nothing but a temporary commitment? Did he hate fighting and learning about weaponry, or was this his way of going against his heritage? Or did he have a family at the other end of the land that he took care of by being part of the Royal Army?

Vonter was glad that Ca'on was going to live. One less soul to mourn, and one more soldier to get to know and maybe even call a friend one day.

25

Sahd knew Draidr would change his mind about working with the animals, and Vonter would agree with him. They needed their information, and their experience. Of course, they would not be able to fight, but he was sure that an alliance with the immortal animals would be a lot more fruitful than they thought. And maybe they had kept a few more secrets from the two Generals and could help with finding out about Dragus and Tessel's respective weaknesses. Sahd knew he had to tell Vonter about the talking animals, even though they had promised Mibb not to.

The rain, howling winds and his thoughts about the impending threat of this evil sorcerer had not helped him to get any sleep at all.

Dragus. Even the name sounded very evil too.

The blanket was scratchy, and his feet would not lie still. Even though he wanted them to, he himself wanted to be still so badly. He wanted to hide away from it all and return to the capital. But that was not possible, he had made promises to his friend, the King, the land, and their people. And he would honour these promises until his death, no question.

His sister, that sweet, gentle, perfectly innocent woman – he needed to make sure that her murderer would be brought to justice. She really was the only reason why he was still alive after all.

When they had been attacked back by the black castle, a tiny part of him had hesitated because he was thinking that this might have been his shot at revenge. But it had not been.

Draidr had been right to call him back and make him run away from the monster. He would have ended up just like the other soldiers.

His men that he had lost so quickly, had not deserved to die in such a cruel way.

But what if he would have been able to finish it right there and then? Would this already be over? Or would he only capture the sorcerer's attention and get killed in another, horrific way? Mibb had said this ... thing was probably just one of many warriors, who knew how many! When they had followed the trail into the forest, his first thought was that only an army could have pushed through the narrow trees like that. Turned out he had been right after all.

A horn announced the arrival of the King. He had to be back from his excursion now. They said that he had left to check out the cursed pond.

But he had been gone for an entire day and night, too long. Sahd assumed that they had checked Tramvil or a different town again and spent the night there. He should probably see them to find out what Vonter had to share and then seek to speak to him in private about the animals, he thought to himself.

A thin voice interrupted his decision making to finally get up.

"There you are, Sahdor. It took me forever to find your tent!"

Sahd looked around. After a breath or two, he found the source of the familiar voice. Mibb, the small squirrel stood at the end of his camp bed, front paws up. The look on the little face was ..., well, annoyed.

"Did anyone see you?" Sahd asked.

"Do not know, do not care."

"Are you okay?" he asked.

Mibb shrugged his shoulders. "Yeah, just thought I'd check on you. Is that King Vonter arriving outside?"

Sahd could not think straight: "How do you ...?"

"It is not important. I think you should convince Vonter to take all his men and go back to the capital as soon as possible. You should make sure that you have a good defence against what's coming."

"What are you not telling me? What do you know?" a quiet tingling started in Sahd's guts.

"I swear, I know nothing. But it is this ... feeling. I told you, we know about magic brewing and cooking something awful up. I do not think we are going to see rainbows and puppies anytime soon! You should get ready for a fight sooner rather than later."

The soldier frowned and pulled his legs closer, then stuck them out of the bed to his right. Sitting on the edge, he rubbed his eyes and stared at Mibb again.

The rodent just looked at him.

"So, you came to warn me about nothing, and now you have moved in? What are you waiting for?"

"Ha! I could ask you the same thing, pal! What are you waiting for? You should go and talk to your King! Now! Lives depend on it!"

He could tell that Mibb was serious, but still, not moving.

"And what are you still doing here, can you please explain to me why you're not with your friends? I thought you animals hated humans, and you wanted to stay away from us?"

Suddenly, the squirrel's expression changed. His concern made way to a different kind of sternness. He looked down and wiped his mouth with one paw, slowly.

"I do not hate you," he mumbled, but then added a little louder: "They asked me to leave and not to return."

"What? Why?" Sahd asked.

"I think I was defending you and your tactful friend too much. Fighting on your side of this battle. They felt I should be with your kind. So, yes, I have failed my family, my community, my kind. And I have no place to go." he summarised without breathing once between his words.

A silence followed that was underlined with the faint voices of men from outside his tent.

"I do not know what to say." Sahd said after a while. "I'm very sorry."

"Do not be sorry! Warn your people! Do whatever you can to be ready! We should not waste any more time."

"We?" asked Sahd getting up.

"Well, I will hide nearby, so no one will notice."

The soldier got dressed and thought about what this meant. "I will speak to the King. But I still do not quite understand what I saw in the forest, and why the other animals do not want to help us."

"I cannot make sense of this all myself, but I think I am better off, and more useful here. With you."

Sahd could not supress a smile. "Is that a compliment?"

Mibb frowned and jumped off the bed. "Shut up. I should stay close to listen to what the King's plans are. Plus, you have weapons. And numbers. I am alone."

Now, that was nearly adorable.

"Fine." Sahd had put on his light leather armour, walked over, and parted the drapes that marked the tent's entrance. Blinded by the sunlight, his sight needed a few moments to adjust. Then, he saw Draidr, and the others surround Vonter and listen to what he had to say. There was a young woman with him, rather slim, but with defined, female curves, long black hair, and strong facial features. She looked like one of the tough ones. A hunter maybe? Sahd moved towards them. From the corner of his eyes, he could see Mibb hiding behind some barrels. He had to smile again. The squirrel was not very subtle. Did he say earlier that he did not care if anyone saw him?

Part of him really wanted to break his promise and tell Vonter all about Mibb and the immortal animals. Particularly, with the newfound hostility that the squireel revealed to him just now, it might not be the best idea to keep this a secret from his King.

As he arrived at the group, Vonter just finished his report: "..., so we rode here, and I am quite glad to see you all. No one turned to stone, then? The rain was no problem?"

Men shook their heads, but they knew what was coming.

Draidr cleared his throat and looked over to Vonter's new companion.

"I am very sorry, Your Grace. But we have lost a lot of men in the White Forest. Apart from Sahd and myself, all of them, actually. All of them turned to stone. It was horrific. A black monster attacked us. We could -" his voice gave in, and Sahd could tell that he would not be able to finish his sentence.

He decided to jump in. "We could only run, Your Grace, to carry the word before you and warn everyone. We have reason to believe that there is a significant number of stone warriors just waiting to attack."

Mixed looks were exchanged amongst the other men, but Vonter stepped in front of him and Draidr, and laid a hand on each of their shoulders. "I am very sorry for losing your men, but we are at war, people die. We need to make sure we do not. Please do not feel bad you ran away. I know you would have saved them if you could have."

Someone murmured something behind him. But Sahd was just glad that the King had said his words.

The last thing they needed was unnecessary blame and accusations.

"The only trouble is, we still do not know exactly what we are up against, and quite frankly, it is making me very nervous. I want to hear your story in detail." Vonter added.

Draidr was faster than Sahd uttering his words: "We had the men prepare for an instant attack on the castle in the White Forest. We will be able to move out as soon as you give the word."

Sahd had to get Draidr and Vonter alone to stop this!

Vonter smiled. "I agree that we should talk first, but I am thinking about retreating to the capital and making sure that we are safe and have more men to form an attack of our own."

Again, some muttering came through to Sahd, but he ignored it. Maybe he would not have to break his promise and talk to his King now about the animals.

He probably would not have believed him either. And seeing as Draidr had chosen to go against what he wanted to propose, he would not be able to count on his fellow soldier's support.

"Let's go inside and share what we know. I think we should consult each other first to make an informed decision." uttered Vonter.

The King was most definitely able to read the mixed emotions of his men. Draidr glanced at Sahd, mouthing his frustration silently, and they followed the King into his tent together with a few other Generals, and the woman hunter.

Sahd thought that he saw Mibb's bushy tail behind the barrels, but he was not so sure anymore.

The rodent was probably already checking the way into the tent by now in order to not miss anything. The lights were gloomy in the large tent of the King and his guard's.

After Vonter took his armour off, and sank into his chair, the other men stood in a half circle facing him, and a servant brought water and bread.

One soldier started by explaining how the search for survivors was progressing, but they had no luck. There were many bodies, most of them torn to shreds, many more missing or turned into stone.

Vonter interjected and explained how he learned so much more about what made the poor men, women and children turn into stone. He introduced the woman from Tramvil as Grunia Pardhua, Daughter of Lartm to everyone and complimented her spirit and intelligence. She blushed modestly. Sahd saw her looking at Vonter a couple of times. The way she held the handle of her sword suggested that she was quite the warrior too.

The King then asked Draidr to describe what happened in the White Forest, and Draidr went into detail how he lost his men, had stumbled through the night, and found the other group, and how they ran away from the black stone warrior.

Sahd did not realise how horrible it must have been for him to hear the men screaming when they turned.

He could still hear the soldier's shaking voice as he explained what happened.

It appeared none of the other men in the tent had seen what Draidr had seen. They had not heard the screams or the agony.

When the stone attacked Sahd's men, Sahd did not even have time to listen, and watch, because he had to run, as fast as he could.

Before Draidr reached the point of the story where they met the talking squirrel, his friend glanced at him. Sahd tried to shake his head as unnoticeably as possible, and to some impact, luckily.

Draidr reported how they ran out of the woods and the stone warrior just lost their trail.

The others seemed to believe him, and he looked at Sahd after he finished.

Sahd decided to mention another detail: "Forgive me, His Grace, but there was something else while I was watching the castle ruins with my men."

He turned to Vonter and explained how he saw some movement in the castle. A man was seen, who was clearly performing magic. This was a lie, of course, but he had to imply at least, that Dragus, the evil sorcerer was behind all of this. He did not want to expose the animals, but this was still vital intel to everyone. He did not mention any names. Vonter needed to hear this.

It was hard to make out what Draidr was thinking, but there was this silent agreement between them. Sahd knew that they would not have to discuss this. It was fine.

Another soldier gave the King the rundown of the numbers of citizens and soldiers in each village, and apart from Sahd's and Draidr's losses, they had only lost a handful men. The most devastating losses were still the violent attack on Buntin and the silent transformation of Tramvil.

After a short discussion about how many men to leave in the surrounding cities, the King made a final announcement.

"We should retreat to the capital and convince as many citizens close to the capital to join us. For the ones that are not able or willing to travel, the Generals should organise guards to be stationed in their villages, but I want as many men as possible guarding the capital.

"And I want my people safe, at least until the mystery with the water has been resolved. As long as we cannot make sense of this threat, I must assume the worst and protect what I can. Please pass this on to your Divisions and search groups. We will leave tonight to make the better part of the way before nightfall, so we're back at the capital as early as possible in the morning."

An older soldier nodded and mumbled something about wise decisions into his beard. Most men looked as if they were glad, they would go back home.

Sahd could almost hear Mibb's sigh of relief somewhere behind the crates.

26

Still experiencing the witch's anguish that filled him up, Fragir's breathing grew heavier. He got up, suddenly feeling uneasy and nervous. He had to do something! Something big.

The sorcerer walked back through the castle and the courtyard at the front and out the main gates towards the trees. At the edge, where the forest began, he turned around towards the dark building, and closed his eyes once again.

Channelling all energies he had in him, and pulling more from the ground beneath his feet, he directed all at summoning the souls inside. Nothing happened for parts of a while. What he was trying to do took up all his concentration, all his Composure. His mind numbed all thoughts, and he let his rage take over, combine with the rage he had picked up through his empathy, and he pushed it all out, pushed her out of his thoughts using the excess to power the spell.

Then, he heard the first rumbling and opened his eyes. The stones of the castle walls started to vibrate and separate. Driven by the torment and pushing of the souls inside the stones, the black rocks started moving. Slow at first, accelerating as the spell went into full swing. They flew up, clashed mid-air, and reassembled themselves almost like bread dough. Like clunky, loud, dusty bread dough.

The entire castle was soon transforming to make up something else entirely. The souls merged and took control of the new structure.

A couple of moments later, the new weapon was almost ready. In front of Fragir, a giant stood, nine houses large and at least six houses wide.

Almost all the stones that had made up the building before, were now part of this warrior's build.

Uglier, chunkier, and much more powerful than Yart had been in the end, this giant housed over 900 souls. The same fiery red lights glowed in two small holes. Hot air was pumping out of a large mouth hole that swallowed all light and promised nothing but darkness. Four thick, almost muscular boulder arms with large fists were ready to smash things into the ground, and the two short legs with flat feet were so massive that one step covered the area of two carriages.

His new toy looked strong!

The witch would have to destroy them all if she planned to fight for the King's precious castle again, he thought.

A new black rock-solid soldier, bigger and stronger than anything in this world!

And Fragir was about to show the world!

For a moment, he lost his balance, exhilarated, and drained, but he was able to catch himself. With dismissing waves, he commanded the big mountain to move, to the capital, crushing that witch.

"Get her!" he screamed.

The bone shattering rumbling disappeared into the dusk, pressing down all trees in its way. Fragir watched the enormous shadow disappear in the East, on its quick journey straight to the capital. The precious home to so many souls, that damned witch, and their army would be crushed, and after that, the kingdom's defences would be crippled severely.

Fragir closed his eyes and followed his new instrument in his mind. The stone monstrosity was galloping on all long four hands, legs up behind it, destroying all that came before its gigantic arms. Within breaths, it had left the White Forest, and it would reach the capital just after sundown. He could feel its meltingly hot core of merged souls, exuding the heat of rage and the excitement of the destruction to follow. He needed to crush the witch and her little blue head!

Suddenly, he sensed something behind him.

He pulled his mind out of the giant and focused on his immediate surroundings. Nothing.

Or was there someone? There was a very quiet rustling sound behind the trees next to the ruins.

"Hello?" he shouted. "Anyone out there? … You know, this is my forest now, and I will find you wherever you go. You might as well just show yourself."

A while passed without anything happening, and just before he was going to use his Composure, the silence was disturbed. Behind the trees, something was moving through the bushes and leaves on the ground. And then, he saw them. The animals of the forest finally showed themselves. But why now, after all this time? They had been surprisingly good at hiding from him. And judging by their faces he could tell that they feared him. A lot.

"Look what we have here. What a nice surprise!" he exclaimed. "What brings the vermin out of their white hideouts into the black streets?"

Their leader stepped forward. It was the fox, standing bravely between Fragir and the other animals.

"We have come before you to talk. We would like to negotiate a truce. We do not share the same values than the humans. We vow to stay out of your dealings. We promise to not tell a soul what we know and in return, we will be left alone."

Fragir could not believe what he was hearing. "Well, well, how very interesting. I am honestly surprised at your stupid courage. Did you really think I would make a deal with you insignificant beings? Why would I do that?"

The fox shifted the weight of his body from the left legs to the right ones. Looking back at the others, he raised his voice again.

"We know who you are, and what you are doing. But we will not get involved or be difficult if we are spared. There is no need to destroy us. We will stay away and let you reign whatever part of this world you want to call your kingdom."

Fragir burst out laughing. What an entertaining delight! When the impulse was over to just strike them down here and now, and he had caught his breath, the animals were still patiently awaiting his answer.

"Oh, so, you are serious? Well, let's say I would accept your terms and leave you be in my forest, what kind of guarantee do I have that you will not rat me out? Apply some ruse to let my guard down and undermine my power in any way?" He could not suppress another series of laughs. "Forgive me, I do not mean to be rude, but it is so ridiculous."

The fox cleared his throat to reply in an earnest tone.

"We keep to our own kind. We do not talk about anything to anyone. We cannot produce any offspring, the legends would not be told, and not live on. There is no reason for us to break the promise."

"Do you think I am completely and utterly daft?" Fragir felt his body tense up and a very comfortable rage cooking up inside him. "I know what you are too. Low lives for eternity, is that not right? Yes, I do remember, you will not die until killed. And that is exactly what I will do to you.

"I do not care about my secrets coming out. By the Ungods, I want the world to know what I have done. I want to crush humanity, destroy them all, and until I do, I want them to know what's coming, and to fear every living breath they have left of their pathetic little lives. I am not sure if you get this, but life itself is what I am trying to get rid of here. Especially immortal life, now that is just disgusting, is it not?"

Some of the animals murmured amongst each other, exchanged looks and a few even stepped back.

Fragir enjoyed their fear, took it all in. "So, just to clarify, you have nothing to offer to me." he said to his own satisfaction. Truly, this would be the last argument, and he could finally kill them. And the fox was able to see it in Fragir's eyes.

"Any last words? I feel like smiting some vermin."

Moments passed as the group processed this is silence, most of them cowering behind the fox in utter helplessness. Their leader was pretending to be strong, staring into the sorcerer's eyes, with no expression.

And then, he moved his mouth without breaking eye contact.

"We will help you. One time."

"How?" Fragir was willing to entertain the idea for exactly one breath.

The fox kept up the confident façade: "We will get you something. Anything you want. One time. And you let us live."

Interesting, he thought. Not so much the others! Behind the fox, a wild discussion arose, mostly protest became louder, and some worried voices were raised beyond hysteria. Fragir, still looking into the fox's fixed stare, thought that that was the reason he best worked alone. He could see that none of the animals approved what their leader had just suggested. Not only was this what was intriguing about the fox, it was also a very agreeable offer as he already had a hundred ideas. Slowly, the man in black raised his hand. Very soon after, the voices went mute, and all eyes were on him.

"Smart move. This is a good offer. Of course, you have no idea if I am going to be true to my word, and not kill you after you have helped me." He winked at the group of small mice who jumped back behind the beavers. "Surely, there is something dreadful and unappealing that I would not like to do myself. So, naturally, I would prefer someone else to do this for me."

"My thoughts exactly," said the fox, unfazed by his group's protests, although he was aware of the silent kicking and nudging from behind, he still looked steadily at Fragir.

"What could you little creatures do for me? I cannot think of anything right now! In what way would I summon you if I decide later what you are useful for?"

"I'm sure we can agree on a way. Just spare us and let us go after we have done what you have asked."

Fragir was considering this deal, of course not without screwing them over once it was done. These feeble animals were entirely harmless. He would use them for this favour and let them think they could live their eternal boring lives in some cave on the edge of the world. Besides, the deal did not say anything about torture. And he felt very inspired by that thought. Pets to play with.

He turned to the side, closed his eyes, and went into his mind. He lifted his consciousness up and shot across the treetops quickly to where his new stone warrior was headed. Within breaths, he saw the giant gallop towards the city walls. But ... something was missing. He did not sense her. The blue witch. Where was she? Had she abandoned the city? As he was watching through the eyes of his smoking creation, how the strong arms were punching through the fields, getting ready to tear down the walls, he could not feel her presence anywhere. In a flash, he pulled himself out again and travelled back into his own body.

For the animals, only very few moments had passed, and he turned back to them, thinking. They did not look very dangerous, so sending them after the witch would be a rather deadly mission. Fun to watch, but pointless. However, they had claws and teeth that, if used strategically, could do some considerable damage in a coordinated attack.

And then, he had an idea. Probably the second-best idea since he was back.

"Alright, I have a task for you to do, but I need you to act quickly. All of you, or the deal is off." he tried to catch every pair of eyes, but it was quite difficult with some of the birds, mainly because of their oddly shaped heads. "You say you do not condone the human way, and you want to help me? The most useful thing at this moment would be capturing the King."

The fox cleared his throat and tilted his head slightly, and the other animals started their murmuring chatter again.

Fragir continued his announcement: "I need you to capture him, alive. I do not mind if you must wound him or drag him here half dead. As long as he is still half alive."

The fox had a glimmer in his eyes. "Give us one breath." he said gracefully and turned around to his followers. Fragir gave them a moment to confer, but he could not help listening in.

"How can you suggest this deal without talking to us?!"

"You are not a true leader!"

"This is the only chance we have at survival; we have to trust him already."

"We came here for a reason."

"... We cannot pick a fight with the humans."

"I do not want to be part of a war that doesn't concern us ...!"

"We have to think of ourselves."

"We should have never come here ..."

And then, one of the wolves spoke up and barked at the group: "This is one simple task! And then we live. Away from this all!"

The fox made use of the silence that followed and said: "I agree. We can do this. We do not have to get involved any more than that. We can track Mibb's trail, find out where the King is, and we can jump him in surprise. We'll make use of the night, when he is asleep, and the guards are less alert."

Fragir found this delicious!

The smaller animals had fear written all over their tiny little faces. This was priceless! The mice and the beavers were not convinced at all, and the ducks backed away from the group until one of the younger wolves jumped behind them and growled.

The fox raised his voice a little bit more forcefully this time: "Everyone in?"

Clearly, not everyone was in, but the foxes and the wolves had this group under their authority.

Fragir had sat down on one of the stones and looked through the strands of hair that had fallen into his face.

"So, what say you?"

"We'll do it," the fox said without turning back to face the sorcerer.

"Good. You have until sunrise. Be sure to be quick." Fragir uttered, and he got up.

He heard the wolves bark and howl, and soon after, all the animals had vanished in the woods.

The darkness had crept up to where they had their negotiations, and it had gotten quite chilling.

The remaining stones looked a bit sad, scattered on the clearing like this. He did not have a home anymore; the castle was gone. But that did not mean that it should remain like this!

With a quick activation of his Composure, he balanced out the nexus of the last cursed souls that were still trapped in the stones around him, and he positioned himself in the centre.

He bent down and pushed his hand into the soil until they were covered, similar as he had done before.

Eyes closed, and drawing energy from his element, he lowered the ground in front of him.

Exactly where the yard of the castle had been before, the earth shifted and formed into a wide, but steeply walled pit. The stones were lifted into the air, and piled up at one side, until he had created a flight of stairs leading from the edge down to the new, lowered ground.

He did not have nearly enough stones, so he laid roots bare that filled the gaps.

A small cave at the bottom would make a good place to retreat and sleep in the warmth of the lower grounds.

At least for the night, and then, he would watch the rest of his stone warrior's venture over the capital tomorrow.

Channelling the ground's energies, he formed his new home. Then, he created a few shadow creatures and positioned them in a protective parameter around the pit. Slowly, he built a small defence up against any living thing.

When he opened his eyes, the work was done, and he stepped down to his new base.

With every step, he could feel how tired he had gotten. This had been a lot of magic, he was wiped.

He sensed the warmth of the surrounding soil, and the cold of the tormented souls that lingered around. Up top, beyond the edges of the pit, he sensed his shadows patrolling through the white trees.

He should get ready for inflicting pain on his Royal guest.

27

"I cannot believe it took us almost the entire day to pack up. What were the men doing?" Vonter sighed. Draidr was kneeling and cutting ripped leather strips off his boot.

"Your Grace, we had quite a lot of bodies to take care of. We did not want to leave them to the wolves."

Vonter instantly felt bad for asking. They would not even make it to Tramvil before it would be dark completely. He had originally decided that they should get to travel for a half day and find a safe place at nightfall. But they would not make it as far as he had hoped. However, the small woods just outside of Tramvil would provide enough shelter without having to set up tents, and it would be a lot easier to get going in the morning. Water reserves were becoming a problem as no one dared to touch the nearby river, even though it had all been safe up until now. Maybe there is just a curse on the Tramvil well and its river, he pondered.

"Let's at least ride for as long as we have daylight, so we will not be back too late tomorrow," Vonter said.

Draidr nodded and rushed away to spread the King's orders.

Vonter looked over to the hills in the South. The last of soft, red light was spreading across the horizon from the West like the slowest tidal wave. Cold, crisp air made its way through his teeth into his throat, and gave way to warm, humid breath a couple of moments later. He liked how the difference in temperature was visible, and how he could try and last his breath as long as humanly possible to create the longest cloud in front of his face. After a few breaths, he lost interest.

He worried about the battles to come; he was sure there would be more than one. If they even would get the chance to go into battle.

Would they stop chasing an invisible enemy? Was he prepared? Was he making the right decisions?

How was Samjya, and how would she react seeing him again?

And the wedding. Vonter wanted to marry this woman and make up for the first time around to be an interrupted event. He was looking forward to finally sleeping next to her, in his own bed. Equally, he was excited but also nervous to go back. He could not wait to see his wife to be again, but he also knew there were a lot of questions about what happened and the co-ordination of the defence of his land. He would be busy. He would not be able to stay safe for her.

Whatever was lurking in the White Forest, was already the greatest challenge of his generation, he was sure of it. And he had not even seen anything or anyone yet. Apart from the stone monster, and that evil sorcerer according to Sahd and Draidr, no one had. No one knew anything of magic anywhere, it would be impossible to predict what powers were directed at the destruction of his kingdom, and how to counteract them. How would they fight magic, without magic?

At least he had his army. Thousands of soldiers that were trained, willing and ready to fight for their King and their people. That had to count for something.

For a few moments, he just stood there and took in the view across the green fields in the East and the Lakes of Llamar. Treetops were bathed in dark red light, and dusk was now very imminent, very few breaths away. He felt a presence behind him. Sahd cleared his throat and stepped next to his friend.

"Draidr has the army almost ready to ride out, Your Grace. We should go."

"Yes, we should." Vonter pressed his lips together.

Something was wrong with Sahd, the soldier seemed anxious.

"What is it?" the King asked.

"We should really get going, but yes, Vonter, I ... need to tell you something. It is going to be a bit hard to believe, trust me, I was taken by surprise myself," he stammered.

He was fixated on something behind Vonter, but the King did not turn around. Instead, he laid a hand on his friend's shoulder and looked him in the eyes steadily. He wanted to let him know that he could tell him anything.

"Draidr and I had help when we escaped. There were friendly creatures in the White Forest." Vonter could not help but smile at this word.

"Creatures? What are you talking about?"

"Well, speaking creatures. Animals."

Was Sahd trying to fool him? But he was being so earnest.

"Animals that can speak? In the White Forest?"

"Yes. Specifically -" Sahd tried to explain, but Vonter had to ask again.

"Speaking animals that were talking to you and Draidr?"

Sahd nodded, but then, he heard a voice behind him. Most definitely the same place that Sahd was looking at earlier.

"Gods, is he always this slow?"

Vonter turned around, and on a branch of the small bush, there was a squirrel. Looking directly at Sahd. Then, it shook its little head and moved its mouth: "I thought Kings were supposed to be wise. He is not really a quick one."

"Mibb!" Sahd was not impressed with the little one being rude like that. But Vonter was distracted by the talking rodent altogether. A living, talking animal from the White Forest!

"Wow!" he did not know how else to respond.

"Yes, I am speaking. What else is new? I'm hoping you can speak in whole sentences, too, so we can communicate?"

"Mibb!" Sahd was clearly deeply embarrassed for the squirrel. "Please forgive him his manners, Your Grace. He has not been in contact with humans in a very long time."

He was throwing warning looks towards Mibb and stepped forward hastily, to reach for Vonter's arm. But he did not need calming down, Vonter liked the little creature and its frank attitude. It was ... refreshing.

"Mibb, is it?" he started. The rodent rolled his eyes and nodded.

"Mibb, it is very nice to meet you. Please forgive me, I have never spoken with an animal before. But feel free to say whatever you like." He stepped back to view the squirrel from top to bottom. It was remarkable.

After just moments, he noticed how he was staring, and Mibb was twitching nervously with his bushy tail, frowning at the man.

"I'm sorry. And yes, also, thank you very much for helping Sahd and Draidr escape."

"Helping them escape? I saved their asses! I risked my life to get them away from the stone monster and brought them safely back to you while you were sunning yourself in the fields."

The rodent scoffed. "I even put everyone else in the White Forest into danger by bringing them to our hideaway. That is more than just a little help! Oh, and did I mention how the others chased me away for it? I am exiled. For saving a couple of humans."

"Others? Wait, Sahd, I thought you had outrun the stone monster without seeing anyone else?" Vonter turned to his fellow soldier.

Sahd looked down to the ground. "I was not quite sure how you would react to this fantastic story, but also, we had promised the animals not to tell anyone else."

"The animals! How many are there?" He turned to Mibb. "You said 'everyone else in the White Forest', who is that?"

Mibb decided that he would not be interrogated: "Sorry, King, not having the questions now. The important thing is that you get back to your castle and defend your people. As soon as you possibly can. Today, now. I will fill you in on the way."

Vonter hesitated a couple of breaths.

Sahd chuckled, and he turned back around to his soldier friend.

"Alright, let's get moving. Signal Draidr to ride ahead with the Second Division as discussed, we will lead the rest," he ordered.

Sahd stepped away to execute the King's will.

"With your permission, I will sit in your hood, undetected by your men, so I can tell you everything," the thin voice proclaimed. The squirrel winked at him as he turned his head.

"That's a very good idea. Hop in."

Sahd was back already, having passed on the message. He probably wanted to keep an eye on Mibb's behaviour but grinned from ear to ear when he saw the two. "You are like friends already."

Vonter could not help but smile as well but couldn't see if Mibb even reacted. He felt the light weight in his hood, moving around a bit to become comfortable and secure. Or so he thought. When he turned towards the horses, he only heard a squeak and hysterical cursing. "Ow! Dear Majesty, do not move so abruptly, I do not want to break my freaking arms."

Vonter and Sahd exchanged amused looks.

"Apologies, Mibb. I will try to be more careful."

When he reached his mount, he looked up the hill where Draidr had just disappeared. The Second Division would arrive before them and secure a resting place for the night. He had also instructed one of the messengers on their fast horse to deliver a note to Sire Graynor at the capital to alert them that they would be coming back and be vigilant about the cursed water.

With a soft jump, Vonter lifted himself up onto his horse, very conscious of the little passenger behind his neck.

Sahd raised his arm as soon as he sat on his mount and the First Division of men started moving to his signal.

Just like the first half of the army, they set out to climb the hill and reach the designated woods near Tramvil soon.

But just as the men started to ride out, Vonter heard something. At first, he could not see where it came from, it was already getting dark quickly. But then, around 500 feet East of where Draidr had led his men up the hill, at the highest point, there was a figure. Someone on a horse. And riding down fast.

The man was screaming on the top of his lungs. Sahd turned and stood next to Vonter quickly, raising his torch. The men made their mounts move towards the young man, who had stopped screaming now, and demanded the last reserves of the horse's energy. When they got closer, and the horses slowed down, Vonter saw the messenger's jacket, and the dried blood on his forehead.

"What happened?" he asked to know. The man was very much out of breath.

"His Grace, my name is Prin, son of Ravin. Apologies for being so late, but there have been developments at the castle that you need to know. I came as fast as I could. There has been an attack. And ... it is about Samjya."

"What about her?" he said with a very bad feeling in his gut.

The man coughed, and Sahd threw a water bottle in his arms. After long gulps and a few deep breaths, Prin started again.

"The castle was attacked, by a ..., well, giant stone monster."

Sahd glanced over to Vonter.

"It was so strong; our men could not defeat it. It broke through the walls and killed many soldiers, women, and children," his eyes filled with tears.

Vonter's heart sank down so hard, that he could feel it break through the ground. "What is it about Samjya?" he was almost too scared to hear the answer.

"She was different. Changed, somehow. No one had seen her in almost two days, and she suddenly ran towards that thing like a ... well, forgive me, His Grace for the choice of word, but she was like a witch, and ... she killed it."

257

The King was speechless.

"She killed it? By herself? With a weapon?" Sahd asked after a short while.

"Not exactly. She had changed into something powerful. People said she had finally revealed her true self! That she was a witch. She was using some sort of magic and shot arrows out of her own hands. In the end, she turned simple wooden poles into ice spears to finish the monster off."

What was happening? The King felt hot and cold shivers running down his back. The more he heard the more unbelievable this became.

"What happened next?" Vonter stammered.

Prin's tears fell silently, and he did not make any other noise until he spoke again: "She left. After the fight, she just ran away. Away from the castle, left the capital, and ran without looking back."

This did not make any sense! Why would she suddenly be able to use magic? And then, leave her new home behind?

Maybe she was seeking out her father, but Vonter would have expected him to have arrived a long time ago. "What about her father?" he asked.

The man shrugged his shoulders. "He was reported missing, I believe. No one had seen him."

"What about the water, has anyone turned to stone?"

Prin looked confused. "No. Stone? What is it with the water?"

Vonter had heard enough. He had to find her!

"Sahd, please make sure the men arrive at the capital as soon as possible, no matter what it takes!"

"Vonter, no, I will not let you go after her, not by yourself! Do not do this!"

But Vonter had already made up his mind.

"Sahd, I need you to do this for me. I have asked many things of you in the time that we have known each other, usually as a friend. And I am asking you to be my friend once again, and as your King I am giving you an order."

Sahd gave him a stern look, then nodded at him and at Mibb, who was apparently peeking over the rim of the hood's fabric without being seen by Prin.

"Please take this young man with you, make sure he gets something to eat when you catch up with the others and keep him safe. Defend the capital, you will act on my behalf and give this authority to Sire Graynor when you arrive at the castle." Vonter added.

Sahd did not protest again and made a hand gesture to Prin so he would follow him. The two started their ascent to follow the Second Division.

Just moments after, as soon as the others were swallowed by the dark night's curtain, Mibb jumped over his shoulder and grabbed the horse's mane to hang on the side of its long neck.

"You know that this is a bad idea?" he said. Vonter nodded silently and turned his horse in the other direction.

"You are going to get killed. Trust me, there are forces at play, which you do not understand."

"You clearly have never been in love," Vonter said. He could not think of anything else to say. His thoughts were all about her. The love of his life. And he could not live with himself if he did not try to help her in this.

Mibb did not have anything else to say either. As soon as the King picked up the speed, he disappeared in his hood again.

They rode for some long breaths' time, the path took them towards the White Forest, and at the next opportunity, Vonter turned North.

It was pitch black by now, and the white trees to his left shone like eerie pillars. The tension he felt did not help his nervousness.

He was really hoping that he would find her before anything else happened. But the problem was, he did not know where to look, or what to do to find her in time.

They did not really talk at first, but Mibb was quite the talkative fellow, so he did not keep quiet for very long.

The squirrel shared his story about how he had become leader of his group and was then chased away after sticking up for Sahd and Draidr.

He also explained how they came to believe that this evil sorcerer named Dragus was responsible and how he was using stone magic and most likely behind all the attacks.

"How long have you been living in the White Forest?"

"All my life. I have never known anything else. Well, there was the time when the forest was not a forest."

That surprised him.

He was under the impression that the White Forest had existed for many hundred years and had been created through magic.

He asked the question and heard Mibb laugh out loud. "Yes, the forest has been there practically forever, but it wasn't this large." Mibb continued to explain how Tessel was betrayed by the human's Elders Council, and she had punished the town for it.

The castle was lost within the trees she erected and how all children were turned into animals.

Vonter could not believe it. "How old are you?"

He was a little bit afraid of the answer.

Mibb moved closer to his ear and said with very apparent pride in his voice: "I am immortal, I have lived around 800 years, I think. I have lost count."

The King gasped. "Seriously? You must have seen a great deal. How does that feel?"

He had to wait for the answer because the squirrel was probably thinking about it.

"Well, we stayed away from the dealings of the world, so we are not really informed of what has been going on outside of the forest. We only heard of the destruction that Sahd and Draidr told us about. Buntin, was it? ... The other animals do not care about the human world though."

"Yeah, you said. I am grateful for your allegiance." he said pondering over the two worlds that came together. "How many animals are there? And what kind?"

"Well, there are about 27 of us left. We have had some losses over the centuries, and some had left and never returned, but it is a mix of foxes, wolves, rabbits, moles and deer, owls, and boars."

Vonter was fascinated: "So, foxes and rabbits live beside one another, peacefully? You have an actual community?"

"Yes, we do see us as different from the other animals, so the carnivorous animals in our group would hunt mortal animals instead of us. We used to be human, but the curse made us immortal, and we have been animals for centuries. We are not like you anymore either. That's why the other animals have decided not to join me. They think that this is your battle to fight, not ours."

The King became genuinely worried for the others. "But surely, destruction of that magnitude will affect you just as much as it affects us sooner or later?"

Mibb squeaked: "Yes, thank you! That's exactly what I told them, but they would not listen. They never will. Maybe … maybe if you tried, maybe they would listen to the King of the humans."

King of the humans, that sounds funny, Vonter thought.

To his left, he suddenly noticed some movement.

Yellow eyes? No, that could not be. Mibb had said that the animals would stay hidden. But there was ... something.

"Mibb?" he shouted, but there was no time for a reaction from his new furry friend. A wolf jumped out from the left, another one from the right, aiming for the horse's throat!

Vonter was almost thrown off, when the horse bucked wildly into the air, and he had a hard time holding on to the reins and keeping himself in the saddle. Despite his horse's attempt to thwart the attack, the wolves' teeth were buried deep into the flesh and caused the mount to stumble.

Some kind of bird scratched his head and face, his sight disappeared for a bit.

He could feel how the horse hit the ground, and fell to the side, crushing his leg beneath its flank. The bones did not break but something snapped!

In anguish, he tried opening his eyes, but something warm and sticky was covering his face. He could feel many claws and paws scratching and pulling at him.

Were the animals out to get him? Why had they left their hideout and decided to get involved? Where was Mibb? Had this been a trap all along?

He tried screaming again, but no luck, they covered his mouth.

The weight was pulled off his leg, and many forces lifted him up. The grip was so tight, that he could barely move. He tried punching and flapping his arms, but it all hurt too much, and he still could not see. They were carrying him away into the dark!

28

No sign of Samjya. But was she still herself? What was she thinking, where was she going?

Yandra did not have any answers, barely any hope, quite a lot of worry. Too much had happened, and her friend was most likely lost.

Darkness was falling over the land. Smoke emerged from the buildings that laid in the path of destruction. The monster and Samjya had left a battlefield.

Out of nowhere, this monstrosity had attacked the city, and no one had been able to stop it. No one except Samjya. But how did she do it? Why? What exactly was happening here? And where had this all come from?

It had to be that flower! They had not been able to find it in the Royal chambers, so it was presumed she had consumed it entirely. Was it giving her magic? Was that the thing that drove her crazy and away from all her loved ones? So many questions.

She was hoping that Vonter would come back any day now with all the answers and the other monsters' heads. But even the thought of more monsters made her so afraid. It shook her again.

A few days ago, she had thought that magic was nothing but a fairy tale. Stories, the Elders told everyone. Now, her best friend had become one, and the rest was all a nightmare!

She noticed how tightly she had been grasping the back rest of the chair and tried to fight away the pain. Looking out of the window made her feel empty and sad, so she decided to stop. To stop hoping? Maybe.

She turned around, thinking about what to do to keep herself busy.

A knock on the door startled her.

Yandra took a deep breath, then she called: "Come in!"

It was Sire Graynor. The expression on his face told her everything that she needed to know. No word. No hope.

She did not fight the tears this time. There was no energy left to fight them. Big drops of water rolled down her cheeks, and she quickly started sobbing uncontrollably. The strong arms of the General wrapped around her shoulders, giving her warmth, and helping her to contain the shivering of her upper body.

The two stayed like this for a couple of moments. After a lot of crying, she noticed how her breathing had calmed down, and her eyes must have poured a whole bucket of tears into his shirt, it was drenched. She blinked away thick tears and pushed her wrist against his shoulder, firstly, to break out of his embrace, and then, to try and dry his shirt with the sleeve of her dress.

Sire Graynor took her wrist and his eyes tried to meet her stare into nothingness. Her nose was blocked, her eyes must have been as puffy as pillows, and she was still not ready to speak. Yandra let him guide her to a chair and sit her down. He moved away for a moment, but only to get her a blanket. He knew she was grateful for the comfort.

She saw him walk up to the window and assessing the scene outside. He was probably using his tactical mind to calculate the damage and plan a more effective defence for next time. But she failed to see any of this in his eyes. He looked tired, empty too, just like her. Or was she just seeing in him what she was feeling all along just so that she was not alone in this?

"I had hoped my messenger would have reached the King and brought news by now. It seems we will have to wait and see when he comes back," Sire Graynor said without a sigh, or any other breathing sound. How was he so contained?

Her throat felt rough, and the voice was breaking when she spoke up. It did not even sound like her voice: "If. You mean if."

An exhausting pause stood between them like an invisible mourning pillar.

For a few moments, Yandra was not even sure if he had heard what she said. But he must have. Her voice had been crackling, but she was convinced it had been easy to understand.

Sire Graynor walked to the far end of the window and watched the men repairing the walls, people collecting what was left in between the ruins. With a shudder, she tried to rid her mind from the images. Enough with the destruction! But she was not able to push entirely away what he was looking at right now, because she had been staring at the outside for a long time.

"Forgive me for asking, but why are you here?" Her voice was almost back to normal. "Shouldn't you be down there, giving orders and making plans?"

"Yes, I should, but I do care about you, Yandra. And Samjya does too. She would want you well and strong when she comes back." he uttered relatively monotonously, without even glancing back at her.

"If, you mean if."

Then, he turned his head and looked at her. "Maybe you should get out of this chamber. Do something useful. It will be helpful."

"Helpful to whom? I do not even know how to walk at this very moment, let alone fold gowns or prepare a meal. And that would not be very useful either! We are defenceless against magic!" She suddenly had a surge of energy inside her. She could finally say what she wanted, it felt as if the words were finally returning after holding out on her.

"My friend ran away, there was nothing that I could do to stop her, nothing! And who knows what happened to her, how she was changed and if she even is still herself? Do you?" she was only getting started. "She attacked you, for the Gods' sake! How does she get back from this, how do we? Why is she not here now, explaining herself? Does she even know what she is doing? Is she in danger? ... Why do not you say anything about this?!!" her words and thoughts drowned in sobbing again.

Her frustration had clearly turned into frustration and anger, more tears and shivering. Sire Graynor was the only person around to vent at. She was taken by surprise by how violently angry she was feeling about Samjya. It had not really occurred to her, but she was so full of fear because she could not understand why she had changed so drastically, why this flower had this effect on her.

She had honestly thought she and Samjya had a deep bond that was unshakable, beyond invented magic even. Sadly, magic was no longer invented. Their whole world had been warped and turned inside out.

The General had become a close friend in the short time that she had known him, that's what she had said before she changed. And she did not even want to imagine how Samjya would react to her Vonter at this point.

Looking at her, with sad, empty eyes, Sire Graynor was clearly at loss to say anything at all. Yes, she noticed the sadness again, that long, lost look that she had seen before, and always. She realised that he was thinking of something else. Someone else. Her anger washed away as fast as it had risen inside her and made room for sympathy. Shame? Sadness. Maybe even pity?

Yandra still had so many different emotions inside her, she did not know how to feel. Her heart was so confused, and she was sure she was not being herself at all.

Suddenly, the bells rang again. Just like yesterday.

She tensed up, and a new kind of shivering came upon her, her eyes instantly jumped to Sire

Graynor, who stepped to the window again, leaning out as far as he could. This time, towards the West. Again?

A new attack, a new monster!

She jumped up, felt her weak knees wobbling, and how cold her shoulders were still, but she slipped out of the blanket anyway to gaze out too. A big cloud of dust was rolling towards the city, and it took Yandra a while to make out what it actually was.

The General recognised it first, and he uttered an unbelievable "By the Gods!!"

Instantly, he ran for the door, grabbing his sword that he had left on the chair by the entrance. He did not even close the door behind him.

Samjya's friend was still deciphering the cloud, and after her eyes had adjusted to the fading light of dusk, and the attacker was getting closer, she could see more and more detail.

It was a new monster, and again, it looked like it was entirely out of stone. But this time, it was a lot bigger. It was hard to determine, but the big mountain of shattering stone was probably bigger than the castle's defending walls were high!

It was running on all fours, like a bearish beast. With an enormous strong back and the biggest shoulders, it was nothing she had ever seen! The glowing eyes were so cold and piercing hot at the same time, that it sent shivers down her spine despite the distance. Loud rumbling was carried across the winds to her ears, and a cloud of dust drew towards her.

The monstrosity stopped, raised both arms, and punched into the wall from the top. The crushing of the hard material made her jump, and she realised quickly how close the attack was.

Stone debris rolled into the streets and crushed the surrounding houses. She could hear some poor souls crying out for help. It was only a few hundred feet away, on the inner rim of the capital, almost by the castle walls! Like toys, the thing chucked bricks and wood, carts, boxes, even people and horses around, effortlessly.

The dust cloud had quickly arrived at the castle, and she had a hard time seeing the soldiers that had passed the walls. Hundreds of men ran out to defend the city, even Sire Graynor was on his horse and overtook most of his men before he passed through the gates.

She could sense it in her guts. This was futile. The attacker was strong, so many houses were already as flat as the ground, and nothing would be able to stop it!

Where was Samjya? Where was Vonter?

Where was everybody?

She turned around, sank down on the ground, pulled the knees to her body and lost herself in clenches of sobbing and fast breathing while she was trying to ignore the vibrations and trembling of the room.

The capital was over, the kingdom was over, her life was over.

It was all happening at once; it was all lost. No hope.

***

Artius Graynor saw the mighty silhouette of this gigantic stone warrior, and for a moment, he could not breathe.

He had not been this close to the previous one, and he was, quite frankly, filled with cold fear. He knew they were going to die, as the arrows did not pierce its skin. The fire kegs that the catapults threw at it did not do any harm either. Even burning oil and the longest spears were pointless.

The soldiers, who got close enough to strike, did not do any damage with their swords, and most of the army were swept away like leaves on a fall day, killed on impact or crushed before, while flung across mid-air.

This was quite the magic! He had seen many things in the last war, but this was by far the most impressive spell that he had ever seen. And he had never been this close to magic either.

In just a few moments, this monster had killed hundreds of his soldiers. He could not just sit in the castle and watch this happen. He decided to fight or die trying.

The massive arms crushed houses, walls and human bodies like matches, the dust and the noise were overwhelming. Just breaths before he reached the giant, he thought to himself, how useless this fight was. There was no escape, no survival, but he still had to try.

He had promised to give his life for the kingdom, for his army and for the King.

And that's exactly what he was going to do. His duty. His honourable sacrifice, even though there was no sense behind it. Nothing would be accomplished by his death; his attack was in vain.

Time stood still, as his horse stumbled across a rolling stone. He jumped out of the saddle. Immediately after landing on his feet, he lunged forward to evade the sweeping motion of one of the arms. It was so fast!

He was not expecting the heavy mass to be moved through the air this quickly. The monster seemed to be fuelled with an incredible amount of rage. The other three arms were punching the buildings and the ground all around. Steamy, moist breaths blew above their heads as it was moving its big stony muscles.

The General rolled onwards, closer to the small stumps of legs, he was aiming for the joints, hoping to damage them with his sword and make the creature lose its balance. He looked up to what had to be its face, and it was not even paying attention to him. Good.

In his approach, his mind circled back to her.

In the last few days, he had been thinking about his late wife a lot, the only woman he had ever loved. Gods, the only woman he had ever touched that way.

Her smile, the elegant twirls when she was dancing, and her luscious hair that fell around her sweet neck at night. All his memories had changed to grey, a distant vision. But the harder they had been to reach over the last decades, the clearer they had become right now. Graynor could see her. As if she was standing right there in the streets, waving at him amidst the terrifying chaos. The unreal comfort drew a smile to his dry lips.

Oh, what he would give for one more kiss.

One last kiss, that made him feel so whole and strong.

She had been everything to him, and he had been cursing the war for taking her away from him.

The year that they had had – never enough.

And the unborn child she had in her …

He had forgiven the Gods, a long time ago.

They would have had their reasons to take her away from him, and they would have had their reasons for sending him into this battle. It was meant to be. He still missed her, like the very first day after her death, even right this moment as he was about to die,

The collapsing library next to him brought his thoughts back to his attacker – it was so big! Higher than ten houses, it had been so easy for it to smash any walls in like it had done and breaking down half of a street was being done without any effort whatsoever within breaths.

When he reached the foot of the monster and raised his sword for the crushing blow aimed at the gap between two stones at its left kneecap, the right leg was lifted in front of him, and the huge creature stepped forward.

The movement was so fast, that Graynor simply could not jump out of the way.

With one step, his life ended. His death became a story that no one would ever be around to tell.

29

When he came to, his head was still spinning, and the night was almost over. The mist was hanging low on the grass between the river and the fields, and the cold ground pressed through his fur like rough tree bark. Mibb was very confused at first as to where he was, but when he saw the white trees, it all came back to him in a flash.

The King had been kidnapped by the animals, his former friends. He had to do something!

His arms and legs were quite clammy, and as he lifted his arms, then legs from the ground, he could feel the moisture of the dew clinging to his fur.

Warm shivers ran down his back, and he stretched his muscles after raising himself up.

It was entirely quiet, not a sound was heard. It was probably normal considering the time of the day, but it had a very looming feel to it. Mibb was not sure whether it would be the calm before the storm or just a simple, quiet morning. But it was more likely to be the first.

With quick and few jumps, he moved closer to the White Forest. Before he jumped in between the first few trees, he hesitated.

What if they were waiting for him to come back?

What would they be ready to do? He had to assume that they knew he had been talking to the King, and that they had seen him with Vonter, but he also remembered to be thrown off out of his hood early in the assault. So, maybe he had just landed on his head in the dark and no one had noticed?

With a quick sigh, he dashed off into the forest and jumped from twig to branch to tree trunk to the next one. He was much quicker in the treetops than on the ground, plus, he could hide away silently in an instant if need be. The full moon made the trees even lighter which helped him see better.

Long times of the day, he was progressing through the woods, checking a few tunnels, and some of the hideouts, carefully. He had to be aware of the moles and owls especially, their hearing was still a lot better than his.

He did not have any luck in the usual caves, until he heard voices. He could see some figures ahead, in the clearing, where the castle ruins were. Or ... had been.

To Mibb's surprise, the ruins were not there anymore. Some random parts and stones of the walls were still there, scattered and spread out. It looked like most of it had been swallowed by the ground!

The round shaped hole in its stead was quite deep, and as he hid in the crown of one of the last trees before him, he could see how the other animals were carrying the unconscious King on their backs. It was not an easy task for them, and as Mibb was changing to the trees further on the right, he had a better angle to see Dragus as well.

Dragus! They had *helped him*?

The mage was standing halfway up the stairs that led down into the hole, almost grinning. In a twisted, sick way. Dragus applauded them and signalled them where to put Vonter. As they all descended into the sorcerer's lair, Mibb lost the view, and he was still too far away to make out the exact words that were spoken.

From the corner of his eye, he noticed Kalia, the older owl, sitting in the tree, turning her head all around and carefully watching the area. Luckily, she had not spotted him yet, and he intended to keep it like that too.

The other owl was probably looking from the other side of the clearing, so there was no way, Mibb would get any closer.

He needed a plan. The owls' night vision was a lot better than his, and it would be not too many breaths before the sun would be in the sky. Vonter might not have that much time!

He slid down the tree and checked the ground from his position to the rim of the hole.

Nothing would give him any cover apart from the occasional stone, but the two watchers in the trees would see him as soon as he stepped out into the clearing, no doubt. His eyes wandered around. Sticks, leaves, stones, nothing around that he could use to get closer. And he needed an idea, fast.

The cool morning breeze blew past his face, and he felt the hairs on top of his ears bend to its gentle force. A leaf was moved next to him, and flew out in the open, followed by a few smaller ones.

That was it! The direction was in almost the right angle, so that could work!

Mibb stepped back silently and carefully, searching the surroundings for a leaf that was large enough so he could hide underneath, but also small enough so that it would be blown over by the light winds passing through the forest. He picked up a few after one another before he decided on the one that he felt was right for his plan. Slowly, he moved into the right position between two trees, hid underneath the leaf by holding it up in a way that he could be unseen from the prying eyes up top, and then, he waited for the right moment.

It seemed like an eternity until the next surge of wind occurred, and some leaves were carried out past the trees. With a cautious jump, Mibb moved forwards, and made sure to tilt the leaf just enough to make the flight look natural.

Or so he thought. But when he landed back on his feet staying close to the other, smaller leaves, he did not hear anything else, so it must have been alright. The waiting without any movement was the hardest part for him. Mibb was not used to standing still for a long time. Probably another squirrel trait.

But obviously, the leaf had to appear to be entirely motionless from the above, so the owls would not become suspicious. It felt like half a day passed before he could move again.

Luckily, the next gust was a bit stronger, and he made good progress towards his desired destination. Jumping up and letting the leaf carry him alongside the others was quite fun. As he landed, he made a few more steps, to catch up with most leaves, and he cowered down again, to hide underneath his cover. He was now about 5 feet from the edge, and he could make out a few of the voices. Mostly, it was Dragus, who was talking to the animals, but he could barely make out the actual words. Again, quite a few moments passed until the next blow of air would enable him to get mobile again.

This time, the wind was turning, so he had to readjust the angle of his glider carefully. Mibb moved once and stopped where the rest of the leaves had landed too. Carefully, he lifted his cover up and noticed he was very close to the edge of the pit. He could see Dragus's face now, even some of the animals. A couple of leaves had been blown over the edge, and Sihgr, the fox, was looking around, maybe not for the first time. Mibb hid his head behind a small root that conveniently had been uncovered from the ground right between him and the others' field of vision. Or so he thought.

Hot and cold shivers ran down his spine, and he had to concentrate hard to not twitch his tail. But no one reacted to him sneaking up, and the owls clearly had not sounded their alarm.

He could now hear everything that was being said.

"That should not be your concern. You should go now." the evil sorcerer ordered.

There was some muttering among the animals, and Sihgr raised his voice: "And we have your word that you will leave us alone as long as we stay clear?"

He knew now why his former friends were doing this, but he could not believe how stupid they were. Surely, they would have discussed the possibility of being betrayed and killed after all?

Mibb would have never let this kind of deal happen. Not under his leadership!

Dragus smiled. His eyes glimmered with sadism and delight. He was planning something. Mibb had to help them!

The animals started to move up the stairs. The fox was still awaiting Dragus's answer, but the man was still facing Vonter, who was lying there, unconscious, completely still, and defenceless. With a swift wave of his hand, the sorcerer raised some roots out the ground, around the King's wrists and ankles, and lifted him up in an almost standing position on the side of the pit, as if he was pinned to the wall. Like in a frame, Vonter was now hanging with arms and legs fully stretched out, still not moving.

Dragus turned to Sihgr: "Yes, now, go!"

But Mibb would not let him have his backstab! With all his courage, he took two steps back, ran to the edge lifted the leaf and angled it like a sail so he would glide down to attack the evil man's face. Since he was almost silently descending from the sky, and neither the animals nor the sorcerer was looking into his direction, only the owls would see him before he made contact, and that was exactly what happened.

Within very few moments, he heard the owls' cries, the animals looked up, confused, until they saw him. Dragus was quite confused; he did not notice Mibb right away. Just before he heard how the others cried out, and saw how they pointed up, Mibb let his battle cry echo in the pit: "Do not trust him, he will kill you all!"

Then, he hit the warlock's face just as he was looking up to him.

Dragus did not have time to raise his arms for any magical defence, let alone use his hands to prevent the squirrel from reaching his face, but as soon as Mibb did, he threw off the leaf and started scratching blindly.

He bit into his hand that wanted to grab him and kicked away any resistance he got from the other side.

Dragus screamed and hit him repeatedly, and then, he got a hold of the tail, pulled him off, and threw him in the air.

Mibb saw his former friends, looking up, scared for him, scared of the sorcerer. Why were they not running away? Dragus's face was all red, mostly scratches, but also bite marks, a bit of blood, and he waved his arms around like a mad man.

When Mibb hit the ground after quite the involuntary flight through the air, he was almost back in the forest again, outside of the pit.

His whole body hurt, his head was spinning, and far off, he heard cursing. A crackling sound came from the lair, and then, silence.

The squirrel looked up. Nothing. But something dropped from the sky. About ten feet from him.

He could not see what it was, but then it happened a second time. This was right in front of him! With big eyes, he raised his head, and recognised one of the owls. Kalia, she had turned into stone, and dropped out of her mid-air flight!

There was no other sound to be heard, so the other animals would have to be stone too!

Mibb had to run! He could not, under any circumstance, be detected. He had to warn the humans!

Despite his pain, he jumped up and ran. As far as he was concerned, he had never run this fast, and he did not look back once. Only a few feet into the woods, he remembered that he would be faster swinging from tree to tree, so he climbed up and jumped.

With tears in his eyes, he moved forward. Away from this place, where he had gotten his friends killed.

Yes, it was his own fault. He should have waited, he should have been more subtle, he should have given them a better warning.

He had to go back to the capital and tell Sahdor. It had been a bad idea to try this alone. Dragus was a lot more likely to kill the King now.

He felt so stupid!

***

Ca'on grunted as Grunia re-positioned the bandage on his arm. He looked strained and as if he was trying very hard to keep his pain inside, and he probably was. The tattoes on his chest didn't hide any of his muscles jolting and jerking as she replaced the wraps and covers.

"Hold still."

In deep concentration, she murmured more to herself than him despite the fact that he was actually very calm considering his amputation. The stitches she had done 2 days ago were starting to heal without infection, not short of a miracle, but they were still sore and tender. She didn't have a lot of experience in this but thinking back to the crying and screaming carpenter who had lost a finger a few years back and painted her mother's studio red with his blood, Ca'on was doing splendidly after having lost an arm.

The new bandage would hold a solid day if it didn't get dirty or wet, and she was glad to have finished it while they still had had some daylight left. Grunia's left hand rested on his chest for a moment while she inspected her finished work. Her eyes met his and she felt a wave of gratefulness and deep respect from the warrior. She wasn't sure if something else flickered up in his gaze, so she moved back a little, placed her hands on her thighs, still on the ground next to Ca'on.

He snickered, which turned into a suppressed cough. "Thank you Grunia. I appreciate you taking care of me."

"You're welcome, I just hope the wound continues to heal. Sorry for the pain I caused you earlier cleaning it." She genuinely felt that the Pirate had been letting himself show any emotion, he was a ruthless and tough soldier after all.

"Do not worry, please." He pushed his upper body up with the one arm and sank down a little as he leant back against a rock, supported by the intact shoulder. "Did I overhear you speak to Victor after Tramvil about where my people are from?"

Grunia was suddenly very aware of her body inside her skin, a hot and cold flash that ran down her spine and how her hands started fidgeting nervously. She might have said something to offend him and was getting ready for a very serious rebuke.

"Don't worry, you haven't done anything wrong - ..." He coughed but tried to smile through it. A few moments later, he continued: "It's just that this whole pirates thing is shtimp. It is not at all how we, the Kan'par came to this land. What you said to the King was just a fantasy, a story."

Ca'on took a few deep breaths. It had to be very tiring to speak, she thought.

"Oh? I remember the people in my hometown talk about this like it was some sort of true story."

"No, it's merely a fairy tale, that's all. We're not quite the Barbarians this makes us." He must have felt the urge to scratch his stump and reminded himself it was not a good idea as his hand reached over but stopped halfway. They looked at each other for a moment, and he tried to make it look like he was going to scratch an itch on his neck.

"We're actually the one and true kin of Cant'un, always have been and never left. At least that is what the Kan'par believe. We don't have faith in your Gods or the Giants that would have created the world, but we think we were molded from sand before any other life."

Grunia was equally interested and wanted to give him a moment to breathe: "From sand? How is that possible?"

"What has been passed down from my ancestors is that the spark of life is in everything living or lifeless. All collides with the spark that gives and takes life, because the spark is life, power and nature."

Ca'on pulled his head to the right and made his neck bones crack. As he did the same to the other side, a small muscle near his mouth pulled it wider for just a breath, then the pain appeared to be gone.

"The lifeless is shaped by wind, water, earth, and fire to create something living.

"The first Kan'par were made with the Kan, meaning sand, and 'par, … life. They cultivated the land, tamed animals, and had families and their traditions. They never settled down for long. There was no need for religion, laws, or weapons. Only when invaders came to these lands, we had to defend ourselves."

Her instinct was to ask more questions, but she sensed there was more to come. Patiently, and without words, she unfolded a blanket from her bag and placed it over his legs and lower stomach.

It had gone dark entirely now, only the low flames of the campfire illuminated his dark skin.

"We developed our own way of fighting, a technique without weapons, the Janh'tan. It's difficult to explain, but we would use pressure points to manipulate the opponent's mobility and organ function."

"That sounds incredible!" Grunia interrupted him. "I knew you were more than just a regular soldier."

Ca'on smirked. "Well, we only show our skills to other Kan'par and the ones blessed by our spiritual leader. We do not share our story with any outsiders either. Our numbers have diminished greatly. Now, centuries later, there are only very few travelling families left in the land, we are still very peaceful kin. I decided to join the army many years ago. I like staying active and practise my fighting skills."

This was fascinating! It was a completely different story than what she had expected. She wondered if there were other stories that had changed over time or were re-told incorrectly and changed because people stopped listening or talking to each other properly.

She also realised that most people in her village had not made any effort to understand the Kan'par at all, they were all just a bunch of tattoed warriors, which was not true. "What about the ink on your skin?" She asked, and quickly added: "If you don't mind me asking?"

The man closed his eyes for the first few words he spoke.

"Not at all. We pay tribute to nature and the sparks that give us and our people life. Each one of us is born with specific signs of life around us. My birth is connected to trees and other plants, still water and a clouded sun, all of which is told on my body as the story of how my life unfolds."

Grunia noticed now the branches and leaves on his chest, vines and waves along his arm and legs, angular patterns framing the images across the natural curves and muscles. She hadn't realised they actually showed specific items and flowed into one another.

Ca'on yawned and she pulled the blanket up towards his chest.

"Rest, my friend. Thank you for sharing your story with me, I will keep it close to my heart."

She meant it. She wasn't sure if he felt a debt to her for patching him up, or if they were destined to have a longer lasting bond than this battle, but her instinct was that he trusted her, and she was starting to trust him. His eyelids closed slowly, and she turned around to face the warmth of the fire. A cold breeze moved her dark hair across the face, and as she moved it away with her fingers, she couldn't help but grin.

All of a sudden, the story of the Pirates of Can'tun felt silly and made up.

30

They saw the smoke from many miles away, covering the moon and stars. Worry and sadness spread among the men, but also the thirst for blood. And water. They had been very anxious and ready for a fight for a long time, and they were ready now. Very tired, but ready.

Sahd would not have had them sleep, instead, they had been riding their horses to exhaustion, all night. And now, that dawn was almost upon them, the big, red flickering was visible at the horizon, smoke had been filling the sky. He even believed that he could smell the fire at this distance.

Exchanging worried looks with Draidr, who had caught up to him, gruelling thoughts raced through his brain without end.

Was the magically changed Samjya back and fighting, or was what they could see the result of a power so big that the entire city had been destroyed? Who had the might to attack the capital like this? It was defended on two rings of thick, concrete walls! How many were dead, how many still alive? Had his sister made it back to the capital only to be killed there in this very moment?

The horses would not be able to keep this speed up, even if it was not that far anymore. They also needed some strength to fight. This was a very tough call to make, Draidr was as undecided as Sahd.

As they were very close to the river, he rode to the front and gave the signal for a break at the bank. The men followed him, and Draidr fell back to lead the Second Division to the river as well. Just a few hundred feet in the East, there was a bridge.

When they were younger, they had spent time there to throw stones onto the riverbed to see how many it took to reach the surface. He did not have to speak to Draidr, his friend knew what the plan was.

Sahd could not stop looking at the enormous echo of the light across the hills. The red glow put the entire riverbank, and everyone's faces into a much more menacing colour.

One of the soldiers announced that he would test the water. The men watched him unmount and lead his mount to the water. It was a very old horse, and not one of the fastest or strongest anymore, so that was a good opportunity.

He did not even have to do anything. The man let the reins go a few feet in front of the river, and his stallion started walking. As its hooves touched the shallow water, nothing happened.

"Wait!" Sahd shouted through the ranks. "Wait for it!"

They did not have any idea how the magic exactly worked. But the horse was drinking peacefully, and then, turned around to its rider. With hesitation, the man touched his horse, and he was fine. No stone, no death.

Some faint cheers were heard, some men kept watching, sceptical.

The soldier then bent down to touch the river's surface himself. Cautiously, he reached with his fingers until they got wet, and again, nothing. More men got off their mounts, and they let them drink. Soon, all the soldiers were drinking too.

Sahd heard more cheering alongside the river, even though some men throughout the Divisions remained sceptical.

"So, Vonter was right, it is only the river that runs through Tramvil. This one seems to be unaffected." Draidr noted.

"Yes. But we should still be careful. I want the men to be back on their horses soon. Every breath we wait means more death there." Sahd was more than just concerned.

He sent his fellow General to check on his Second Division.

While he was gone, Sahd decided the First Division was to cross the shallow river, the others would take the bridge.

It was too narrow to take all of them, and he was grateful for the river to not be a threat to them.

Now, almost all their men had unmounted, led their horses to the water in the usual, coordinated manner, or sat down to have something to eat. Sahd saw some of them lie down for a quick nap, even though this was a very quick stop. A few grim, hungry faces looked back at him.

Draidr came back on his horse. "Nothing to report, other than the men are complaining about the journey. They are saying they will arrive too tired to fight, but everyone knows that this is necessary."

"They are worried about their families too." Sahd said. "Some of us have already lost everyone in our family. Every one of our friends."

He was fighting the wetness in his eyes, but Draidr could tell. They had been friends for too long. "I am very sorry, Sahd. But we will avenge them all. We will defend the capital and our kingdom."

"Or whatever is left of it." said Sahd with a bitter sneer.

No one spoke for the next few breaths. His heart sank low, and so did his mood. Watching the men at the brink of exhaustion did not help.

What good was a tired army? The only way they would be useful if their body and mind was in the right place to fight. But he had to be hopeful. They needed to get to the capital as quickly as possible and save as many lives as they could, at whatever cost.

He would let them rest for a bit more.

"I had a thing with a servant from the castle." Draidr said after some silence.

"What?" Sahd was not in the mood for this kind of talk.

"She was so beautiful, modest. She smelled so nice." he continued; Sahd barely reacted. "What would I give for one more night with her? One more night."

Sahd kept quiet.

"I wonder where she is now. And if she is thinking of me, the soldier fighting for her.

"She might imagine I am heroic and return to her protecting the capital, or she's been raped and killed by the enemy, and I am to never see her again. Fate has a funny way of playing with love and war."

"What are you talking about?" Sahd burst out angrily. "Are you seriously talking about this right now? We're all afraid of our lives and you're lamenting about this last sex you have had and how it could have been so much more if we would not die today?"

"Sahd, I was just making conversation. I guess seeing that bridge again brought back memories of us talking about girls. You know, like we used to, ... I'm sorry if my silly thoughts offended you. We all have our reasons to fight. Mine happens to be the sweet servant girl."

Draidr must have realised how his voice had become louder, and he stopped himself. After a few breaths, he added in a quieter manner: "I am sure she is still alive."

"Your girl?" Sahd was confused now.

"Minher. And your nephews."

Sahd had to look away from his friend.

"Didn't she want to come to the capital for the wedding?" Draidr continued.

Sahd sighed. "Yes, but she had changed her mind just the week before. She did not have a dress and she did not want to travel that far."

A big lump blocked the next words from coming out. He swallowed it and blinked the tears away. "We had arranged for next month to go to Tramvil for the big fair market. ... She was crazy about those little vases."

"The Cecisi, the dark clay vases with blue engravements. I know. My foster mother had a few. She almost ripped my ear off with the slaps I got for breaking one of them." his friend tried to lighten the mood.

"Really? Minher had some too, would not let me touch them. I do not care for this stuff anyway. I was just interested in spending a nice day in Tramvil with her. She hardly ever got out of Buntin; you know."

"Kids." Draidr nodded his head.

"I am not blaming my mother to bolt. It is too much."

Sahd never heard his friend talk like that. "Really?"

"Well, children are loud, dirty, and annoying little brats, are they not?" Draidr was rolling a leaf between his fingers until it crumbled. "They are anything but grateful and keep asking for more. I would not have the patience for any of that."

"You would not want a family? With your servant girl?" Sahd wanted to know.

"Nah, I would just screw them up."

"True."

They both laughed.

He thought about the women that he had met in his life, and all the excuses he had made for not staying with them, not having a family, not even thinking about anything serious in his life. All these years, he had seen himself as a lone wolf. Running solo through thick and thin, no baggage or weights to hold him down. And the weird thing was, he never missed any of it.

The army had always been the priority, and it had kept him sane and sober. Most importantly, the latter. And busy. It became very apparent now how he had kept himself busy not thinking about his life. Aimlessly, he had become a cog in this machine, eager and willing, but to what extent?

He felt that if he had concentrated on living just a little bit more, spent a bit longer on human interaction, maybe his life would have been richer and fuller. He would not have ended up right here and now, and maybe he and his loved ones would not have been exposed to these attacks, living in the woods somewhere with his wife and children.

How would he have felt then, about the hypothetical life he'd have in the army, about to die for King and kingdom when the capital was under attack? He might have found this all daring and mortifying. These attacks did not spare women and children, and they did make the men fight even harder.

Maybe Draidr was right, and love and war were entangled in an inseparable way.

He shook the thought and noticed how his friend had been staring at him, trying to read his mind.

Sahd cleared his throat and got up, walking to his horse. Its breathing had calmed down, and the sweat on its back had gone cold.

Draidr followed him to his horse and looked like he wanted to say something, but Sahd was quicker: "Let's give the signal to continue."

He did not wait for a reaction, instead, he whistled to let the men around them know to get ready.

A few feet over, he saw Grunia, the young woman from Tramvil, climbing onto her mount. Their eyes met for a few moments.

He had not actually talked to her at all yet. Sahd had overheard Vonter mentioning that she was a seamstress. She seemed so confident in her thin armour and the sword on her side, he would have sworn she was a soldier. She was quite impressive.

Her long, black hair was tied behind her head, and the bandana she was wearing made her look like a pirate. Her movements and gestures however were soft and unassuming, and there was a hesitation in her eyes. Her lips were pressed together, and Sahd could not help but think she probably was very good at hiding her fear.

For the journey, she had been taking care of Ca'on, the other strange pirate man with one arm. She was good with him, tending to his wounds, and making sure they did not fall too far behind.

Suddenly, she smiled a little in his direction, barely noticeable. Sahd did not feel like smiling back. Draidr swung his torch on the far left, and most of the men were on their horses by now. Sahd whistled again and made his way across the shallow river.

He led the First Division through the flowing water, while the Second Division turned to the narrow bridge to the right, they could use the additional few moments of waiting as their break had been shorter anyway.

The cold water splashed up his legs and reached his knees easily, but his horse had the strength to strut through, same as the others. Within a couple of breaths, he was on the other side and pushed his mount to gallop up the hill. The city was still a bit of a ride away, and they had to hurry.

With an orange glimmer, the sun was almost visible in the East, and they would be able to see the capital in the distance in a clear line of sight just behind the next hilltop.

As he turned around, the Division followed him up the long hill, some faster than others. On this side of the bridge, he could see Draidr's torch. A small light in the dark, far back, and so faint, he did not know what was about to happen to them.

***

She had felt the change, it was like a towering fire, smoldering across the sky.

Her power had not been compromised, on the contrary, it was still going strong!

The change tasted amazingly. She was very happy with his rage.

He wasn't even aware of it helping her plan.

Her plan for the end of the mortals.

The girl was almost ripe. Ready for the taking. Ready for the next phase.

She was the perfect candidate, always had been. Innocent, loving, ever-so-trusting.

Her love was undying, so it was required to be undone.

There was poetry in the turn, in the warp, in the twisting of truth.

Truth was not true. *It was all a lie, and they had no clue.*

She knew, her alone, and it was a great burden. Her life was not one of truth.

Nothing was truth. It was all so futile. But she made *it* count anyway.

The move *was next,* her move *alone. Long time plan, finally,* the harvest.

The move was *inevitable. Her* skin stretched *and it became a thin* veil. *Slim. Just mist.*

And through.

Her heart was pounding.

Very strange sensations overcame her.

Not real, not right, but it was at least physical.

Somehow. Not quite on the same plane.

The girl was almost ripe.

Just, one, more, pain, one, more.

Undying, unliving, that's how it was going to be done.

31

Vonter became conscious again and knew instantly that something was wrong. He could sense how he was tied up, arms and legs apart, his hurting back against a soft wall of sorts. He felt like he had bruises and cuts all over his body, and he was struggling to open his eyes. There was a surge of ache coming from the left side of his forehead, and something was not right with his knee. When he tried moving it, a suppressed sound of pain left his mouth, and he regretted it right away.

Whoever had captured him, was probably watching, or at least close, and he would not want to admit how much pain he was in. When Vonter was finally able to open his eyes, he realised how bright it was. Was it already the next day?

The light was blinding, it took him long to get his bearings. Memories of the violence came back. They had been attacked by wolves in the dark of the night. So, he had to have been unconscious the entire night, even longer.

The animals must have carried him here, but why keep him alive, he wondered. Why had they tied him up, standing upright to a wall, and to what end? Vonter looked around for clues. He was in some sort of hole in the ground, just the naked sky above him. The almost perfect circle was about 50 feet wide, and the hole must have been at last 20 feet deep. There was no way he could tell where he was. No white trees, so probably not in the White Forest.

This hole looked like an old hideout. Long buried, recently excavated perhaps. Not many items were lying around, there was an old chair that probably had not been used in a while. A broken shelf with old pottery and rags. Some large, black rocks were lying scattered on the ground, and a small table was next to him, covered with shiny and rusty knives, nails, tongs, and other torture instruments that made his stomach turn. They certainly had plans for him!

Then, he saw the animals. Or some of them, at least. He made out a fox, two wolves and a couple of other small creatures. They were stone too. Other lumps of stone suggested there had been many more. So, this was the same curse! The immortals had been killed after doing their part, getting him here? Or had something else happened?

Dirty cloth was hanging in some places on the round wall, and there were stairs leading up to the surface. The steps looked like they had grown naturally, most of them were stone, some looked like roots and sticks, even though they were more of less old and worn, it all appeared so ... fresh, as if it had been hastily created by someone. And Vonter could see now that the wall looked solid, but it was mere soil. The opening was literally a hole in the earth, so precise, someone must have cut it with a gigantic sword or something, almost surgical.

He still could not make out anything beyond the edge of his artificial horizon, so he had no idea where he was. By the light in the sky, he guessed that it had to be early morning, the sun was not visible, but probably high enough by now to vanquish the typical morning dampness.

Looking above his head, he could see that plant roots had been wrapped around his wrists, they were very tight. Again, he would have thought they had grown like this naturally, very robust, but new. That could not be. It was not natural. His ankles were fixed the same way, though he noticed that looking down hurt his head.

With both of his feet sunk down on the ground, he was able to put some weight on his left leg, the right knee did not feel fine at all, it was probably severely bruised, maybe even broken. But standing on one leg was taking off the pressure on the wrists. The smallest of movements were more painful than he expected, there were definitely lots of bruises and wounds all over his body!

He glanced over to the torture arsenal once more. Vonter took a few deep breaths. He did not have the time to panic. The restraints were too tight and strong, he would not be able to free himself.

There was nothing for him to reach to, and he was most likely not in the position to stand up, let alone walk. Maybe he did have the time to panic.

Where was Mibb? He could not see the little furball anywhere.

Maybe he got away, had followed him, and was hiding in a safe spot to get him out. He probably had a plan by now. With his sharp teeth, he could nibble through the roots and get him out!

He swallowed his panic and fear and cleared his throat quietly. With his heart beating louder and faster, he whispered: "Mibb? Are you there?"

Suddenly, from the corner of his eye, he saw movement.

But instead of the trustworthy squirrel, some of the knives and nails were lifted into the air. As if an invisible power was controlling them, they floated towards Vonter! The pointy ends were directed at him, slowly getting closer.

His breathing got heavier, and the heart was pounding. Who was doing this?

And then, without warning, the sharp metals thrusted forwards and hit him hard, the nails and knives entered his legs and arms.

A few were pushed in quickly, others slowly; a nail pushed into his stomach, a knife in his legs was even turned around sideways to make the pain more intense.

He had never felt such agony, it made him wail loudly. Not only did he not recognise his own voice, but it was also as if his inner animalistic self was forced to leave his body through his throat. He wanted out and away so badly.

Tears ran down his face, but he tried to keep his eyes open, so he could see what was happening.

The cloth to his right was lifted and from a hidden cave behind it, a young man appeared. He had brown hair that had grown out up to his shoulders, brown stubble, and dark brown eyes.

On his lean body, he wore a dark red linen shirt that looked like it had dried blood on it. The black trousers were tight, and dirty from soil and dust.

He was a little shorter than the King, but he had quite the confident look on his face. Vonter could feel that there was a dark power inside him, something very strong. His eyes showed delight and disgust at the same time.

There was a definitive reason why Vonter had been captured by this man. Was this Dragus, the infamous evil sorcerer?

"Hello. What an honour, the King, in my humble home?" his voice was soft, but cold.

"You mean, in your little outside lavatory?" Vonter replied between his teeth. His throat was dry and hurting. Not as much as the cuts and stabbings though. "Who are you, what do you want with me?" he demanded to know. "Tell me!"

The man circled him, paced around him slowly, like a tiger about to pounce. Never breaking eye contact, he just stared at the King with barely any expression other than more coldness. After a few moments, he spoke again.

"Right. You would not be able to recognise me, but we go back." he said with a dark undertone.

"We do?" Vonter had no clue what the man was talking about.

"Not you and me so much in person. But you know, your Blood. Your kin. I have been seeking revenge for hundreds of years now. The way your Blood hurt me was unbearable. And I wanted to repay the favour. Well, your family is already dead."

He was still confused. "I do not know what you want from me."

"Your family murdered my family! It was YOUR ancestors who destroyed my life! YOU created this curse I live in, and YOU are responsible for this!"

The knives in his body turned again, slowly, through the mist of pain and his tears, he saw how the man clenched his thin hands to fists and raised them up.

Nails were driven into his flesh deeper than before. He screamed again at the top of his lungs.

"Shut the FUCK up and do not interrupt me! I am not done! Your people have destroyed me, and you are going to pay for it. I have already killed thousands, in Buntin, Tramvil and your capital will be next! Your precious kingdom will be crushed. I will destroy every life in this realm, and I'll make you watch. And then, I am going to release you to live out your sad little mortal life in agony and loneliness."

This man was crazy! He clearly had the power to cause the destruction that Vonter had seen, but it was unimaginable what he was talking about! He refused to believe that this was possible.

And then, his thoughts jumped to Samjya. His Queen Bride, the woman of his dreams that he had left in his castle, would he ever see her again? If he had that much power, she was doomed, and so was everyone else he cared about. Still, he did not understand this man.

"But I do not know anything about you. How have we destroyed your life?"

"Are you not listening? Your kind. Royal Blood." He said the last word as if it was the most disgusting and delicious thing in the world at the same time.

"You know. When the King killed my family centuries ago. You know. They teach you these things in Little Prince and Princess School, do they not?" the man shouted. The disgust was mixed with a menacing sarcasm that Vonter never experienced before.

A tingling frustration grew in the back of his head. "I do not know anything about this. And how am I even the one to blame for this?"

His captor did not react at first, but he stopped pacing and stared at Vonter for a long while. And then, the fine thread of his patience had to have snapped, because he jumped at him: "LIAR!"

With his cold hands, he pressed on Vonter's throat tightly, and sealed off the flow of air. The body weight that was pushed against his stomach was applied to a rusty nail and moved deeper inside his torso.

The King became dizzy, and for what felt like a very long time, he pulled on his arms even though it was pointless. He had the impression of his wrists getting pulled apart and throat getting crushed entirely. His head was filled with a rushing sound, blood pumped through his brain in a panic.

And then, as quickly as it had started, it was over. The hands moved away, and with deep breaths, interrupted by coughing and spitting, he gasped for air. When he lifted his head, the attacker had his back turned to him. The black veil in his eyes faded, and he was able to breathe normally again after a little while.

"Please believe me, I had nothing to do with this. I do not even know which King this was, I do not know who you are."

The man faced him again and Vonter could see that something had changed. A deep sigh was audible, and their eyes met.

"Alright, I'll tell you. King Brunn killed my relatives. We were a very powerful family of sorcerers. We kept to ourselves, kept our magic pure. The humans always hated us for our magic. You know, the unknown breeds fear. Especially among the simple minded, when life is so short as yours."

Vonter vaguely remembered stories about families of sorcerers and sourceresses, who had studied the world and its natural and magical laws for thousands of years. Their magic vanished a very long time ago, no one could remember when. If he had only paid more attention to these old stories.

"Why?" Vonter immediately regretted interrupting him.

"Because we became too powerful! They were afraid in their feeble little minds! And jealous of the things that we could do! And how we made life easy for ourselves."

He snickered quietly.

"There was always friction between us and the mortals. King Brunn came to visit my father, to negotiate a truce, and for years to come, we had a good relationship.

"On my mother's birthday, they sent over food that was poisoned. Not just any poison, it was the only poison that would kill an immortal. Everyone died except me and my sister."

He paused for a moment.

"But just imagine, you come home, and you find your family dead. I was only 12 years old, my sister just a little older. In the days to come, we found out that aunts and uncles had also been killed. Just like that. We were all alone, scared, hunted, and most of all, feared and hated. We started practising our magic in secret, hiding away, not speaking for years, because we thought they would hear us and kill us. We ate wild animals and fruit so no one would see and recognise us.

"My sister wasn't ready for taking care of us like that. It drove her mad. And I understood. Humans are nothing but weak cowards. Their shame stinks up to the sky and back. Kings and Queens are the worst, sitting on their entitled seats above everyone else, making up the rules." He chuckled, but there was no amusement in his eyes.

"I swore to take revenge. We killed the King, and his precious children. One survived, and we hunted him down until we lost his trail. But we did not give up. We battled armies and climbed over the Desert Mountains, we burned and buried cities, by the Ungods, half the kingdom. Nothing could stop us.

"And nothing will. Without my sister, I must finish this. I will destroy you and every other life. I cannot stand your smell, you dirty mortal."

The young sorcerer moved to the small table a few feet from where he was standing.

"What's your name?" Vonter asked with a slight trembling in his voice. He was wondering if the full name would help him remember the story.

"Fragir Tyrus Crim." he answered without looking up.

No. That did not help.

Vonter had believed his name was Dragus? Was he lying?

Hadn't Mibb mentioned the name Fragir?

What was his plan? What was he going to do with him?

As if he had heard his thoughts, Fragir exclaimed: "I am not Dragus. Dragus is dead. He was weak, he did not deserve to live! And I am creating a new world. I am having the capital destroyed as we speak, and I am going to show you all the bodies. My wild warrior will stomp on town after town, and I will show you what it feels to lose it all. And I am going to make you watch it all. I am going to keep you alive, and slowly, painfully, you will go mad. Destroying your kind like yours destroyed mine. Until then, we have some time to kill."

He arrived at the table, but instead of picking up a knife with his hand, he moved it with his mind, just about moving his hand with minimal motion. Without any apparent effort, he let the sharp blade levitate through the air and made it stop right before it was touching Vonter's leg.

"Now, tell me about this blue witch of yours."

32

About 160 years earlier

Fragir felt lucky.

Like every morning, the chickens had a couple of eggs for his breakfast, the garden was lush with salad, potatoes, and radish, and he had caught a big fish yesterday, which would make an amazing dinner tonight. A feast. This day was going to be beautiful. He loved the mild climate by the coast, a bit of sunshine and quiet.

He had been able to live in complete isolation here ever since he could remember, far away from the troubles of the world, in this peaceful, abandoned village. The mortals had forgotten about this place, and he thought it was best to stay away from them. And he was more than content by himself. No screaming souls.

Living close to humans had been too exhausting. As a sorcerer who was versed in dealing with souls, his empathy was strong, and most of the time, thoughts and emotions could run so high that it would be too much, even for him. As a child, he had always struggled with his impeccable talent. He had been the most gifted mage of his generation by far, but it came at a great price. Of course, they had taught him how to deal with the pressure, but it was always a struggle.

Lots of memories of his young years were blurry, like his family or how he was raised – he did not even know how old he was. At least 600 years, that's how long he had been here. The only thing he did remember how much he had suffered, the pain and agony of feeling and hearing, tasting, and breathing everything and everyone around him. All by himself was the only way he could live now. He could not imagine anything else.

When he had found the Forgotten Villages as no one ever called them as they were, well, forgotten, they had been in much worse condition. A few of the smaller, more weathered houses, he completely ignored, but he had lived in and taken parts, tools, and supplies from more promising buildings to begin with.

The house he had finally chosen was the biggest of them, with a spacious kitchen, a large balcony and nice, comfortable furniture. He had repaired a lot, and it had been quite the undertaking. Sure, it was all still a bit run down, but he had made it work for himself.

Happily.

Sometimes he was surprised that it had never become boring, being all by himself in the same village for all this time. But he could not think of anything that he would miss.

With a cheerful melody on his lips, he wandered down to the sea for his daily meditation and stared at the clouds for a good while. Not only did this kill some time, but it was also a very good way to relax and focus.

On his way back, he found a flower that appeared to be quite interesting. It would look great in his house, he thought to himself. So, he unearthed the small root and took it home with him. He found a nice pot and placed it in the centre of the dinner table.

The simple life. Bliss.

For the better part of a day, he read on his balcony in the shade, until he got tired.

After a small nap, he decided to prepare for the evening and walked across the old bridge over the stream to collect some wood for the night fire.

He was almost done for the day, but he sensed something else. Something new.

Carefully, he walked towards a bush at the edge of the forest. Something was moving there, and without warning, the source of the noise stood in front of him.

A boy, well, a young man, really, barely in his twenties, dirt on his face, ripped clothes, and a missing shoe, was out of his breath and quite starved.

But there was a panic in his eyes that suggested he had not seen another man in quite some time. And the emotions he picked up from his soul were ... troubled, to say the least.

Before Fragir could say anything, the boy jumped out of the way to the left and ran away from the bridge to the Southeast.

He shouted after him: "Wait!" and the young one turned around, so Fragir took a few steps towards him. Suddenly, a huge gush of water was lifted out of the little stream and hit the sorcerer with full force from behind.

When he got back up again, fully soaked, the man was gone.

That was some power! This boy was a sorcerer just like him!

He stared at the edge of the forest where the boy had vanished. Should he have gone after him? He shrugged his shoulders. He was probably already quite far, and it was probably for the best. He was better off alone, he thought, walking back to his solitary home in the Forgotten Villages.

A few weeks later, he baked himself an apple cake using the fruit from his apple garden. It was a lovely fall day, and he was in a baking mood. After making a mess in the kitchen, Fragir went upstairs and napped some time on the balcony.

When he walked back into the kitchen, the cake was gone. Thinking that a bird or a deer might have pushed it down the windowsill, he left the house and wandered around the back. But he could not even find the plate in the grass. And then, he heard something behind him in the bushes.

He used his Composure to find the noises.

It was him!

The boy from before!

And he was so hungry.

With the power of his mind, Fragir lifted a bread roll and some goat's cheese from the kitchen table, made them float out the window, past his face and straight into the bushes.

He could sense that the boy was more than surprised, but he also sensed that he gratefully accepted the food. The sorcerer smiled and left him to himself.

As he turned around to leave him be, he could feel how the boy started to think. There was a lot of worry, and darkness. Insecurity and insincerity, even.

But Fragir sensed something else too, some greater power that he had never felt before. This young man was already a mighty sorcerer, for sure. And with that trick he pulled off the time they had met, Fragir was also sure that his element was water.

He had never met anyone like him – yes, there had been his parents and his teachers, the White Circle of Ancients, priests, and sorcerers of the same blood. But not a young boy with a display of such a strong soul.

Yes, it was his soul. It was old and powerful, very inspiring, and radiant. That boy would make quite the influential master one day!

Fragir's Composure picked up that the boy had sneaked away, back beyond the river.

He did not want to follow him; he probably had his reasons for staying away from him. And really, Fragir wanted to stay by himself. It was probably the best for him.

Again, a couple of weeks passed, and one night, during a terrible thunderstorm and times of rainfall, a knock on the door woke Fragir from his deep sleep. He checked who it was first using the sight of his Composure, and then, he went downstairs and opened the door without hesitation.

"Excuse me, good man, I am not a beggar..." he started.

The young man was entirely drenched, hungry, shivering and half naked. A large wound gaping across his chest, and blood dripping down on the wooden planks outside the door, Fragir needn't to hear another word.

He waved the boy into his home, and already commanded a jug of water, clean cloths, and some alcohol to levitate across the room to where the couch was.

He signalled the young man to lie down and tended to his injury with soft and slow movements. There was a lot of blood. Fragir cleared his throat.

"Where are you from? I have not seen you up until a weeks ago."

"I ran away. I did not do anything wrong, just wanted to get away from mor... – I mean, people. I do not like them." the boy stuttered.

Fragir smiled. "So, you have been living by yourself? Where?"

He shrugged his shoulders and looked away.

"Why did not you try and find a house, grow food, go hunting?"

"I do not know. I mean, I do not know how. And I never learned, and so, I have no money. I am very sorry; I will not be able to pay for this. ... Besides, I wanted to get away from -" he obviously felt quite embarrassed about taking on the older man's help.

"Mortals." Fragir finished his sentence.

The boy's eyes met his, and then, he squinted, sucking in air through his teeth sharply.

Fragir had not paid attention to his hands for a moment. "Sorry, I will be more careful" the sorcerer snickered softly. He turned his focus back on the wound.

"How long have you been living here?" the boy asked after a short pause.

Fragir thought about his answer for a moment. He honestly did not know.

"A lot of centuries. I stopped counting them. I also feel I need to stay away from humans. They make me feel uncomfortable, I can hear what they are thinking, and I can feel what they are feeling. It can get very messy and awful. So, that's something we have in common. One of the many things we have in common, I believe. You are very special."

This noticeably made the young man quite uncomfortable. His arms and legs became even tenser, and he inspected the vastness of the grey wall again.

"Do not be ashamed, you should embrace and nurture your powers, they can do a lot of good."

The young man suppressed a laugh. "Is that so?"

"Of course. I suspect on your own all this time, and no training, no one has ever told you that you can actually heal yourself?"

The younger man looked at him.

"It is called Composure. It is the power that holds everything together, including your bones and your flesh. It is inside every mortal and immortal being. And as a sorcerer, you can channel yours, manipulate yourself and even others. I bet at this moment you feel you cannot control your powers at all?

"Like ... they control you?" he added after another pause.

The boy turned to face the spot on the wall yet again.

"But trust me, you are always in control, whether you know it or not. You alone guide your life in the direction it is going. Take control, and you are never lost. Take control and you always have a choice.

"This is the first lesson. I suggest you have a good rest tonight, sleep as long as you need to, here, and I will make you a big breakfast when you wake up. I am more than happy to help you learn to take care of yourself, if you follow my rules and agree to work on your powers."

"Are you a Sire?" the young man's voice was still not entirely trusting.

Fragir could not help but smile. "We do not carry the silly titles of the mortals. But yes, back in my day, I had been instructed by the White Circle of Ancients to choose carefully who to train and how to train them properly. The basis is made of wisdom, honesty, and honour. You will understand soon.

"But you should get some rest first. I will explain it all tomorrow, and you can decide then. Eat this, and sleep." with these words, he made an apple fly over to the couch, grabbed the bloody cloth, and left the water for the boy to drink.

He put it all away in the kitchen and as he was climbing the stairs back up again, he heard the boy say with a quiet voice: "Dragus. ... It is my name. Dragus."

"Nice to meet you, Dragus. I am Fragir."

The next morning, Fragir checked on Dragus before he got up, and it seemed not only did the boy have amazing healing capabilities, but he also displayed a very curious nature. While the sorcerer was still upstairs, Dragus apparently had snooped through the entire ground floor and was tinkering around with his kitchen herbs.

As he came down, he saw how the young man was rearranging the teas. "What are you doing?"

Dragus was startled and looked guilty. "I'm sorry. I did not mean to impose..."

"It is okay. Breakfast?"

There was nodding, impatient waiting around the hot pan and fruit cutting, which Dragus had never done before – quite entertaining actually –, then, vigorous devouring of the fresh food, while Fragir explained the house rules he wanted his new friend to follow.

They were very reasonable and fair, and finally, after he had also explained what he would teach him, the young man agreed to stick around.

Dragus helped clear the table after the meal. When he moved the flower that Fragir had found a couple of days ago, the sorcerer said to his new pupil: "Oh, that can stay there, I picked the flower for the table."

Dragus hesitated, but then he shyly replied: "Forgive me, but this flower needs more light, less shade. It should stand on the windowsill. It will not bloom on the table."

The first few months went by quickly.

Fragir grew quite fond of his young apprentice. He only had gotten the permission to call him that a few days ago, Dragus was still convinced that he would take off very soon and continue to try it on his own again.

He saw this as a temporary measure and was not really planning on sticking around for too long. Fragir would let him, it was not his intention to pressure him into anything. He could sense the darkness still, Dragus's soul had lived through some tough whiles.

Sometimes, the rough emotions would jump at him. And despite his reservations towards his uncontrollable empathy, he endured it. Fragir felt that training the young sorcerer was worth it.

At the same time, he stressed the importance of finishing his training in magic, it was imperative to securing the stability of his powers.

Dragus would be able to achieve so much more, and the magic he would use, would be so much more powerful. And he could sense that the young man understood.

As suspected, Dragus had the strongest connection to water, and he quickly learned to regain his Composure with this element.

For years, he had controlled water without conscious intent, but now, he was able to steer his magic.

Luckily, Fragir remembered enough from his own education to responsibly teach a young one. He even remembered the exam rituals, so he felt more than confident he could pass him as a fully trained Water Sorcerer.

Dragus had trouble being patient though. Not unusual whenever the element water was involved. And more often than not, he reminded Fragir of himself when he was younger.

Stacking stones on top of each other, understanding and using the telekenisis of the Composure, meditating in the core element to increase it, potions, and herbs, and learning powerful spells, it was all tough to follow through to perfection.

Even with his talent of understanding and using the language of plants, Dragus had a long way to go to become a successful healer.

The ambition to reach the top was there, faint at first, but growing quickly.

Especially an easy success was often followed by frustration when the next task or lesson was not that easy.

And Fragir was glad that he had decided to be his mentor, and not continued his lonely life.

The company was highly appreciated and filled him with joy and pride. He finally had a purpose again.

"You know, I am very happy that I came across you, Fragir." Dragus said one day. "You are a very kind and gentle person. Helpful, considerate, and so generous. Full of wisdom and quite the resourceful teacher."

"Thank you, boy. But please concentrate on the water. You do not want it to shower down on me."

Fragir laughed.

Dragus had been with him over 3 years now, and he was wondering if he would actually leave him soon like he kept saying, or if he would stay to conclude his training.

He was hoping for the young sorcerer's sake, that the tasks, exercises, and challenges were interesting and demanding enough to quench his thirst for knowledge.

Fragir was sitting with crossed legs on a small hill, while his apprentice was standing a few feet away, staring at the round shape of water floating mid-air above Fragir's head. The amount was impressive.

He had asked Dragus to create a large ball of liquid out of thin air, and keep it contained several feet above the ground. He was now able to control as much water as you would need to fill three houses.

With all his concentration, he held it in the air, tight like a bottle.

After a while, the young sorcerer waved his hands and turned the entire form of water into a massive white cloud that drifted off blown gently West by the winds across the ocean.

Small rainbows danced across the water surface.

"Very good. And remember, it is all a circle. What goes up, comes back down, and all your actions influence this. You – ..."

"I cannot stop it; I can only change its course. I know."
Dragus smiled proudly.

"I think I am getting pretty good at this. Can we do more potions? I think they are my favourite part!"

Fragir smiled.

Of course, the answer was yes.

33

6 days ago

He did not know what was wrong. Maybe he was trying too hard. For a multitude of breaths, he had been staring at the same spot on the dark grey patch of grass. No luck in making it green again. But he did not understand what was holding him back!

Dragus was able to create water out of just air, make any plant grow faster, but to multiply a couple of grass leaves, that was impossible?

Taking a deep breath, he told himself to not let the frustration take over, he had to be gentle. Nature was a mighty force at his will, but only if he was able to control the smallest dust particle of a mountain. Fragir had him pick a single drop out of the ocean, bring it to the surface and into his hand many times. He had mastered that task, and so would he master this one. He only needed more time.

With a sigh, he decided to leave it for the day, got up and turned around to walk back to the house. Today, he had said he would prepare the evening meal, and it was already getting dark.

On his way, he picked some apples from the small orchard that he and his mentor had planted many decades ago. The trees had kept short and fruitful crowns, but that was not exactly a challenge for Dragus.

Within his first few decades with Fragir, he had tripled the size of the garden, and increased the harvest significantly. It filled him with pride to have built something this amazing and simple simultaneously with another person. He never thought he would share anything with anyone anymore. Too painful, the memories, betrayal, the rejection.

Fragir was different.

Maybe because he was the only other sorcerer that Dragus had ever met. Maybe because he was the only one who would have taken him in when he was in dire need. Or maybe because he had become a father figure without guilt, shame, or pressure, and Dragus had simply been lost and lonely. Anything that he had been imagining a family would be, he had found here, in the Forgotten Villages, surrounded by the White Forest. Where no mortal bothered to look anymore.

Sometimes, he wondered how long it would take the people to remember or rediscover this corner of their world. And then, he thought this may even have been the effect of a spell. He found it hard to believe that an entire group of villages had become so forgotten that no one ever came here. Maybe they had stories and legends about this place, but none that Dragus would have heard.

So, here they lived, at the edge of the world, moving earth and water, growing fruit and vegetables, hunting game and bore, and all this far away from the mortals and the troubles they brought.

It was a good life.

When he arrived at the house, he saw Fragir having a nap in the hammock in the front.

The book had slid off his belly and was lying pages down on the floor. Using his Composure, he determined which pages had a certain humidity to them and folded the corner of the first page that was dryer than the others, placing the book on the table. He knew Fragir would have issues finding the page again he had looked at last.

He went inside and started to prepare his stew. With precision and care, he used chicken, potatoes, carrots, celery, and the apples.

His master woke up and joined him in setting the table just moments before the food was done.

They ate in silence, Fragir was usually not very talkative after his naps, but then, they went outside to practise some more water control.

Dragus had made very good progress in his studies and practices. He was almost ready, his mentor kept saying. But he did not want things to change. They had built something powerful and peaceful here.

Taking away the long periods of days filled with training and lessons would change their days forever. They had become a nice little routine, rituals of tradition.

Whether being "ready" meant, ready for a final exam, and they would finish their lessons, or whether that meant Dragus would have to leave, he did not know, and Fragir did not say.

This uncertainty made him feel uneasy. His previous life had been uncertain for a long time, but now that he knew what being home and having a family meant, he was not ready to give that up just yet.

One morning, Fragir woke him up before dawn and asked him to meet him outside by the old oak tree. He suddenly knew this was the day. His moment. The ultimate test.

"So, you have learned all I can teach you, young student."

"I am not that young anymore, old man. 186 years, to be exact." Dragus grinned.

"Very true. And today, you will prove to me if you have mastered your magic, your element and how powerful you have become."

"What happens then?"

"Patience, my boy. Let's focus on the task at hand. I have three challenges for you. This is what my mentor asked of me before I became what I am today, and this is what his mentor asked of him too. This final trial of a sorcerer's abilities goes back millennia and has proven to bring forth the most powerful magic throughout the land."

Dragus's smile had vanished.

He suddenly felt so small.

After all, he was just himself.

A young, naïve man, who dabbled with water, plants, and herbs. He had fought off bears with natural explosives, grown a fertile garden, redirected rivers and cured animals of life-threatening diseases and injuries. But this had all been achieved only with the support of his mentor.

"So, what is the first task you would like me to do?" he wanted to know.

"We will test your Composure first, then, you will prove yourself in your potion magic talents, and lastly, your element, water. And you will have only until sundown to complete these tests."

Fragir took off his scarf and blindfolded his apprentice. He used a second scarf to make sure the ears were entirely covered too.

In his mind, Dragus heard the older man's voice: "I want you to unearth the old oak in the old market square and plant it down the hill by the seashore."

He could not believe what he was hearing! Of course, the Composure made it possible for him to see, feel and touch things, but he had never lifted a tree out of the ground! Let alone without his natural senses. While Fragir was turning him around a couple of times to make him dizzy, he wondered how long this might take him.

Immediately after he stopped spinning, he focused his Composure on the tree. He sensed Fragir's heartbeat to his right, sitting on a stone, just watching, calm and patient, as always.

Dragus found the oak a couple of moments later. He touched it all with his magical sense, from the leaves on the top to the bark and the density of the stump, and all roots from the thickest end to their thinnest tips.

He tried to get a feeling not only for the overall dimensions, but also for the weight. It was hardly possible with all this earth around; the roots were too complex and deep. He had to calculate how much force to apply to the weight of the surrounding soil and the fine roots in order not to damage them.

Instead of focussing too much on the tree, he moved on to the beach. The sand stretched from the hill to the ocean for several hundred feet.

Taking the tides into account, he thought a good spot should be around 40 feet from the hill. There was still a bit of adjacent vegetation, and deep below, he could sense an underground water channel, which would provide enough salt-free nutrition for the old oak. The acid levels in the soil were also quite like the current spot of the tree, so the transition would not be too difficult for this mature plant.

Dragus started digging. Not with his hands, of course, but in his mind, he made the sand move apart and he pushed deeper and deeper. After a while, he had produced a hole that was 15 feet wide in diameter and a solid 20 feet deep, almost reaching the water channel.

When the Water Sorcerer was happy with the size, he spent a couple of breaths' time softening the ground in the hole, to make it easier on the tree to grab hold of its new surroundings.

Going back to the oak with his Composure's focus, he noticed Fragir's unchanged heartbeat again. His demeanour was so serene. Dragus knew that he was able to sense everything that he sensed. And he was most likely tapping into his soul and thoughts to see the method that Dragus used to go about the task.

He started digging around the old tree trunk, laying bare the largest roots first. He opened the earth up in a large area, so the wooden underground network was exposed. It took him longer than he expected. His forehead became sweaty. He had never used his Composure like this, but he knew that he could do it. In his mind, he could feel Fragir smile. For him, it was hard to tell why, he was not empathic like his mentor.

But Dragus concentrated on the oak again and grabbed the roots at the bottom. He also secured the tree further up top and pulled on the twigs and leaves at the highest points spreading the lifting points evenly so no branches would rip off.

He did not want the tree to tip upside down mid-air, and he could already feel how the weight was in a delicate balance throughout the object of his attention. Focussing all his strength on raising the tree out of its known surroundings, he forgot everything else around him.

Only when the oak began to move up, he actually understood what he was doing. A tree that was hundreds of years old was ripped out of its ground, the home that it had for centuries, away from all its dependent symbionts, to which it had grown attached over decades. He should not really challenge his mentor on this, but for the tree, it was not the best thing to do.

He could feel the lush leaves, withered, resistant bark and strong roots. It was amazing how he could experience the weight, texture, and vitality of this tree in its entirety. This was such a unique moment, one that he most likely would never get to feel again.

Slowly, he moved the oak across the grass and beyond the edge off the hill. Dragus could sense the effect of how its weight put a strain on his Composure, and the pearls of sweat on his forehead that started to connect and gave in to gravity.

By the time the tree was just levitating above the newly dug hole at the beach, his face, the neck, and his back were quite sweaty. Fatigue crept into his mind.

But with a lot of confidence still, he moved the tree down into its new habitat. Gently, without putting too much pressure on the fine ends of the roots, he let the tree down as slowly as he could, held it in position for a moment, and pushed soil and sand back into the ground, surrounding the tree trunk and its roots.

By making sure the earth was not too tight and pressed around the tree, it would make it a lot easier for the roots to find their places. Up top, where the tree had a thicker bark, he used more pressure to secure the weight of the crown and protect the tree against a high tide and storms.

And suddenly, Dragus realised that he was done.

He could not believe his eyes, when he took off his blindfold. The tree had moved to his will. Well, to his mentor's bidding.

Fragir was pleased. "Well done, apprentice."

"Let me finish it properly." Dragus suggested, and he closed the hole in the ground where the tree had been before. He also moved some of the larger mushrooms and fern plants close to the oak again, so they would not dry out without their symbiont.

Fragir patted his shoulder in appreciation.

"Let's move on to the next task, I suppose this will be rather easy for you." the older sorcerer said.

"So why do not you think of something more challenging?"

"Because this is what you are good at anyway. The best that I have ever seen." he answered, smiling yet again. He handed him a note. "Mix these potions without using your Composure. All the fresh and natural ingredients needed must not be taken out of our stock at home. Tools and containers may be taken from the house. And remember, you only have until sundown."

Dragus wondered how it was already after noon. He was not aware that it had taken him almost half a day to move the tree! And on the piece of paper, he could see quite the list of potions. He would have to get going right now and rush himself.

After all, he did not know what the remaining task would ask of him and how much time he would need for its completion.

Quickly, he set off into the woods to get the first herbs and plants, wood types and animal fur and claws. He had to kill two rabbits, a boar and a stag with his bow and arrow, which cost him quite some time.

Many of the ingredients were easy to find, but some, he had to dig deep, climb high and run far.

Another wuarter of a day passed easily, and he still was not quite finished.

Naturally, only the potions' names were listed, but he knew all of them by heart. He only had to think about what was required for a split breath. This really was his thing, which made it a lot easier for him. He had this natural aptitude for potions and herbs.

The props and tools he needed, he was allowed to retrieve from the house, bottles, bags, spoons, corks, satchels, and such likes.

He placed them all into a box and ran back up the hill. He used the small dent in the ground as a fireplace, stacked some firewood and prepared the ingredients he had to heat up.

While they were roasting in a pan, he rushed down to the beach and collected the rest of the herbs and rocks he needed.

For the next long time of breaths, he cooked, mixed, and mashed together what he had to, and prepared the spells and potions. When he had finished the full list, the sun was quite low, he maybe had just a little time left for the last part of his test.

Fragir checked the list twice and nodded in agreement with his student. "Well done, Dragus. All accounted for, and as instructed, without Composure."

"We do not have a lot of time left before sundown; I should learn what you ask of me next." he wanted to know.

"Yes, but I have all the confidence that you will be able to do this in the last breaths of daylight."

Fragir positioned himself between the dying fire and the newly planted oak and took a deep breath. "The third part of your final test will prove how well you can control your element. As you know, there is a significant amount of water in our bodies. Using only your power over the water, I want you to strike me down. Push me as hard and far as you can."

It took Dragus a moment to process what he just heard. He hesitated.

Fragir smiled. Again. It was a very trusting, trusted smile. He was serious.

"But I thought using magic against another sorcerer is forbidden?" Dragus had a very bad feeling about this.

"It is, but you have my explicit permission. You will only use the push on the water that's coursing through my body. Just push me to the ground and your final exam will be over and passed."

He was not sure at all what to do. What if he hurt his mentor? It had to hurt at least a little bit when the water in his body was used to control his physical shell, for a mortal that must be excruciatingly painful, he thought. He had never tried to focus on water in his body, let alone someone else's, this was a whole new level for him. And he didn't have a lot of time left!

"Fragir, please. I do not think I can do it. I do not want to do it. Think of something else, anything else, please. I fear this will hurt you more than we both expect."

His mentor placed a hand on his shoulder. "Dragus, if I did not believe you could do it, I would not ask you to do it. And I will be fine, trust me on this. Hit me!"

Dragus blinked away small tears and tried to overcome his insecurity. With doubtful focus, he tried to get a sense for the water inside Fragir. "Do not doubt this. You need to be in this a hundred percent! Just ignore the rest, do not focus on me, just on the water."

He tried, he really tried. For many breaths, he fought the urge to turn around and run back to the house. There was no use, he had to admit it to himself. He could not do this, he should not be doing this, it was wrong.

As he turned around and a shudder ran down his back, Fragir's tone became sharper: "Dragus, you need to do this. All you have learned about magic will be for nothing, and I will not let you undertake another test again. It is imperative that you finish your challenges."

"Yes, I know, but I will not push you, I cannot!" his heart was flooded with cold and hot emotions, he was not sure what to feel anymore.

"Forget your emotions, just get on with it, the sun is almost down!"

"No!" he shouted this time. He had never shouted at Fragir before. He also noticed how he was shaking. What was happening?

"Do not do this Dragus, do not get in the way of yourself. You know you want to master your element, and you need to master your element. This is the most important task! And you must learn to put your personal feelings aside, no matter what the task at hand."

The apprentice turned around to his friend again. "This makes sense. It is logical, but I have never used my magic against you, and you know, you have taught me never to do it – I cannot go through with it!"

Fragir suddenly stepped forward and pushed his shoulders back so hard that Dragus fell on his back to the ground. He had not expected that. But the older sorcerer was taller and stronger than him.

On the ground, looking up to Fragir's determined eyes, he decided to give this another try. He got up, and pulled his element focus together again.

He could sense the fluids, all the acids, blood, and plasma, and he tried to get into the tiniest cells. At this point, Fragir could potentially feel him touching around inside, but there was not much of a physical effect based merely on Dragus's probing yet.

Focussing on this was not easy. He had to concentrate on many details and movements. All thoughts and feeling had to be blocked out entirely. Only then, he could see what he was doing. Long moments passed without anyone saying a word.

Doubt and frustration, even confusion about the whole reasoning behind this washed over him again. He did not want to do this.

"Stop thinking doubt and worry. Make this happen right now. You are ready." And Dragus let it go.

He pushed without holding back.

It was so easy, suddenly.

A scream of despair and relief came across his lips, and he opened his eyes.

He saw Fragir thrusted through the air several feet and right into the crown of the old oak! The young apprentice was shocked and amazed at his power. He felt so drained and exhilarated in equal parts!

Almost completely hidden inside the leaves, with quite the velocity in his flight, the old sorcerer had to have hit the tree quite hard. But he was smiling. "Well, congratulat- ..." he started, but was immediately interrupted.

A blinding, dark red light appeared in his eyes, illuminating the surrounding leaves in the tree. Loud, earth-shattering thunder was heard and a short breath later, a bright red flash emitted from Fragir's body, burning away all leaves and twigs of the poor old tree.

Another set of thundering cracks were heard, and a shock wave hit Dragus so hard, that he was blasted back a few feet. Worse even, he bummed his head against a rock!

He sensed his Composure was low. The water was too far for him to refill it.

With a buzzing in his head, and feeling almost sick from dizziness, he lifted himself off the ground again, and he saw a red, glowing, brightly sizzling Fragir levitate out of the dead tree towards him.

His entire aura had changed. Dragus did not recognise his friend and mentor at all. The eyes were suddenly cold, no light, no hope, just hatred, pure hatred. He emitted a darkness, full of pain and rage. The way he held his arms, and his head was on his neck, he looked like a different person altogether.

And his voice was different. Deeper.

"Well, I have to say, it is good to be myself again. I guess I must thank you, before I kill you, you whiny little embarrassment." he said just before he arrived in front of Dragus.

"What? What happened?" he stammered.

"You lifted the curse. No idea how, but I'm myself again."

He did not understand.

Fragir had always been someone else?

How was that even possible?

That must have been a trick!

Another test?

"I cannot wait to rip you apart!" the earth sorcerer said, getting ready for his attack.

Dragus felt the water call him, but Fragir was in his way.

The dark sorcerer would never let him pass.

Was the only way back into the Forest?

He looked around. No hiding. No weapon.

"This is the part when you start running before I kill you." Fragir whispered.

Dragus believed him.

34

Sahd knew they were too late to win this battle long before they got there. As soon as they had passed the small hills behind the river, it had become clear to everyone that the capital had taken a lot of damage, and most of its army had been killed already. There was so much smoke and fire, it was hard to tell how many soldiers they were up against.

The closer they got, the bigger became his worry. They could hear the loud rumbling of walls and buildings being crushed, and when they were almost there, it was so loud, he could barely hear the men shouting over it organising their formations.

Smoke drew teary drops into his eyes, and more than once, he coughed because of it. Just outside the Southern walls, his horse stepped over the first dead. Severed limbs, crushed heads, blood everywhere, it was a massacre. Sometimes, he would see legs or arms twitching from underneath large parts of a building. A small child was crushed in between a tree and a big stone, and one woman was so flat that she had to have been waltzed over by a very heavy carriage, both as lifeless as most of the bodies they encountered.

Sahd also spotted very few survivors, hiding away behind stones and half-destroyed buildings. A small group of people were running down the roads to the East, hoping to find shelter in the woods or the next village maybe. He signalled for the healers to be called to assist the wounded, but knowing his diligent soldiers, they were already on it.

Draidr had vanished from his right-hand side to lead the Second Division from a slightly different angle, but Sahd could still make out his loud voice over the sounds somewhere in the smoke.

Suddenly, he noticed Grunia next to him. She tried to smile nervously and raised her voice.

"Where is the enemy?" she shouted.

"I do not know, we need to get to the castle!" he replied, going into his horse's sides. Before he turned his horse to get up the hill, he let a third of his Division fall behind so they would secure the South, sent one third around the front gate to get in from the West, and commanded the rest to follow him and Grunia.

"Are you sure you want to be in front with me? What about Ca'on?" he screamed at the top of his lungs. She waved his questions away and raised her sword, ready to follow him.

"Where did you learn to fight, woman?" he wanted to know.

She almost smiled: "My father was a soldier before he had his own business. And I learn quickly."

"You're not scared?"

"You are not, General?" she asked right back, but Sahd could tell that she was putting a brave face on to mask her fear. It was probably best not to think about it too much. He barely did.

Climbing over fresh ruins, jumping over bodies and splintered wood, his horse had trouble getting through the mess. This was similar to Buntin, but a lot hastier, as if the force that was crushing the capital was rushing it, or it was not paying attention to it all. But there were a lot more dead.

And suddenly, a breeze parted the thick cloud of smoke and gave way to a horrifying scene than let chills run up down Sahd's back.

The inner walls to the castle were breached in two spots, massive holes each.

A giant force had crushed its way through buildings like the girl's school, the blacksmith's home and one of the biggest warehouses in the capital. Inside the walls, lots of market stalls, people and stone constructions flattened beyond recognition, fires everywhere and stones big like houses that only at a second glance were recognisable as part of something else.

Startled, he had to stop his horse, which also most definitely saved his life.

Grunia stopped next to him, and she got especially lucky. With a loud rumbling sound, a small house rolled from his left to the right just behind what was left of the walls right before he went through. The massive construction missed Grunia's mount by just a few inches, and it stumbled backwards a few steps.

Not even five feet in front of Sahd, the attacker appeared in the smoke. And it became apparent why the destruction was such a devastatingly large area throughout the city.

It was an at least fifteen houses high and five houses wide, black stone creature, fuming with energy and as fast as a raging bear, with two small legs that were easily hidden by the debris of the flattened entrance hall of the castle. Four enormous arms swung through the air and punched their way through everything that was in front of them.

The monstrosity had something of a face too, but the two relatively small lights in its shapeless head were only accompanied by a large gaping hole. It reminded Sahd of the stone warrior who had attacked and chased them back in the White Forest, only this was the grotesquely ugly, bigger, and stronger brother from some nightmare.

And just one short instant after they had stopped before entering the inner walls, this thing was turning around like a tornado, hitting, and crushing everything in its wake. A fruit stand flew just past them, merely a foot away from Grunia's horse, which reared up and almost threw her off.

Hot air was pushed in their direction as the thing turned its head, looking over the remnants of the walls as it noticed the three hundred soldiers behind Sahd. He ordered to attack and regretted it two breaths later.

While he let a few soldiers take positions to the left and right, the monster had turned around fully, getting ready for its blow. But his men did not hesitate and flanked it from two sides.

Unlucky for most, the punches and strikes of the giant stone fists were catastrophic. With just one blow, it killed dozens of men, and its actions did not even look very strenuous.

Quickly, Sahd saw half of his Division either crushed like foul fruit or land on the floor with broken necks. That thing was ruthless!

From behind it, he could see Draidr's Second Division climbing up the hill to attack from behind, but it must have sensed the approach. With another round swing it killed at least two hundred soldiers within mere breaths.

Sahd stayed back at first; he saw Grunia was still struggling with getting her horse under control, and he needed to get a better view of what was happening in the castle. He had to check for Vonter or Samjya.

Going the long way around, he rode his horse up on the steep hill just between the gardens and jumped off to climb the balconies. While the attacker was busy with the army, he climbed up the fences and swung himself onto the first platform. He entered the corridor through the small kitchen window and rushed through the empty rooms. Even the dining hall was empty. From the inside the battle noises sounded pretty far, but ever so often, the foundation or the walls of the castle would be hit, and then, it all shattered like in an earthquake. After running down corridor after corridor, he reached the main stairs.

The entrance hall had been half destroyed, and he could see the stone warrior easily, ploughing through human bodies just a few feet from where he was now. Climbing over stones and broken furniture, he aimed to get up the stairs, but then he stopped halfway. On the top of the stairs, he saw a woman. One of the Royal servants.

"Hello?" he shouted up to her. She barely reacted. Her eyes focused on him, but her expressionless face made him nervous. She had been crying for a long time. Her dress was creased, with many blood streaks and smears on it. Her hands shivered uncontrollably. "What's your name?" he shouted over the noise.

She had to think about it, or it took her a few moments to get her head straight. "I'm Yandra."

Sahd remembered that name. She was Samjya's friend.

"What happened?" he asked, fearing the obvious answer.

"I failed her. She left and never came back. She left us to die." she stammered with a dry, crackling voice.

"Who did? Samjya?" Sahd asked.

He slowly ascended until he was on the same level as her. When he almost reached her, her eyes caught up with his, slowly, filled with tears.

"She was in my care, and I failed her. Everyone died because she left."

"I heard what happened, how she averted the first attack and saved the capital. Where is she now?" he gently put his hands on Yandra's shoulders.

She started weeping, and her knees gave in.

Holding her steady and turning around to the open front of the building, he thought how he did not have time for this.

Samjya was clearly not here, nor were her fantastical powers, so they had to come up with a plan to save as many people as possible. He thought retreat was the only option by now.

Without warning her, Sahd clasped Yandra's upper body and legs, pulled her up and carried her down the stairs.

As the monster was a bit further from the castle now, he figured using the front entrance was safe enough. He could see the numbers of soldiers shrinking around the monster's feet, but he did not have time to think about that now. He had to find more survivors.

"Where is Sire Graynor? What is with the Royal Guard? Any others?" he shouted at her while he exited through the large hole in the building front.

Yandra only looked down at her bloody dress and whimpered: "Gone. Everyone's …"

Rushing down the ruins and climbing down the debris of the walls, he saw Grunia, who was doing something in the middle of the marketplace. When she saw him, she waved him over.

"Help me!" she only shouted, pulling on a large board stuck in the ground.

Sahd sat Yandra on the side and saw how the wood had wedged a woman's leg into the ground, leaving her immobile. Without hesitation, he assisted Grunia to push it up, and free the woman. She let out a cry, but the stone warrior was distracted enough not to hear it.

"I found this merchant and his family; they have secured a carriage! Let's get them in and out of the city." the young seamstress suggested. "Where is the rest of the Royal Army?"

"All gone. We need more power. The army is not strong enough." Sahd replied, while he pushed Yandra onto the open wagon despite her protesting. Some more people had seen them and had taken refuge in the old cart. This was hardly a carriage.

"You should go with them; you are not that experienced with the sword, and this will turn very ugly!" he urged her to go with the others.

But Grunia turned around, hit the horse on its back to make it run out of the danger zone, and declared: "I found a catapult that should still work. It looks like you will need someone to operate it with you."

There was an idea! This might at least inflict some damage. Sahd had been desperately trying to come up with something to attack this thing. Their army was entirely useless!

He followed the young woman back to the castle and helped her get some stones off the installation. It was one of the older models, more robust and slower than the newer catapults, but it would do its job splendidly.

They did not see much ammunition, but he could easily stack up some stones that had come off the walls. Grunia turned out to be more than useful, she knew how to get the catapult ready for the shot and used the right knots to secure it! She even found some oil and suitable cloth that they could light up.

"Told you, fast learner." she grinned.

Some shouting caught Sahd's attention just as he was about to adjust the angle of their weapon.

He saw Draidr running towards them. Sahd stopped on top of the catapult and in the direction of his friend. The monster was just behind him, killing soldiers and destroying the capital.

"Retreat! We must retreat!" his fellow soldier screamed.

Sahd shouted back: "We are using the catapult!"

Draidr was almost with them now. "No, Sahd, there is no use. This thing is too powerful, we cannot fight it. We have lost almost every living soul in this damned city. We need to get out of here. Find Vonter and Samjya."

"If we do not try to kill it, it will move on to the next city and the next! We need to try." Sahd exclaimed and stepped back, ready to fire the catapult. Grunia nodded, and Draidr went aside to make room for them to rotate the machine.

When he and the young woman thought the catapult to be in a good position, he loaded it up and waited for the right moment to pull the lever. Just instants before the monster got ready for another tornado attack, they fired.

The rocks hit the monster full force, and made it tumble. The men cheered and rushed closer, Sahd could see many arrows with ropes on them, trying to wrap around its neck to pull it down, some fire, and spears. They had just been waiting for a chance like this to bring the thing to its knees.

Unfortunately, the four arms were quite useful to prevent the monster from falling entirely, and without any effort whatsoever, it was able to keep its balance.

Worse even, its rage was fuelled. With a loud roar, it turned towards the three single defenders, and got ready for a sprint leaving the roughly 100 soldiers behind it.

"Run!" Draidr's voice was shrieking.

As Sahdor and Grunia were knocked off the wall of it breaking, he saw Draidr vanish behind a wall of rubble and smashed into the ground by one of the black fists. He could not have survived that.

35

She had known and felt it long before she had reached the top of hill. Not only was the black cloud of smoke a dead giveaway, but it was also only logical whoever was behind the capital attack to retaliate. Samjya might have killed the first attacker, but now that the enemy had sent more, it was very clear: they wanted to crush her kingdom.

From above the valley, she could see it all. How the army was almost fully defeated within instants, and how buildings, landmarks and castle walls were destroyed in the process. Bugs.

For a long time, she just stood there and watched. The image had something quite calming to it. The loud sounds of battle and destruction, and the images of fires, smoke and the monster's swings and jumps throughout the capital were quite beautiful in the morning's sun. She had been out for so long, keeping away from bugs, trying to find Vonter. But she was not able to sense him anywhere near her. Only when she did not find him in the Planes of Llamar or near Buntin, she decided to return to the capital. Maybe he was down there, defending and fighting this new attacker.

What kind of force was this? Did the bugs bring this upon themselves? After all, the land was hers now. They should bow down to her and her power. And anyone threatening her land should be punished.

She could not care less about the pesky bugs. They were just breathing, eating, screwing, crying, and feeling just too damn much. It was more than annoying. She grew impatiently upset with herself and the bugs. What was their purpose anyway, why were there so many of them? All they ever did was always for themselves, no regards to nature, no respect for any other forces in this world. Everything was so loud and tough all the time. Everything was so damn important to them. Because it was *them*. Bugs.

Her skin was crawling with uneasy frustration, and her hair just would not stay out of her face! With a deep sigh, she brushed her blonde-blue mane back, and she tugged her dress down while she looked up.

Wouldn't it be amazing not having to walk? Maybe she could just fly? Fly away from all of this, and never come back, yes, that's what she would love to do.

It would be amazing not to feel anything anymore, and just be away. It pained her to think of her father. And it pained her even more that Vonter, the love of her miserable life, had left her just like he had left her family to die.

Samjya wanted to find him though. She wanted to face him one more time. She had to find out if he had this all set up for her, to find nothing but pain and misery, or if he really loved her and was simply too busy to send her a message. The King was likely dead by now, lost in battle forever, probably even crushed by one of these stone monsters. If not, she would want to have a word.

But she would not let this demon destroy her kingdom.

She decided to stop this destruction and kill it. And then, to find whoever was behind it and kill them too. This was her world, and hers alone. She would not let anyone or anything else take control over it.

As she descended into the valley, she could feel the intensity of pain and suffering in her head grow. Ugh, it was so annoyingly stressing. These bugs should just stop.

She realised that she was floating! She did not even have to think about it. It was like flying! With her feet just a few inches above the ground, she moved quickly and smoothly towards the capital.

The destruction was very impressive. The city, just like Buntin, was practically flattened, houses, churches, mansions, shops, and all the other silly things that the bugs had come up with in their lifetimes. Just wood and stone walls around them while they celebrated, killed, prayed, and abused privately. As if anyone else cared about the bugs in their dirty little holes.

The new stone attacker was a lot larger and wider though! The legs were at least twice as thick, and this time, it had four arms that punched and swung independently, inflicting a multiple amount of damage all around!

Samjya reached the inner walls when it was about to jump down on the building again. The front entrance hall and the main body of the castle had already been crushed.

With an easy, swift hand gesture, she threw a small ice ball at it. The crackling energy formed inside her fist without her even thinking about it. And just as quickly as the energy came to be, it was already released and shooting through the air. It was not a very powerful blast, but it caught the black giant's attention when it hit its massive shoulders.

Something happened when it turned around. It ... recognised her. *He* recognised her. Was this the same entity that had attacked the capital before? There was something ... *someone* very familiar behind these hot eyes of the stone monster. A slow, dark growling grew louder, like a dog that would try and get more and more intimidating. It did not work on her, and that was probably what made him even angrier.

The demon got ready to jump her, and he did!

He used his lower arms to lift himself off the ground with a quick bounce, and his weight turned him into an earth-shattering cannon ball.

Of course, it was not difficult for Samjya to evade this, and she already created a few cannon balls herself drawing the cold atmosphere around together with her new powers and making up sharp, freezing, white and blue weapons out of thin air.

His attempts to dodge these attacks were quite successful, but it also meant that his four arms were busy being swung around, and she would not be able to get close. Up in the air, it was easier to keep a safe distance. She was flying! Effortlessly!

"Samjya!"

She summoned more and more spears, ice balls, spiky nets, and frozen shrapnel pieces up in the air ready to rain down. When she had quite the arsenal floating around her, she closed her eyes for a breath's time to concentrate on getting enthralled with power herself. She let everything she had fall on her enemy. Crushing ice and hot stone clashed in whirring explosions and shattering rumbles.

Circling her opponent just a few feet above the ground, she was careful to stay out of his arms' reach. Pulling out all energies that she could pick up on in the sky and around the ruins, she covered herself in and outside of her body. The cold gave her a certain amount of comfort, and was energising, electrifying her.

The humidity around her created a static that was ready for her to burst. And just when she sensed her weapons to almost have been used up, she opened her eyes again and dived in for the attack. In between the wildly swinging arms, she swooped onto the monster's head and unleashed the full power that she had stored by punching the skull. The impact was immense.

Her swings unloaded in loud bangs, and the combination between hot and cold temperatures sizzled around her fists and arms. With each punch, she dealt more and more damage, cracking and freeze burning the black stone! While his arms were still veering off the cold bullets, balls, and spears, she had almost bashed in the hard, clunky head.

Samjya was hit unexpectedly with the back of one of the hands. She swirled through the air, then caught herself about ten feet away from the giant. He turned his head immediately, while she stabilised her flight mid-air getting ready to rain the next wave down on him.

But this time, he changed his strategy and let the ice hit him on all sides. Instead of blocking them, he rolled and jumped forward and chased her across the Royal courtyard, destroying more constructs and plants in his way. And he was a lot quicker than she expected!

"Samjya!"

It was just about to throw a rock at her. With a quick wave of her hand, Samjya destroyed that rock quickly using a white power ball of ice. She could tell, by looking into the eyes in his flat face that he was thinking about what he should do next. But that did not take very long.

The stone monster grabbed rocks and large stones from the ground and threw them up to Samjya. As soon as they left his hands, he picked up the next ones and threw them up. Easily, she dodged and destroyed the first few rocks, but soon, it was like a rain from below. The thing was digging itself in, it would probably raise all the ruins if it could.

Samjya hardly had time to shoot back. Occasionally, she managed to bolt an ice ball down, maybe a spear, but the attack was becoming more and more fast paced.

"Samjya!"

The first time she got hit, she brushed it off. It did not hurt. But she soon got struck by rocks and other objects more often, and then, a big one really hurt. From one moment to the next, the upside-down rain stopped, and all she could see was dust and smoke beneath her. And then, the attack reached a new stage.

From within the clouds beneath her feet, she saw movement. Carefully, she descended in the hopes of seeing what her opponent was up to, when small, rock-solid hands grabbed her ankle.

Amid the mist, the warrior had divided himself up into several small ones, and they had climbed on top of each other to reach her – with success.

The top stone soldier grabbed her ankle and they let themselves fall! While Samjya was pulled to the ground, she saw at least a hundred small stone men. The giant was gone, and she could sense a small fraction of his energy inside the others.

She hit the ground hard, being distracted like she was, and suddenly, she was surrounded by the black, smoky soldiers. Quickly, the Queen Bride jumped to her feet and found herself attacked from all sides. Punches, kicks, the new army became quite the curse!

Samjya grew impatient. This was getting tedious. With a couple of large radius blasts of ice and wind, she pushed back, repelling all stones, until she had some breathing room around herself. It took her some time, and quite some energy to push them back.

There were so many!

Taking aim to strike the ugly bastards down for good, she created icy bullets and shot them around. One by one, she pierced their stone bodies and shattered them into pieces.

Her energy was fluctuating under the enormous pressure, but she hardly paid attention to that. While she was shooting all around, she started to collate cold just above the ground to freeze their feet. Covering the lower half with thick, dry ice, they were not able to move around like before. Their legs were stuck to the ground, and they started to realize what was happening, because they tried punching the ice off their bodies. Samjya was quicker.

Within a few moments, she had them all covered in thick, unbreakable ice. As soon as the things could not move anymore, she levitated back up into the air.

"Samjya!"

She smiled down into those tiny little lights inside the stone and ice and crafted a freezing whirlwind between her hands.

Mounted with hardened ice picks ruins from the castle, and other debris that she picked up around her, she started to push her new wave of attack into the frozen stone army, burning and piercing their skulls and bodies. Through the icy barrier, she could feel the vibration of their pained screams below, muffled and still roaring.

These were live bugs, tortured souls, she realised. Condemned to do someone's bidding. She did not care.

"SAMJYA!"

Drilling further into the stone shells, she was able to sense the heat inside. There were so many souls in them, heating and charging the stones, and she was intending to bring them all out.

She broke out in sweat, and her chest became soaking wet working through the massive material. The thick, hot stone was no match for her cold, hard fists channelling cutting winds and punches. And just as she was about to stop for an instant to catch her breath, she went through!

Shrill, deeply resonating, and hot and cold souls blasted out of the small openings, in one soldier first, then the next, and the next. Their life essence rushed into the sky.

Samjya could not let them get away and being assimilated again. She froze them mid-air. Like flying balloons that suddenly got extremely heavy, they dropped to the ground. But these were no balloons, the shattering burst through the air like a multi-echoed howling. She had to make sure that these things would not come back to life.

She was probably freezing hundreds of souls, and the flow of light orbs ebbed. She concentrated her energy on filling the remaining moving stones entirely with ice and pressurising them. A last surge in her power let not only the stones burst, but also her own ice cover, the big flameless explosion destroyed it all into a million different pieces. Debris of ice and rocks was scattering the ruins and hitting the few still standing walls.

Then, silence.

The stone soldiers were gone, disassembled, destroyed, crushed, or exploded. She looked around. A few bugs had emerged from their cover and stared at her in disbelief, fear? They did not understand her powers. And they never would, she thought.

There were not many survivors at all, the entire capital was flat like the ground. There was just half a house, a bit of walls here and there, and only a small part of the castle left, the rest was ruins and fire.

"Sa…mjya!"

Who was that? Had she been hearing this voice before?

She was still puzzled by all these thoughts and emotions around her. Mostly pain and suffering, some relief. But she felt something else, too. She turned around to locate the source.

It was one of the bugs feeling something. Loudly.

Why was that so distracting, what was her problem? She should not be experiencing emotions at all. It was wrong.

Samjya's glance brushed the ground around the ruins. A handful of bugs had survived the attack and were rushing West to safety.

But she could not quite pinpoint the direction where this strong emotion was from.

She looked around, and at first, she could not see anyone who was close enough, who would dare to be close enough. While she was floating back down, she noticed a bug, long, brown hair, under a large piece of ice shrapnel and surrounded by dark red blood.

She had been pierced with the sharp end and pushed down by its weight. Her face was somehow familiar. But she could not think of how and why.

"Samjya! My dearest friend. What happened to you?" the bug sighed under great pain. Samjya could feel the amount of discomfort that if this had been her, would have made her cry out in agony. But now, she was much stronger. Now, she was not even fazed by this bug's injuries and her suffering.

"Samjya, you're bleeding."

The Queen looked down on herself. Her dress was full of blood and dirt. She realized she was having nosebleeds, quite badly.

And that was not all.

Her arms and legs had cuts and bruises on them. She truly had not been aware of this. There was no pain. No bother.

She did not feel a thing, physically. But all the emotions and thoughts of the bugs were still calling out to her, reeling her in, telling her to listen and ... help?

No, she had defended her kingdom. The enemy was gone, and the danger was over. For now.

She could not locate Vonter, and all she wanted now, was to get answers. And get to the ones responsible for this! She wanted to kill them.

She did not have the patience to deal with pesky bugs. Without paying any more attention to any of them, she turned around, floated away, just a few feet above the ground.

Southeast again. Just away from all these feelings.

She did not miss a thing she used to know.

She was going up to a place where the world was small. No one had to know.

36

Yandra had watched her old friend, the witch. She had been fighting like a demonic whirlwind, a fury with magical snow powers, suffocating the stone warriors in ice and driving out their possessing ghosts. She had also caused the destruction that injured her.

Hit by shards of frozen masses, Yandra had been pinned down and stabbed many times.

But now that Samjya's demonic face had vanished from her ill-defined field of vision, the icy sharpness was mixed with warm syrup.

Yandra did not feel any pain anymore.

There was no physical sensation, and the emotional scars were all gone. All her thoughts washed away with the feelings in her limbs and her heart.

Wishing she could have been there for her friend earlier, better. Staying true to her promise to Samjya's father in making sure she would let nothing get in her way of caring for his daughter.

Even her regrets of not getting through Sire Graynor's protective armour and start a romance of her own, it all went away like the blizzard making space for the warm summer winds. Smooth, warming winds.

She knew the warmth was blood.

But that was the Gods' plans, was not it?

She knew Samjya could have saved her.

But she was not her friend anymore. Just like that. She had not heard her shout.

And now, Yandra's voice was silent. There was no strength left.

Warmth dissipated once more, and she was aware of one final physicality.

An icicle, bleeding her out while she was unable to shout her name.

***

The little squirrel was not able to enjoy the sunshine warming his pelt after the soul freezing night and morning he had. He could not forget the looks on his friends' faces when they turned to stone. He could not forget the pleasure Dragus took in killing. He could not forget how lucky he had been to have survived. Or maybe unlucky? Of course, he felt guilty, he should have died with them.

Mibb's anger was not only directed at himself, but also at Sihgr, who had put everyone else in danger without thinking about the risks. He would have never even thought of a deal with the sorcerer. He could not believe how reckless they all had been.

He had heard about the risk he was taking from the river to turn him into stone, but he did not care anymore. It was the quickest way to ride the flow of the water towards the capital on a piece of bark that he had found at the edge of the woods. And it was rather nice, not having to move. But by sitting on a boat going down the river, his mind was not occupied well enough. He was not doing anything else than just waiting for time to pass.

So, he waited. He had waited for so many things in the 800 and something years of being a squirrel. Sometimes, he thought it all went by too quickly. Sometimes, he wished to have died centuries ago with the other townspeople. Not that he had grown to hate his life, but a shorter life might have been ... easier.

And now, he almost wished he had died with his kind. Now, Mibb was the only one left. The very last immortal animal from the White Forest. Everyone else was gone.

He wondered if the spell could potentially be reversed once Dragus would be defeated.

The humans did not have any magic whatsoever, as far as he knew. They would have an army though. That would have to count for something.

There was not much certainty that the humans would have the power themselves to fight a powerful sorcerer like this. But maybe Sahd had an idea.

The squirrel was staring at the front rim of the wooden means of transportation, watching out for any splashes that might kill him, or stones in the way that might obstruct his safe passing.

He just had to get to the capital and warn Sahd and the soldiers – if it was not too late already. They had to know where the King was and try and rescue him. As he looked up to check how far he had come, he saw the giant smoke cloud hanging low over the fields. That was not a good sign.

Mibb feared for his new friends.

**

Sahd looked at Grunia, and Grunia looked at Sahd. They had seen Draidr being drowned in a massive landslide of stone, punched into the ground. His friend was dead.

He could not say anything.

And then, right after, Samjya had shown up like a flying witch destroying the menace. She had looked so intimidating and mad... And as quickly as she had shown up, she had disappeared again. Where had she gone, and most importantly, what had become of her? He could not say anything at all.

"What was that?" Grunia stammered as soon as the flying fury had disappeared. The monster army alone was a shock to her, but she also had seen Samjya for the first time, Vonter's soon to be wife, who had changed into something completely supernatural.

Without wasting another moment, Sahd jumped up and ran to Yandra. She was still breathing, eyes open. There was so much blood around her!

Icy shards and stones had blasted into her frail body and made her bleed. There was so much blood.

Sahd pulled some linen cloths from under a beam and placed it gently over the wounds, around the ice shards.

Samjya's friend did not make a sound, but he could tell, she wanted to speak. He tried to sooth her: "Yandra, do not."

He could not keep it in anymore, still in disbelief of what he had just witnessed. His vision got blurry.

"That witch, it looked like she did not care for her at all. For anyone here. ... Maybe she was just killing that thing ... these things, and moved on?" Grunia offered, but Sahd would not accept her explanation.

"No, Yandra helped raise Samjya, they were best friends. Something is seriously messed up! She was turned into something *inhuman* ..." he fought his tears and clenched his teeth. This was unbearable. Too much loss.

He turned his head away. He did not understand any of this. So many people killed. Good men, women, and children. The army, ... he did not even want to know how many men were left.

Blinking away the wetness in his eyes, he pressed down on the cloth and looked around. Very little movement among the soldiers' bodies told him that they would not have many survivors. He had to find the King.

After a long pause of silence, he turned to Grunia again. She was close to tears too. Having lost all and seeing the capital fall like this was very tough on anyone, him included. And the seamstress was not even used to fighting.

Sahd was surprised she was keeping it together at all. She noticed his stare. Slightly embarrassed, she brushed dust off her leather clothes. She grabbed the sword handle again without pulling the weapon out.

"What now?" she said impatiently.

"We will gather as many soldiers as possible, build a defence, and find Vonter." Sahd answered motionless.

"You are kidding, right?" his new friend almost laughed. "There are barely any survivors out there. How big do you think the defences and the search parties will be?"

Sahd stopped her talking with a sinister stare.

"Shut up and help me. We need to help this woman. And then, we need every weapon left!"

*   *   *

The White Forest was a slim line a few miles out, on the other side of the valley. Distance was not a problem for her. But suddenly, she had become very tired, and flying had taken quite a lot of energy out of her. Gradually, she felt more and more drained, as if she had not eaten in days. Come to think of it, the last thing she remembered eating, was the flower.

She decided to stop floating, and as her feet touched the ground, she registered the warm sand under her toes. It was an odd sensation. Such a normal thing, and yet, so interesting. She found herself staring at the ground beneath her feet for a few moments.

Samjya was now walking down the foot path towards Tramvil, her feet more dragging across the ground than actual walking. The sun was high in the sky and very warm. There was a warming breeze from the South, but she was drawn West. She wanted to be alone, and not run into any bugs.

There was something … in her, a thought. A lingering thought. She
was not sure what it was. It had to do something
… with …

Maybe a faint memory? Something she had forgotten.

Vonter came to mind, the love of her life. The one who had left her behind. If she had not left the castle, she would surely have died like the other bugs. Had that been his plan all along, to get rid of her?

Or had he genuinely been fighting to defend his kingdom – and had he maybe even been killed in the attack? Her mind kept circling around the same questions, all the time. She was beyond frustration though. She did not know anything. And maybe that was okay.

She did not want to think about Vonter, and it bugged her that she did. Naturally, she would want to forget about him. He had left her behind, he clearly did not want anything to do with her. He was just a bug like all the others. Insignificant. He was not worth a thought. Not one single thought.

But he had made the decision to postpone the wedding and go to war. He had left her behind without a single word. Like a coward, he had disappeared. Vonter did not even have the nerve to tell her that he did not want her anymore. He did not want her anymore. He left and was to never come back.

Bugs.

He had left her behind.

He left her!

Her legs gave in, and she dropped to her knees, her hand stopping her from falling entirely. Dizzy and confused, she raised her arm to gently rub her forehead. A piercing pain rushed through her arm, down from the shoulder, preventing her hand to reach her head. She tried to raise her arm and hold her shoulder, but even that was painful. And then, the tears came. Wet on her face, they turned to small icy drops on their way to the ground as soon as they left her cheeks.

She cried for a long time.

She realised that she was still in love with him. And the time that they had spent together was too short.

Too short for a bug's life, he probably did not have a clue of what he was doing to her. Why had he left her?

Samjya sobbed and tried to breathe at the same time. It was difficult, so she heaved and pushed air out as hard as she could. Something was blocking her throat. Something that

was not there before. Or was her throat just closing?

No, there was definitely something there,

sharp and

itching. She coughed, but it would not work. She scratched her throat on the outside, it was really that bad!

Desperate for air, a wave of painful coughs erupted from inside her, and when she opened her eyes again, the ground beneath her face was bloody.

There was so much blood. She believed for a breath, she had vomited, but it was blood, that had clogged up her throat. She was able to breathe again. There was something else in the puddle.

Covered in blood and in between the frozen tears, there was some sort of splinter, or shard. It was almost as large as her hand, grey and shimmering blue under the drips of the dark red liquid. It took her a while to see it clearly. Was that the thing that had been in her throat?

With trembling hands, she reached down to touch it. It was very hard, and rough. Like an old shard of glass, really, but very dull in colour except for the blue shine to it. Whatever this was, it was unlikely that it was important now, she thought to herself, and tossed it aside.

Bugs.

Wiping tears and blood off her face, she noticed again how dirty her dress had become. She looked around, nothing felt real, it was suddenly so bright and hot. Yet, she was freezing on the inside.

She had to get away!

Samjya tried to get up. It took her a few attempts. Her legs and knees hurt like cursed too! What was happening? She did not understand.

But there was something else ... again, in the back of her head. An idea, a drop, a tree, something

... – No.

She could not grasp it.

Bugs.

She slowly started walking again. All her joints hurt, and her head was buzzing.

It was all so strenuous, but she felt she needed to put more distance between her and the villages, so many bugs had died, but a lot of them still roamed around.

All the emotions and thoughts that she had picked up, kept resurfacing. Like waves, every little feeling washed back ashore and muddled her up like the sand on a beach.

Why did she have to feel these things? She was not interested in bugs and their peskiness. She did not care for them, nor did she want to know what they were thinking. Some stuck with her longer than others, like the woman that had lost her lover, or the girl with no parents feeling all alone in this world before she died. There were a couple of boys soil their pants before the monster had splattered their skulls across the school yard, and an old man having sex with his much younger wife, thinking of all the other girls that he could have been with instead of her when the attacker had torn down their house. All distant flickers in the back of her head. But still, very annoying. Screwing bugs.

Carefully, she tried walking a bit faster. Her feet hurt less, but her mind became more and more foggy.

Bugs.

The sun was too hot now, blinding her. Squinting her eyes, she stumbled down the footpath towards the White Forest. In the shade, it would be a lot cooler, and no bug ever went in there. She remembered that from...

The White Forest was too scary. White trees covering almost half of the land, apparently created by...

Many tales had been told about this forest, and legend had it that...

She did not remember. And she was too tired to think these thoughts.

But this forest would be perfect for Samjya to hide away from all the bugs.

Like a magnetic haven, the white pillars pulled her closer.

The rocks and the river next to the road looked so far away, and the White Forest was moving towards her. The sky was bending down almost rhythmically. A soft, white cloud framed her vision, and she realised that she was not being herself. Bugs.

Maybe she needed some water?

Losing her balance when she turned to the left to face the river, she fell to her knees again.

She could smell the water. It was so cold and fresh. It was calling her.

Samjya crawled down the riverbank until her hands reached the water. She bent down and – hit her head on ice!

The flowing water had turned into crystal clear ice, just one short moment before she wanted to drink it. How was that possible?

Frustrated, she started punching the frozen surface. It took her five blows to break through. The cold water under the layer that she had opened, was very refreshing. She cupped the water in her hand and moved it to her mouth, drinking lavishly.

Bugs! After gulping down quite a lot of fluid, she leaned back and caught her breath. She was able to focus again. Her environment was less cloudy, and her breathing was normal.

But unfortunately, she could sense the bugs yet again. Those screwing bugs, thinking and feeling their pathetic misery!

Samjya got back up and started walking. She ignored the frozen river, the pain in her legs, arms and shoulder, and the harsh spikes of pain in her spine.

She concentrated on the edge of the White Forest again. It was still a few hundred feet away, but she felt a lot better, and confident that she would make it before nightfall.

And there it was again, this
thought. A memory. The
fish. A heart. Wind.

Samjya knew – *remembered* that she had been different before. One of *them*!

How was that possible?

She had to find Vonter!

***

Mibb could not wait any longer. He hadn't realised the river would become so voluminous towards the capital. The gap was getting wider and scarily more dangerous with his little boat rocking up and down, slowly drifting away from the shore and mid-stream.

The river was carrying him towards a little drop and the larger rocks guided the water in rough bends and turns downhill. The gushing water grew wilder each moment, and he had to jump off – he did not want to turn to stone.

This leap of faith took all his courage, and when his little paws caught the impact, and clawed deep into the soft earth beneath the grass, he could have kissed the ground.

Instead, he ran up the hill and climbed one of the pillars of the capital's protective wall that had not been crushed entirely.

He had heard great things from this place, Sahd had told Mibb how it was for him to live here, but there was no life to be seen. The soldier had described large, brick homes, tall shops and taverns and a fantastic castle with white and gold pillars.

He had never seen such a large settlement, he could not even make out the end of the buildings afar, or what was left of them.

Ruins as far as he could fathom. Almost all of the capital had been destroyed. Most houses had been crushed to stones. Stones had been crushed to rubble.

He saw burning fires, dust clouds and so much smoke. This place must have been magnificent, for sure, but it reminded him a lot more of his hometown and how the castle was left in ruins back then after Tessel was done with them.

He did not see any people. No soldiers, no men, women, or children that ran around or were injured. It seemed as if he was too late.

Not a single person was standing in the ghost town. No, that could not be true!

And then, he noticed blood, body parts and corpses in between the ruins. Yes, he was too late!

Mibb's little heart began to race, and he leaped to the right, following the wall alongside the edge of the capital. Here, some buildings were still intact, but again, no life in sight. He saw a horse carriage pressed into a wooden stable, and a large chunk of stone that had rolled down an alley and it looked like it had mowed down people, animals, and several walls in the process.

The little squirrel just hoped that Sahd was still alive! There was quite a body count between the stones, trees, and other strange items the mortals had built and collected in their short lives.

Further East, he could finally see some movement.

His instinct made him hesitate. The danger could still be around. He squinted and tried to pierce the smoke with his eyes.

Soldiers were carrying things, and there were horses. No fighting, and more importantly, humans. Chances were, one of them had already heard of him, so they would not waste his time by trying to understand how there could be a speaking squirrel. Mibb decided to go there first.

Jumping from house to house, using carriages and stalls, all demolished and pushed into the ground, he moved forward, quickly, but also nervous about what he would find. He tried to avoid jumping on the dead, but more than once, his feet would touch one, and he would try and not look at them.

Blood, intestines, and crushed heads were not what he had signed up for when he decided to aid the humans.

So far, he had not been much help. He had not planned to throw up either.

It gave him goosebumps to think of all the people that had been killed. There had not been that much death around him since every adult in his hometown had gotten killed. And that was a witch's curse, not a brutal incident like this.

The attack had to have been immense, the humans seemed to be lucky to have a few survivors at all.

345

As he arrived at the group of soldiers, he could see that they were not great in numbers at all. There was really just a handful of armoured humans at work. Maybe another 50 men and women were collecting weapons, bandaging their wounds, and tending to the other injured. One of the guards had calmed down a few horses and brought them over.

No one paid attention to the searching squirrel, and Mibb could not see Sahd at first. Grunia was the first one to see him. Her wave was shy, and she looked around before she ran over to him.

They had not talked to each other directly at Buntin. He had only heard Sahd mention her name when he talked to her before they had split up.

"Hello, little fella. You are Mibb, right? That, or I am talking to a wild animal." she tried to joke. "You look rather rattled?"

Rattled? She was still getting used to the idea of a talking animal, so Mibb decided not to make a fuss. "Do not patronise me. Where is Sahdor?" he replied snappily.

She backed away and turned her head. "Sorry, he went behind the castle. His friend Draidr

… did not make it. He wanted to find his body, ... Er, ..." she stopped herself.

"Thanks." Mibb was in a hurry after all, so he started running into the direction that she pointed. The Royal residence looked like it had been cut in half. He guessed that the front had been flattened like most of the capital. There was some gold and white in between the rubble.

The back side to the massive building was almost intact. There were some parts of tall walls and towers, decorated with fine reliefs and small statues. Yes, this place must have been very impressive.

It did not take him long to find Sahd. He was standing by himself next to a well.

The ground in front of him had been moved just recently, and two wooden crosses were sticking out of the ground. The squirrel could see that he had been crying.

"Sahdor. I am so sorry." he said, gently placing his paw on Sahd's boot.

His human friend looked down and smiled. "Mibb, you're alive."

Sahd's voice was a bit distant, his eyes not really paying attention to anything in front of him. The glance went right through the squirrel. He could feel the soldier's loss.

"I am. But I am afraid for the King." he blurted out.

Sahd's face darkened in worry: "What do you mean, is he hurt?"

"Worse. He is being held captive and tortured by Dragus. I am not sure why. We must help him!" The soldier pulled himself out of his thoughts and turned to face Mibb, eyes focused.

"Yes, we should. We are getting ready. I do not have a lot of men, but they should be ready by now. It is in White Forest?"

He nodded, and Sahd started to move back to the other soldiers. "We need horses."

Mibb was glad to hear that he did not have to travel by himself again – by land or water.

37

More blood.

All he could see was red when he was not close to blacking out. Fragir knew his torture skills.

Vonter had lost all sense of time and space. He had been weeping from pain and begging for death, but the evil sorcerer would not let him die. He had also lost count how many times he had broken his bones and put them back together very excruciatingly – he was not sure how that was possible, but it was the most painful thing he had ever felt!

"You know, Vonter, I am quite impressed. Hardly anyone has ever resisted for this long."

He did not understand what Fragir wanted from him. There was no witch, had not been in years. And certainly not one that he knew about. It was more likely that Fragir was asking about Samjya if she really had defeated a stone monster.

But Vonter did not know anything about his future Queen's whereabouts, or the fight other than what Prin had told him. He would not be able to tell the sorcerer anything. He did not know how she was capable of what he had heard, and he certainly did not know where she was.

The King could barely speak, the words just slurred out in between his teeth. "I do not know anything about a witch, we do not have witches!"

"LIAR!" Fragir screamed again. He had finally lost his patience.

And again, the piercing pain of daggers, needles and spears penetrating his stomach, legs and arms jolted through him. There were more of them, and they went deeper and moved around within the wounds.

Vonter did not have the energy to scream anymore. Just before he would have passed out, he felt how Fragir was patting his cheek. He was going to keep him conscious for as long as possible and start over and over and over.

Vonter had his eyes closed, but he could feel how close Fragir was. His torturer's breath was hot on his face.

"This might be your last few breaths, noble King. Tell me who this witch is, and I will let you die. I will drive my hand into your chest, rip your heart out and eat it. It'll be the last thing you'll see. Just tell me what I want to know. Or I can eat the other organs first, you know the ones that you don't need to survive."

Vonter did not really have a voice when he opened his mouth, so the sounds he made were a flat whisper. This exhausted all his strength reserves, and he lost track of what he was saying.

Slowly, he opened his swollen eyes. Warm sunlight around the sorcerer's face told him it was day, and he could almost make out the features on the face in front of his. For a few moments, he thought that was it. Fragir did not move, did not say anything.

But that was not it. Indescribable pain shot through his arm as, yet another weapon was driven into his hand. A silent scream passed his dry lips before he finally passed out again.

This time, it was different though.

His mind did not go dark entirely.

He was probably not quite unconscious, but somehow, in a different place. It was cold and he felt like he was levitating and being pushed down in the same moment. It was a sensation that was completely new to him.

As if he had been pulled into a different world. Or pushed?

A small, white light, moving in the distance. Some kind of ball?

As it got closer, its shape began to change. It changed into something ... human. The shape was glowingly light blue and white, but it glowed a little weaker the more human it became.

Vonter could see that it was a man, the figure became clearer, and he quickly recognised him. It was Fragir.

Same long, brown hair, almost down to his shoulders, a short, well-kept beard, and soft, brown eyes, he was a bit shorter than himself, and slim. He wore the same clothes.

It was only now that he started to notice some subtle differences, Fragir had an off expression on his face, he looked scared, hunted. His movements were softer somehow, more careful. But his legs were not going through the stepping motions. Maybe he was not moving. It was as if the space around them was shrinking.

It was all so different, hearing, seeing, tasting, even feeling his own body was very odd, he could not sense his own limbs!

"We do not have much time. I'm Dragus."

Fragir/Dragus's mouth was not moving, and his voice was an odd echo, distorted and hollow in this place. It made him dizzy, but somehow, it was a comforting version of the same voice that his captor had.

What do you want?

Vonter could not speak. He did not have any power over his body at all.

"Please do not talk, this connection is very fragile, and we need to be careful. Try not to think too much." the echo explained.

Well, that's easy, the King thought to himself.

"I'm a prisoner, in many ways different from you, but just as much a prisoner as you are right now. If we work together, we can help each other."

A prisoner?

Vonter could not help but stare at his eyes. They were demanding, intense. Deep.

Somehow, he felt like he could let himself fall into them, they made him experience a warm, soothing calmness. Looking into these eyes made him feel like nothing else before. As if these eyes were made to make him feel at home. There was still a haunted sadness that covered the light in some way, like a veil that did not show him the entire brightness.

But how was this someone else when his torturer and this person looked exactly the same? Yes, the spirit, the way he spoke, and his eyes were very different from Fragir's, but why should Vonter trust him?

He would never be sure to believe a word out of his mouth!

The face was very familiar, and that was the face of the man who had hurt him in the past day or however long he had been captive. He had this metallic taste in his mouth. Blood?

He could swear there was actual metal on his tongue.

Still, he could not move. What was going on?

"Stop thinking, please, he can sense your thoughts. Just stop. Let go of all."

Fragir/Dragus's face showed more dramatic despair, and he moved closer.

Vonter thought, this had to be a trick.

This man had to be a somehow less evil version of himself, made to make him feel secure and safe before he got the information he wanted!

His mouth half opened, Fragir/Dragus came so close that their noses almost touched.

Vonter should have felt his breath on his face, but there was nothing. He came to believe that there was no sense in touching, it would simply not be possible. He was not able to move or defend himself. The more it was a surprise to him what Fragir/Dragus said next.

"We need to try and touch each other." the echo explained hastily. "Only with a connection to the physical realm, I can escape this and pull myself back into my own body."

His body? What was he talking about?

Dragus/Fragir widened his eyes. "Please stop asking questions, he is almost onto us. I am not Fragir. He is merely using my body. Please, we need to try this. Now."

It was difficult to see what was true and what an illusion was.

Clearly, this situation was otherworldly, and he would not be able to tell if this was Fragir's making, this "Dragus" luring him into a new trap – or if this was what he had been waiting for, an escape.

But if he decided to help this man, how would he do it?

He could not flex a single muscle, except for his eyeballs.

He would not even know how to tell one arm to move.

The beginning of a smile appeared on Dragus/Fragir's face, and the piercing eyes grew softer. "You are starting to trust me. Good."

No, I did not think that, Vonter corrected him in his mind.

"Well, you are starting to think about it. That's all I can ask for right now. It is going to be difficult. You will have to be my anchor."

Anchor? What ... and how? He tried to be short in his thoughts.

Dragus/Fragir moved even closer. His nose was now next to Vonter's, almost touching. And he felt something else. Something new. Even warmer.

"The only thing you need to do is, think about your life at home, what makes you feel safe and happy, and then lean forward with as much effort as you can summon."

Home? The capital that was most likely under attack, his men dying? His Samjya, who probably had been turning into a witch? Or even his body that was being mutilated right this moment?

These things filled him with fear. He was close to giving up.

"Do not." the voice urged him. "I need you. Please let's help each other. Once I can pull myself out through our connection, I will be able to battle him, cast his soul out, reclaim my body." So, Fragir has been using your body? The reply was a much blunter echo.

"Yes, that's what I have been trying to explain to you. We have been captured by the same man, who needs to be stopped."

Had the room become smaller? The temperature had been rising. The King was very warm.

It was quite stuffy, like on a hot summer night just before the thunderstorm.

He felt as if the entire fabric of this world was putting pressure on him on all sides.

Vonter wanted to scream, fall to the ground, and just give in to the discomfort.

He inspected Dragus's eyes again. The sadness had not disappeared, but it had given way to … a hopeful glimmer?

And it began. There was a very gentle change inside of him. His body weight was shifted, forwards. It was not against his will, but he was also not in control either. In a way, he felt it was the right thing, maybe the only right decision that he had made since he left the castle a few days ago. Or ever in his life! There was an existential weight to it, a big reason.

Was this it? His ultimate decision, the meaning of life? Maybe he was supposed to end up here and help this stranger that looked exactly like the villain of the story. Maybe his role was to fight evil from the inside.

Strangely, he felt Dragus was telling the truth. That Vonter was doing the right thing to help them both.

It was now getting hot. He could feel the heat building up around him. If this would be reality, he would be sweating like a pig by now. What was going on? Was this...?

He suddenly noticed, how his upper body, very slowly but steadily, leaned forward. His face was so close to Dragus's that his nose was now touching it. Vonter did not feel anything in particular, but looking down on his nose, he could see how it started to press against his skin.

His mouth was almost touching Dragus's lips!

A bit more and they would be kissing!

What was Dragus thinking?

"A little bit more." his voice whispered in his ear now.

The heat was unbearable.

He wanted to scream his lungs out and not breathe that heavy air anymore! He wanted to scrape his skin off and not sweat like this anymore!

While leaning forward, even closer to this man, he thought of his body, how it was hurt in all places, and he was so close to dying. His heart was getting slower! There was a darkness creeping in from all sides!

He did not want to die. He did not want to burn up here, and have his life ended by the sorcerer back there. Whatever this was, he wanted to leave this place and return home.

He wanted to see Samjya again. His familiar, amazing, beautiful Samjya, whom he would marry on the spot. But first, he had to help this man. And help himself.

As soon as his lips touched Dragus's lips, the heat was gone.

He could physically feel the other man's mouth, the gentle, soft tickle of his stubble, and the taste of metal, meat, flowers, water, salt, fruit, and the fullest wine, all at once.

For a few breaths, everything stopped, and the simple touch of lips became it all: a full body sigh of whirring purity, that moved his form away from the ground, the dimensions, the very being of it all.

It was lifting, liberating, and inspiring, bending matter and time with light and force beyond everything he had ever felt!

This was the right choice, he could feel how his restraints were loosened, and the heat and the pain evaporated, he was filled with a gentle, cooling comfort. Like a thick, liquid curtain that was pulled, the surroundings moved away, and the pit reappeared, earthly smells and the afternoon air were back.

The dizzying bliss was interrupted, by a high toned, shrill scream. Furious, full of pain and violence, this tore a rip into the moment like no weapon ever could.

Fragir?

Vonter's senses returned fully to where he had been before: The hole in the ground, somewhere in the forest.

He could see that his capturer had backed away, bent over forward, holding his chest, in pain, struggling with ... something.

The restraints had indeed been removed, and because his legs gave in, the King fell to his knees, relieved. But when his glance moved up to the sky, he saw the most terrifying thing in his life.

And an ice-cold chill like he had never felt before, ran down his neck and back.

It was Samjya.

It was her, no doubt, but she was changed and didn't look human anymore. Blue hair, light blue skin, her back slightly hunched with shoulders dropped and naked arms holding her lower chest.

Her dress had been ripped and had dirt stains and dried blood all over it. She did not look like herself, but it was her.

Her eyes ... They were crystal blue and glowing with the coldest emotion he had ever recognised. The warm, kind person that he had known, was not the one standing on the edge of the hole in the ground looking down on him.

Her mouth was half open, and he noticed now that she was shivering violently. Her hands reached out as if she had planned to pull him up with a sheer thought but could not because she was too weak.

Vonter could not imagine what might have happened to her, and what had changed her so drastically, but she had become some*thing* completely different. He was scared for her, and of her. But that was not the worst part.

In her eyes, and the tears that rolled down her face, he could see that she had not intended to pull him up. She was hurt in a way he never thought she would be hurt.

He had never seen this kind of pain, it was crushing her very self, wiping her out! A pain, that had become physical, and immobilised her completely. Betrayal?

The King raised his hand to touch his lips. Was it the kiss?

Did that really happen?

His heart sunk even lower, and the cold conquered him entirely. He started to shudder. He could not take his eyes off Samjya, and she was staring at him.

Vonter could not believe this. What had become of them?

Fragir growled. Almost clawing his eyes out, he fell to the side, hitting himself, and hot air sizzled above him, it smelled like burnt skin.

This woke them both out of their frozen postures that may have lasted only one short breath, but it had felt like an eternity.

Vonter tried to say her name, but Samjya jerked forward, almost losing her balance. Her mouth opened fully and again, the same loud and shrill scream full of fury and pain was heard. It was so powerful though that Vonter thought he sensed vibrations across the grounds and air was pushed away into all directions.

So, she had seen the kiss? Samjya abruptly turned her head, focused on Fragir and with a third bone shattering cry, she extended her arms at him, and started to shine in a pulsing, light blue glow.

His Queen Bride was charging up some sort of energy!

She was quickly surrounded by gusts of wind that turned into a little cyclone. Cold air dissipated into all directions, and blue light formed at the end of her fingers that quickly became a shard of ice.

Samjya's cry grew in intensity and when she released the freezing weapon, it was like a part of her life essence left her hands. The icy energy shot down and hit Fragir and Vonter full throttle.

They both winced, blue and white smoke started to build up between them and all around, and Fragir's eyes turned from red to green and then white.

Covered in a thin, blue crust, he just fell to the ground, and did not move anymore. Vonter was a little further away from her, so her freeze power didn't hit him as hard, but his knees got weak, and he lost his balance.

Vonter looked up and saw that Samjya stared down in exhaustion and disgust. She was not even looking at her future husband, just somewhere on the ground, trembling again. Her breathing became faster, and she opened her mouth for another scream. But this time, nothing could be heard. Before a sound left her mouth, large, green flashes surrounded her, and then, she was gone!

She vanished into thin air, and the flashes disappeared with her! Just like that! Silence fell over the scene like death. Eyes wide open, Vonter still could not believe what he had witnessed.

He gasped for air, as he did not appear to have been breathing in the eternity that had just passed. Tears formed in the corner of his eyes.

The pain of his wounds came back in a devastating surge. At the same time, he was aware of his heart that had just been frozen like ice.

How could he do this to the love of his life? How did she change? Where did she go?

He sunk down in himself and started crying. Clenching the muscles in his stomach, of the limbs, and even his throat, he let it all out, the frustration, the terror, and the stress of the last few days. Most of all, his love for Samjya. And how he had destroyed the one good thing that he could have come home to. Home. This was an empty expression now.

Coughing up blood and vomit, he was exhausted after he did not know for how long he had been crying. His face was numb, and everything hurt. He would not survive this; he did not want to survive this. He did not want to be anywhere in this world right now.

Yet, his arms made the beginning. The pain was tremendous.

Reaching forward, and finding a steady position on the soil, he pushed his torso up, moved his legs closer and tried to put some weight on them. It worked, until he tried getting up fully.

His legs were weak, and he lost his footing quickly. But as he leaned against the wall that had held him tight before, he was able to limp around the lifeless body of the sorcerer and towards the stairs.

He put his hand on the roots on the wall and placed his foot on the first step that was a black stone. It took him quite a while to get up there, and as soon as his head reached the level of the ground, he could see where he was.

The white trees surrounded the clearing in an almost symmetric way. It was the White Forest after all! It was hard to tell whether this was deep inside the woods or further to the edge, but the trees were rather tall. The sun had started its decent slowly, and it was still quite warm. And very quiet.

No animals were heard or seen. Except for a few stone animals on the white grass that harboured a few black stones. Some ruins of something long forgotten. He made sure not to get too close to the animals. Suddenly, Vonter could see a lot of them around and at the bottom of the pit too, close to where he had been tied up.

Fragir had really killed everyone and everything in his way! Or was it Dragus?

He pulled himself up the last few steps, and rested on the white, dry grass. A few moments passed for him to catch his breath. Every muscle, every bone in his body hurt immensely, he was not in the condition to travel. At least not without a mount.

With great effort, he turned around on his stomach and looked over to the spot where Samjya had vanished. A black, burnt spot of grass was the only evidence of her existence – Vonter was hoping that this had been just a nightmare, and that he would wake up next to her.

But then, he moved a finger without care, and the pain reminded him of the reality. He stared back down into Fragir's lair, checking that the body was not getting up again.

How was he supposed to get out of the woods alive? Where was Samjya? What had he done?

He gave in to the exhaustion and closed his eyes. Just a few moments of rest, and he would try and get away from this place.

And if he never woke up again, that would be fine with him just as well. There was no reason to go on, Fragir had won.

He had lost it all.

38

"Quietly! We do not want him to hear us!" Mibb whispered into Sahd's ear. The General had signalled the soldiers to stay behind and was crouching in between the white trees. He thought he was doing a good job, but he could not really compete with the lightweight of a squirrel.

"I know, I am being careful!" he hissed back at his rodent friend. "I cannot hear anything!" he added.

The little voice next to his ear was thoughtful: "Yeah, very suspicious. ... There it is!" he pointed straight ahead. Now, Sahd could see it as well. The light behind the trees about twelve feet out was a lot brighter. The clearing Mibb had mentioned. He slowed down now and tried to be even more noiseless. Of course, dried leaves and sticks were not helpful, but he ignored the little sounds and sighs from his companion.

And then, he arrived at the last line of trees, and he spotted a wide, round hole in the ground, in the middle of the white grass. On the opposite side, there was a man, face down, not moving.

"Is that ...?" he lost his words. Without thinking, he got up, and despite Mibb's whispered protests, he ran out into the open.

"Do not do that! Are you crazy? ... This could be a trap! ..." he could not hear the rest as he had left the trees and the hiding squirrel behind. Within moments, he had carefully circled around the hole, avoiding the stone animals around the pit. He saw a second figure on the lower ground, not moving. It was so silent, that he was almost sure there was no one here anymore.

Stepping closer to the person on his level, he recognised his friend. Vonter was barely breathing, and bleeding from multiple wounds.

"Healer!" he screamed on the top of his lungs. He did not care about the threat from the sorcerer.

He slowly turned his King around to lie on his back. There were many stab wounds and cuts, and a lot of blood. It was a wonder Vonter was still alive.

A few breaths later, some soldiers rushed out into the clear from where he had come and were surprised to see the pit and the hurt King. Their healer, however, was quick to kneel at Vonter's side and started to inspect the injuries at once.

"Will he survive?" Sahd asked. He could not disguise the shaking in his voice.

"Not sure. I will have to patch up a lot here. Will take some time."

Sahd sighed. His glance wandered down the stairs to the other body. Just before he had decided to go down there and check this man's life signs, Mibb jumped in front of his face.

He was still whispering: "Careful! That's him! That's Dragus!"

"He is not moving! He might be dead." Sahd suggested.

The squirrel was not convinced and shook his head violently. "Not possible! This is a trap; we need to leave. Now!" he had almost screamed the last word, wildly looking back down and up into Sahd's face.

It reminded him of Draidr's warning the first time they had been in the White Forest. His friend, who had been crushed by the enemy, had had the same naked fear in his eyes. With gestures and more protests, Mibb was urging him not to do what he was planning to do. He had to make sure.

Sahd moved to the top of the stairs and carefully, stepped on the first few roots and started to climb down into the pit.

It was an odd structure, man made, but so perfectly smooth, and the steps seemed rather sturdy, even though they did not look it. The pit was cut out like a round cake, but it looked like it had always been like that.

He could barely take off his eyes from the lifeless body on the ground.

Dragus was young, long brown hair, slim and short, and covered in something. It looked like grey-blue dust. Halfway towards him, he looked back up again, and registered Mibb's scared eyes just on the top of the pit. The furry creature was so terrified!

Sahd turned and moved closer to the sorcerer.

His hand was one with the sword handle, more than ready to take it out and finish the bastard.

He bent down to see if he was breathing, but he was not. Instead, the General noticed how the entire man was covered in this strange dust. As he got closer, he realised that it was ice!

Dragus was frozen, and the outside was a layer of hardened, blue ice! Sahd was too afraid to touch it, but there was no apparent sign of life, no breathing.

Maybe Samjya defeated him and saved the King? And then, she would have left him to die – just like she had done with Yandra?

That would make sense in a bizarre way, but where was she now?

Sahd drew his sword and raised the handle in front of his face, pointing the blade down. With a determined thrust, he slashed the sword straight into the sorcerer's back.

For Draidr. And Minher. And Vonter. And the countless lives lost, in stone and otherwise!

The ice coat broke open, the flesh was pierced bloodlessly, and bone matter cracked. Still, no movement, no sound. That might have done no difference to an already dead man.

But Sahd had wanted to make sure. The point was, that Dragus was not alive anymore, and they could focus on getting the King back to the capital.

"Dragus is dead. Frozen." he announced.

He pulled out his weapon and turned around without a second look. More relieved, he climbed the stairs back up and re-joined the healer and a more than nervous Mibb.

The little rodent was clearly sceptical and kept looking back down a few times.

The soldiers had taken position to protect them from potential other dangers from within the woods, and when Sahd sat down next to Vonter, some of them relaxed as well. The healer was very much immersed into his work, and Sahd did not want to disturb him. So, he decided to just sit there and wait.

His mind kept playing the same images repeatedly.

His sister and her children, all those people in Buntin and Tramvil, the capital, his childhood friend Draidr.

He did not want Vonter to die too. He could not let that happen! But there was nothing he could do except wait. Too much had happened over the last few days. He just wanted it to stop. The killing and the dying, it was enough! Sahd sincerely hoped that with Dragus's death, this was all over now.

A light breeze blew through the treetops, but down here, it was rather still. One of the soldiers coughed a few times after drinking from the waterskin too quickly. It slid from his hand, fell down into the pit and rolled into the middle.

The other soldiers let out a muffled laugh and argued who should go down to get it back. Mibb had apparently decided to stop obsessing over Dragus, and had one paw placed on Sahd's leg, watching him.

Then, the healer sighed and looked up. "Sahd."

"Yes?" he was ripped out of empty thoughts. "What do you think?"

"I do not know if he is going to make it, to be honest, the injuries are very grave. He has lost a lot of blood, and the breathing is flat."

The answer was not what they had been waiting to hear.

A moment of silence stood between them. Sahd did not know what to feel.

"We should not move him right now. Might be best to wait out the night."

Some soldiers turned around, they clearly did not like the idea of spending a night in the White Forest. Sahd and his small friend exchanged a long look. They each had paid a high price.

"Anything for the King." Sahd mumbled.

A voice behind them startled everyone. "Maybe I can help him?"

"DRAGUS!" Mibb shrieked, and the soldiers turned all their weapons towards the sorcerer.

He had woken up! And there he was, shivering, barely alive but standing at the top of the stairs.

Sahd rushed up to his feet as well, drawn sword, ready to strike. "I stabbed you in the back! You were dead!" his heart was pounding.

Dragus was fighting the pain, almost struggling to keep standing.

"KILL HIM! DON'T HESITATE!" the squirrel was in a frenzy, hiding behind Sahd's boot, jumping up and down, scratching the back of his legs.

Dragus raised his hands slowly and stepped back, almost falling back down the hole. "I'm not dead, I can heal myself. But please believe me, I am not going to harm you. I am not the person you think I am."

"HE IS LYING! HE IS LYING!" Mibb was furious.

"QUIET, MIBB!" Sahd wanted some time to think this through. He asked the man: "What did you say?"

The sorcerer started again.

"I am not trying to harm you. I did not hurt Vonter. Please believe me. We helped each other."

"How?" the soldier wanted to know. "How can I trust you are telling the truth?"

"I do not know how. But I know you can. My name is Dragus. I was betrayed by Fragir, he took over my body and used it for a lot of death and destruction. I saw it all. And felt it all." the emotions in his eyes seemed genuine.

"LIAR! IT'S A TRAP!" Mibb started again.

Sahd almost kicked him.

"Mibb! Stop! Let me handle it!" he barked without turning around, eyes fixed on Dragus. "You killed so many people. You killed my best friend, my sister, and most likely our King!" Sahd was fighting his tears. Was his revenge not done after all?

"Again, my friend, it was not me. Fragir had control over my body, he used me for all his terrible crimes. I'm Dragus, and I can help him." the wounded sorcerer coughed.

If he was indeed setting a trap for them, it was a bit too elaborate. He could have striked them down already or turned them into stone like the animals. And he seemed very badly injured too.

Dragus continued: "Please, I am not your enemy. Fragir is gone. For good, I think. And believe me when I say that I can save your King. Our King."

The soldiers stayed tense and alert, but Sahd lowered his weapon.

"What do you think you can do to help?"

Some whispers and mumbling came up behind him, but he ignored them. Dragus was not exactly in a good shape either. He could barely stand. How would he be able to help the King?

"I can use magic to heal his wounds, the deadly ones at least. This will weaken me even more, but I have great self-healing powers if you can spare some more water. I can regenerate myself over time. I will be unconscious. You may do with me as you please."

Sahd considered the offer. He kept his eyes on Dragus while he spoke: "What do you say, healer?"

"I certainly cannot speak for magic, but there is a big chance that -"

Dragus interrupted him: "He will die."

Sahd hesitated still. He had soldiers surrounding him that probably would not support this, and Mibb was literally biting his boot's rim and growling in protest.

He raised his sword again and stepped forward.

"I will keep my sword next to your face. Try one devious action, and I will slice it off!" he exclaimed and gave way to Vonter, without moving the blade away from the sorcerer's skull.

Dragus smiled nervously and limped slowly off the stairs across the white grass. Sahd followed him with his sword, carefully watching his every move.

Mibb growled some more in disagreement, clenched around his leg.

Apparently in great pain, the sorcerer bent down and extended his arms above the King. Some soldiers stepped closer as well, ready to attack.

Dragus closed his eyes. Summoning a glow, a warm, golden light left his hands and travelled into Vonter's body. It only lasted a few moments, and just as fluidly as the light had appeared, it vanished again. Most of Vonter's cuts and bruises were gone!

Dragus fainted and fell next to the King into the grass. The healer and Sahd rushed down to check on Vonter. He seemed fine, even his breathing was stronger now!

Sahd turned to Dragus. He was breathing too, barely visible though. He was very pale and entirely still. This had to have him drained significantly.

Mibb jumped on Sahd's shoulder: "That was very risky!"

"Yeah, it was. But I knew he would not try anything. He has had every chance before." Sahd replied. He looked back to Vonter just began to open his eyes.

The healer held him down by the shoulder. "Slowly, His Grace. You were gravely injured."

Apart from some weakness, Vonter looked quite healthy and well!

"How do you feel?" Sahd asked impatiently.

The King cleared his throat: "Water!"

Someone handed Sahd a waterskin, and he passed it on. Vonter drank greedily and gasped for air after he was done.

"I feel fine. Thirsty. ..." he drank more. "What happened? What are you all doing here?"

Mibb let out a sigh of relief, and most of the soldiers relaxed again.

"You were tortured by Dragus, ... Fragir." he corrected himself. "Mibb brought us here."

"Fragir." Vonter seemed to remember. He raised his upper body more and discovered the sorcerer's body. "Dragus." he said, deep in thoughts.

"So, ... that man was telling the truth? How Fragir just used his body?"

"Yes, Dragus helped me escape. – ..." and then Vonter remember something else. He turned his head quickly, and because he could not see behind the men around him, he jumped up and pushed through them, still very shaky. He tumbled a few feet away, and stopped in front of a black, burnt patch on the ground next to the pit.

"Careful!" the healer said, but everyone ignored him.

Sahd followed Vonter, and tried to support the weakened King, but he would not let him. There was a very apparent pain in his face, the fighting of tears.

In shock, as if he was checking that it was real, he touched the black grass tenderly.

Staring down in tears, he whispered: "Samjya. ... Where did you go?"

39

Her scream filled the airless space around her, but it could not release anything. The pain was ripping her apart. Samjya could feel how her insides were crushed and pulled, she felt sick, burning up and ice cold all at once. Green sparks burned off her face, arms, and legs, and melted into thin air.

In her stomach, a large stone grew and stretched her skin. The ribs squeezed tighter and pressed her lungs flat, and her heart was beating so hard that it exploded out of her chest.

Physically, it felt like that, and the scream was not helping a little bit even. It was a pointless act, a feeble attempt of a reaction to her found again humanity. No release.

Yes, she felt quite intensely herself again, even if it was the unbearably hurting self. When she gasped for air, the flow of air felt somehow unreal, empty. Her mouth and throat did not respond the way they should, her bosom shook with every sob.

After crying for a long time, Samjya opened her swollen eyes. It was dark. There was nothing around her. Still struggling to normalise her breathing, she turned around. Nothing.

She looked up and down. Nothing.

Where was she? Why was there so much darkness?

She looked down on herself, and she could see herself perfectly without light.

Her dress was still ripped, and she could see her bare, dirty, bruised feet and legs. But her skin was white again. No blue veins and no glow!

Even her hair was blonde again.

Frizzy, and dirty, but the normal colour. So, it was not darkness?

Wiping off her tears, she only dried the cheeks for more.

The panic went as quickly as it had come. But she could not stop crying. Her whole body felt cramped up, she could hardly stand.

All she wanted to do was to roll up into a little ball and disappear. This nothingness should just swallow her up already, she thought to herself.

And without a warning, flashes of memories jumped into her mind. Breaking out of her chambers, fighting off stone monsters twice, Yandra's face when she laid there dying, Vonter, how he was covered in cuts and bruises, about to be burnt alive by the evil sorcerer, and he *kissed* him!

Of course, she had seen men kiss before, but never like that. She knew how Vonter had kissed her and how happy it had made him. This was different, bigger, profound.

She could feel it, still and always, but with a different intensity now. It was just like the feelings she had picked up from the other people, and it would not go away!

She could feel what he had felt, and to him, the kiss was so much more than he ever had felt for her. Something a lot purer she thought than what she held in her heart for him. But it was nothing compared to what this kiss was to her beloved King, how it had made him feel.

That was the worst of it all. And it broke her heart. It was the hardest break, right through the middle. She could feel that too.

It was bleeding out inside her chest, filling her with hot, heavy blood, and making her full. Filled. Fed up. It hardened and froze her from the inside. She was burning up and freezing to death at the same time.

"Calm now."

Who was that? It was a woman's voice, old and warm. But there was nothing. So, she was not alone?

"Be still, my child."

She did not recognise the voice. Was this someone she knew? How could this person be here with her when there was just nothingness? It sounded as if she was standing right next to her, one moment. And somewhere else in the next.

"You are safe now. I will take care of you."

Samjya did not feel entirely comfortable, and she was still too upset to speak. Instead, she tried taking a step. It worked. She could feel the flat, smooth ground beneath her naked feet.

As she reached down to touch the floor next to her foot, she could not feel anything, there was just nothing, of course. It was as if she was standing on the edge of a cliff, but as soon as she moved her foot forwards, there was solid matter below her.

Carefully, she took more steps and began to walk, then run. She could not tell if she was in fact moving away from her spot or if she was going anywhere in particular at all, but her feet carried her inside nothing to more nothing. It was pointless. Just like her scream, she realised that it was in vain. There was no escape from herself, her emotions, or her slowly decaying heart.

"Do not worry, you will not have to run anymore."

The voice was behind her, and then, in front of her.

"I am here to help. You are ready. You can trust me."

Samjya stopped. She swallowed a few tears and tried to overcome her heavy breaths. Speaking was still difficult, but after a long and complicated sound to clear her throat, she could utter a few words.

"Where am I?" she wheezed.

"You're in my mind. Not physically, but your body is in transition."

"In transition?"

"Yes, have you not noticed? You are becoming something else, something far better. My child, I am making you what you were meant to be. Powerful."

"I do not understand."

Was this her ... mother? Everything inside of her was rearing against this.

"The ambrosia, the flower you ate."

"What do you mean?"

"It is the food of the Gods. It gave you your powers. I did not think you would eat it completely though."

The voice chuckled, still moving around. Samjya suddenly felt tricked into this. She had not agreed to this. Was Vonter in on this?

"Vonter gave me the flower."

"I was the one who sold it to him so he could give it to you on your wedding day. Samjya, I have had big plans for you, for a while."

"How? Why me?" the Queen Bride stammered. She remembered Vonter's story about how he bought the flower from this old merchant. Was this woman a witch? How long had she planned this? There was a moment of silence, and for a breath, she thought this woman had disappeared.

"You are the purest human I have seen in a long time. And you were so rare, I had to use this opportunity. I am so glad it worked out in the way it did, my child. You are ready, oh so ready. Truth is not true, and you will see for yourself!"

"Why do you keep calling me your child?"

"You are my child. I love you."

She did not know what to say or believe. This was crazy. This was not her mother!

"What am I doing here, where are we? And what is my body changing into?" Samjya's heart was beating faster again.

"I wanted to talk to you before your next step in your new life. You will see, it will make sense. Your journey will be a bit more painful for a while, but I will be there for you the entire way."

Samjya's heart was beating louder and faster, and her legs were kicking almost uncontrollably.

"No. I want out. I do not want this. Let me go."

"My child, that's not possible, I am afraid. You have made your choices."

The voice was still friendly and comforting, but the effect was lost on Samjya.

"My choices? Ever since I got this flower, all my actions were driven by fear, sadness, and isolation! I did not have choices!"

"Of course, you did. You always have a choice, my dear. You chose fear. You chose sadness, and you chose to give in to isolation. I only gave you the tools to work through pain and to fight back with power. Pure power."

"No. I will not accept this. You destroyed it all!"

The woman's tone hardened slightly: "I did not destroy anything. You did. You alone are responsible for your actions."

"LET ME GO!"

Samjya started running again. She wanted to leave all this behind, forget this all ever happened, and go back to her own life. Making her own decisions!

But what if this woman was right? Was Samjya alone responsible for everything that happened to her? It was hard to believe her. She kept saying that Samjya was safe and that she could trust her, but she could not even see her. And she did not know what was happening to her body, what she was changing into.

After what had felt like a very long time, in a crazy, distant nightmare, she was finally feeling human again. It was barely bearable, and the pain was almost killing her instantly, but she wanted her humanity back. She did not want some witch's help!

"Samjya, please stop running. I will release you in a bit; your new body is almost ready for you. You will not remember this conversation, but just know, I love you, my creature."

"A new body? No, wait. You cannot do this to me! Please do not!"

There was no point in begging, crying, or demanding in her situation, but she did it anyway. "Please do not do this. I just want to go back to how it was all before."

"We all want that." The voice was suddenly very stern and cold. "But change is the only thing you can depend on in this world."

"Please! Let me go! I do not want this! I do not want this!"

The nothingness around Samjya started to crumble.

Behind the matterless, there was a light-blue shimmer, like a different room that let its light shine through a curtain. It all fell apart quickly.

The pain washed back into her heart forcefully. All the destruction in her kingdom, Vonter's betrayal and that horrible woman's violation of her life course, it drowned her.

More and more cold light broke through the barriers, and blue and green pulsing flashes burst through the openings.

Samjya was not hit, but the cold froze her anyway. Still, so very still.

The flashing, blinding light came closer, circled her in a whirring thunderstorm, and just like she had vanished from the pit in the White Forest, she left the nothingness like nothing ever was.

40

Vonter's trusted horse walked steadily, and the continuous rocking had put him in a numb trance, deeply sunken into sombre thoughts and empty emotion that became gradually tainted with the harshness of reality.

That kiss.

Samjya.

What had he done to his poor Samjya?

Has he put the kingdom second with his actions?

How could he go on like this?

It was over.

He was not fit to be a King anymore, surely.

It was almost dark. He had not noticed how much time had passed, and he did not care. His love was gone, his kingdom was in ruins, and so many people had died. Nothing mattered anymore. He did not care about how Sahd and his men had rescued him and how Dragus had healed his wounds. They should have just left him for dead.

When his vision and his hearing could not ignore the surroundings anymore, he looked around. The soldiers around him moved slowly like mute figures. Even the flag of the Proud Steed appeared a lot more subdued than usual. Sahd rode in front of him, talking to the little squirrel.

Vonter turned his head to look at him.

The man he had kissed.

Has that really happened? It had felt real. More real than anything else, but kind of surreal. Like it had not happened, but he felt like it had.

This man was the culprit who had destroyed this world, and at the same time, he was not.

That kiss.

Samjya.

The man who had him break Samjya's heart.

The man who had saved his life, and whose life he had saved. And everyone else's.

Dragus remained unconscious or asleep from his last action.

His body had been strapped to the horse, almost like a sack of potatoes, he was probably still in the process of healing himself as they travelled back to the capital.

Vonter did not understand how this terrible magic had been able to bring so much suffering into his kingdom. Dragus would have a lot of explaining to do. Fragir had to pay. If he was still alive somewhere inside him.

That kiss.

Samjya.

There was no trace of his Queen Bride, he did not even know if she was still alive.

What had changed her?

How had she found him in the forest?

Why had not she talked to him?

Where was she now?

There were so many questions that would remain unanswered. And it was like Sahd said, there was no chance he would have been able to find her now. If she really vanished into thin air, it would not make sense to comb through the entire kingdom.

They were down thousands of soldiers; he had been told that there were only about 500 men and women of the Royal Guard left. They had to secure the castle, make sure the defences were up, and get the word out to the other towns and villages.

As his mind began to clear, the emotions kept swinging back into play.

He could not shake the look on Samjya's face. Her pain, unlike anything he had ever seen.

He still could not believe it.

Mibb startled him by jumping from Sahd's horse to Vonter's without announcement.

"Oh, Mibb, you scared me!"

"I called over three times, and you did not react!" the squirrel answered slightly annoyed.

"My apologies." Vonter replied.

"Yes, you say that a lot! ... How are you holding up? Sahd is concerned about you, His Grace."

He could not say.

As much as he was weighed down by the multitude of feelings and unbelievable impressions of the last few days, as empty was his mind. No words could be enough to give an answer.

"You know, Mibb, I have never felt like this before."

The rodent was probably just interested in one thing: "How does it feel to be back from the dead?"

Right. There was that. He did not remember to be dead or gone, even. All he remembered was the physical and emotional pain, and the suffering that he went through, and had caused.

"I do not know. I do not recall anything from the other side if you mean that? I am not even sure there is such a thing as 'the other side'."

The small rodent seemed rather disappointed. "I was hoping you would have seen something. I'm immortal, so I have had time to think about it a lot. I do not think there is something, really.

"Once you're dead, you're dead, that's it. And maybe that is true, and all there is. Unless, you come back, of course. It would be good to hear if that's all there is. I for one -"

"Mibb, why do you not go check on our prisoner?" Sahd interrupted the rodent in a stern tone. The soldier had fallen back and appeared next to Vonter.

The talking squirrel understood the hint, and climbed over Vonter's shoulder to jump to Dragus, via two other horses.

"Thanks, my friend." the King said quietly. "My head still hurts from processing all this." he sighed.

Sahd smiled and nodded silently. The following silence was very solemn, welcome almost. They rode side by side for a number of breaths until Sahd could not be quiet anymore. Vonter knew his friend too well.

"Your Grace, you've met Dragus, I mean ... Fragir. How was he?"

The King was honestly surprised by this question. "Why do you ask?"

"My sister and her children are still missing. I am thinking of the worst, really. I want to know what kind of man would do something like this. Who would be capable in killing so many and creating such powerful magic? I want to understand this monster."

He thought about this for a moment.

"Fragir was ... driven. Hurt. He would not stop. His motivation was so determined, and he was the pure embodiment of hate. He was consumed by pain and loneliness."

He paused, and Sahd wanted to say something, but Vonter stopped him with a gesture.

"The most striking thing I thought, was that there was no joy. No pleasure or enjoyment at all, even in the bad things he did... I think he was more than just a crazy person. Very scary and unpredictable.

"He and Dragus had a shared past, and I could feel how Dragus was innocent in all this. I do not know any details, of course. He will have to tell us once he is conscious again."

"At least Fragir got what he deserved. ... Do you think he is really gone?" Sahd asked with a sceptical look back to Dragus.

"Oh, you think we might carry him home with us right now?" Vonter pondered on that idea for a moment. "Well, you could be right, I do not have a clue about how magic works, no one does. Dragus surely thought that Fragir is gone, is not that what he told you? I trust him, I think."

"Why? Because he saved your life?" Sahd sounded unconvinced.

Vonter ignored his tone: "Twice, indeed."

Another moment of silence stood between them.

"I'm very sorry about Draidr. I know he was your best friend, even before we met." he heard himself say.

Sahd did not react. He was probably still dealing with what had happened.

He could tell that his friend had quite a few reasons to not be entirely present in the now – especially not trusting when it came to the sorcerer. The confusion between Dragus and Fragir did not make things any easier, certainly. It was good that Sahd was still suspicious about him.

Vonter did not trust himself now, really.

His judgement was probably not the best.

That kiss.

Samjya.

He was still very confused. It was not something that he would admit to anyone, though. What they needed was a leader. Their King. Even if Vonter was not up for it.

The overwhelming regret and shame came back in a large wave of lethargic cold.

When they reached the peak of the next hill, he could see where the dark smoke came from. The capital was pretty much just a pile of rock from what he could see.

His heart sank into the deep dark of where Fragir had kept his captured souls. He felt nothing but darkness and despair.

His thoughts returned to Draidr, his lost friend, and Samjya, his one and only.

How was he going to continue without them?

How could he continue after letting down his people?

Rebuilding was one challenge, protecting what was left seemed impossible.

That kiss.

Samjya.

***

24589 hardly took their eyes off the screen.

The system was adding up the points of the plot as it happened automatically, no input needed.

With the concentration and serenity of every other analyst, they had been watching the unfolding events with scrutiny.

Everyone liked watching the live feed. It was good entertainment this time around.

"I like how most of our new Creators are guiding the chains of events. It adds a certain subjective complexity to the storylines." they said.

The white room was empty apart from a workstation with two large desks, one with various keyboards, lights, and switches. The other one with touchscreens and holographic emulators. There was no light source, door, or window to distract them from productivity. The two analysts were working one desk each, with ease and full confidence.

29691 nodded discreetly with the same level of gratified tranquillity. They never changed the expression on their face. "True, the upgrade is pleasing. The trojan was a welcome addition, it is interesting how it all spreads."

"We need to keep an eye on the glitches, they have not fixed any of them." **24589** added.

"Yes, I have seen the updates from Level 8, they are working on the repeating anomalies as they have isolated the patterns. At least it's just some food and pets, nothing too major. They estimate 90 FLE for the completion as general maintenance takes precedence."

"Of course."

29691 turned around to check the meters on the other wall of the system's indicator lights. "Do you think She will notice?", they asked.

24589 still did not move their eyes away from the screen. "Probably. But She has lost Her mind and all direction of the plot. We might as well see how it plays out and then delete Her permanently. It is better to have them clean the glitches than risking the integrity of the grid right now."

A chime was heard from one of the speakers in the corner.

Two other analysts entered the room through a door on the back side of the spacious room, sliding open from within the wall automatically. They wore the same white clothes, one of them glasses, the other one an earpiece.

As soon as their steps had taken them closer to the workstations, **24589** and **29691** stepped back and almost, simultaneously, reached into their coat pockets.

While the other two took over their positions in monitoring without a single word, **24589** pulled out a pair of glasses and placed them on their nose. With a tap on the rim, they activated the live feed in a small portion of their field of vision.

29691 pulled out an earpiece that connected to an implant in the side of their skull as soon as it was placed in their ear.

The left eye turned white as the live feed started to play. "You do not have the latest augment yet?"

24589 carried the same emotion on their face as the analyst left the room the same way the others had come. "Once I have enough credits in my account. I only need to watch another 7,100 FLE."

Their glasses had a permanent counter towards the goal they had set. It was important to work with a goal in mind to spend and earn the time.

They stepped through the door behind them, and turned right, walking down the empty, white corridor.

The automatic door closed behind them silently, leaving no visible trace of itself in the wall.

They had left the other two alone for the next 0.8 FLE, carrying on their work making sure Cant'un would not end prematurely.

The story will continue in

THE DRAGON OF ICE

Printed in Great Britain
by Amazon

29044310R00219